Henrytown

Books by Mardi Oakley Medawar

Tay-Bodal *series*
Death at Rainy Mountain
Witch of the Palo Duro

Novels
Rainwater on the White Road
Remembering the Osage Kid
The Glory Days of Buffalo Egbert

Henrytown

Mardi Oakley Medawar

SPEAKING VOLUMES, LLC
NAPLES, FLORIDA
2020

Henrytown

Cover design by Hannah Linder

ISBN 978-1-64540-315-9

For Cherry Weiner

A great agent, and a decades long friend.
It's been a marvelous journey.

Author's Note

This novel is a work of fiction. To my knowledge, Henrytown, Louisiana does not exist. Therefore, any resemblance to anyone now living or deceased is entirely coincidental.

Mardi Oakley Medawar

Chapter One

In the year of 1935, rail was the principle means of travel. For the nation's Depression weary down-and-outs, traveling by rail meant hiding inside box cars. For the country's minority of well-offs, rail travel meant private sleeper cabins and dining cars. Aaron Brooks, one of these lucky few, was in the confining hallway of the train's passenger car with most of his upper body leaning out of the "Slide Down to Open," window. It was Monday, May Twenty-Third, and Aaron was just barely twenty-two years old. This was his first trip into the wilds of Louisiana.

From the age of seven Aaron had felt the call of God on his life, this call propelling him from the children's seating section towards the Brooks Family pew, which happened to be front row pew on the far side of the sanctuary, a two storied auditorium of the largest church in Atlanta. It was an ancient and dignified building, so grand and stately that General Sherman had flatly refused to burn it down with the rest of Atlanta because the Union General could too easily imagine God Himself in residence. Aaron's unusual intrusion into the adult area caused embarrassment and consternation among the adults filling the Brooks' family pew, most especially for his father, Professor of Georgian History, Dr. Albert Brooks, PhD. Aaron kept his request almost painfully precise.

"Father, Mother, I should very much like to be baptized."

His mother, Emilia Brooks stood, and, like Hannah of old when presenting her son Samuel to the High Priest Eli, she held her son's small hand as she walked with Aaron toward the altar, and it was there that she gave her only son to God.

During the passing years, and much to his father's chagrin, Aaron's religious zeal steadily increased. The jewel in Dr. Brooks' parental martyr's crown appeared when Arron was seventeen and newly graduated from high school. At the dinner table, and in the company of their invited dinner guests, Aaron announced that he'd declined the invitation of admittance into the University of Georgia, his father's alma mater and employer. Aaron's decision came as a back-molar grinding disappointment as he then went on to state that he would instead be attending a small and less than impressive seminary. Emilia had gloried in the applause of their dinner guests. It was too late for fatherly rebuff, intimidation, or even bribery. Instead, Dr. Brooks ate the remainder of his meal without noticing a single morsel.

And off to the seminary Aaron did go. A voracious student, Aaron thrived. Upon entering his fourth and final year, his father, still hoping to salvage a modicum of dignity from the situation, made it his business to push his son's name forward as a candidate for associate pastor of the illustrious and historically important Atlanta Church. But on the night of Aaron's graduation and just seconds before his father was prepared to share with him the glorious news of the associate pastoral appointment, his son rather enthusiastically announced his acceptance of an interim appointment to a church that was somewhere off in the swampy bogs of Louisiana. When asked how he'd even found such a questionable position, Aaron blithely replied, "Oh, it was listed on the difficult placement board. Meaning of course, the church is either very small, or in an awkward locale. I was told the church met both criteria. Still, I felt led to accept the position."

"And the length of this interim-ship?"

"Six months. And then the church will either vote to retain me or carry on the search."

Standing tall in the seminary's cap and gown and clutching his rolled and ribbon tied diploma, Aaron was positively glowing. He went on to relate that the dean himself had written a letter of recommendation to the church's deacons. The very public conversation, what with graduates and their families milling all about meant that Dr. Brooks could not decry his son's ludicrous plans. The only option was to turn and walk away before his rising temper caused a scandal.

In his father's study the very next morning and standing squarely in the center of the huge oriental carpet, Aaron prayed for calm. His father only ever raised his voice when he felt pushed beyond the limits of his patience. On this particular morning, his father was most certainly raising his voice and directly into Aaron's set face.

"Please tell me this church is not in New Orleans!" his father roared. "That city is little more than a human cesspool. No amount of preaching from a newly graduated seminarian will stir so much as a ripple on the surface of all that filth."

"The church is not in New Orleans, Father. It's further north."

"Shreveport?"

"No sir. It's somewhere in the center of the state in a place named, Henrytown."

"What?"

"Henrytown, Sir."

"Oh, for the love of Saint Peter! What would ever possess anyone to name a town so absurdly?"

"Apparently a gentleman named Henry who very much wanted to have a town named after himself."

"Do not be flippant with me young man. I am down to my very last nerve and you are playing hob with it. And then there's your poor mother who has locked herself inside her bedroom where, I'm told, she is prostrate with grief. And who could blame her? Her only child has proven himself to be infernally pig headed."

Dr. Brooks turned away from his son before he did something even more outrageous than raise his voice. Coming to his grand oak desk, he sat down in the throne-like leather chair. To calm himself further he pretended to organize the carefully typed pages that his secretary had left for his approval. The pages were his latest manuscript. His first publication had been on the genealogies of Atlanta's great families. This new effort comprised the complete history of Georgia and was a work he had every reason to believe would become the lasting word on the subject. The feel of the papers gave him a sense of coming success as well as richly deserved acclaim, all of which calmed his embattled nerves. Then too, the imperial grandfather clock standing off in the far corner of the imposing room sent forth its steady rhythmic ticking of the brass pendulum, a sound which never failed to soothe. Feeling closer to civility, he looked up at his son.

Aaron was a tall, rakishly slender, and startlingly handsome, young man. A veritable throng of young ladies from excellent families had vied for his attention and yet, Aaron merely greeted each young lady cordially and then went cheerfully—and obliviously—on his way. Dr. Brooks felt a fresh wave of temper swelling as he thought of the brilliant marriage, the illustrious pastorate that could, with simply a word, belong to his son. Yet he was throwing it all away without the slightest twinge of remorse. The sunlight streaming in through the bay windows highlighted Aaron's golden wavy hair. Along with his deeply blue eyes he appeared remarkably angelic: Which, to Dr. Brooks' way of thinking, was ninety percent of Aaron's problem. He'd looked angelic from birth and his mother Emilia just couldn't seem to stop herself from calling him that.

"Oh, my precious, precious angel," were the very words she invariably used whenever beginning a conversation with their son. After Aaron, Emilia had suffered five separate miscarriages, then never conceived again. Subsequently, Emilia poured herself into her only child.

Dr. Brooks took a deep breath and counted slowly as he let the breath go. Able now to speak in a softer, albeit clipped, tone he said,

"Six months. I will fund you for the entire period of your interim-ship. After that time, if this church decides that it will indeed have you as its permanent pastor and, if you yourself persist in this…calling…you will then be cut off from any further allowance."

"Thank you, Father."

Dr. Brooks busied himself again with the manuscript pages. "Do not thank me. I'm doing this entirely for the sake of your mother."

"Understood sir."

Three days later, his parents saw him off on the train. His mother way crying as she fussed over him. His father was. . . formal, stiffly shaking his hand, as he requested Aaron telephone as soon as possible to assure his mother of his safe arrival. In the years that followed, Aaron would often wonder that if either of them had but known that this would be their final moments together as a family, if father and son would have behaved any differently. Somehow, he could never quite convince himself of their final parting as being otherwise.

The sign stuck to a pole that leaned dangerously close in toward the tracks had originally been white with black lettering. Over the years, and because of the dust and soot from many a passing train, the sign was now a dingy brown and the black lettering an unhealthy gray. Still craning from the window in an attempt to absorb every second of this adventure, Aaron could just make out the sign's message:

Henrytown, Louisiana Pop. 645
642 Saints - 3 Old Soreheads

The depot office itself was very small. There wasn't a public convenience or waiting rooms. The depot was a wide, uncovered boardwalk. As the locomotive noisily slowed, Aaron could see only one man standing on the boardwalk. He was a weathered looking man wearing a white shirt, bib overalls and wide brimmed gray hat. Aaron had not been expecting a public welcome, but at the very least he had counted on a show of the church deacons. Determined not to allow disappointment to dampen his excitement, Aaron retrieved his suitcase from the sleeper compartment and hurriedly descended the train's metal steps.

After coming to stand on the boardwalk, he and the other man simply stared at one another. Then the one-man reception committee rather lazily sauntered toward him and, in a dialect Aaron could only just make out, the man said, "Hey young'un. Can you tell me if you seen a parson on the train?"

Aaron set the suitcase down on the boardwalk. He stood a good head taller than the man who was unabashedly looking him up and down. Aaron was wearing a white linen suit and shirt and a bold blue tie. On his feet were blue socks and highly polished white Oxfords. The blue socks and tie were to please his mother who was ever so fond of matching his clothing accessories to the blueness of his eyes. He was also wearing a white, wide brimmed hat. All of this was considered to be the norm of Atlanta summer attire. The man's blatant study of every inch of him was beginning to make him feel uncomfortable in his clothing.

Answering the man in his soft Georgian drawl, Aaron said, "To my knowledge I was the only pastor on the train."

The man tilted his head slightly to the left as his narrowed eyes with a new interest. "Then *you* be Pastor Brooks?"

Aaron expelled a deep breath and then forcibly, he put on his brightest smile. "Yes. I am indeed he."

"Good-gobbledygoo!" the man exclaimed. "What are ya? Twelve?"

Instantly deflated, Aaron answered, "No sir. I happen to be twenty-two years of age."

"Well I'll be a suck-egg mule."

Having absolutely no idea what that might be, Aaron chose not to respond.

The man relieved the silence when he pointed to the suitcase and asked, "That grip the onliest thing you got?"

"Uhm…no…I have two trunks in the freight car."

The man tugging the brim of his hat said, "Right Pastor. You go on ahead an get in that truck over there an' I'll go wrestle with them packin' trunks."

Within minutes, the man, along with three of the freight car porters, had the trunks and the suitcase loaded into the bed of the black Model-T truck. Sweating profusely, the man climbed behind the steering wheel and after a quick swipe of his brow with his forearm turned to face Aaron. "My name's Yancy. Yancy Flowers."

"I am both very pleased and very grateful to meet you Mr. Flowers."

"Uh-huh," Yancy returned, as he put the truck into gear and the truck set off in the blinding speed of fifteen miles per. As they proceeded along the only paved road in all of Henrytown, Yancy pointed out the places of interest. There weren't many. A scant series of one storied buildings lined both sides of the road that was apparently Henrytown's main street.

"On your left is the movin' pictures show, and just by that is the feed and grain. My uncle owns it. Next to that is the Mackie's Grocery. On the other side of the street is the general mercantile and then on the corner is the post office. On the next stretch after the intersection is the Blue Bayou Café and the barber shop. Directly across the street is the knit and quilt store and right after that is the lady's hair parlor. Everything was kinda set up that a'way so's the ladies can have one side of the road and can also keep their eyes on their men while they're getting their hair all spiffed up."

"And that's important? Keeping an eye on their men?"

A secret smile played the thin lips of the man named Yancy. "Yeah Pastor, it purely is."

"And where's the church?"

"Hold your water. We're comin' on it."

Aaron's heart soared when he spotted the postcard perfect brick church sitting in the shade of towering pines. Evidently Yancy did not miss Aaron's excitement.

"That's the Methodist."

"Oh." Aaron nervously cleared his throat. "And our church?"

"Just a bit more up the road."

The pavement came to an abrupt end just after the welcoming drive into the Methodist church. Barely beyond the center of the Methodist church's neatly mowed lawn, the road became a pothole littered hard-pan; and from that point on the truck jounced along like a reeling drunk at the even more cautious speed of six mph. As promised, after a few moments, Aaron spotted the church: A white clapboard building with a stubby steeple. All of it stood high off the ground, resting on brick support columns. A set of stairs and a modest porch provided the means of entrance into the building. The church was surrounded in a semi-circle of huge pine trees, their height and width managing to block out the blue sky and the white orb of the sun.

"Had to build her high up," Yancy said in a voice loud enough to be heard over the rattling of the truck. "It can get a bit soupy out here when it rains. All of us here in LaSalle Parish are mostly English and with just enough French in us to make us interesting. Just below us in Avoyelles Parish, is where everybody is either pure Paris French or Cajuns."

"I'm sorry," Aarons shouted back. "What exactly is a Cajun?"

Yancy pealed laughter. “Oh, you gonna find out son. I can gaur-on-tee you dat.” And, again, he laughed.

Chapter Two

The suit jacket was off, neatly placed inside the truck. The tie was loosed. Aaron was standing in the back of the truck bed while Yancy stood in the knee-deep grasses and weeds that passed as the pastorate lawn. The house Aaron was to live in was set just as high off the ground as the church and the pastorate was conveniently located about an eighth of a mile behind the church, both church and house shared the same strip of dry dusty road. Amazingly, the pastorate looked to be much larger than the church. As an unmarried man, the house was far and away more than he'd been expecting as accommodation. But he couldn't think about that for the moment. The first order of business was the unloading of his trunks. Trouble was, both trunks were extremely heavy. At the station depot it had taken the combined efforts of four men and one highly enthusiastic youth to load said trunks. In the pastorate yard, there were only two men, the younger one with scant upper body strength and the older, as wiry as a whip snake. Which meant the unloading wasn't progressing at all well. Aaron pushed while Yancy pulled yet still, the trunk barely moved.

"What in the world's in this thing?" Yancy yelled. "Did you stuff a fat wife inside to save money on the train fare?"

Tired and so hot that his sweat soaked shirt clung to him, Aaron paused long enough to arm eye-stinging sweat from his brow. "Mr. Flowers, I'm not married."

"Well then what in the tarnation did you pack?"

"Books," Aaron answered. "And a typewriter. I hadn't realized they would be quite so heavy."

"Tha's cause you a gentleman," Yancy scoffed. "Gentlemen's got others to do all the heavy tote'n for 'em." With that, Yancy simply gave up. He removed his hat and with a kerchief pulled from his back pocket, wiped the sweat from the top of his head. He returned hat to head and glared at Aaron. "We need more help." Yancy turned and walked toward the brick steps leading up to the covered porch. "Come on in the house boy. It's yours so ya may as well see it from the inside."

Grateful for any excuse to abandon the unloading, Aaron jumped down off the flatbed and hurriedly followed.

The deep covered porch wrapped around the entire outside of the house. There were six rocking chairs set off to the right side of the front door. Yancy stood with the screen door propped open as he fished around inside each of his overall's pockets, eventually finding the key. After turning the lock and opening the door, he passed the key back to Aaron.

"Around here we don't usually keep the doors locked, but this place has been sittin' empty for a bit. Head deacon said for us to lock it up otherwise, can't never tell who we might find livin' in."

Aaron looked at the key in his hand. The streets of Atlanta were filled with soup kitchens and homeless families. Atlanta was not the exception, the Depression was a national crisis and any empty building, even in such a remote corner of the United States, would have been too tempting for those desperate for shelter.

As if reading the younger man's thoughts, Yancy said, "Hard times is hard times Pastor. Especially here in Henrytown."

The living room was very large and fully furnished. Two overstuffed settees and three matching wing backed chairs made a cozy grouping as the couches opposed each other and the chairs filled in the gaps. A mahogany coffee table rested on a worn rug in the center of the furniture grouping. A closed upright piano stood against the wall and within steps away from the closed French doors that divided the living room from the dining room. Through the small glassed windows of the French doors Aaron could see a large oval shaped dark oak table surrounded by twelve chairs. Directly behind the table stood a china cupboard and off to the far side of that stood a pie safe. None of the furniture was covered with dust protecting sheeting, yet there didn't appear to be a speck of dust on any of it. Even to his bachelor's somewhat oblivious eye, the house was immaculate.

While Yancy made for the candlestick telephone on its special stand in the corner of the living room, Aaron walked toward the closed door on the left and opening it, discovered the pastorate study. There was a roll top desk and chair as well as a wing backed chair that matched the living room chairs. Lace curtains covered the four windows in the room and pull shades were half closed directly behind the curtains. There was a standing lamp next to the wing backed chair. A banker's lamp was on the desktop and hanging from the center of the ceiling was a wood and wicker woven ceiling fan with a protruding white globe. By playing with the wall mounted two buttoned light switch, Aaron could turn on both the fan and the light inside the globe. All in all, it was the perfect room for devotional time, sermon preparation, counseling troubled souls and, Aaron's passion, Bible study. Yancy's sudden laughing and then the loud, one sided conversation, caught Aaron's attention.

"Well sugar-bean, ya'll gonna have to talk about Miz Lizzie's bunions some other time. Right now I need the line to call Everett." A slight pause as Yancy listened. "Yeah, he's here." Yancy turned at the waist as Aaron stepped back into the living room. The long body of the telephone was in Yancy's right hand and the receiver or listening tube was in his left and pressed against his ear as he eyed Aaron and spoke into the mouthpiece. "What does he look like?" Yancy's eyes squinted. "Well, I guess you could say he's a pretty boy, but he's kinda on the skinny side." Yancy barked a laugh. "Naw, naw, he got golden hair." Another pause, then, "Keeps sayin' he ain't."

Even at the distance between them, Aaron could hear a succession of clicks as the women who had been tying up the party line rapidly hung up their phones. The newly vacated line noisily thrummed through the receiver in Yancy's hand as he said to Aaron, "You maybe want to wash up a mite. Women are hot footin' it over here an' just as fast as they can run."

Aaron turned and walked out of the room, out of the house and down the brick steps. Again at the truck, he retrieved his suitcase. As he came into the living room, suitcase in hand, Yancy's back was turned to the entrance doorway and he was again laughing loudly into the telephone.

"Oh you know that! Tha's what I been talkin' about! This boy don't have a prayer." *Pause* "Naw, naw, naw. Him being a preacher man only makes everything worse. Means he got to stand there an' be polite. You don't want to miss this sight. An' bring me some good strong help for his blamed trunks."

Yancy hung up the earpiece on the telephone arm and set the telephone back on its stand. He was still chuckling when he turned and spotted Aaron. A nanosecond later, he was slapping a hand to his chest and exclaiming, "Boy! You must be half cat. You need to be more noisy when you come into a room."

"I apologize," Aaron said. "If you could show me to the bedroom, I'd like to change into less travel worn clothing."

Yancy led the way, saying over his shoulder, "They's only one bedroom these days." Opening the French doors, Aaron tagging behind as they passed through the dining room, then into the spacious kitchen. As they passed by the walk-in pantry, Yancy went left and into a room that looked very much like a lady's sitting/sewing room, complete with dressmaker's dummy and treadle sewing machine. Through the opposing door they entered another room which turned out to be the master bedroom. Yancy tossed his head slightly, indicating a door on the right. "That there door is for the sleeping porch."

"Excuse me?" he said as he laid his case on the wide wrought iron bed.

Yancy stood in the center of the large bedroom. "Sleeping porch," he said with an air of exasperation. "You don't have them things in Georgia?"

Aaron raised his hands slightly as he shrugged his shoulders. "Sorry. I've never heard of a sleeping porch so I suppose the answer to your question would be, no."

"Well here in Louisiana, the summer nights are mostly more like breathin' hot water than what you'd call air. Makes sleeping in the house real bad. That means we all got a sleeping porch. There's five beds out there so you got your choice. Pastor Ed built this house long time ago when him an' his wife first come here. He built it out of money from his own pocket. The house kept getting bigger with each baby. They were blessed with four, two boys, two girls. Then the babies grew up and went their way. Finally, Miss Shirley—Pastor Ed's wife—she passed and then he passed two months after her. None of the children wanted the house, so they deeded it over to the church. Tha's how come you got a nice place to live instead of havin' to make do with a room in somebody else's house."

"But the house has only the one bedroom?"

"It used to have four. This here room was Pastor Ed's an' Miss Shirley's. The second bedroom was a nursery before it became Miss Shirley's sewing room. We passed that one when we come by the kitchen. The third bedroom, what is now the study, was for the boys. The fourth room was the girls'. Miss Shirley had it emptied when the last daughter left an' then they put in shelving for linens and quilts an' such.

But back when the kids all lived here, they all slept out on the sleepin' porch during the summertimes. They used to play like they was camping.

Yancy looked around the room with a reverent awe. "This house has known lots of love and laughter." Then he looked meaningfully at Aaron. "An' this house will bless you too; if you let it."

Aaron was about to reply when a series of car horns shocked the moment.

"We got company!" Yancy cried.

Now alone Aaron explored further, going back into the sewing room and opening the door in the center of the far wall. With that, he discovered the house's central hallway. At the bottom end of the narrow hall he could see the interior of the pastorate study through its partially opened hallway door. There were three more doors along the right of the hallway. There was only one closed door on the left and when trying to open it, the attempt was blocked by something heavy on the other side. He then correctly assumed the cause to be the upright piano in the living room. Turning to investigate the center door on the right, to his immense relief, he found the bathroom with a claw-foot bathtub, a toilet with an overhead cistern and pull chain, a pedestal sink with hot and cold taps and three freestanding cupboards. In a cupboard next to the sink he found wash cloths and hand towels. Removing his soiled shirt, he took a quick sink bath and then raced back to the master bedroom. All the while he could hear raucous male voices coming from the front porch. In agitated stress, he redressed in a fresh shirt and then, while still working the buttons, he set off. Had he allowed himself a moment to think it through, he would have gone back down the hallway and emerged into the living room via the study. Instead, he blundered into the kitchen that was now filled with women.

The women varied in ages and sizes, yet all of them looked as if they'd dressed in their very best springtime dresses. Had Aaron been one who was given to notice such things, he would have immediately noticed that except for the variations of color that the cotton material, high waist, near-ankle length dresses, were identical. This meant that each dress had to have been home sewn. The ladies also wore the same dark gray three-quarter inch heeled, shoes. As there was only one hairdresser in Henrytown, they each had the same hair style: Wavy Bob. Yet, for a Depression Era back-of-the-bayou type town, the ladies were indeed stylish.

And silent.

In describing the new preacher Yancy had said, "Boy" but none of the women had taken the term all that seriously. Yancy was as old as dust. Next to him, Methuselah could have passed for a boy. He'd also said that the preacher was pretty, but that infernal man hadn't prepared them for even the half of it. What that idiot man should have said was, "Movie Star" because as they openly gapped, that was the one thought that flitted through each and every Wavy Bobbed head.

"*Our new preacher's a movie star*!"

Then en masse they remembered the most important piece of information. Their new preacher was not married. And that thought was followed very rapidly by, "*Thank you Jesus*!"

Aaron was stammering his apologies for having intruded when he suddenly found himself inside a crush of jabbering females.

"You look half starved to death!"

"You like pecan pie? I brought one."

"My peach cobbler is better because I canned them peaches special just last fall. And peaches are so hard to come by you know. Would you like a nice bowl?"

"Not till he's had proper food first!"

"We got chicken—"

"An' ham!"

Yancy's voice sounded above the female squabbling. "Ya'll get off that boy!"

Inside the crush, Aaron all but quivered with relief as Yancy hauled him to freedom. As the women watched their quarry escape, their circle compressed, bringing them in shoulder to shoulder.

"What you think?" Thelma Lewis asked in a near whisper.

Myra Waters was the first to answer. "I believe he's the answer to every mama's prayer." Index finger rapidly tapping breastbone, she finished, "Especially this here mama's prayers."

"And I think," Edna Flowers, cousin-by-marriage to Yancy, said, "If that boy-child can preach half as good as he looks, we're gonna need a bigger church."

On the front porch Aaron was treated to the only unoccupied rocker. The men present numbered twenty. The oldest men, all of them in overalls, occupied the remaining rocking chairs while the younger males, all of them wearing denim jeans and short sleeved shirts, made do with roosting on the porch's top wooden railing. As the screen door was the only hindrance between the porch and the house, the men could clearly hear the sudden eruption of laughter from the kitchen.

The oldest man, and sitting at Aaron's left, turned at the waist and said, "Son, you're toast."

Before Arron could respond to the man on his left, the man on his right chimed in. "Them hens is cluckin' an' tha's a fact. Preacher, you done stirred up the whole dern hen house."

Among the young men sitting on the railing was one that looked very much like a younger version of Yancy Flowers. Grinning as he looked at Aaron, he said, "Daddy? Have you spoken to him of Libby?"

Daddy did indeed turn out to be none other than Yancy Flowers who coughed and then peevishly replied, "Didn't have time to think about it on account of my being too busy killing myself with the man's trunks." Yancy looked out toward the yard. "Speakin' of which, while we got so many young bucks lookin' to get themselves fed, they might as well go on ahead an' deal with them trunks right now."

"Aw, Daddy—"

"Don't you—'Aw Daddy' me, Casper Flowers. You opened your mouth and now you got my boot in it. You get your sorry self on down from there and get the pastor his trunks."

The porch railing emptied of four young men who filed passed Yancy and descended the steps.

"Ya'll remember to lift with your legs now," one of the men called after them. "Don't be messin' up your backs. A bad back will haunt you all your life."

Casper waved a hand in the air. "Thanks for the advice."

"You're more'n welcome, young'un."

As Aaron rose to follow, a hand on his arm stayed him, the man on his left shaking his head no, as he said, "Liftin' is their chore. Preachin' is yours. Besides, you got to stay nice an' pretty for the ladies."

Aaron blushed scarlet as the other men laughed.

The first trunk had been deposited in the study and now the second, and heaviest of the two, was being carried casket style, on the shoulders of the four strapping young men. As they came up the front steps, Aaron finally managed to escape the old man in the next rocker and literally on the run, he arrived just in time to open and then hold back the screen door as the young men, and the trunk, passed through.

In the study, the trunk was set down next to the first, and with a thump. Aaron quickly began shaking hands with each of the four men who were very close to his own age. As they shook hands, each young man said his name and Aaron added a mental identity tag; a trick he'd learned in seminary for remembering a multitude of names and faces.

"Casper." *Thirty year younger version of Yancy Flowers.*

"David." *Blond Charles Atlas advertisement.*

"Leon." *Good looking face, crooked front teeth.*

"Archie." *Bright red hair, wonderful smile.*

Aaron was in the midst of thanking each man for his strenuous effort when a female voice announced that the meal was ready for the blessing. This pronouncement caused a stampede from both the porch and the study, Casper being the only one to think of grabbing the new pastor by the arm and hauling him along with the thundering male herd.

In Georgia, the main meals were breakfast, luncheon and dinner. In Louisiana, he was quickly learning, the meals were known as breakfast, dinner and supper. The assortment of foods, the stack of plates, along with napkins and utensils, had been laid out on the dining room table buffet style. Before any plate or fork could be lifted, everyone waited for Aaron to bless the meal. From the eager expressions of the young men, Aaron sensed it would be wise to keep the blessing brief.

"Our Father, we thank you for Your goodness and Your bounty. I ask that you especially bless the lovely hands that prepared each dish. We thank You for your great mercy and for the wonderful fellowship we are enjoying this day. In Jesus' Name . . ."

"AMEN!" everyone said.

And then the buffet became something on the order of semi-organized mayhem as plates and utensils were snatched up and everyone proceeded to help themselves. Aaron decided it would be best to wait, but he needn't have bothered with humble decorum. The ladies were taking care of his plate, and, when it was handed to him it was so loaded he could barely manage carrying it. With their own plates taken care of, the men began to head back to the front porch, leaving the women to sit daintily at the dining table. Careful not to spill anything, Aaron followed the men.

The rocking chair he'd previously occupied was again waiting for him, but Aaron walked on by, going for the company of the young men sitting on the series of steps. He stopped at the top riser, sitting down next to Casper. The older men on the porch began holding sway on Louisiana's favorite topic . . . politics.

The eldest of the group was known as "Grumpy" even though he'd been introduced as Mr. Edward. Apparently, his nickname stemmed from the fact that he was completely edentulous, the absolute loss of teeth causing his chin to meet the tip of his nose. Still, Grumpy was doing a great job of eating a crisply fried chicken leg. Grumpy had a lot to say about the Kingfish—Huey P. Long's nickname—and how the Kingfish was going to clean up Washington D.C. now that Governor Long had been voted in as United States Senator Long. Good times were coming, and the American people would soon be sending their thank you's to none other than the Kingfish of Louisiana.

Grumpy's opinion was not met with a unanimous approval. An argument ensued. Following Casper's lead, Aaron too concentrated on the mountain of potato salad on his plate. But still, Grumpy seemed determined to press the issue.

"Preacher? Ya'll up in Georgia ever hear of our Huey P.?"

"Yessir, Mr. Edward. We have indeed."

"An' just what has Georgia gotta say about him?"

Aaron set his plate on the porch flooring and answered slowly, well aware that Mr. Edward's question was more on the order of a challenge, and that every ear was finely tuned to visiting pastor's response. Failing to believe that this was a group of men would be at all receptive to his father's view that the newly sworn Right Honorable Senator from

Louisiana was nothing more than a thorough-going Dishonorable Scallywag, Aaron proceeded with supreme caution.

"Georgia believes absolutely in State's Rights. Therefore, Georgia supports absolutely Louisiana's right to elect into any office anyone it so chooses."

Yancy, sitting happily in the rocker that Aaron had shunned, laughed heartily and then said, "You sure you a preaching man? You sound more like a politician!"

Aaron blushed. "Perhaps," he stammered, "once I am more personally invested in Louisiana's interests, my opinions will be less vague."

"Yeah," Yancy agreed. "But the smartest thing you can ever do is stay just like you are. Old Grumpy here's been known to shoot people who don't much agree with him."

"That reminds me," Grumpy said to Yancy. "For you not ever voting for the Kingfish even once, I'm still owin' you a twenty-two bullet square between your eyes. I'm not so good at drivin' no more so one of these first days I'd appreciate you comin' on pass my house so's I can let ya have it."

"Can't do it this week, Grump," Yancy drily replied.

"Tha's all right," the old man said with a wave of his hand as he settled back in the rocker. "Just give me a call whenever you're ready an' I'll get Ole Bertha primed an' loaded."

The other men were laughing, but Aaron looked worriedly to Casper. "It's all right," Casper whispered. "Threatenin' to shoot people is how Ole Grumpy communicates. Besides, he's half blind and can't never find his gun."

Chapter Three

It was quite dark when the last of the vehicles drove away. The unkempt lawn, on which the vehicles had haphazardly parked, deserted. The men had all shaken his hand with vice like grips, while the ladies had gushed, each giving him a motherly hug along with instructions on just how and where the leftover foods had been stored. These women, he'd learned, were the very same ladies who had worked to make the house sparkling clean and the bed dressed with fresh sheets. Aaron stood on the edge of the porch and leaned on a support column watching as the lights of the cars and trucks faded and then winked out. Now in the absence of the welcoming crowd, the isolation of the house was uncomfortable.

Never before had he been so completely alone. It was a positively eerie sensation. Outside of the noise-some bullfrogs, there was such a nothingness. Atlanta was a crowd of people; his parents' home a never ending procession of guests. The nonstop presence of people had always annoyed the studious Aaron and there had been many an evening when he'd prayed for just one night of—nothingness. Now his prayer had been answered, and much to his chagrin, the nothingness he'd longed for was rather unnerving. He was entirely alone in a strange wilderness.

But then he remembered a lecture on the wilderness being God's proving ground. For Moses it had been forty years before God spoke to him from the burning bush. For Jesus it had been forty days and nights confronting Evil head-on. And for Paul, it had been three years, relearning everything he thought he'd known before God allowed him to become an apostle. Aaron knew all of this as a head fact. He'd even written his pre-grad thesis on this very subject. But a head fact and reality were miles apart. As crickets chirped and frogs . . . frogged . . . as well as other noises that he'd no idea of, he realized something else. The wilderness is not silent. Actually, it's a bit rackus. And more than a tad unnerving.

He turned and went to the first available rocking chair and sat down. Then the enormity of what he'd done caused fear to grip his heart. He was alone. He was a stranger in a strange country. The evil twins, Fear and Doubt, rushed into the void. "Father!" he cried out in utter panic. "I don't think I can do this!! I'm so afraid!"

He did not remember falling asleep. What he did remember was becoming mosquito bait and taking a hurried refuge inside the house. He also remembered locking the front door and turning off the living room's lights. From there he'd made his way to the bedroom. Because of the heat, he chose to wear only light cotton pajama bottoms. Then he'd dropped to his knees as he continued the agonizing conversation with his Lord. At some point he'd climbed onto the bed and, then as he lay there, a wonderful sense of peace settled over him. And now here he was, coming awake in the early morning to find the sun turning the lowered window shades a bright yellow. Somewhere just beyond the opened windows behind the shades he heard the gentle music of calling bobwhites. From some corner of his mind he recalled his fourth grade Sunday school teacher talking about Noah's Ark.

"God told Noah to gather two of every kind of animal, but He told him to gather seven pairs of every species of birds. Now, can anyone tell me why He'd say that to Noah?"

Aaron raised a hand, and she nodded her consent.

"Because God loves birds the very, very best!"

His teacher had laughed.

Laying there and listening to the bobwhites, he blessed God for the inclusion of seven pairs of bobwhites on the Ark. And with his eyes closed, he gloried in the beauty of their private language, as well as the fact that he had not only gone to sleep in a strange house and in an even stranger country, but amazingly, that he'd slept through the night feeling entirely secure. In a voice barely above a whisper he said, "Thank You Father. I love You so much."

The bedsprings creaked as he finally rolled out of the bed. He began this new morning in the same way he began every morning—with a series of stretches, beginning with toe touches to work out any kinks in his back. He was on his sixth toe touch when he heard a burring sound. He came up straight to his full height and extended his arms over his head. The distinct burring was heard again. Was it only his imagination or was he actually hearing the telephone? Well, if it was, it certainly didn't sound like any telephone he'd ever heard before. This sounded like a series of four quick burrs, and then a long pause of silence and then two more quick burrs. Telephones simply didn't ring like that. Not in his experience at any rate. He finished his series of ten toe touches and just before starting the deep knee bends, the irritating burring started up again. This time he decided he should investigate.

Annoyed by the interruption in his morning routine, Aaron opened the bedroom door and padded barefoot through the kitchen. The telephone was just sitting there on its stand in the living room absolutely silent, the very personification of innocence. But as he turned away, the thing began to burr. Again, not a true ringing but a series of four short burrings, pause, pause, pause, and two more short burrs. Cautiously lifting the receiver tube from its cradle, he was about to say a whispery hello, when from the listening bell, he heard the sound of a very angry male voice.

"Pastor Brooks, this is Deacon Winters. Did you forget to call your mama?"

"Excuse me?"

A derisive snort, then, "Pastor, your mama has kept the whole parish in turmoil. She is convinced you're dead. She said she kept calling the pastorate but that you weren't answerin', which to her mind meant that you've got to be dead."

"Oh, I do apologize," Aaron said. "I was asleep. I must have been too exhausted to hear the telephone."

"Well good for you cause I sure kept on hearin' it. An' I'd truly appreciate you calling your mama this very minute so's that maybe I can get myself an hour's rest."

Deacon Winters hung up.

His cheeks puffing slightly, he rapidly tapped the receiver's cradle arm to signal his need for attention from the trunkline operator. A young woman immediately answered. Caught off guard by her promptness, he stammered, "Ahh—yes, good morning . . . and then he heard the operator giggle. Feeling somewhat sheepish he said, "Um—I wonder if it might be possible at this hour to place a collect call to Atlanta?"

Not bothering to ask for any other information, the operator said, "Right away, Pastor. I'll ring you back as soon as I have your mama on the line."

"Thank you." As he was about to hang up, a thought occurred. "By the way, you wouldn't happen to know how to make coffee would you?"

Libby Flowers, the nineteen-year-old daughter of Yancy, and the younger sister of Casper, clamped her hand firmly over the bulky head set's speaking horn, as she fought laughter. When able to contain herself, she removed her hand and proceeded to give him precise instructions for using the drip style coffee pot. She also told him exactly where he'd find the canister containing freshly ground coffee.

Not really certain he'd followed all of that, Aaron asked anxiously, "And you will be calling again soon? I only ask because I'm not completely certain I can manage most of the instructions."

Oh, good heavens! The man's pitiful! Now more concerned than amused, Libby said, "Just don't forget that you have to light the burner with a match while you're turning the knob on the stove."

"That's important is it?"

"Only if you don't intend to blow up the whole house."

"Oh. Right. Then that is important isn't it?"

"Pastor? I'm gonna wait on the line while you go light the stove and put the water kettle on the burner. If I hear a big boom, I'll send the fire brigade."

"What about my call?"

"Your mama can wait another five minutes. Now just go do what I said."

"You are very kind," Aaron replied. Then he set the receiver down alongside on the telephone. Four minutes later he was back on the line and sounding enormously pleased with himself, that he'd done everything just as she said.

"And did you remember to put water in the kettle?"

"Drat!"

Her elbow resting on the edge of the desk and her forehead resting against the palm of her hand she said a dispirited tone, "Do not turn the burner off. Just take the kettle to the sink, take the top off the kettle, turn on the water spigot and fill the kettle. Then you put the top back on the kettle and then you set the kettle back on the burner."

"Won't that be dangerous? Those flames are rather high."

"Turn 'em down! Not off, just down until you put the kettle on the burner."

"Oh. Right. And will you be good enough to wait again?"

“Yes,” Libby sighed wearily. While listening to his footsteps fading, she said, “No wonder his mama was tellin everybody her son was dead. The man could kill himself just makin’ coffee!”

The board buzzed and Libby plugged into the separate line and heard the voice of her Aunt Connie. “Good morning darling.”

“Morning Aunt Connie.”

“Could you ring me over to Ethel?”

“No ma’am. The line’s gonna be tied up with a long-distance call.”

“Is he finally callin’ his mama?”

“Yes ma’am.”

“Be sure you let me know how that goes.”

“Yes ma’am. Gotta clear the board now.”

“I swear Libby Flowers, you are just as smart as a bug knowing how to do all this modern stuff.”

“Thank you, Aunt Connie.”

Libby pulled the plug on her auntie.

In the kitchen Aaron looked at the two separate spigots, one for hot, one for cold. It came to him that as his ambition was to heat the water to boiling that he might be well ahead of the game if he began the process by using the hot water spigot. He also decided that just in case this wasn’t the correct procedure, he wouldn’t tell the highly patient telephone operator. As the water poured into the kettle, he thanked God for the tender mercy of sparing him the danger of actually ever meeting this unknown woman. His humiliation would be astronomical. But, as she was most probably in yet another town that he’d never heard of, this embarrassment would be happily contained to addressing her over the telephone line. However, it was just a little galling to know that far off in *Somewhere Else, Louisiana*, there would always be that disembodied female voice who would clearly know exactly who he was; that he was domestically incompetent; and that his mother was an excessive worrier.

After setting the kettle back on the burner and dutifully turning up the flames beneath it, Aaron went back to the phone to report his success.

The board was buzzing like a swarm of angry bees, but Libby ignored it as she carefully instructed him in the final steps of this coffee making business. "Louisiana coffee is strong. You don't want to use more than six tablespoons of grounds or you'll be making yourself a pot of goo. You put the grounds in the top half of the pot and, when the water boils, you carefully pour the water over the grounds and let it drip down into the bottom half of the pot. Do you think you can do all that?"

"Yes," he replied confidently. "You've been very thorough. Now, how does one go about making toast?"

Libby's reply quashed his certainty that this unknown young woman was far, far away. "You don't," she said with finality. "What you do is you let me put the call through to your mama and then you wait for me to turn up on your doorstep."

Before he could gather his wits, she was gone. Alarmed now, Aaron hung up the receiver and ran to change his clothing and brush his teeth.

Aaron was Atlanta dapper; fresh white trousers that stylishly flowed down and across the arched section of his summer white oxfords, and a white shirt with the sleeves rolled up to the elbows. To break the tedium of all that whiteness, he was also wearing his beloved red suspenders: His ownership of something so daring was a secret he'd kept from his parents—most especially, Father. He was finally enjoying a cup of coffee—which he'd made practically all by himself—and sitting quietly as he listened to his mother's teary voice coming through the receiver. It was no good assuring her that he was quite all right because she was his mother and she didn't want to hear that her one and only child could cope without her. So, Aaron was silent, and he was patient. Before she forced herself to hang up, she said, "Aaron, I want you to check inside all of your books. I put special book markers in each and every one of them."

"Yes, Mother."

"Do this immediately, Aaron. It's very, very important."

"Now?"

"This very instant, yes. And now I'll say good-bye, but I'll be expecting a call on Sunday afternoon. I'll want to hear all about your first service."

After ending the conversation, Aaron dutifully went into the pastorate study and, after, finding the trunk keys, he opened up the heaviest trunk. He removed the typewriter's case, setting it in the center of the opened roll-top desk. Then he went back to the waiting books, lifting one and fluttering the pages. Things flew out: Three twenty dollar bills. He set the bills on the desk and then he repeated the process until all of the books from both trunks had been rifled through. Each and every book contained twenty dollar bills; some only two, others three or more. The cash had quickly stacked up on the desk as the emptied books were neatly arranged on the shelves of the tall bookcase. When the trunks were emptied Aaron sat in the swiveled desk chair dazedly staring at the pile of bills.

The exact amount was, five thousand, eight hundred dollars. This he knew, was the entire horde of what his mother called her, "Pin Money." Years ago she'd told him of the custom of Pin Money; a custom in which all mother's instructed their daughters on the eve of their weddings. Men erroneously believed that the mother-daughter-prenuptial talk was about the bride's marital duty to her husband . . . but, no. In an age when all of the bride's worldly goods immediately became the sole property of her husband, the mothers went to great pains to teach their daughters just how to skim the household accounts. The brides were also given hat boxes labeled "Buttons" in which, they were told, to hide the purloined stash. This custom was to prepare the daughters against the dark side of marriage. If the husband turned out to be a brute, a drunk or a gambler, the wife would then have a private resource. Pin Money was, in effect, a woman's security in a very insecure and completely masculine-biased world. Thus, the stack of bills currently in Aaron's possession was the whole of his mother's worldly worth, and each cunningly pilfered dollar represented Emilia Brooks' complete investment of herself in her son.

Stunned, Aaron could only stare, at all that money. Added to this was, of course, was the six hundred dollars his father had given him as an advance of his final allowance. Therefore, Aaron had, in his immediate possession, six thousand, and four hundred dollars! That was more money than he'd ever seen. He jumped up from the chair, urgently seeking a secure hiding place for the newly found filthy lucre. That's also when he realized that having a lot of money also meant having a lot of panic. In this untrustworthy economic age, his father wouldn't have entered a bank even with a gun stuck to his head. Ergo, his father had a home safe. Oh, and how Aaron now envied him that. Several possible hiding places flitted through his mind but then completely vanished with the sound of a vehicle pulling into the yard. He hurriedly slammed the desktop and raced out of the study. Using the house's skeleton key, he locked the study's door just as his arriving visitors were climbing the porch steps. A familiar feminine voice called through the screened door.

"Hey Pastor Brooks! The toast cavalry has arrived!"

Aaron stepped into the living room. And then he saw clearly the young woman he'd previously hoped he would never be forced to actually meet.

And, to use the Atlanta vernacular, she was a PIP! The sunlight set fire to the strawberry hued, curly, shoulder length hair. The nose was pert and well freckled. The eyes were huge, dark brown and sparkling with mischief. Her smile was playful and with tiny dimples set in each corner. Her complexion was so creamy that she looked like a terribly expensive Heirloom China Doll.

There was a young man standing beside her, but Aaron was so captivated by the young woman that he wouldn't have been able to describe her escort even if the police later tried to beat it out of him. The very most he would have been able to confess was, "He seemed rather surly."

"Pastor Brooks?" That now wonderfully familiar voice chirped.

With a jolt Aaron came back to himself.

There was a note of laughter in her voice when she asked, "Is it all right if we come in?"

"Oh, good heavens!" Aaron cried as he released the hook latch.

Libby walked in first. She knew this house like a second home. When Pastor Ed's children were young, sleepovers were always on the sleeping porch and Libby couldn't count the many sleepovers she'd attended. Pastor Ed's once boisterous family was gone now. Pastor Ed Wallace had been from one of the oldest families in Livingston Parish, one of the parishes of Louisiana's Plantation Country. Instead of being a sugar baron, Pastor Ed had chosen the simple, godly life. His two grown sons had subsequently chosen the life their father had abandoned, idolizing their paternal uncle Jefferson Wallace, patriarch of the Wallace family.

Eldest daughter Martha-Anne had married a paternal third—or possibly fourth—cousin. At any rate, she hadn't needed to change her last name. And she lived in a house about five times bigger than the house she'd been raised in. Youngest daughter Sarah-Marie, always the talent of the family, was studying art in New York City. Sarah-Marie was still a wonderful friend, always sending Libby colorful post cards and Kodak photos of her glamorous life in a big city.

Libby forced herself to smile brightly and shake off the missing, her childhood friend. She stuck out her hand to greet the house's new occupant.

"Hello Pastor Brooks. I'm Libby. Do you still have coffee?"

While shaking her hand, Aaron took in every five-foot, three inched detail. She was a slender girl dressed in a white blouse with capped short sleeves and high waist gray cotton trousers and brown penny-loafers. All of this was the current fashion craze created by the rebellious young film star Katherine Hepburn. While they shook hands, with her left she pointed her thumb behind her shoulder indicating the surly escort. "And this big lump is Seth Lewis."

Aaron knew he'd more or less greeted the escort, Seth Something, but beyond that he had no idea.

And . . . he still couldn't describe him.

With great reluctance he relinquished Libby's hand and then followed her like a devoted puppy as she led the way to the kitchen.

Seth didn't like the new preacher, not even a little bit. The guy was too young, too good looking and too . . . not married. Besides, Seth wasn't exactly what you would call, a churchgoer. As Libby played at being an expert cook (she most certainly wasn't—the girl couldn't even parboil a crawdad), Seth helped himself (not that anyone noticed) to a cup from the china cupboard and then poured tepid coffee into it. He then decided to wait for Libby on the porch. (Again, not that either of them would notice.) On leaving the kitchen, his last sight was both Libby and the preacher being on their hands and knees in front of the stove, Libby showing the preacher the magical wonders of the broiler. Seth shook his head and left them to it.

Aaron, had rarely, if ever, had the occasion to enter in his parent's kitchen where the cook and the cook's helper reigned supreme. Even his mother had only ever dared to invade the kitchen on Monday mornings to settle the weekly menu. In the seminary, the kitchen was always locked against marauding seminarians. Ergo, the propane stove was proving to be something of a marvel. And now knowing that the thing could also to be extremely lethal, he did his best to listen carefully while watching Libby's every move. Within minutes he felt yet a new thrill of accomplishment when he mastered the craft of lighting the boiler. Then Libby was again on the move. Aaron jumped to his feet, staying with her.

"This is the bread box, but in the spring and summer you want to avoid it." She retrieved the loaf of home baked bread. "The church ladies will make sure you get a fresh loaf every Saturday. And then you put it straight inside the ice box, not the bread box, or by Thursday you'll be eating green mold."

From a drawer beneath the work counter she extracted the bread knife and proceeded to slice the bread. "Get the butter dish out of the ice box please."

Aaron all but ran across the room to the electrified ice box. With the door opened, and cool air brushing his chest, he was stymied. "What exactly am I looking for?"

"Oh, for heaven's sake!"

They were both bent at the waist and shoulder to shoulder as they examined the darkened maw of the ice box. Brand new ice boxes—now called Refrigerators—came with a light that popped on whenever the door was opened. This was not a fancy refrigerator. This was a decade old Sears-Roebuck electric ice box. Consequently, no modern interior lighting.

"You see this little plate?" she asked. "That's the butter dish."

"And what's that big hard looking white lump?"

"That's the butter."

"Shouldn't butter be yellow and in very small squares?"

"Only in Atlanta and Baton Rouge."

"Oh."

"Here in the backwoods, butter is a big white lump."

"Oh."

She retrieved the plate containing the big white lump and they both straightened. "And now we put it on the bread."

Aaron was appalled. "What? All of it?"

"No," she said, elongating the word.

Libby gave Aaron the job of toast watching, which involved him being crouched before the boiler, literally watching the bread turn brown and the little white blobs of butter melting into the bread. Libby stood at the stovetop scrambling eggs. Then she showed him how to put the eggs and the toast on a plate and shove the platter into the stove's warming section. As soon as this final step was completed, she announced her departure.

"If you don't mind my saying so," she said. "You are going to need some help around here. I have a cousin who's a widow lady and she could do with the work. And she has a strapping son who can keep the yard cut down. You could probably get the pair of them for about ten dollars a month." She began to talk faster to put off any objections. "Now I know the church is only paying you twenty dollars a month, but my cousin and her son would save you from killing yourself and they'd work really hard and they're very dependable."

He had a smile that could stop a feminine heart mid-beat. So, when he smiled, Libby felt her heart stop mid-beat. It restarted when he said,

"I believe I will be able to make do quite nicely on ten dollars so, if your cousin and her son are willing, I would receive them most gratefully."

"So that's a yes?"

"That is indeed a yes."

So happy that her second cousin—her daddy's first cousin—was finally having some good luck, Libby couldn't stop herself from giving the new preacher a hug.

Her flinging herself against him took Aaron by complete surprise. With her arms around his waist and her head bumped hard against his chest, he had no idea what he should do, so his own arms sort of hung in mid-air like a large bird preparing to launch itself into a thermal. Before his dazed brain could instruct him to fold his arms around her, she was gone and running for the living room. Aaron followed and listened as she spoke into the telephone.

"Is Miss Mabel in the Nest?" To Aaron she quietly whispered, "It's the Crow's Nest. They tie up the line every day except Sunday and always from eight in the mornings to about four. There can be anywhere from two to forty of them on the line at once but, you'll get used to it." Back into the phone. "Well, if she does come on, will you please tell her that Libby said that the new preacher said he'd sure be pleased if she would come to work for him as his housekeeper? And says he needs Bubba-X too." She listened for five seconds and then she squealed, "Yes I know!"

Aaron did not know the mysterious something that Libby had just happily professed to know. She hadn't bothered to tell him.

His mind still in something of a blur from the unexpected hug, he foggily realized that she was shaking his hand with all the force of one priming a rusty pump. "You're not going to regret this, Preacher. And your mama can stop worrying. Come to think of it, the whole parish can stop worrying. I'll have Seth pass me by Miss Mabel's house just in case she didn't get the word. I'm sure she'll be here by midafternoon. And Daddy said to tell you he would pass by."

"Daddy?"

"Yeah. Yancy Flowers." She gave him a quizzical look. "You did know I'm Yancy Flowers' daughter didn't ya?"

"Ahhh . . . no."

"Well, I am."

"And that would make Casper—"

"My idiot brother."

Aaron's face turned an alarming shade of scarlet. Seeing the sudden flush of color, Libby hooted, "This whole time I've been here bossing you around and you really didn't know me from a squirrel?!"

"No—ah—, I afraid I didn't. B-b-but," he stammered, "I did find you to be a very knowledgeable person."

She leaned in close in order to avoid Seth's eavesdropping from the porch. "Don't be embarrassed," she smiled. Aaron momentarily phased out again. The sight of those adorable little dimples made his head feel swimmy. But she didn't notice because still speaking in a confiding whisper she said, "Everybody is related to everybody in LaSalle Parish. And it will also be good for you to understand that what people don't know about you, they'll make up, so with Miss Mabel here to look after you, you'll avoid some very unhealthy rumor and strife."

"I will?"

"Yes. Miss Mabel will see to it. Just think of her as your gossip killing guardian angel who also cooks, cleans and washes. You're gonna be just fine Pastor."

In the truck with the breeze coming through the opened window, Libby's mind was in a happy whirl. Then she heard Seth.

"He's got jug ears."

Her eyes wide Libby demanded, “Who has jug ears?”

“That preacher. He looks more like a milk pitcher than a preacher.”

“Seth Lewis! Don’t you dare blaspheme like that.”

“Libby, that ain’t blasphemin.”

“It’s getting mighty close, so stop it.” Fuming with anger she said more to herself than to Seth, “His hair’s cut too short on the sides is all.” In a snit, she turned her face away, allowing the cool air to refresh her face as the truck rolled along. *And he definitely does not have jug ears*!

Seth gripped the steering wheel. He had been liking Libby Flowers since they were both six years old. True, he’d never thought of doing anything seriously about it, but that didn’t mean he couldn’t get jealous if he put his mind to it. And now he was putting his mind to it. After moments of silence, Seth chanced a glance in Libby’s direction. She was smiling and twirling a lock of hair with her fingers. That’s when Seth knew that Libby had outgrown their childhood romance. She might be in the truck with him, but for all intents and purposes, Libby was long gone.

Chapter Four

The Louisiana expression, "pass by your house" doesn't actually mean that someone will cruise slowly on by admiring your yard's blazing display of azaleas. No, what it means is that someone is coming to visit. Therefore, around midmorning when Yancy passed by the parsonage, he brought people with him. One of the people was a dumpling of a woman with a deeply dimpled smile. The second person was a hulking mass of manhood of an undeterminable age, anywhere from twenty to fifty. Yancy did not wait for the new preacher to invite them in. He simply opened the screened door and held it like a gentleman while his cousin Mabel walked on through. The hulking mass, followed in after Yancy.

Miss Mabel was seated on one of the settees when she looked up at Aaron and asked, "Ya'll got a pitcher of tea in the icebox?"

Just as Aaron was opening his mouth to profusely apologize, Yancy, who was standing alongside of, and dwarfed by, the bulk of humanity, quickly spoke for Aaron. "Now Miss Maple-Sugar," Yancy paused long enough to wink at Aaron and say, "Maple-Sugar is what I always call her." And then back to Maple-Sugar . . . huh . . . Miss Mabel. "You know this boy's only just now learned how to make coffee. How's he supposed to know how to make tea? Tha's why he needin' you."

"Oh. tha's right," she tisked. "An' tha's why I brought some lemons from my tree. So why am I sitting here like a guest?" She wobbled to her feet. "I'll be in the kitchen if ya'll need me." Given her girth, she was amazingly spry. She was more than halfway to the kitchen when Yancy introduced the other male in the room.

"This here is Bubba X. His real name is Charles, but he was the tenth baby of the family, so he's used to bein' called Bubba. His daddy had a peculiar fondness for the Roman *numericals*, tha's why he got the X. Now, I know he looks right stupid, and he kinda is, but the boy can do anything once something is explained to him. You tell him what job you want doin' an just how you're wantin' it done, and he'll do it, no questions asked. An' truth be told, he's a long sight better at fixin' an mendin' than any professional builder I ever met. Folks around here set great store in what-all Bubba X can do. I've known him to mend everything from a dead automobile to a leaky roof, an even durin' a hurricane. And there ain't nobody who can tend a better yard. But if he ain't watched, he will eat you out of house and home. So, you make it plain to Maple-Sugar that her boy only gets one plate for his dinner-time."

Yancy turned to Bubba X. "You know where the shed is. The lawn mower blades most probably need sharpening, so you go on now. I gotta take the preacher somewhere's." Bubba shuffled out and without . . . as the old spiritual is wont to proclaim . . . ever uttering a mumbling word. The screened door banged shut behind Bubba X as Aaron was asking, "Where am I going?"

"Over to my cousin Fred's. He sells automobiles an' you truly gonna need one. Don't bother wearing your suit jacket. It's too hot a day for that. Just come on like you are. Now, go say bye to Mabel cause it'll hurt her feelings if you don't; I'll be in the truck."

Upon Yancy's exit, Aaron first hurried to his office, retrieved five hundred dollars, stuffing the cash into his front pocket. All of his money had been separated into six rolls and all six were tightly secured with rubber bands. Like a squirrel stashing acorns, he had hidden each roll in a different desk drawer and the roll top of the desk, he locked. After securing the desk he also locked both doors to the office, and then he sprinted off to the kitchen where he found Miss Mabel already with several pots of steaming something on the stove while she busily mixed up something else entirely inside a very large bowl. Aaron dutifully repeated everything that Yancy had said, adding, “Oh, and my office is not on your list of responsibilities.”

She looked at him with a puzzled expression. “Are you sayin’ you don’t want me to dust or nothin’ inside the study room?”

“Yes, but not to worry. When the room gets too awful, I’ll let you know. But in the meantime, I’m trying to organize my study so, I’d prefer nothing to be disturbed.”

Whipping to a froth whatever it was in the bowl, she sighed wearily. “Preacherin’s a hard business. Don’t you be frettin’, I’ll leave ya in peace. But be sure to yell when it gets knee deep in there.”

“Yes ma’am. I certainly shall.”

There was a momentary lull and then she stopped whipping the batter in the bowl. “Okay, sweetheart. You done told me what all needed sayin’. You can go on now.”

As the truck began its bone jarring journey, Aaron asked, “Would it be possible to make a brief stop at the church?”

Yancy glanced at Aaron, a hint of a smile playing his lips. “Itchin’ to see it are ya?”

“To be perfectly honest, I am.”

“Well, can’t say I blame ya. If I was startin’ a new job somewhere’s, I’d want to take a peek at the worksite. But I gotta warn ya, we’re a plain folk and the church is what we are; plain and simple.”

“It is my profound belief,” Aaron replied, “that where His children have gathered, our Lord is in glad attendance.”

Yancy looked at Aaron with what seemed to be a newly found approval. Turning into the church’s narrow drive, Yancy was easing the truck into a rolling stop when Aaron threw open the passenger door and bolted out of the cab. Yancy yelled through the driver’s side window.

"Preacher! You might want to wait for me. I'm the one with the door key!"

Aaron stood in the center of the aisle, quietly absorbing every detail of the sanctuary. It was very small and held the faint, yet not unpleasant, odors of humid air and age. The pews were rough hewn wood; the pulpit the same. Four windows lined each side of the walls; the mullioned panes of glass covered over with what looked to be oil cloth, Aaron guessed that the covering was to keep the strong sunlight, and its heat, off of the worshipers. Still, the coverings allowed in enough light to bathe the sanctuary a rich ocher.

Two ceiling fans with light globes hung just over the center pews. Additional lighting came by way of the evenly spaced wall mounted kerosene lamps. An upright piano stood against the wall off to the left of the pulpit. The pianist, who was yet still unknown to Aaron, had light via two small kerosene lamps that were safely gripped by the brass arms extending from either side of the piano's music shelf. Oddly, the music shelf was bare and the only hymnal that Aaron could see anywhere rested on top of the piano. And apparently, the church did not boast a choir for there wasn't room in the sanctuary for a loft, nor was there a baptistery which by tradition was always directly behind the choir loft. As there was no other door beyond the front entrance, Aaron felt safe in the assumption that the church lacked Sunday school facilities. But it was the Cross behind the pulpit, as well as the altar directly before the pulpit, that were the sanctuary's featured attractions. The Cross and the altar had, most obviously, been created by the same wood-crafting artist; the lines of each straight and true, the carvings of dogwood blossoms on each elegantly simple yet so very breathtakingly delicate. Any cathedral would have felt itself enormously blessed to have one, or at best, both of these on display.

Yancy cleared his throat and in a reverent tone, said, "A man named Nester Lantry made the Cross and the altar. He had a pure love for the legend of the dogwood tree; how thousands of years ago the dogwood was the strongest and straightest of all the trees, until it was used as the wood to make Christ's cross. Ever since that time, it's been weak and spindly, but it blooms every spring to celebrate Christ's resurrection."

"That's truly a beautiful legend," Aaron replied. He looked back at the Cross with a new appreciation for its quiet message and its lovingly crafted detail. "I shall very much enjoy meeting Mr. Lantry and thanking him for his marvelous contribution to this, my first pastorate."

Yancy turned his hat in his hands, "You'll have to do the thankin' in eternity son. Tha's where he's at right now, an' tha's where you'll find him one fine day. An' knowin' that man like I do, I know he's gonna be mighty proud to be meetin' you too."

With great reverence Aaron approached the altar, coming to kneel before it. Wordlessly, Yancy followed and knelt beside Aaron. With his head bowed and tears escaping his closed lids, Aaron softly prayed aloud.

"Father, thank You for the splendor of this wonderful church. May You and You alone be glorified in every service, in every prayer. May we all, Your children of Henrytown Free Church, be obedient to Your will. May You give us the strength to equal each and every challenge that You send as we strive to bear witness of Your beloved Son, our Advocate, our Blessed Redeemer. And it is in that Name, Jesus, we are privileged to pray, in all faith believing. Amen."

"Amen," Yancy repeated.

Before rising to their feet, Yancy turned his head, looking fully at the young pastor and said, "I believe you're gonna do for us, Preacher. Yessir, I believe you're gonna do us just fine."

They were entering Henrytown when Yancy suddenly became atypically chatty. "Now I wanna warn you ahead of time about Fred. He's a church deacon, but he can act like a pure heathen when it comes to sellin'. So, while you're lookin' over his automobiles, only believe ever second or third word comin' out of his head. An' make sure you don't jump at the first price he mentions. Also, ya gotta be careful of his 'add-on's'."

"What are those?"

"Fred's, *extras*. That man would charge for the air in the tires if he thought he could get away with it. So, whatever he says is 'extra', you just hold to the same price you want to pay and don't let him push you around. Truth be told, Old Fred's kinda got it in his rabbit mind that all preachers are pitiful easy to bamboozle."

Aaron laughed heartily. "I believe Mr. Fred is long overdue for a well-deserved shock."

Yancy was laughing as he replied, "You get him, Preach. Me? I believe I'm just gonna stand back and watch."

If there was one article of clothing that immediately symbolized a particular decade, then for the 1930's that article would be the Fedora. The Fedora came in a wide variety of colors and fabrics, the grey wool being in the cheapest price range and favored by men of modest means. Yancy Flowers' inexpensive grey Fedora grew like a weed among the pair of snow-white Fedoras being worn by the other two men as the trio walked down an aisle of parked motor cars.

Mr. Fred of *Fred's Friendly Auto Sales* was a jolly salesman with a nose finely tuned to the scent of cash money. His sense of smell was uncanny really, owing to the fact that Aaron had more than enough money in his pocket to pay in full for every car on offer. However, ninety percent of those autos looked as if they'd also need the services of *Fred's Towing* soon after leaving the lot.

Unfortunately for Mr. Fred, Aaron had, in his late teenaged years, picked up a bit of knowledge concerning the modern automobile. This knowledge he'd gained at his friend Fredrick (Buster) Cullpepper's house (actually, it was a mansion house). Aaron and Buster had spent countless hours inside the detached garage—formerly the stables—happily stripping down and then subsequently rebuilding a Model T simply because Buster's father had thought this would be an excellent way to keep two adolescent males well out of summertime trouble. On the basis of that knowledge, the newly ordained pastor was able to recognize an automotive stinker when he saw one. While they walked the line of autos, Mr. Fred stayed on Aaron like a bloodhound relentlessly tracking an escapee from Angola.

"Fords are all I sell," Mr. Fred heartily declared.

He was a man of portly proportions and the sweltering heat had him huffing for breath and sweating profusely. Still the huffing and sweating did little to deter his enthusiastic banter.

"An' Fords are all I'll take in trade. Can't never go wrong with a Ford. No sir. The world would stop spinning faster than a Ford will quit runnin'."

Mr. Fred stopped and grabbed Aaron by his elbow. Aaron waited while Mr. Fred collected a wheezing breath.

"Tell me just one thing, young man. Now, I'm not a nosy person by nature, but in your case I just gotta ask, do all brand-new preachers wear red suspenders?"

"Only the unmarried ones," Aaron replied.

Mr. Fred brayed laughter. "I see! Kinda like a peacock showing the ladies his fine feathers. Ya know it's good to be a member of a church that's finally got itself a preacher with a sense of style. Yessir, them suspenders are lady catchers all right. Course, your face ain't short in the looks department."

"Thank you."

Mr. Fred took a stronger hold of Aaron's arm. "Well given the fact that you could start courting any day now, you're gonna be needin' a saloon-type car. Saloons are a better bet when it comes to sparkin'." He let go of the elbow, wrapping an arm around Aaron's shoulders while propelling them both in a new direction. "I got one just over here that ought to do ya."

Aaron dug in his heels, impeding Mr. Fred's romp toward yet another stinker. "I'd rather we had a look at the silver-gray coupe in the showroom window."

"What!?" Mr. Fred squawked. His arm fell away from Aaron as his heavy black brows met at the bridge of his considerable nose. Friendly Fred looked more menacing than friendly. "Now son, have you any idea how much a brand spankin' new car like that's gonna cost?"

"Yes. In Atlanta they sell for three hundred dollars."

"Three hundred dollars!" Mr. Fred's face turned quite florid. He looked as if he were on the verge of a massive stroke. "Son! That's a five-hundred-dollar car."

"On my graduation from the seminary, my parents gifted me with a bit of cash to help me get started in my new vocation. I currently have that gift inside my pocket. The price you are currently proposing is with the inclusion of a sizable interest on a long-term loan. An immediate cash payment, which I have on my person, effectively cancels any amount above factory pricing."

"B-But there's the radio—"

"Standard."

"The white wall tires—"

"Standard."

"Rust protection on the undercarriage—"

"Applied at the factory."

"The extensive warranty—"

"Made available by the Ford Motor Company."

"Tax an' licenses—"

"Which I can pay myself at the town hall for a five-dollar filing fee."

The two men then stared at each other for several eerily silent moments. Finally, Mr. Fred found his, now not quite so jovial, voice. "Three hundred an' fifty."

"Three hundred and five and you file the tax and licenses."

Mr. Fred wiped a hand over his mouth to prevent slipping a stream of curse words currently itching his tongue. "Preacher, there is no point in us arguing about this. I am not going down, not even by one penny, from three twenty-five."

Aaron paused to consider, then said. "That is an exorbitant amount Mr. Fred. But I shall pay it on the condition that as a member of my congregation you will agree to put ten of that extra twenty-five dollars into the church offering plate."

Well that just about tore Mr. Fred all to pieces. "Tarnation Preacher! You're killing me!"

"No sir," Aaron said evenly. "It is not within my power to kill anyone. If you are feeling close to perishing, that's the Lord's business. I have merely made an honest and above board offer of three hundred and twenty-five dollars today in your hand with stipulation that ten of those dollars be rightfully tithed to God, making the entire transaction a total of three hundred and fifteen dollars to you and ten for God. It's entirely your decision to either make the agreement or respectfully decline. This refusal on your part also means that I am then free to go to another dealership, preferably one that is not associated with our church . . ."

It was at this point that Yancy, who had been enjoying himself immensely, chimed in. "Next town over's got a Chevrolet dealer. An' right next door to him is the Oldsmobile man. Both of them lots are owned by Catholic people and them Frenchies are pure partial to a hard trade."

"Three twenty-five less ten for the offering!!" Mr. Fred thundered. In a high sulk, Mr. Fred stuck out his hand to shake on the deal.

Aaron looked down at the hand. "I'm afraid that before any deal is struck I must first test drive the car in question."

Yancy had to hurry away before he laughed like a fool.

It was a brand new two door saloon style Ford V-8. The model name was Tudor. Seated on the client's side of Mr. Fred's desk, Aaron carefully read the automobile's brochure.

The Tudor model is distinctive with modern line and remarkable riding comfort combined with the outstanding performance of the V-8 engine.

With enormous satisfaction, Aaron looked beyond the office window while salesman Fred quietly beavered away at the sales agreement paperwork. Through the window Aaron watched as Yancy slowly circled the new luxury automobile. He was intently inspecting each detail from the covered spare tire holder on the top of the trunk to the double lights on the front fenders. The car was so expensive that Yancy was afraid to get too close. He paused on the driver's side of the car and looked down at the running board's rubber mat that was a lighter gray than the silvery gray car paint. When he felt he was being watched, he looked up and met Aaron's gaze. Then the young preacher smiled and nodded, giving quiet consent for Yancy to have a better look inside. Yancy took a step nearer the car and put his hand on the door handle. Easing inside, he felt a thrill he hadn't known since the first time his wife Mildred had allowed him to hold her hand.

***

Hours later, Yancy was at home and at the supper table and talking nonstop about how he'd personally witnessed the Preacher slicker Mr. Fred down to the bone. Libby picked at the food on her plate while she pressed back a smile and listened to every word coming out of Daddy.

"I'm gonna tell you what," Daddy said, wiping tears of mirth from his eyes as he concluded his tale, "that boy is purely something. He may look so young that he don't know top from bottom, but don't let that ever, ever fool you. He's a sharp as a finely stropped blade."

"Did he get a good car?" Libby asked.

"He got the pick of Fred's litter." Yancy slapped the supper table as he wheezed laughter, "An', he's got Fred puttin' ten of those dollars into the offerin' plate! He stood right there and made Fred write a tithe promise into the contract! I thought Fred was gonna pop a vein. Funniest thing I ever heard of in my whole life! A sales contract with a built-in tithe clause. Which reminds me," Yancy said as he cut the slab of meat loaf on his plate, "I'm going over to the barber shop first thing in the morning."

"Why?" Mildred, his wife asked. "You just had a haircut last week."

"Good gobbledygoo!" Yancy cried. "Who said anything about a haircut?"

And then it twigged. "Oh," she said with a roll of her eyes. "Man-gossip."

"*Men* talk, Mildred," he said peevishly. "*Women* gossip, an' usually while they're either camped out on the party-line or while sittin' under hair dryers with curlers stuck all up on their heads. Are you hearin' the difference here?"

"No, but I do know when to stand corrected."

"Uh-huh. You shore do," Yancy agreed, missing entirely the fact that his wife and daughter were quietly laughing behind pressed lips.

Ralph Winters, the head deacon of Henrytown Free Church, knew all about the interim pastor's brand-new automobile. He should, he'd been on the telephone with Fred Flowers for nearly every minute of all the live long afternoon listening to Fred complain about how that "young'un pastor" had bamboozled him and just how Christian is something like that supposed to be anyhow? But that was Fred. Anytime he got the red licked off his Tootsie Pop, he commenced to boo-hooin'.

With the Depression deepening, a depression that had stricken the State of Louisiana years before it had gone national, Winter's Sawmill was still the biggest employer in Henrytown. It was true however, that Ralph's current employee record had slowly devolved to the bare minimum crew of fifteen men. Thanks in total to Huey P. Long's many building projects, the demand for high grade lumber was now on a steady increase and Ralph always came in with the lowest bids. That was because Ralph wasn't as glued to reforestation as was the Urania Mill. That mill had been founded in 1893 by Henry Hardtner, the man now being hailed as the father of reforestation. Ralph failed to comprehend the point of reforestation. The way he reasoned, you cut down one pine and three more would just naturally pop up in its place, and all by themselves. Ralph simply could not see the need to employ a team of men to follow behind the clear cutters with the sole job of digging holes and setting down two-year-old baby pine trees. All in the world that accomplished was less profit on the sale of cut timber. Ralph Winters was not a man that anyone would readily accuse of being a far-seeing individual. Truth be told, he had never been blessed with the ability to see beyond what was immediately set before him. And what was immediately before him at the moment was the increasing difficulty of the new preacher-boy.

He had just gotten over the galling fact that the preacher's mama had kept him awake for most of the night with her tearful phoning of his private home number. Something he knew had been maliciously achieved by that impudent operator, Libby Flowers. None of the Flowers people cared for their nearest neighbor, Ralph Winters. The trouble between the two close neighbors had started over the fence that the Flowers claimed was well over their property line. Well, maybe it was by a couple of inches here and there, but big fat woo. Then when Ralph had laid Yancy off from the mill, they immediately went to yelling that Yancy's lay off was yet another personal attack against the Flowers' family. Well, Ralph had had to lay off a bunch of other men too, but that sad fact didn't stop them from spewing bile. Of late, they were declaring that Ralph had used the town's dependence on the mill, to swing the congregational vote in his favor as head deacon.

All right, so what if he had? He was used to bossing men, and he knew how to get things done. All Yancy wanted to do was pray. Like reforestation, Ralph couldn't see the point of praying when he could simply roll up his sleeves and see things got done without troubling the Lord over every little picayune detail. Like when the church needed a new preacher, Ralph found them a new preacher, and—at half the cost of hiring a full-grown preacher with a wife and a bunch of kids in tow. Problem solved.

Ironically, Fred Flowers of Fred's (claptrap) Autos, had been one of Ralph's main supporters in the "let's hire a newly ordained seminarian" idea, but now Fred was squawking because the newly ordained seminarian, wasn't nearly as green as Fred had been counting on. Instead of unloading a clunker at considerable interest on the in-house loan, the boy had plunked down cash money and had driven off in Fred's one and only brand-new showroom car. And, while leaving Fred to suffer the narrowest profit margin he'd ever experienced in his whole double-dealing life. But the corker was that the preacher-boy had gotten, in writing, Fred's promise of putting a chunk of his profit into the offering plate.

Now, I don't care where you're from, that was as slick as goose grease.

Ralph had made all the conciliatory noises over the phone, but in his mind, he was thinking that if that preacher-boy wasn't already employed, Ralph would take him like a shot into the milling business. Anyone who could get the better of a grafter like Fred Flowers, would definitely be an asset in writing up contracts and bids. But no, the boy had gone over to the "Cloth."

What a waste. And what a tremendous pain in the old bohunkus!

Ralph sighed wearily as he came to the conclusion that there was no way around it. He was going to have to meet the new preacher face to face and let that young man know straight from the get-go just who was boss of Henrytown Free Church.

Chapter Five

During his late teens and then into his seminary years, Aaron had been allowed to use his father's second car as his own. Consequently, this was his first experience as a real car owner. If he could be any prouder driving his very own car, there wouldn't be a button left on his shirt. He parked on the east side of the house where it would sit in the shade and be close to the porch's kitchen door. He had been so careful of his new car while running Miss Mabel's errand at the grocery store that he'd even turned down the offer of help from store owner's son. Aaron's biggest fear was that the teenaged boy might accidentally bump the car or scratch the paint with the sharp corners of the wooden carry crates. And then while crying on the inside, he'd have to virtuously forgive the lad, even though it might take a long, long time for him to actually mean it. Fearing this scenario, Aaron had left the store owner and his son simply standing behind the counter while he made two trips from store to car, carrying the loaded crates all by himself.

The only worry left had been driving the main street without any traffic incidents. And then came the angst-riddled and vigilant slow crawl along the seemingly endless dirt road with its horrifying amount of deep pot-holes and unusually high level of threatening gravel.

Brand new cars certainly came with an inordinate amount of brand-new anxieties.

The crates were safely sitting on the newly mown lawn. Aaron saw not one sign of Bubba X to lend him a hand. He stood there for a moment, in no real hurry to leave his new car, but also wondering if he should try carrying both crates at once or if he should, as he had at the store, simply carry them one at a time. The difference in both situations was that now there were the considerable amount of stair steps up to the porch and each crate was on its own, quite heavy. He was on the verge of a decision when he spotted a big black car coming cautiously, but steadily, up the pothole beleaguered road. Newly infected with the Overly Protective of My Car germ, Aaron easily recognized a fellow sufferer. But the strange thing about this proud car owner was that the time was going on five, the precise time when the Yancy Flowers family were taking their seats at the supper table and when he, along with Bubba X and Miss Mabel, should be sitting down to theirs. According to southern custom, this was not the hour for receiving uninvited callers. The big black car came to a stop on the newly manicured lawn. The driver's door opened and out stepped a man of medium height wearing a well-tailored gray suit and a rather daring paisley tie and a gray hat that exactly matched the suit. As he crossed the lawn, the man said, "I'm Deacon Winters."

Mabel could not believe her eyes. Mr. Ralph Winters was totin' and fetchin', for her! In her view, that was akin to having Huey P. *Himself* carrying a crate of baking goods and a flour sack! It was all she could do not to curtsy as Mr. Winters walked into the kitchen. And by way of the backdoor no less! Meanwhile, Bubba, seated at the table and waiting to be fed had not deigned to look up from the dining room table. The only thing plaguing Bubba's mind was that the food was all laid out and within reach and yet his plate remained empty. After a hard day of strenuous labor, he was not concerned in the least that Mr. Ralph Winters was having to lift his hand to carry something all by himself. Bubba promptly wondered, what with her being all fired up over Mr. Ralph an' all, if Mama would even notice it if he stole a wedge of cornbread.

Mabel was wringing her hands while the two men set the crates on the kitchen's worktable. "I'm real sorry Mr. Ralph—," she began to say, but Aaron interrupted her.

"What smells so wonderful Miss Mabel?'

"Oh that? That's just a fried-up chicken, some hoppin'-john, and cornbread and egg puddin' with meringue."

Aaron, his back turned on Mr. Winters, and stood facing Miss Mabel with his hands on his hips. "That sounds like a veritable feast. With the exception of that hopping something. Whatever is that?"

"Oh, that's just what we call black-eyed peas, an' onion, an' rice and bacon all cooked up together."

"It sounds splendid."

Miss Mabel looked pleasantly embarrassed as she waved a hand. "It's just plain old country food, but it does go real good with fried chicken."

"Well I for one am famished." Aaron rounded on their unexpected guest. "And you are most welcome to share in our evening meal."

"Well I didn't—"

"Nonsense," Aaron scoffed. "You've come all this way, it's only polite to feed you. Miss Mabel, would you set another plate please?"

Aaron had barely said Amen to the blessing when Bubba lunged for the chicken platter. During the meal Aaron and Ralph Winters carried on a conversation as if they were the only two people at the dining table.

"So, you own a sawmill?"

"Yes, I do."

"That's impressive."

Ralph sat back in the chair, pushing his emptied plate toward the center of the table. "It used to be. That was back in the first years of the twenties when the whole country was booming. But the twenties are long since gone. What we've got now is the hard times business of hanging on until things turn around again."

Aaron lifted the tea glass and took a drink. Setting the glass down he asked, "And when, as an astute businessman, do you see the national economy eventually righting itself?"

"That's the two-thousand-dollar question, Pastor. To think about the economy, you have to go beyond what's happening here in Louisiana or, even in America. You've got to keep up with what's happening around the world."

Aaron studied his head deacon with a renewed interest. The man before him looked quite relaxed and casual, suit jacket off and draping the back of the chair; tie loosened, top buttons on his shirt open, and sitting with his thumbs inside his belt as he spoke at length on global dynamics and their effects on even a town as remote as Henrytown, Louisiana. He was a about three inches shorter in height than Aaron and he was an angular man of about fifty-five with graying hair. He seemed to be an educated and highly intelligent man. But there was a nagging something about him that made Aaron uneasy. Aaron tuned back in just as their supper guest was winding down his soliloquy.

"Usually it takes something equally cataclysmic in order for an existing disaster to balance out. At this point in time, I can't even begin to imagine anything worse than what's already going on. I don't have even one idea what the waiting-in-the-wings misfortune might prove to be. I'm just praying that the passage of time, not a worse upheaval, will level things out."

Aaron drained his tea glass, set it down and patting his stomach looked at the very uncomfortable Miss Mabel as she concentrated just as hard as she knew how on what she perceived to be cultured lady-like table manners. Her son, Bubba X had long ago finished his plate and having done so, sat staring up at the far wall's dado railing as if there was something unique and quite intriguing about it. With Bubba staring and Miss Mabel doing her best to de-bone an unwilling chicken thigh with a knife and a fork (never mind that all three of the men hadn't had any qualms about using their fingers) it was evident that both mother and son were suffering. A merciful man, Aaron decided that it was time to take them home. He looked back to Ralph Winters.

"Mr. Ralph, I can't say how much I've enjoyed sharing a meal with you and getting to know the church's head deacon."

"Well, that's all I came for Pastor. I believe it's important to get to know even our *temporary* pastor face to face, and he, the person he'll essentially be answering to."

And there it was. Aaron couldn't stop the smile that was beginning to spread across his face. There were a few things he could have easily said to Mr. Winters, but the sound advice from his favorite professor came rather forcibly to his mind. "*Follow the example of Jesus when He dealt with the Pharisees: Never complain; never explain. Simply get on with our Father's will of preaching the gospel and trust Him absolutely to sort out the rest.*"

"Indeed," Aaron casually replied. "And I do beg your pardon for cutting this meeting short." Looking to Miss Mabel he said softly. "I'll help you clear the table and then I'll drive you and Bubba home."

She looked positively relieved to be finished with the ordeal of sophisticated dining. "Now Preacher, you don't hafta help me with the dishes. I put 'em out; I can pick 'em right back up again."

Aaron remained firm. "You and Bubba have had a long day. Clearing the table is the least I can do." Then he looked to Ralph Winters. "Deacon, would you be so kind as to pitch in?"

Ralph Winters looked stunned. And trapped. Stammering slightly, he answered, "W-well, not at all. I'd be pleased."

Ten minutes later and the supper dishes were in the sink to soak overnight and Miss Mabel and Bubba X were in the preacher's new car. Ralph was in his and while inching along down the long dusty road and following the pastor's brand new car's tail lights, he couldn't stop himself from wondering if he'd made any point with the young man or, if the new preacher had just slickered him as easily as he'd slickered Fred Flowers.

Libby Flowers was on duty at the telephone exchange trunk line. She liked the night shift because it was typically quiet, and she could concentrate on her correspondence secretarial course. She could type as fast as a blizzard, but the shorthand study was like learning a foreign language. What she needed was to have someone dictate to her so she could gain speed. But Mama was shy about dictating even a grocery list; Daddy could never think of a word to say, and Casper was given to dictating rude jokes. So, there she sat going over the "Dear Mr. Brown," notebook dictation yet again when the trunk-line buzzed. With a sigh, she put aside the course book and dictation notepad and plugged into the lighted number. Before she could even say, "Number please," Cousin Mabel's voice was sounding in her earphone.

"Ring up your daddy's line for me. I got news."

Libby swiftly obliged, staying on the line so that she could listen in. Within five minutes Libby knew every last detail of the big happenings at the parsonage and her father's rather strong reactions to this information. None of this sounded all that healthy for Pastor Aaron's wellbeing. Libby went off the line leaving her father and Mabel to talk further, sans her silent presence. Her hand shaking, she plugged into Aaron's line.

Aaron was in his study going over his notes for his upcoming Wednesday night sermon when the phone in the living room began its peculiar coded burring. Expelling a long breathe, he put his notes aside and left the study.

Libby stopped herself from using his first name when he answered. "Pastor, this is Libby Flowers. I thought I'd better call you and tell you one or two things you may not be prepared for."

Aaron was grinning. She sounded all breathy and conspiratorial. Then too, he was remembering her strawberry hair and freckles. Until now he'd had no idea just how much he liked freckles.

"My cousin Mabel is on the line with Daddy right this very minute and she's telling him all about the supper you had with Ralph Winters. Now there's just a few things you have to know about Daddy and Mr. Ralph—"

"Would that something be that both men consider Henrytown Free Church to be each man's private property?"

Libby was a little taken aback by his quick and highly accurate discernment. "Well that's the start of it, yes. But are you aware of their feud?"

"Well no," he admitted. "But one thing typically follows the other in these cases." Worried now that she would hang up, he hastily added, "Just how would you advise me to proceed in this state of affairs?"

"Me?" she squeaked. "I wasn't calling to give you advice; I only wanted to warn you."

"Yes, but you are the daughter of one man, and you have a long-time knowledge of the second. I've only known your father for one day and I've only known Mr. Winters for about an hour. In either case, that's only long enough to surmise the situation. It's certainly not long enough to come up with a viable solution."

Libby thought it over. Another part of her brain wondered how one would shorthand write the word, *viable*. Casting that thought to the side she said, "I don't want to be a traitor to my daddy."

“Absolutely not,” he agreed.

“And I have to admit that I do not like Mr. Winters at all, so any information I give you may not be completely unbiased.”

“I deeply appreciate and admire your frankness.”

Libby took a deep breath as she thought for a moment, then she said, “Daddy’s house and Mr. Ralph’s house are only about a quarter of a mile apart. Last year Mr. Ralph put up a trestle fence between his property and Daddy’s which has brought on the feud because Daddy said that Mr. Ralph helped himself to nearly a foot of land that isn’t his. That doesn’t sound like much, but, when you consider that he’s talking about a foot of land stretching out for over five acres, that’s quite a chuck of property. It’s hard for Daddy to fight back because he can’t afford lawyers the way Mr. Ralph can. Then just last year Mr. Ralph beat Daddy in the vote for head deacon. That’s when Daddy publicly accused Mr. Ralph of being a low-down land thief and they haven’t spoken a civil word since. The pair of them going to the same church makes Sunday worship kinda uncomfortable for the most of the congregation but real interesting for the remainder. Then here comes you, a young lamb to the slaughter so to speak.

“Now my daddy is a wonderful Christian man and I love the breath right out of him, but to get even with Mr. Ralph, he will not be above making you look like you are the second son he didn’t know he had. To counter that, Mr. Ralph is going to try to make you look like you are deep inside his pocket.”

“But I’m neither of those things.”

Libby wanted to pull her hair out by the roots. “That doesn’t matter. Around here it’s how something looks, not how something might actually be. Now you take the case of Eugenia Hampton—”

“Who?”

"Will you please just listen? Eugenia Hampton is someone from around here who ended up having to move over to Shreveport. And all that happened right after Eugenia got it into her head that she wanted to be thought of as prettier than she actually is, and so she started wearing dresses that were way too tight across the bosoms. Then came the bright red lipstick, cheek rouge and heavy mascara. Next thing to happen was her going to the beauty parlor and getting her hair permed. And it was a terrible perm! Bless her heart, Eugenia went from sweet looking to tacky and outlandish. I mean, the girl was so over made up that if she'd visited New Orleans, she would have attracted a sizable gang of romantically inclined street mimes!"

Trying to contain the mounting threat of laughter, Aaron squeezed his eyes tightly shut and bit down hard on his lower lip. Still, adorably dimpled Libby was on a relentless roll.

"And it was for the very reason that she suddenly looked so outlandish that people started saying all manner of outlandish things about her. Things that weren't true at all, but that didn't matter. Before that poor girl knew what was happening, her reputation was completely ruined. Finally, she had to move to Shreveport where she didn't know a living soul."

Suddenly concerned about a young woman he'd never met he asked, "And then what happened?"

"Well, according to her Mama, she got a job working for a dentist and she's back to being sweet looking again."

"Oh, that is good news."

"Well, at her job she has to wear a smock all the time, so it was good-bye to the too tight dresses. Plus, she's also got a very nice boyfriend who's a dental student."

"Praise God for all things coming right in the end," Aaron said, enormously relieved for Miss Eugenia Hampton. "So, what exactly are you advising me to learn from this lesson?"

Oh for heaven's sake! *This is nothing but the coffee fiasco all over again*. "What I'm saying," she managed through partially gritted teeth, "is that you've been seen riding with Daddy all over town and now you've had Mr. Winters over for a private supper. You cannot do things like that and not expect to split the congregation even more than it is."

"May I please say a word on behalf of the defense?"

"To me," she demanded, "or to the whole church?"

"Only to you. That is, if you don't mind."

"Fine."

"To begin, your father's kindness to me has been a very real blessing. Without that kindness, I'd still be dragging my trunks around Henrytown and wondering where I might be going with them. Secondly, Mr. Winters simply appeared on my doorstep and stayed for supper. Now, those are the facts. How you would suggest I proceed?"

Libby had a long, quiet think. Then she said, "I don't know how to reach Mr. Ralph, but I do know how to reach Daddy. If I were you, I'd think up a sermon on the Lord's Prayer . . . about forgiving us or debts."

"Drat!"

What's wrong?"

"I was going to speak on the call of Moses. Following your advice, which is excellent by the way, means that I have to begin again and it's a bit laborious to write out all the notes and then apply my hunt and peck typing skills."

"Uhm . . ." Libby said shyly. "I'm slow with dictation, but I'm a fairly fast typist."

"Really?"

"Yes. I'm studying to be a secretary."

Aaron's heart began to race. "Do you think you could apply those skills, say, tomorrow? I'd be more than happy to pay for your services."

"Don't be ridiculous. I'm the one making you rewrite your sermon. The least I can do is help." She had another quick think. She couldn't ask her father to drive her over and Seth wouldn't do it again even if she begged. Then a thought occurred. "Are you picking up Mabel and Bubba X in the morning?"

"Yes. Now that I have the means, I'm solely responsible for picking them up and taking them home."

"Good. I'll be at Mabel's house and I'll ride with them. What time?"

His face became scrunched as he answered in a questioning tone, "Seven?" His face happily un-scrunched as she quickly said that she would see him at seven. After Libby rang off, Aaron finally allowed himself the laughter he'd bravely battled down. And when that laughter made him weak, he sat on the upright piano bench and really let loose. Wiping his tear swollen eyes with the heel of his hand, he said softly and repeatedly, "Romantically inclined street mimes!! Oh, that girl, that girl."

Mabel was very surprised when Libby turned up on her doorstep just as she and Bubba were stepping out to wait for the preacher. Mabel was about to question her younger cousin when just then, the pastor turned up and almost five minutes early.

The preacher's new car was like riding in a royal carriage and Mabel sat like a queen in the back seat next to her son. Libby rode in the front compartment next to the pastor. But the thing that began to peak Mabel's further interest was that the pair in the front were acting as if they were completely alone in the car.

"I found this station," Aaron said as he turned on the radio. "This is the most interesting music I've ever heard. What is it?"

"Zydeco. That's Cajun," Libby replied. "This radio program comes out of Baton Rouge."

"And just what is that 'zigging' sound in the music?"

"That's a washboard. Cajuns wear a washboard on their chests and scratch a spoon handle against the metal scrub board to the rhythm of the music."

"How fascinating."

"It's even more fascinating to watch them."

"Can we see that sometime?"

"I don't see why not," Libby said with a slight shrug of her shoulders. "We're not that far from Avoyelles Parish and there are plenty of Cajuns living there."

"Then we definitely need to plan a day trip to Avoyelles Parish," the Aaron said decisively.

Her ears finely tuned in to the conversation, Mabel did not miss any of the "we's" being tossed around so casually. This situation between the pastor and Libby needed some very careful watching. And Mabel couldn't help but wonder how Seth Lewis would appreciate hearing his Libby making plans with another man, even if that other man *was* a preacher. She just couldn't believe that Seth would sit still for any of that for a single solitary second.

At the parsonage, Mabel cooked breakfast and after the meal, everyone fanned out. Bubba X was tilling the overgrown kitchen garden and Aaron and Libby were held up in the study. Mabel decided that instead of tackling the kitchen she would carpet sweep the living room rug and run the feather duster over all the furniture.

Thus engaged with the push sweeper, Mabel was able to see directly inside the pastor's study. He was seated in the chair belonging to the desk and Libby was in the wing backed chair. He was talking and she was writing in a notebook. Then it twigged with Mabel.

Libby's trying out her hand at bein' a professional secretary!

Oh, that just thrilled Mabel to the very core. She knew how badly Libby wanted to be a secretary; how she'd used nearly every dime she made from being a switchboard girl to pay for her correspondence courses. All in the world Libby needed was for someone to give her a chance at the job that she'd been studying so hard for. And now it seemed Libby was getting that chance.

Well no wonder those two had been making plans for trips and things. As his secretary, Libby would just naturally need to go where her boss went so she could take notes for him. But now fearing Seth's hot-tempered reaction to it all, Mabel decided quite firmly that he'd never hear a word of it from her. Libby had every right in the world to better herself and a blind-jealous Seth Lewis had no right to stop her.

With that Mabel also decided that the living room rug had been swept just about as clean as it was ever going to be. And too, the room's furniture no longer looked dusty. Carrying the sweeper by its long handle she took it and herself off to the kitchen where the sink full of dishes patiently waited.

Dinnertime was peculiar. Mabel had reheated the hoppin'-john from last night's supper and baked a fresh pan of cornbread. She'd also sliced up a platter full of fresh cucumbers and tomatoes. All of this was to be washed down by veritable gallons of iced tea. She and her son sat at one end of the table while Libby and the pastor sat at the other end; Libby with her notebook, he with a Bible and two big books that Mabel had no idea about. As Bubba X made rapid work of his plate, almost swallowing his meal completely whole, Mabel picked at her plate and watched the pair at the other end of the table. It was a wonder that those two could eat and work at the same time, but they did. Then without so much as a word to her, they were jumping up from the table and carrying the books and notebooks and running back to the study. From the dining room Mabel could hear his voice but couldn't make out his words because Libby was banging loudly on the type writing machine. It was as if the noonday meal had never happened. Mabel took a sip of tea as she tried not to have hurt feelings.

But they could have at least said something about the cornbread. It tasted to me like the best batch I ever made.

Mabel and Bubba rarely, if ever, attended Wednesday night services, however they were in attendance for this particular service: As was nearly the entire population of Henrytown, which included the Right Reverend Phillip Waite of Henrytown's United Methodist Church. The early supper at the parsonage had been just about as strange as their noontime dinner. Mabel had served cold fried chicken, slaw, butter beans and leftover cornbread and once again, with the exception of Bubba, her efforts felt wasted. Libby and the preacher looked like a pair of nervous fleas. Following the meal, the preacher drove them to their respective homes. It had been left to Yancy to haul Mabel and Bubba to the church in his truck, Mabel squeezing into the cab next to Mildred. Bubba X, while reasonably tidy in a clean shirt and trousers, made do with riding in the flatbed. Casper and Libby followed their parents in Casper's truck. Both trucks arrived at church and in a reasonable gathering time but, to everyone's chagrin, the churchyard was already so jammed that they'd had to park quite distance from the building.

The small sanctuary was filled to the rafters, many of those attending having to stand alongside the walls. The windows were opened, but the evening air was thick with heat and humidity. It also was a tad cloying, what with every unattached woman and girl from no less than ten miles around had liberally doused themselves with conflicting perfumes. The only pew that wasn't completely filled was the front family pew. That pew had once been reserved for Pastor Wallace's family, but tonight only the pianist and Mabel and Bubba X were expected to sit there. Pastor Aaron had insisted on it. Mabel was trying to get used to being seated in such a prominent place when, low and behold, the Methodist Right Reverend came in and sat right down on the pew with them. Then if that wasn't enough to beat everything half to death, Mr. Ralph Winters and his family and immediate friends were filling up the pew directly behind her. Mabel didn't know whether to cry or go blind because she could almost feel Mr. Ralph staring at the back of her head and wondering how it was that the preacher's housekeeper was suddenly more important than the richest man in town. Yet, there was nothing for it but to brazen it out. It had been the preacher himself who had asked her to do him the honor of sitting on the first pew and, as he smiled at her from his place in the highbacked chair near the pulpit, Mabel began to feel important. She elbowed Bubba, forcing him to sit up straight as she smiled back at Pastor Aaron.

Chapter Six

The joy of a small-town church is that everyone knows everyone. The sorrow of a small-town church is that everyone knows everyone. Aaron had only been in the town and in the church for less than five minutes, yet, he was the lone reason why people who may or may not get along, willingly squeezed in together in the limited space. On this night old disagreements were laid aside as the kerosene wall lights glowed merrily and the sanctuary faintly buzzed with anticipation. Above heads the ceiling fans struggled to stir the sweltering air. Women were also fanning themselves with the cardboard fans that could always be found in the pew rack. The fans were stuck on flat wooden handles and on one side was a colorful print of Jesus standing at the door knocking while the other side there was printing that read, *Over the Jordan Funeral Home—Myrtle Hedge, Louisiana.*

Above the soft hum off voices, the pianist played a nice selection, but no one was listening. They were too busy craning their necks in order to get a look at the pastor. From his vantage point, being seated in the pastor's chair, Aaron had more than ample opportunity to view the congregation. They gawked and he smiled. Aaron was not amazed that there were those who, for various reasons, were determined to be in the immediate vicinity of the head deacon, Ralph Winters. Encouragingly, the greater number of men and women were simply attempting a better ogle of the pastor and these persons seemed without guile.

There was a group of young men who looked definitely out of place. Aaron guessed that the reason they attended had more to do with the high presence of young women. The third pew in particular had been claimed by a significant bevy of local beauties. Yet what Aaron found most interesting about the third pew was that the entire gaggle seemed to be suffering the same type of vision difficulty. Each and every one of them continuously blinked in a rather disturbing manner. He had no way of knowing that the young women gazing up at him were intentionally following movie magazine advice in what had been hailed as the Wide-Eyed look.

As far as the young ladies of Henrytown were concerned, Hollywood magazines were a veritable gold-mine of beauty tips. This month's issue was all about eyes. There was one female star celebrated as The Perfect Wife . . . as Miss Loy was famous for her, "wide innocent eyes that sparkled with life and a hint of mischief." So, the dauntless young ladies of pew three had loaded on the mascara and had spent days practicing the wide eye look. It was a lot of work really, and it involved popping the eyes whenever forced to blink. The swarm of young women blinking in this fashion—and almost entirely in sync—would have been thrilled to know that their attempts for notice were a triumph. Just as the glamour magazine had promised, Pastor Aaron had most certainly noticed them. And needing relief from the highly peculiar sight, he hurriedly began scanning the faces of the entire congregation until, seated on the very last pew, he found . . . Libby.

Libby didn't wear mascara. She believed her pale skin and fair hair meant that blackened eyelashes would make her look ridiculous. Her make up case contained a bottle of vanilla scented body lotion and one lone tube of a light tangerine lipstick. And Aaron thought she was stunning. And too, for reasons he couldn't fathom, she reminded him of his most favorite summertime treat, vanilla ice cream.

Edna Flowers (cousin-in-law to Yancy and one of the ladies who met Aaron on the day of his arrival) was the church pianist. She was also quite gifted at keeping the thing reasonably tuned. Miss Edna played by ear. If you could hum it, she could play it. Her favorite hymns were *Sweet Hour of Prayer* and *I Come to the Garden*. She played these with some regularity, but tonight she played them in honor of Aaron's first sermon. As she was coming up on the very last stanza of *I Come to the Garden*, a man Aaron had yet to meet walked up to the piano and turned through the pages of the church's one and only hymnal. After stopping at a specific page, he raised a hand and the congregation stood. Then in a hurried, nasally voice the man sing-songed, "Sweet hour of prayer, sweet hour of prayer, that calls me from a world of care." The congregation immediately began to sing the line. When the congregation approached the end, the man again called out in his unique style, "And bids me at my Father's throne . . ."

Aaron realized that this man was the church cantor! The reason the church didn't have hymnals was because it had this man. Aaron had read about this style of service in the books concerning early American church services, as in pre-Revolutionary War early. He'd never imagined he'd ever be privileged to witness such a service. What a thrill it was, like a jolt of lightning striking the top of his head and exiting the soles of his feet, leaving in its quickening wake a restlessness in his spirit. As part of her pianist duties, Edna was to nod to the pastor whenever the musical portion of the service was about to conclude. But before she could do so, the young pastor startled her and everybody else when he took off in a run for the pulpit. His appearance behind the pulpit was so abrupt, they instantly stopped singing and sat down.

On the pulpit were his Bible and the prepared sermon. Gripping the sides of the pulpit as if hanging on for dear life, Aaron lifted his voice in prayer. Aaron did not memorize prayers, nor did he read them. Prayer was his heart connecting with God's. Aaron was in such an enlivened state that, although he prayed aloud, it remained a very private conversation. At the concluding "Amen," he opened his eyes; he was a trifle taken aback. Reverend Waite was standing as well as Miss Mabel and Bubba but, with the exception of these three, the sanctuary looked deserted. Aaron felt the sting of humiliation—and then he began hearing softly speaking masculine voices sounding their own amen, and with that, people began to reappear, reseating themselves in the pews or standing along the walls.

They were kneeling! The true devotion of such an action filled his heart with unbridled joy. It was because of that overwhelming joy that he pushed aside the carefully outlined and typed sermon.

Libby's eyes flared and popped almost as widely as the Wide Eyed girls on the third pew when Aaron began to speak. Having typed the sermon twice, Libby knew the service order, and, according to that order Aaron should now be directing everyone to Matthew 6:33. But instead he was simply talking!

Seth Lewis, seated with the Rowdy Boys was listening, and with a smirk. But as he listened, the smirk gradually faded. The young pastor was talking about the Jesus he knew, the Jesus he cherished and followed. How Jesus, God incarnate had lived and walked among His people, His special creations. And people responded by coming to Him from all walks of life. He turned no one away who truly came seeking a close personal relationship with their creator. And Jesus broke all the rules; lepers were untouchables, Jesus touched lepers. Dead people were considered unclean, but He not only touched dead people, He brought them back into life. He was not a scribe or a priest, but He taught the people anyway. He also fed the hungry and He wept with those who were marginalized, were rejected, were helpless. Aaron then said that if we wanted to be like Jesus, we will have to love what Jesus loved. And what Jesus loves is . . . us.

Seth swallowed hard, there was a burning in his chest he'd never felt before. As far as he was concerned, he and Aaron were the only two in the building and, that Aaron had been speaking directly to him. Seth was so caught up in what he was hearing, that it came as a shock when he heard Aaron say, "Reverend Waite? My beloved brother in Christ, would you do me the honor of offering the closing prayer?"

As the Methodist minister haltingly began, Edna Flowers was fighting tears. Then she realized that she had her pianist duties to attend to and as the minister began to pray, she quickly rushed to the piano. As the minister pronounced "Amen," without pausing to think she began to play *Tis So Sweet to Trust In Jesus*.

When Aaron stepped down to stand before the altar, the storm that had been building throughout the service had made its way forward and was directly over the church. Lightening cracked and flashed, filling the sanctuary with a shock of blinding light. And Seth Lewis found himself running up the aisle to meet Aaron at the altar. He crashed into Aaron with such force that he almost sent Aaron flying backwards. Then the two held on to one another, both weeping. And finally, and forever, Aaron would be more than able to precisely describe the young man who had previously been nothing more than a hazy presence; for he was now the very same young man who held onto him for dear life while he sobbed more loudly than the thunder.

As the storm worsened, few in the sanctuary noticed. Wild Boy Seth's run to the altar had been more a jolt than the deadly lighting. And most especially for Libby who had been certain to the core that Seth would die a thoroughgoing pagan. Lost inside the mob of standing people, she climbed up on the pew bench and then stood on tiptoe in order to see over the slow-moving tide of heads. Seth's dash had set off an eagerness in others to rededicate their lives, hence the parade down the aisle. This evening had merely been meant to be a normal Wednesday night service along with the interim pastor's formal introduction. (Alright, and it had also been meant to be a bit of a stinger, sermon-wise.) Instead Aaron had gone entirely off script and the odd result had the feel of a good old-fashioned revival. The only things missing were the tent and the store-bought ice cream in Dixie Cups with those cute little wooden spoons attached to the lids.

A baffled Libby thought back on the sermon. Pastor Wallace had been a pulpit banging, hell-fire breathing preacher. Truth be told, his sermons had always scared the living whey out of her. In sharp contrast, Aaron had barely raised his voice and the only way she could describe the gist of the off-the-cuff message, was that it had sounded to her to be all so perfectly logical. But still, there had been something else inside that refined Atlanta accent. Something other than the elegant patrician drawl that had so captivated the assembly. Whatever that something had been, it had drawn such close attention that those sitting in the pews had been eerily quiet, barely breathing so as not to miss a single word. And those standing along the walls hadn't budged or even twitched. And after the closing prayer, there was all this hugging going on. And among folks who hadn't spoken to one another in years!

Libby wasn't the only one to be confused. Head deacon Ralph Winters had listened to the sermon with a smug satisfaction. Ralph was convinced that the young preacher's silly sermon would find that young man being handed his hat as well as a strong encouragement to drive his brand-new car straight back to Atlanta. Yet instead, there was a long line of people waiting their turn to hug his neck. What in the world was wrong with these crackers? Didn't they know sorry preaching when they heard it? Had they been entirely bamboozled by the sound of all that snooty high-born speaking? And what was all that he'd been saying about Jesus. Ralph didn't know. His mind had wandered off to the details of the new contract bid still waiting on his desk.

Aaron was busy shaking hands with those anxious to meet him while Seth stood next to him like an overly-protective guardian angel. Seth was being hugged by ladies and having his hand shook by the men as he maintained a back to back stance with Aaron. No one voiced it, but the wonderment of a renowned hell-raiser like Seth Lewis coming to the Lord was a miracle right up there with the loves and the fishes.

As it was for Seth, as when he'd held on to Aaron, and felt all of the internal darkness he'd known for most his adolescent and then into his adult life, melting away. Everything had become clearer, brighter. Now the only things Seth Lewis wanted for himself was this clarity and this brightness that he found in his new belief in Jesus.

The storm finally passed, but not before a lot more noise and light flickering, both outside with the lightening and on the inside with the sensitive electric bulbs. At long last people were braving the inclement weather by making the dash for their vehicles. Seth was still with Aaron in the doorway, watching the parade of departing cars and trucks. It felt natural to him, hanging around with Pastor Aaron. After all, as of tonight, Pastor Aaron was the only friend his own age that Seth probably had left in this world. The Rowdy Boys, his Patch working cronies who were also on work furlough from the oil field, had come to church with him, hoping to either get a girl or enjoy a good laugh at the new preacher's expense. Seconds after Seth had made a blind run for the altar, they were making a blind run for the door. There were no second chances with the Rowdy Boys. You were either completely with them or completely against them. In their collective opinion, Seth had just galloped himself on over to the opposition's side.

Aaron turned and walked back into the sanctuary to turn off the lights. Seth took on the kerosene lamps turning down and extinguishing the wicks. Aaron looked back over his shoulder. "Seth? How much Bible do you know?"

Seth turned his shamed face away from Aaron's penetrating gaze and in a low tone admitted, "I don't even have a Bible."

Aaron was not surprised. They eventually met together in the vestibule and, when Aaron pushed the bottom button, that light went off and he and Seth moved out to the partially covered porch while Aaron turned the key in the door lock. "If you're not tired," Aaron offered. "We can go over to the parsonage for coffee. I have a spare Bible I'd be more than honored to give you."

Seth answered the candlestick telephone. "Oh, hey Libby!" Seth chirped. "You'll never guess what. Aaron just gave me my very own Bible. It's white and it's brand new. He said he got it as a present from when he graduated the seminary, but he's already got a favorite Bible so he let me have the brand new one."

Seth listened for a second before answering her question. "He's in the kitchen makin' coffee. Want me to get him for ya?" Seth didn't wait for a response and with the telephone's speaker against his chest he yelled, "Hey Aaron! Libby's on the phone."

In the headset Libby heard a muffled, "Okay," and then Seth's voice was again loud and clear in her ear.

"He said to tell you he'll call you in the morning. Right now, he's got all he can do with watching the water boil."

"Oh, for heaven's sake!" she snapped. Fit to be tied, she pulled the plug and disconnected the call. Of all the people in the parish that she could have readily named as competition for Aaron's attention, not once had Seth Lewis' name made the list. But now it would seem he was turning in to her primary rival and Libby just did not know how she felt about that.

Aaron was still in the kitchen and focused on kettle watching when a loud knocking sounded on the front door. Seth dutifully answered it, his eyes flaring wide at the sight of Casper Flowers and Archie Lofthouse.

"Hey ya'll—"

The pair, soaked to the skin, wordlessly steamed by Seth, coming fully into the living room. The three young men stared at each other until Archie finally nudged Casper.

"We didn't get a chance to talk to you at the service," Casper said. "So, after we dumped off our families, we came looking for you."

Seth tensed. He knew he'd alienated his rowdy Patch friends, but he hadn't thought that he might have also alienated the pair of church-boys.

"It's not all that often we get a brand-new brother," Casper continued, his voice thick with emotion. "But that's what you are to us, Seth. You're our brand-new brother. Welcome to the Family."

Aaron was carefully carrying the tray containing the drip coffee pot, cream pitcher, sugar bowl and two cups. His progress into the dining room came to a halt when he saw the three young men in the living room hugging each other and sobbing. Aaron carefully set the tray on the dining table and quietly returned to the kitchen where he retrieved two more cups and then waited until he heard the sounds of animated conversation. "Hey fellows!" he called as he reappeared in the dining room. "Is there anyone here brave enough to try drinking my coffee?"

The coffee was a mite too strong but those around the table didn't seem to mind. One of these fine days Aaron was certain he would perfect the art of coffee making, but tonight he and the threesome would simply have to suffer through his painful learning process. However, the pain Aaron experienced was in his sides because he couldn't remember a time when he'd laughed so hard or so much. First the trio had teased him about his mother hunting him down by way of long-distance phone calls, and then they'd put the boot in about Libby needing to run to the rescue before Aaron blew himself to Glory just trying to light a stove.

"Yes," Aaron said as he laughed softly. "Libby has been a bit of a Godsend."

"Don't never tell her that," Casper warned. "I know she's my kid sister an ever'thing, but the truth is, she can be as hot natured as a Louisiana red pepper pod. She might be little in size, but she can be downright scary when she's riled. An' just let her get it into her pod brain that you can't do without her and she'll lord it over you for life."

"She's never been mean with me," Seth said.

"Seth Lewis," Archie said. "There's no liars in heaven."

"I ain't lying!"

"Yeah you are," Casper and Archie said in an amazing unison.

Looking only at Archie, Casper said in a tone that could only be compared to the dryness of the Gobi Desert, "Seems this boy's entirely forgotten the Great Crawdad Debacle."

Aaron was laughing again, Casper's humor bordered on merciless.

"Libby was about seven at the time an' it was the beginning of summer and Mama was already half crazy with us kids being out of school, even though school had only been out for less than a week. So, before she found herself on trial for killing her children plus all the neighbors' children, she sent us boys out with our BB guns to hunt for a brace of squirrels. And, she sent Libby out with a bucket, a bent safety pin and some bacon rind to fish up some crawdads. Well, squirrel-wise, we weren't having much hunting luck because BB's are slow and squirrels are fast, but Libby was at the mud-pond catching crawdads faster than a Cajun. So, after a couple of hours of missing every squirrel in LaSalle Parish, we decided to call the whole thing quits.

"We came out of the woods only to see Libby staggering up the dirt road and totin' that bucket with both hands and lookin' like she was about ready to expire under the load. So, ole Seth here passes me his BB gun and runs over to help her." Casper turned at the waist and looked at Seth. "That's about the age and time that you decided you were gonna impress her with your manliness, isn't it?"

"Yeah," Seth agreed.

"An' how's that been workin for ya?"

"Frankly, not real well."

Casper slapped the table-top and became more animated in both his tone and his body language. "That's what I've been sayin' to ya for years! Libby's not your normal female. She's an entirely separate species; a pure spawn of the Pepper People. I'm swearin' to ya Seth, it must have been while Mama was working in her kitchen garden that she found Libby comin' into full pepper bud. An' knowin' how Mama is, she must have said, 'Oh, isn't she sweet?' whereupon she dusted off the evil pepper pod baby and brought it on into the house. That's the only thing that explains my sister's non-normality as a human female." Casper wagged his finger in Seth's face and dared, "Now you just go ahead an' show me one thing able to impress or intimidate a red pepper pod an' I'll kiss it."

Aaron's fingers massaged his forehead. In a gentle tone, he brought Casper back to the subject of the story. "You were saying about the crawdads, Casper?"

"What? Oh yeah." Casper turned away from Seth and faced Aaron. "Well, Masculine-Boy here ran to Libby and relieved her of the heavy bucket. But he didn't stop there, *nooo* because stopping there would have been just too easy. No; what he did was go on to try to explain to her all about centrifugal force, something he'd just learned about in the fourth grade. But the key to this story is that Libby was only just goin' into the second grade so of course she had no idea what he was talkin' about. So that's when he decided he'd show her. Only that bucket was too heavy for him to get a good centrifugal whirl on it, an' while he was slingin' that bucket around tryin' to build up speed, centrifugal-wise, crawdads started flyin' out of it in all kinds of different directions. But, to Seth's credit, I got to admit that those mud-bugs were flyin' through the air way faster that our guns could fire BB's."

"That's the truth," Archie said. "One of those crawdads popped me hard right on my face."

Aaron was laughing so hard he hurt.

"Oh, it did not!" Seth protested. "At most it was just a glancing blow."

"Was not! It left a crawdad shaped purple bruise that I carried for a week or more. Folks were swearing it was a late-blooming birthmark."

Aaron was now fighting for air.

"Yeah," Casper said, recapturing the conversation, "but the upshot of this tale of woe is that when Seth finally emptied Libby's bucket of every last hard fished for crawdad, she promptly grabbed that bucket out of his idiot hand and beaned him with it on the side of his even more idiot head. He's been trying to make it up with her ever since." Casper turned back to Seth. "You're just wastin' your time on that one my brother. Red Pepper Pod People never forget nothin'."

"Just give it time," Seth said.

"You've had ten years!" Casper cried. "That's an entire decade, Seth. An' the girl still can't eat a crawdad without first griping about *Seth the Malicious Crawdad Slinger*!" Realizing that he hadn't quite crippled the new preacher with his lethal humor, Casper asked, "Hey Preach? Wanna hear how our wonder-boy Seth accidently gave Libby the mumps for her sixteenth birthday? For two weeks," he said, holding up two fingers as a visual aid, "that girl's ears and shoulders were all melted together." His arm settled back on the table. "But what really made her just as mad as the snapper turtle she looked like, was that Seth never even once got the mumps. He did a lot of griping about how he couldn't eat a pickle, but essentially all he did was carry the mumps. And just as dutifully as he knew how, he carried the mumps to Libby. So there she was, sweet sixteen and didn't nobody—not even Mama!—wanted to kiss that!"

The other three were rolling as Casper mournfully shook his head and finished, "Seth truly does have a lot to answer for, Libby-wise."

It was almost two in the morning when Seth, Casper and Archie finally left, and an exhausted Aaron dragged himself into his pajamas and fell across the bed in a heap. It was nearing six a.m. when the now all too familiar ring of the telephone woke him up.

"I have several messages for you," Libby said crisply. "I didn't put the calls through because of the lateness of the hour, so I simply took messages."

"I'm very grateful. It was a long night."

"Yes, well, you're in for a longer day," she said, sounding very officious. "First off, Daddy said to tell you that he's bringing my cousins Mabel and Bubba so you don't have to bother fetching them yourself. Then Miss Cornelia Faraday called in. Apparently she's dying. Again. Of late she's been dying about once a month, but last night she was convinced that this was it; this time she's truly shedding her mortal coil. She's expecting you to rush to her bedside the instant you hear this summons. However, if you'd deign to take my humble advice, I'd advise that you first enjoy a big breakfast. Miss Cornelia Faraday might be the first lady of Henrytown, but she isn't known for her gracious hospitality."

Libby's caustic remarks were beginning to cut Aaron's brain into paper thin slices.

"Next, you need to call Charlie Bean. He and his wife are having marital strife."

"Did he give any indication of the type of strife?"

"Not a word," she answered coolly. "Which means it could be anything from bankruptcy to adultery. Were I prone to make suggestions to a person such as yourself, I would suggest that you make Charlie your first call of the day."

"What about this Miss Cornelia you mentioned?"

"Oh, for heaven's sake! Miss Cornelia can wait awhile longer to sing her bi-monthly swan song. It's not like she doesn't know that thing by heart."

This was simply one acerbic comment too far. "Libby?" he asked impatiently. "Why are you angry with me? And so very early in the morning?"

"I'm not angry with you," she sniffed.

Her clipped denial plucked the last cord of his patience. "Libby Flowers," he said quite firmly. "I am exhausted. I'm still in my pajamas and I am yet to have a cup of coffee. In brief, I am in no fit condition to put up with feminine high jinx."

Libby gasped so violently that she almost swallowed her tongue. "Feminine high jinx!" she shouted into the speaking-horn. "Did I understand you correctly?"

"Yes," he shouted into the telephone speaker. "You most certainly did."

"Well, I have never been spoken to like that in my whole entire life—"

"After nineteen whole years of life, isn't it high time you were?"

"Good day Pastor Brooks!"

"Good morning Miss Flowers!"

And seconds later, Aaron who had never fought with a woman before, and Libby who had never known man nor boy she'd ever cared enough about to fight with, were each worrying just how in the world one would go about making it up with the other.

At going on seven, Aaron was dressed in a clean shirt and a pair of not-so-nearly-as-clean white trousers that were held in place by his beloved red suspenders. He was now enjoying a cup of coffee as he stood inside the sleeping porch. Something had to be done regarding his laundry situation and he was coming to the conclusion that the sleeping porch was crucial to solving this problem.

"Hello to the house!" Yancy shouted through the screened door. Then he opened the door to allow Mabel to enter. Bubba wasn't with them. Seconds after jumping out of the back of the truck and retrieving the flat of small plant containers, Bubba X had gone off to work in the kitchen garden. Mabel headed straight for the kitchen with Yancy walking a few paces behind her. Just as single minded as her gardening son, Mabel donned the apron and set about putting bacon in the frying pan while Yancy wandered on out to the sleeping porch and came to stand alongside Aaron.

"Morning to ya Preacher."

"Oh, good morning Yancy!" Aaron said, trying to sound more cheerful than he felt.

"Whatcha doin'?"

"Mentally measuring," Aaron said. He placed the emptied coffee cup on the small end table near one of the beds. Then with his hands on his hips, he turned his back to Yancy as he thought out loud. "There's more than enough room out here. The only problem I can ascertain would be the plumbing."

"Would you mind backing up that wonderment just a hair?"

"Oh!" Aaron said, as if amazed he hadn't made himself clear. "I'm thinking of turning this space into a laundry facility. All that's needed is to find a new home for the beds, move a washing machine in, hang some drying lines, set up an ironing board and then this back porch becomes an all weathers laundry room."

"Well, that does sound pretty slick all right," Yancy agreed. "But shouldn't you wait to hear from the deacon committee if you're gonna be kept on as the permanent preacher before you commence to redecorate?"

Aaron considered for a moment and then said, "No. I'm afraid the challenge of my laundry can't wait that long. As a matter of fact, it can't wait out the week." Aaron walked hurriedly passed Yancy. "Is that bacon I smell? Praise God! I'm starving!"

Normally Libby slept in the afternoons, her lengthy naps beginning just after the noonday dinnertime meal. Yesterday she missed her nap because she'd been playing secretary to Aaron (which had turned out to be a complete waste of her time!) and then the early part of the evening had been spent in church. Soon after the service, she'd then had to pull her telephone operator shift and after such a busy day and evening she'd taken her work shift with only the resilience of youth to see her through. After she'd been awake all night long—and taking messages for Aaron—she'd then had to hear him complain about not having any more than only four hours of sleep (oh poor baby!).

She'd been so angry and upset during noontime dinner that she'd barely slept at all during her badly needed nap. And now here she was at suppertime waiting for Daddy to say something meaningful as in, "*That preacher looked so downcast and mournful. I can't for the life of me imagine what could be making him so sad.*"

But . . . no. What Daddy was going on about was how Aaron was turning the parsonage sleeping porch into a laundry room. Libby felt on the verge of losing her mind.

She hated it that every word coming out of her daddy's mouth centered on Aaron's laundry plans. Hadn't Aaron confided in her father about their . . . hers and Aaron's . . . current difficulty? Or maybe Aaron didn't see any difficulty. Maybe he just didn't care that she was upset. Maybe to him she was merely one more girl in the congregation dreaming about the handsome preacher. Well, now it was all she could do not to cry! Instead she stood up and announced, "I'm going to work."

Her parents watched her storm away from the table. As she opened the front door, her father called after her, "You're gonna be more than an hour too early!"

"I don't care!"

Her parents jumped in their chairs as the door slammed behind her.

Mildred looked confusedly at her husband. "What is wrong with that child?"

"I 'spect it's the same thing that's wrong with him," he answered.

"Him who?" Mildred demanded.

"Him, the preacher. All this morning, he was slamming doors too."

Mildred felt her temper rising. "Yancy Flowers! Why in the world did you not say that in front of your daughter?"

Yancy chuckled in his throat as he loaded his fork with butter beans. "Guess I was more curious as to how she would react, an' now I know."

Mildred threw her napkin down beside her plate. "You just beat everything half to death, you know that?"

Yancy chuckled again. "Yep."

Chapter Seven

Yancy hadn't stayed with Aaron all that long. He'd entirely missed the fact that, whereas Aaron's day may have begun with slamming doors, his sour mood gradually ended as his attentions began to focus on Bubba X. There was just something about the man that didn't quite ring true. Aaron hadn't had any desire to bend himself over and creep along beside Bubba during the exploration of the underbelly of the house because, quite frankly, Aaron was now down to his very last clean shirt, and too, he had a secret aversion to spiders. In answer to Aaron's voiced concerns about the dangers to his shirt during the subterranean crawl, Mabel had piped right up with her kindly offer to launder his other shirts in the sink. Briefly put, the idea of her mauling his expensive clothing against a rough washboard was a thoroughly unbearable notion. Aside from the treasure of cash nicely stored inside his office, he was, for all intents and purposes, quite poor. He knew that too much attention would be drawn if he, on a modest pastor's salary, continually replaced items the well-intentioned Miss Mabel had mauled to death with new and equally high-quality clothing. Therefore, he would have to take extra good care of the clothing he currently owned. A washing machine would be kinder to the fabrics. Hence, a washing machine was an extremely wise investment. And too, like the new car, easily explained as a portion of the monies given as a graduation gift. Happily, all of that was perfectly true.

It was this inspired idea of a washing machine that had sent Bubba X into a hunched-over saunter under the house. Meanwhile, Aaron was standing on the outside, and with his arms stretched upward and pressed against the side of the house, while he leaned in as far forward as his rotator cuffs would allow. He plainly saw the large and hanging spider webs and he said a quiet prayer for Bubba's safety.

"I'm followin' the mains," Bubba X said. "All the plumbing starts up from the ground well. Then it splits off with a pipe going into and out of the hot water boiler. An' then you got all that feeding into the bigger piping that goes out to the septic pit. So, what I'm gonna do now is follow the two separate water supply pipes comin' from the kitchen."

Bubba was quiet for a few moments as he hunched along beneath the house. When he stopped walking, he started talking.

"Appears to me that to move water along from the kitchen and out to the back porch, you're gonna need some yards of new copper pipes, elbow joints, solder an' a solder iron and about thirty or forty hang clamps to keep the pipes tight. That many hang clamps is gonna be pricey, but if them pipes ain't clamped down tight, you're gonna hear some mighty big bangin' noises ever time your washing machine's pulling water."

Bubba was squinting, scratching his thumbnail along the elbow joint of one of the kitchen pipes. He was so intent on this challenging project that a normally silent and intentionally slack-jawed Bubba hadn't considered just how he badly was foiling a life-long ruse. Instead of making any mention of Bubba's pretense, Aaron posed another question.

"Bubba? How much would you say a new washing machine ought to cost?"

"Thirty dollars," he said without bothering to look back to Aaron.

"You sure about that, Bubba?"

"Yeah. Certain sure. Them machines don't come cheap." Brushing his hands free of dust, Bubba X now looked at Aaron. "These here kitchen pipes could do with a re-solder. They gonna go all leaky if we don't see to 'em right quick."

"Whatever you say, Bubba. You're in charge."

"Okay then," Bubba said with his typical dullard's intonation. "Need some flux."

"Excuse me?"

"Flux. For the solder. Won't nothing hold together without the flux."

Aaron was extremely impressed with Bubba X. True, he was more of an eater than a talker and he wasn't what anyone would describe as fashion conscious, but the man could do just about anything he turned his hand to. Aaron could only wonder at the dark reason behind Bubba's subterfuge for the man was most assuredly *not* simpleminded. Aaron believed that at some point he would learn the why's and wherefore's of it all, but until that time he was more than content to feel blessed to have a such surprisingly bright and capable Bubba X in his employment. A moment after he returned to his office and closed the door, Aaron counted out fifty dollars for the cost of the washing machine as well as the supplies Bubba X needed. Then he counted out an extra twenty dollars: ten dollars for the current month's wages and an extra ten as an advance. He was putting the money in separate pockets when he heard Mabel calling.

"Breakfast! You two come running you hear?"

Being called to breakfast was an ordinary, and some might hazard to say a truly unimportant occurrence. But Mabel's voice had come at the precise moment that Aaron had paused to listen to the soft sounds of bees and the humming birds working the blooms of the crepe myrtle and bottle brush bushes that stood so thick and lush just outside the study's opened windows. Hearing God's creatures working diligently at their nectar gathering, and then Miss Mabel as she called her menfolk to their own type of nectar, he was struck by the hominess of the day. The thought of sitting down to breakfast with Mabel and Bubba X also seemed natural and normal, as if the three of them had been doing this for years. The truly baffling spat with Libby was now completely forgotten and there was the beginnings of a smile on his face as he called back to Mabel, “I’m on my way!”

Aaron was about to finish up his telephone call to a Mr. Charlie Bean when Seth, Casper and Archie breezed in. They each greeted him with “Morning, Preach,” as they strode by him, the trio intent on the kitchen. Less than a minute later, Aaron was occupied with assuring Mr. Bean that the late night call was not a bother. Then he heard Mabel’s irritated squawking sounding loudly from the kitchen.

In Mabel’s hard-won wisdom, young men were more trouble than a blessing and what her kitchen did not need were three more of them. But, there they were anyway. “Ever’ one of ya’ll just keep your dirty fingers outta my cake batter bowl or I’ll give each one of you wretched boys a hard slap upside the head!”

“Any bacon left?” Casper asked.

“Casper Flowers,” Mabel sighed wearily. “If ya’ll will just go on an’ get busy with takin down them sleepin’ beds, I’ll make some toast and strawberry jelly bacon sandwiches.”

“Thank you Miss Mabel,” they cried. And then there was the sound of boots thumping off to the far end of the house.

Having rung off with Mr. Bean, Aaron clicked the receiver arm until he heard the operator (who, thankfully, was not Libby) come on the line. “Yes, could you connect me to Miss Faraday please?”

Two minutes into the conversation with Miss Faraday, Aaron was in complete agreement with Libby. Miss Cornelia Faraday was not physically dying. What Miss Faraday was suffering from, however, was infinitely worse than an impending demise. And it was worse because Aaron believed absolutely in the Lord Christ’s opinion on death; that there was no such thing; that physical death was simply the departing from one world and the entrance into another. But in this world, there was the reality of heartache and pain, and Miss Cornelia Faraday sounded as if she suffered from a great deal of both.

There were two more minutes of his listening to the pitiful mewling in his ear when it occurred to Aaron just how he might be able to help Miss Faraday. In a soft, sympathetic tone he said, "Miss Cornelia, I can be at your house in about three hours. Do you think you can hold on until then, sweetheart?"

"Yes," she whimpered, feeling a warm glow from having been addressed as sweetheart. "I feel I'll have just about enough breath to last until you can get here."

"Well that's just fine. Now you just make sure to keep yourself comfortable on the settee. Maybe have a restful nap. I'll be there directly."

"You'll need to let yourself into the house," she said weakly. "I don't believe I have the strength to get up and greet you properly at the door."

"Miss Cornelia, please do not worry about courtesies. I'll be able to take care of opening the door. You just have yourself a nice, peaceful nap."

"Thank you, Pastor. I believe I shall."

The instant Miss Cornelia Faraday hung up her phone, she threw back the afghan coverlet, bolted from the settee and raced off to her bedroom where she spent the next half hour dressing and primping. Then she went to the kitchen and made certain she had enough cold fried chicken and ham and a big pitcher of tea on the shelves in the walk-in electric refrigerated room. After that, she got busy boiling a dozen eggs in order to make some deviled eggs. While the eggs were boiling, she diced up a whole head of cabbage for the cole slaw that would do nicely with the cold chicken and ham. The entire time she busied herself, she hummed a variety of hymns and wondered if she might just have enough time to bake a pecan pie.

***

Aaron had no difficulty in finding the department store in the nearby town of Myrtle Hedge. It was a big two-story brick building that sprawled along almost 50 percent of the north side of the main street. The painted lettering on the sign that stretched across three spacious display windows announced: Chandler's, Est. 1887. Aaron parked in front of the department store. Standing on the sidewalk, he paused a moment to look at the store's large windows, each with a separate department theme.

One window was dedicated to the ladies' apparel department, the posed mannequins wearing dresses of appealing styles. The second window was for the men's department featuring male type mannequins dressed for formal as well as informal occasions. But it was the third and biggest window where he lingered. This was the window dedicated to housewares. This larger window had a male mannequin sitting on the sofa and a younger looking male resting in an easy chair, the furniture grouped in front of a faux fireplace. What drew his eye was the female mannequin in the mock kitchen area. This mannequin was bent at the waist as if checking on something inside the modern oven. The stove was ultra-modern, putting to shame the stove Aaron was just learning to operate. But it was the appliance behind the female mannequin that captured his heart . . . a true beauty of a washing machine. The machine stood on four curved legs with roller balled feet. It had a big round tub able to handle the largest loads of laundry and set into a rectangular mounting were double rollers for squeezing out excess rinse water. And like the mythical siren's song, the washing machine seductively beckoned.

Aaron knew all about the operation of washing machines. At seminary everyone shared the laundry facility which had two machines. The cardinal rule at seminary was that students were at all times to present themselves clean and tidy. Not only that, but one had to change one's bed sheets twice a week: Wednesdays and Saturdays. All seminarians were responsible for his own laundry. There were no exceptions. Rich students and scholarship students shared the same laundry room fate. One of the machines was designated for dark clothing and the other for sheets and lighter colored fabrics. The laundry day machine usage was on a monitored schedule that was strictly adhered to. After four years in seminary Aaron had not only graduated with an impressive grade point average, but he'd come out of there a real dab hand at washing and ironing. And now he was going to purchase his own very private washer and hopefully, one of those brand-new electric steam irons he'd heard so much about. It was simply so thrilling that he was very nearly all aquiver.

Twenty minutes later he came out of the store carrying a box containing his very own snazzy electric steaming iron and the sales slip and warranty for his very own washing machine. He was followed by a male store clerk carrying the ironing board, which had been given as a thank you by the store owner for Aaron's full cash payment for the expensive appliances. The washing machine was scheduled to be delivered the next day by the store's van. If Bubba had the plumbing sorted, by this time tomorrow Aaron would be looking forward to running his first load of laundry. Life was good. Mr. and Mrs. Bean had agreed to marriage counseling, Aaron had been highly successful in his shopping spree, and now, it was on to Miss Cornelia's.

Chapter Eight

As a joke, they had begun calling themselves, The Preacher's Boys. However, the joke had faded as the title became a mutually held identity. It was amazing that after only three days Aaron had become their hero. He was a man their own age and from a privileged station in life, but as he'd casually said, "Paul counted all earthly gain as trash when compared to the richness of knowing and serving Jesus. As do I."

None of them had ever known anyone who talked like Aaron. Nor had they ever known a pastor who laughed, as he did, at the top of his lungs without a hint of embarrassment. Without ever realizing it, all three young men, Archie Lofthouse, Seth Lewis and Casper Flowers, had, until just recently, lived lives that had been starving to death for a true image of Christ. After spending an entire evening in Aaron's company, they were now able to imagine Christ laughing and joking, but mostly they were beginning to feel Christ's presence when all four of them were together.

After depositing the last sections of the sleeping porch beds into the feed and grain store's storage barn, the trio, Archie Lofthouse, Seth Lewis and Casper Flowers, slid the barn doors together. Casper clamped the padlock and for all intents and purposes, their slave labors were completed. However, the "Preach" had also asked them to meet him at Miss Cornelia Faraday's for "luncheon". Now that request was just flatout peculiar. At no time in any of their collective lives had they ever so much as stepped a toe inside the sprawling house owned by Miss Cornelia. They were not alone in this for rarely, if indeed ever, had anyone in Henrytown been invited to pay a social call on Miss Cornelia.

It wasn't because she was a horrible or spiteful person; it was that, because of her social station, she simply wasn't the type the people of Henrytown felt especially at ease with. Nobody knew just how much money the woman had. All of her private banking was done through a bank in Baton Rouge, but rumor hath it that she had way too much money for a puny La Salle Parish bank to handle. It was also said that the run on the banks hadn't fazed her because she had her own personal vault in the Baton Rouge bank. As mentioned, all of this banking and hidden money business was strictly speculation and buck-wild-rumor. Yet, the exact brass tacks were: in her day Miss Cornelia had been the unrivaled beauty of LaSalle Parish. And, in his day, Cedric Faraday, her beloved and late lamented daddy, had been one of the wealthiest men in nearly all of Louisiana.

From the day she turned sixteen, the day she'd traded pigtails for her enduring upswept coiffure, Miss Cornelia had been in the constant company of wealthy and highly attentive beaus. The prevailing mystery swirling around Miss Cornelia was that despite her advantages of looks and money, why she'd never married. What was known was that she'd gone off to an all girl's type of finishing school in New Orleans and three years later she'd come home to care for her ailing father. After he passed, she had then remained to dutifully care for her highly nervous natured mother.

Nervous natured or not, it had taken almost two decades for her flibbertigibbet of a mother to flibber her last gibbet. By then, Miss Cornelia was forty, well passed marriageable age. As understandable as her years of selfless devotion might seem, it was also widely known that during the decades' stretch between the funerals of her parents that Miss Cornelia had continued to attract streams of admiring bachelors. For reasons known only to herself, she'd turned one and all away. Rapidly following her mother's death, Miss Cornelia closed off two wings of the great house, dismissed the staff and shut herself off from society. Overnight the town's opinion of Saint Cornelia radically changed to Peculiar Miss Cornelia. (And the fired staff happily shared tidbits of Miss Cornelia's eccentricities even though some of what was said was about a four mile walk away from the truth.)

Miss Cornelia's parents had been staunch Methodists, but she left that congregation and began regularly attending the Free Church. No one knew the why of it, and Miss Cornelia was not forthcoming. But Sunday after Sunday, there she sat, alone but regal in the pew, the other members of the congregation far too shy to impose themselves on the great lady of Henrytown. And their shyness left Miss Cornelia to become what is known by clericals as a clandestine Christian; someone who slips in, sits alone, then slips out. While on the whole these are a no muss, no fuss type of congregates, they are, for their pastors, the most worrying.

Now nearing her sixties Miss Cornelia Faraday was unknowingly worrying her brand new pastor. From the little information he'd gleaned during the morning from Miss Mabel, he had been able to ascertain that Miss Cornelia—called such not because of her spinsterhood but because in the south the title of Miss is applied to both the married and the unmarried ladies—was considered to be the town's pariah. Mabel, who knew everyone's business, knew only that Miss Cornelia's interests consisted of going to church every Sunday morning, belonging to the Book-of-the-Month mail order club, bossing around gardener Mr. Tanner, and her once-a-week cleaner, Carla Hicks. Outside of these two staff persons, no one could put a name to another soul Miss Cornelia ever actually spoke to. However, of late, and this according to Libby, Miss Cornelia had been putting through a lot of calls to the doctor and bringing him on the run at all hours of the day and night.

The three brand new Brothers in the Lord were standing near Casper's truck, Archie, removing his hat that had seen better days, and with the tips of his fingers vigorously scrubbing his thick mop of flame red hair. This brisk exercise left all of that coppery red hair standing wildly on end.

"Waddaya'll think we outta do?" Casper asked.

"Well I been thinkin' on it," Seth drawled. "An' what I been thinkin' is this. The Preach has only been in town for about a week an' first thing he does is get me saved, an' now he's sayin' that we all gotta meet him over at Miss Cornelia's for dinnertime. So now I'm kinda worryin' about the three of us just turnin' up for dinner at Miss Cornelia's like it's just as natural as a thing as it can be."

Casper scratched at his earlobe and grimaced as he said, "Tha's a mighty twisty road you're travelin', Seth. Does it finally empty out somewheres? And in my near future?"

"Yeah," Seth laughed. "It ends with the three of us climbing back into the truck and goin' over to Miss Cornelia's, if for no other reason than it gives us the opportunity to tell ever'body in town that we did it."

"Lord have mercy," Archie sighed as he stopped checking his unruly hair for the fleas he imagined he'd picked up inside the storage barn. There was a lot of old and moldy stuff in that barn. Fleas were known to make a home inside old and moldy stuff while waiting for something tasty to wander by, say something as tasty as Archie's noggin. He was more than convinced that they had sailed right on by Casper and Seth in one bodacious flea-jump for his head. Donning his hat, he said gloomily, "If Miss Cornelia really does feed us, an' I'm sayin' inside the house, not just outside on the front porch like we're a bunch of no account field hands, my mama's gonna pester me half to death with about four hundred million-zillion questions." Setting his face like flint, Archie finished, “An’ I am not lookin’ forward to that. No sir. I’m not looking forward to that not even a little bit.”

Casper slapped his hands against the sides of his legs as he exclaimed, “Well we just can’t let Aaron go in there all by himself!”

“I say we can,” Archie countered.

To whit Casper and Seth hollered, “Get in the truck Arch!”

The unhappy trio took their own sweet time during the drive through town, but to their mutual chagrin they eventually arrived at Miss Cornelia’s. As there was no sign of the preacher’s spiffy new car, they remained in the truck. At the end of ten minutes when a hint of reprieve wafted through the snowy blooms of the huge magnolia trees in Miss Cornelia’s front yard, Seth was stretching forth his hand to key the ignition when behold and lo, they spotted Aaron’s car. Seth slumped back against the bench.

Aaron parked, exited the car and walked toward the truck. Clad in his customary white fedora, white oxfords, white trousers and shirt and bright red suspenders, Aaron’s sunny manner was apparent as his long legs strode toward the truck. Stopping at the driver’s side, and with one foot settling on the running board, he said cheerily through the cab’s opened window, “Hello you fellows!”

This greeting left the three with the need to wonder, yet again, why Aaron invariably said, “You fellows.” Didn’t anybody in Atlanta ever say, “Ya’ll?” What kind of Southerner didn’t say, “Ya’ll”?

Casper, in the Louisianan roundabout way of asking a question, lent a voice to their mutually held quandary. Leaning around Seth in order to speak to Aaron, he said, “Hey Preach? Answer me something. After the Yankees burned down Atlanta, was it them that rebuilt it again after they’d run all the real Southerners out?”

Aaron's pale eyebrows shot straight up to meet the inner band of his hat. "Why no, indeed. Atlanta was rebuilt by the old families and they accomplished this despite the heavy taxation the Northerners continually imposed. I assure you, Atlanta remains a thoroughly Southern city. Why would you ask?"

"Oh, no reason," Casper answered. "It was just one of them historical things I never could get straight inside my head."

Any lingering discomfiture, as well as further conversation, was put to an end by the cicadas beginning yet another wave of their distinctive, as well as deafening, buzz. Aaron opened the truck's driver side door and Seth reluctantly hauled himself out. At the same time, the passenger's side door opened, and Archie and Casper stepped out. The three followed behind Aaron as he walked himself up the center cement pathway that was dappled by the shade of the magnolia trees. He went onward and then upward, bounding the set of brick steps that fed up to the substantial and covered front porch.

Casper, Seth and Archie were taken aback when the preacher did not knock or employ the bell-pull but simply opened the very solid front door and then stepped inside the house. The three followed but more slowly, and unable to shake the suspicion that they were unwittingly in on a daylight burglary. They deliberately remained in the foyer, their hats held respectfully in their hands, watching as Aaron walked on down the hallway and then opened a set of sliding doors.

Never in all their young lives had they been inside such a grand home. For one thing, there was the spotlessness of it. Then there was the fact that the larger portion of the foyer dead ended at a curving staircase. There was nothing beyond the staircase, no visible avenue of escape through a back door. That was unsettling as well as highly claustrophobic. Louisiana architects had a fondness for shotgun style houses.

Meaning that a man could stand at either end of the entrance hallway and fire a shotgun straight through the house without ever disturbing anything a wife or a mother might consider important to her life. This was not a shotgun house. To escape Miss Cornelia's house, a person would have to know just which of the several closed doors on either side of the foyer hallway might hold the clue to the nearest back exit. Yet Aaron had not hesitated. As if guided by an inner compass, he'd walked to the double sliding doors, which were up a ways and on the right and had stepped on through.

Well, Casper reasoned, Aaron's own daddy was said to be a very rich man, and as such, he'd more than likely been raised up in a house just as grand as this. The three could hear him speaking and then they caught the faint sound of a feminine response. Not knowing what they should do, they contented themselves with simply standing like three exceptionally masculine statues while each gave the impressive foyer a good looking over.

Archie was rather intent in this pursuit, taking in every detail—all purely for his mama's sake of course. The interior of the house was nothing that Casper had been expecting. For years he'd harbored the notion that behind the formidable front door lay a house shrouded in a sinister gloom. He'd also believed that it was haunted, and *everybody* knew that haunted houses were heavily curtained with nasty, long hanging spider webs. Yet this foyer was not at all eerie. As a matter of fact, this house was the pure spit of the house his own mama used to talk about, the house she'd gone into when she was only a girl of fifteen and while training for what she called "service." Years later, Casper understood that "service," meant being a housemaid. But that house Mama had talked so much about was a long way off in New Orleans, and in a mysterious place known as the Garden District. His mama had only lived in it for a year and then, when she'd come back to Henrytown for a visit with her parents, she'd ended up marrying Yancy Flowers. Mama said goodbye to "service" to strangers and hello to "service" to a husband and two squalling kids. But that big house she'd once lived in, be it ever so briefly, left a lasting impression. An impression she'd happily discuss at length, that is, whenever anybody would let her.

Clearly remembering his mother's details, Casper's gaze traveled along the wall to the left where there was a long table with highly polished silver candlesticks standing like gleaming soldiers on either side of a large vase that contained an arrangement of freshly-cut blue hydrangeas. On the wall just above the tallest of the blooms hung an oval mirror inside a gilded frame. Beneath the vase was a slender, oblong shaped little blue tray with raised white figures. Thanks to his mother, Casper knew that this was called Wedgwood and this type of tray was meant for what his mama said was calling cards. When rich persons called on each other, they always left their cards in the tray. Why, he didn't know. Rich people were a little odd.

On the left, directly opposite the table, there stood a tidy white fireplace with blue delft tiling. On either side of the fireplace were two high backed Queen Anne chairs. This was where his mama said unexpected guests were requested to remain while waiting to be received. And Casper, knowing all the local lore of the young and beautiful Miss Cornelia, could imagine many young men sitting and waiting to either be received or turned away. In either case, the swains would have left their calling cards in the fancy little Wedgewood tray.

Archie, not one easily given to romantic notions, was more interested in the foyer's flooring. It looked to be pure marble but cut into large squares of black and white and laid out in checkerboard fashion. Boy-hidey, on a rainy day a couple of children could have themselves a fine old time playing a game of human-being checkers.

Seth's attention was on the stairway. Not even in magazine photographs had he ever seen anything like those stairs. On the first landing, there was a floor standing candelabra holding eight big fat candles. The light of those candles had to be a pure blessing on a dark night because even now in the middle of the day, that staircase just kept on climbing upward until it disappeared into the shadows. Without those night candles, one misstep would cause a tumble that would really put a hurt on a person's entire day. Seth dearly longed to climb those stairs to see just what was up on the second floor. However, he knew he didn't dare. His boots would leave dirt marks on the runner rug that was held tightly into place on each riser by a long brass rod.

Casper, now staring up into the electricity converted crystal chandelier, spoke for all of them when he said, wonderment evident; "Miss Cornelia's daddy musta gave a big pile of money for this place."

"You know that," Seth agreed. "This place is so grand it makes me wonder if heaven didn't come as something of a disappointment to the man."

The next thing they knew, Aaron's head was poking out from around the side of the opened doorway. "You fellows come in here and meet Miss Cornelia."

By the way Miss Cornelia's hands trembled, the Preacher's Boys could tell that she was just as flustered to be formally meeting them as they were her. But there was something noticeably different in the way she stared at Archie. Then her right hand went to her chest and clutched the big cameo broach pinned to the neckline of her dress. In a soft and halting voice she said, not questioned mind you, but said like a known fact, "You're related to Archibald Lofthouse."

"Yes Ma'am," Archie replied as humbly as if addressing a queen. "He was my grandpaw."

Miss Cornelia held onto that cameo, like it was for dear life, as she slowly lowered her head and said in a near whisper, "I was . . . grieved . . . by your loss."

This was immediately followed by a silent pall. And that's the only way to describe it. It was a big old *P-A-L-L*, as in, big fat dark cloud. Never mind that practically every dab of the day's bright sunlight was streaming in through the French windows that opened up to a wonderfully private sitting garden. The noon day sunlight might have been inside the formal parlor, but it suddenly felt as if it wasn't strong enough to warmup a worm. Archie was quickly realizing that he was somehow responsible for all this *P-A-L-L* business, and how, he simply didn't know. Had he been the more observant sort, every morning when looking into the bathroom mirror he might have noticed the uncanny resemblance between himself and the old sepia print of his much younger grandfather. Sadly, Archie was not overly observant. Therefore, at the moment all he could do was stand there wondering just how he had unwittingly faux pas-*ed*.

Miss Cornelia was looking at Archie again when she asked, "Young man? Would you mind very much smiling?"

"Excuse me, Ma'am?"

She did not respond, she just kept staring and waiting for the requested smile. Unfortunately, Archie couldn't think of a single thing to smile about.

That's when Aaron, who, seated on the ottoman directly in front of the couch on which Miss Cornelia regally sprawled, placed his hand on her free hand and asked, "Miss Cornelia did you hear the church has just voted to take back the Humility pin that was awarded to Casper's daddy, Mister Yancy Flowers?"

Miss Cornelia at first looked stunned, and then her expression became a question mark.

"Well they had to," Aaron hurried on to explain. "If Yancy Flowers is the sort of man proud enough to accept such a pin, then just how humble could he be?"

Miss Cornelia, along with the Preacher's Boys exploded into laughter. And as they laughed, it thrilled Miss Cornelia's heart to see Archie Lofthouse's truly exquisite smile.

Chapter Nine

The four young men remained with Miss Cornelia for almost three hours. Contrary to popular Henrytown fiction, she was not a stingy hostess. The fact was, the woman kept feeding them until they all felt as fattened up as a gaggle of geese headed off for the butcher shop. And judging by the way she continually hopped on and off the settee, it was also evident the woman was anything but on her last legs. Trying to force down yet another deviled egg, Aaron rightly believed that his initial impression had indeed been correct. The true cause of the lady's health concerns was . . . loneliness.

If the amount of food she had prepared was any indication, then despite Miss Cornelia's chosen cloistered lifestyle, deep down she was a woman who was quietly desperate to feel connected. The underlying dilemma was a problem Aaron was all too familiar with: Miss Cornelia's station within the community. She was a wealthy antebellum maiden lady in a small town that had been reduced to hardscrabble penury. As such, there were many in town who simply envied or deeply resented her privileged circumstance. Then there were those who were either beggars or out-and-out swindlers, all of them anxious to line up at her door and prey on her kindly nature and fat bank account. Acutely aware of her own vulnerability, her tireless eye for vigilance had resulted in splendid isolation. However, God did not create His children to be alone. But neither did He approve of His children, simply for the sake of companionship, being placed in a situation where they were easily used or abused. Ergo, this problem truly was something of a stumper.

Aaron was dwelling on Miss Cornelia's predicament and what, if anything he could possibly do to help her, all the while the lady in question was being regaled by Archie with yet another tale about his grandfather; a subject Miss Cornelia found oddly fascinating. It was merely by happenstance, or so Aaron believed at the time, that he noticed the freestanding needle work frame that had been tucked, almost secretively, into a distant corner of the room. Following this clue, he then took notice of the fine needle point chair and pillow coverings that were positively everywhere. The pillow coverings were foremost on his mind as he rose and casually, and unnoticed by the others, left the conversation. He was standing before the stitching frame and looking at the excellence of Miss Cornelia's work when he spoke, rudely interrupting Archie.

"Miss Cornelia," the unexpected summons effectively broke the conversational flow. With everyone's attention redirected toward him, Aaron said, "You my dear lady are a true artist. I can't help but wonder if you wouldn't mind using your gift in the Lord's service?"

Miss Cornelia was genuinely flustered yet again, but not in a big fat dark *P-A-L-L* kind of way. This time she was looking at Aaron with an expression that suggested hopeful anticipation.

"I'm sorry Pastor, but I truly do not understand your meaning."

His hands clasped behind his back, Aaron, looking deep in thought, made a slow walk back toward the group. When he spoke again, his words were carefully measured.

"Last evening I noticed that ours is a congregation given to kneeling during prayer." He stopped, looming over the reclining Miss Cornelia. "Kneeling during prayer is a habit I deeply wish to encourage because I am of the opinion that kneeling before the LORD God of All, is the only true attitude of a supplicant." Aaron paused, taking in a deep breath before continuing on. "Therefore, given the expertise of your skill and the artistry of your designs, I can't help but wonder if the congregation wouldn't welcome the chance to kneel upon such excellent cushions as your talent so easily produces."

Miss Cornelia, who was again beginning to look as delicately fragile as a porcelain figurine, was on the verge of declining the proposal and to stave her off, Aaron raised a silencing hand. "My dear lady, I quite understand the magnitude of such a notion, but I'm also certain that there's more than a fair share of ladies within the congregation who might be more than willing to aid you in such an endeavor. All they are lacking really is the proper leadership and, of course, a genuine artistic flair. After closely examining the excellence of your work, I've concluded that you, Miss Cornelia, have been blessed with both of these attributes."

His smile was so warm, so affectionate that for several moments she simply couldn't speak. To her immense relief, he carried on.

"I wouldn't be so bold as to press you for an answer at this moment, however, I would encourage you to be in prayer regarding a suitable cushion design and then the possibility of forming a league of ladies to help with the needlepoint work."

Archie, knowing full well that his own mother would give her eyeteeth to be inside this house, couldn't help but jump at this, his mother's one golden opportunity. "My mama purely loves to do needle work. She'd be the first one to volunteer."

"Well my mama's just as good at it as your mama is," Casper said. "An' she's even won a prize."

"This is not a competition," Aaron said firmly. Turning toward the three young men, he continued. "Fellows, I am merely proposing to Miss Cornelia that she should consider this service. It is a highly important ministry and it's not one to be entered into lightly. Until Miss Cornelia confides to me her final decision, you must not rush home with any news of this to your mothers."

"But . . ." Miss Cornelia shyly interjected, "If you *really* feel my small talents might be of some use, then Pastor, how could I possibly refuse?"

Aaron's smile caused her heart to leap. "Miss Cornelia, I can think of no one better suited to carry out such a valuable service to our congregation."

Before coming to Louisiana, Aaron had never eaten so many meals that included beans. It would appear that Miss Mabel had a bean dish for every type of entree. Tonight it was lima beans with the roast pork and roasted wedges of sweet potatoes. To some relief she'd made wheat flour biscuits in lieu of the unrelenting presence of corn meal.

"I tell ya what," Casper declared over his plate. "I have not eaten nearly so good as I have for this whole live-long day."

Archie and Seth put the Amen to that pronouncement. Bubba said not a word, but the speed of his fork most certainly spoke volumes.

Miss Mabel gushed, "I purely do love cooking for a houseful of hungry boys." Her head bobbled proudly as self-satisfied smirking lips puckered just enough to take sips of iced tea. Unwisely, Miss Mabel went fishing for more compliments. "The food over to Miss Cornelia's waddn't so fancy you boys couldn't eat any of it was it?"

Miss Mabel shouldn't have dipped her bait into the bigger pond because the instant she did, her moment of culinary glory was shot to smithereens. Aaron tried not to smile, or recall Proverbs 16:18 *Pride goeth before destruction, and a haughty spirit before a fall*, as he concentrated on Miss Mabel's simple fare. However Archie, Seth and Casper, and rather unfortunately, tried to outdo one another as they regaled a thoroughly unenthused Miss Mabel of the sights they'd seen inside the grand old house and the refined taste of the foods Miss Cornelia had made with her very own hands.

"She's really sweet!" Seth declared.

"And she loves to joke," Archie said.

"Yeah," Casper chimed in. "Who knew Miss Cornelia was such a fun-time kinda gal!"

As they went on, Miss Mabel quickly became mighty sick of the entire conversation. To her relief, a car horn sounded in the front yard.

Aaron made haste to excuse himself from the table. He'd only just made it out onto the porch when he spotted Libby storming her way up the steps.

"I want to talk to you," she said, her tone threatening.

The porch was back lit by the lights shimmering out from the living room windows, those windows encased along what was commonly known as the porch's house-wall. On the two tables set in between the spacing of porch rocking chairs, a pair of coal oil lanterns emitted a warm glow. Yet the combined richness of the porch lighting was hardly more than a frail protest against the solid wall of darkness that stood so robust and resolute just beyond the porch railing. Sweeping his right arm to the side to convey a silent invitation, Aaron indicated the rockers. She moved passed him, taking a seat in the second rocker. Mystified by her paying a call at such an hour and in such an apparent bad humor, he claimed the rocker next to hers and, from that point onward, neither of them chose to be the first to recognize the other's existence.

As for her part in the drama, the only noise coming from Libby's direction was the squeaky agitation of the rocking chair. Her arms were defensively crossed at her midriff as she looked straight ahead into the darkness. The more he didn't so much as even try to speak to her, the madder she got and the madder she got the more quickly and nosily the rocking chair moved.

Conversely, Aaron rocked his chair only ever so slightly. His long and lanky body held the posture of one perfectly relaxed; hands resting comfortably against his upper thighs. He looked for all the world exactly what he'd been born to be, the unflappable Georgian Gentleman, secure within his social strata and entirely comfortable within its timeless grace and courtly demeanor. Albeit, underneath all of this he was becoming more than weary of Libby's ill attitude and even more weary of her need to foist this attitude off onto him. Miss Mabel's food might have been a bit too plain after the afternoon's enjoyment of the finer foods, but he was hungry and Miss Mabel's supper was at least filling. Not to mention that it was, because of the cooling and gelatinizing process, growing even less palatable by the second. If all Libby Flowers intended to do was pull a pout, then he felt sorely tempted to simply leave her to it. She could then pout to her heart's content while he grappled with the meal of slightly burnt sweet potatoes, near tasteless roast pork, watery lima beans (beans which at the same time were strangely dry in the middle) and biscuits (actually, the biscuits were surprisingly delicious).

With an inward groan, he remembered that he was Libby's pastor. Abandoning one of The Shepherd's lambs in favor of a biscuit was sadly not an option. Yet now Aaron couldn't stop thinking about biscuits; hot and melting with butter and dripping great gooey globs of fig preserves. How perfectly marvelous!

Drat! Now I can't think of anything other than those biscuits.

Casper was eating a biscuit exactly like that, but he didn't actually taste it as he stared off at the distant doorway. The main door was propped open, but the screened door was shut. Other than the occasional flutter of a moth against the screen, he couldn't see anything beyond it. Minutes earlier he'd heard his sister's voice. He was also very well acquainted with that *special* tone of hers. He had no idea who had shoved a button up Libby's nose this time but, knowing his sister's angry voice as well as only a brother can, he knew someone most certainly had. He couldn't help but think that her arrival at the parsonage could be something of an indicator of just who that person might have actually been.

That just doesn't make any sense at all. The man's only been here five days! What could he have done in five days that's worthy enough to send her off into one of her stupid fits? Casper didn't attempt to even hazard a guess but at the moment the prevailing issue—because like it or not, he was her older brother, sworn to protect and all that—was that things were sounding mighty quiet out there on the porch.

Then Seth said, "Ya know? Things are soundin' mighty quiet out there on the porch."

Fearful that he'd suddenly developed an echo inside his brain, Casper rapidly shook his head in an effort to clear it; then in annoyance he looked at Seth across the table.

Seth was sitting half turned in the chair, his body now more in line with the front door than the dining table.

"Libby's quite a girl," he said in a lowered tone. This comment wasn't actually intended to be directed to anyone in particular, but the other four pairs of ears were finely tuned in. "I always did like her. Couldn't ever get her to like me back though." Seth stood and with an edge in his tone said, "I'm gonna go see what's goin' on out there."

Casper immediately stood and Archie, muttering "Oh have mercy," stood up beside Casper. A heartbeat later both were walking with haste in the pursuit of Seth.

Mabel, worried to no end, because she knew what a hellion Seth Lewis could be when pushed, scuttled a step or two behind Casper and Archie. The screen door banged shut behind Seth, and then after Casper, and then again after Archie; the door taking a bit of a pounding with each slam. Mabel chose to stand just inside the door and peer out through the screen. Meanwhile, at the table, Bubba was pulling the biscuit tray closer to his plate.

"What's going on out here?" Seth demanded of the stone silent pair.

Aaron calmly rose from the chair and as Casper and Archie arrived on the scene, he just as calmly replied, "Well, as you can clearly see, nothing very much. Miss Libby arrived, announced her intention to speak to me, we sat down, and, apart from the tree frogs which sound to be in exceptionally good voice tonight, I have since been the recipient of remorseless silence."

"Oh boo-hoo," Libby snipped.

Aaron briefly glanced down at her, then he turned away and asked of Casper. "Is there any hope at all that a biscuit has been left on the bread tray?"

"Yeah," Casper shrugged. "But Bubba X is guardin' the tray. You might wanna step lively if you want one."

Aaron walked for the door just as Mabel fled away from it, shouting as she hurried toward the dining room, "Bubba! Them biscuits are for the preacher!"

Libby had planned on having it out with Aaron and during the drive she had rehearsed exactly what she was going to say—and to his face—the instant she arrived at the parsonage. Trouble was, during all of this planning and rehearsing she'd entirely forgotten what Aaron looked like. This was remedied when she was steaming up the brick and concrete steps. Sadly, the re-acquaintance with his unnerving good looks had completely, well, unnerved her.

I should have telephoned this in, she thought as she began to weep into her hankie. Aaron had simply walked away, leaving her to be surrounded by Archie, Casper and Seth. *He thinks I'm an utter fool! And I am! I am an utter fool*!

Libby was tipping her head back and Casper, knowing what that meant, rushed to say, "Libby? Sweetheart? Please don't cry. You know cryin' makes you look kinda cute—like that little cartoon penguin—but honey, you don't stay like that. You know what you look like when the little penguin disappears and honey, you just don't want to be doing any of that in front of people, most especially, men-people."

Libby's mouth opened until it looked like a dark and ever widening maw. And then there was that . . . sound . . . which was loud. Very, very loud, and on par with either a wonky fire siren or a randy donkey's mating bray.

Archie jumped back. "Great day in the morning!" he yelped. "What in the world is she doin'?"

Casper hollered over his sister's din, "Welcome to the Flowers' family secret." He quickly looked at Seth who was now staring at Libby with a thoroughly alarmed expression. "Seth! This is not a vow breaker. This right here don't let you out of your thinking about proposing to my sister. We all heard you say you're sweet on her. We're witnesses."

Seth yelled loudly to Casper, his voice barely covering Libby's extraordinary din. "How long can she keep this up?"

Casper increased his volume but still, his was only a trace louder than his strident sister. "Depends on how mad she is. The record so far is a whole day. But I can't be sure 'cause I only know about the first half of that day on account of Daddy finally stuffing her into the truck and driving her off. He swears blind that they were just barely this side of Alexandria before she finally quit."

Libby paused long enough to take a deep breath and then let go again.

Casper increased his volume. "Well—if you wanna know the wretched truth, Daddy takin' her off like that made the sudden peace in the house pert-near exquisite."

A panicked riddle Seth yelled, "What are we supposed to do?"

"One of us could take her for a ride I guess."

"She's your sister!" Archie countered. "You do it!"

Casper promptly responded, "I am not getting into a confined space with none of this. Besides, I'm only her brother." He glared at Seth who was still staring down at Libby with an expression that bordered on abject horror. "Seems to me, the fella always claimin' that he likes my sister so much ought to be the first one puttin' his hand up for the task."

It was about that time that when like Daniel walking into the lion's den (but with a half-eaten biscuit in hand), Aaron wandered out onto the porch. Happy to be eating his biscuit, he seemed completely deaf to the obnoxious sounds shattering the peace of the night. Still, Casper felt the overpowering need to apologize for his sister's unseemly blaring. Trouble was, with Aaron's reappearance, Libby's wailing had risen to such an earsplitting level that now Casper could not out shout her. Aaron swallowed his bite of biscuit and raised his biscuit free hand to put Casper on pause.

"Hold on," Aaron said. Bending at the waist he patted the back of Libby's hand that was holding a white-knuckled grip on the rocker's arm rest. In a tone that could only be described as unruffled, he said, "Libby, my dear you're simply going to have to be quiet. I can't hear Casper."

The effect was instantaneous. Her shut eyes popped fully open. And her mouth, which had been so unhinged that it had taken on the aspect of a canyon, snapped as tightly closed as a Five and Ten Cents Store coin purse. Not only was Libby suddenly dead calm, but all of nature seemed to have gone there with her. The overall effect could only be described as, spine-chilling.

Again, Aaron did not seem to notice. "Would you fellows mind going back inside the house? I'd like to speak to Libby—"

The three were gone, the screen door banging hard behind them. Aaron nonchalantly took another bite of his biscuit and sat down next to Libby.

The trio were in a high trot toward the dining room when Seth half whispered to Casper, "Couldn't Aaron even hear that? I mean, he was just as calm as a May morning. Libby was screaming her lungs loose an' all he did was stand there eating a biscuit!" Having reached the dining room table, Seth sat down in a chair and armed a film of sweat from his brow." So, you know what I'm thinking?" he asked no one in particular. "I'm thinking that the perfect man for Libby could be right now sittin' on the porch with her."

From the other side of the table Casper expelled a dispirited sigh. "Does this mean you are formally withdrawing your suit?"

Seth looked sheepish. "Well . . . yeah!"

"Ya know," Casper drawled, "I can't help but feel that this has more to do with a pert little blond named Verda-Louise from over in Olla, who just happened to be visitin' your cousin for all of last summer."

Seth shook his head. "Well . . . truth be told, Verda and I have exchanged a few letters. But in my defense, the girl writes a real interesting letter and she has a truly fine hand. Her capital B's and P's are a true wonder."

"Really?" Archie said.

"Oh yeah," Seth answered. "They're pure artistry." Then snapping back into the moment, he hollered at Casper, "Besides! I had no earthly idea Libby could carry on like that!"

Casper slapped the tabletop. "Seth Lewis! I have been tellin you for years that you don't know my sister half as well as think you do!"

Archie added his own bewilderment to the conversation. "Wonder how he got her to go all quiet like that?" Another puzzlement occurred as Archie looked around the room. "An' I wonder where Miss Mabel an' Bubba X have got to."

"They're Flowers family," Casper grunted. "That means they know when it's time to hide."

Aaron finished his biscuit. Even lukewarm it was still delicious. He was thinking that he should speak to Miss Mabel about making more biscuits than cornbread when he looked over at Libby and said, "I can't say I care very much for our arguing. Most especially when I'm so mystified as to why we're arguing."

"You mean you really don't know?" When he continued to look baffled, and in that gorgeous way of his, Libby had to physically muster her courage in order to speak her piece.

Aaron said not a word as she started in—primarily because he knew she had to get all of the hurt and bitterness out before he could reason with her. He was also wondering if she would be finished in time for him to have another biscuit before the bread platter was emptied. As she wound down and drifted to a stop, he said evenly, "I want to thank you for speaking so frankly—but is that all? Are you certain there isn't anything else you'd care to add?"

Libby did a quick mental check list, her thumb touching the tips of her fingers as she ticked the topics off. A) Worked so hard, B) Wasn't even thanked, C) Her efforts were cast aside as if of no importance . . . Oh! D!) She'd forgotten Item D.!

"Oh!" she cried. "You made me lose confidence in the one thing I'm trying so hard to be good at."

"And what would that be?"

"A professional secretary."

"I see." Aaron pursed his lips as he had a brief think. "Well, as far as I'm able to determine, you will make quite an excellent secretary.

However, I myself am not in the position to offer you employment that is even remotely on par with your already achieved skills level. The most I can afford is a one day per week typing position at say," he twisted his lips to the side as he thought his money situation through. "Two dollars per week. I know that's not an adequate amount—"

"Really!?" she squealed. "You're hiring me to typewrite for you?"

Aaron held up his hands in surrender. "Yes, but I can only afford your service one day per week an—"

Libby's chair careened wildly as she flew out of it and put a choking hug on Aaron's neck. He hurriedly stood, primarily because he was becoming desperate to breathe; but his real hope was that by standing he would dislodge her. This did not prove to be the case. Libby had such a tenacious hold on him that when he came to stand, she came up right along with him, her feet dangling above the porch boards. Before Aaron's need for air became acute, Casper, by some miracle, was there and disengaging his sister.

"Sorry Preach," he said as he dislodged Libby. "She's a hugger."

Aaron's hand gently explored his throat, most especially the esophagus, which he feared had suffered some lasting damage. Rasping more than speaking he managed to say, "I've just offered Libby a part-time position as my typist."

Casper nodded as he set his sister down between himself and Seth. All eyes were on Aaron as he formally addressed Casper. As this was a contractual moment, Seth and Archie assumed somber attitudes as Aaron spoke to Casper, the male representative of the Flower's family. All four chose to ignore the fact that Libby was practically dancing.

"Her employment will be each Friday from morning until afternoon and of course you have my guarantee that she will be well chaperoned throughout her working hours. Her transport and luncheons will also be provided."

Casper's teeth worried the corner of his mouth as he listened, his anger with his sister reaching a new high. When Aaron finished speaking, Casper looked down at Libby and yelled, "You just beat everything half to death, do you know that?" Startled, Libby looked as if she were about to restart her infamous hollering, but Casper beat her to the proverbial—"Don't you start all that up again Libby Flowers 'cause I swear if I hear so much as a tiny boo-hoo comin' out of you, I'll turn you right over my knee."

Libby gasped sharply. "I'm tellin' Mama."

As Casper walked away and began to descend the porch steps, he yelled, "You just go ahead on an' tell her anything you want to. I can tell her a few things my own self."

Libby went after her brother. Archie and Seth made haste for Seth's truck. To Aaron, left alone on the porch, it was as if all of the four young people had just stepped off the edge of the earth and into pitch black nothingness. Yet even in the void, Aaron could clearly hear Libby and Casper arguing as truck doors opened and slammed. From behind him there came the noise of a stampede as Miss Mabel and Bubba flew by Aaron with a speed he would have never dreamed they possessed. As Miss Mabel launched her bulk into the darkness, he heard her calling, "Libby Flowers!! You give me an' your cousin a ride pass my house."

"Okay then, come on."

Aaron sat down as the lights of the two trucks flashed on and gears were heard being engaged. He smiled as he heard them all call out, "Good night Preach!" But the best part was Miss Mabel's farewell.

"There's four biscuits waitin' for ya in the oven warmer!!"

Chapter Ten

The advantage Bubba X enjoyed by wearing the expression of one who didn't have two functioning brain cells to rub together was that, if he kept his mouth firmly shut, he was made privy to a lot of interesting conversations. Oh, practically everybody in the parish knew that when it came to working with his hands, Bubba X was a magician; it was just mentally that the boy was a bubble off from level.

The widely held belief of his mental incapability did not wound Bubba's feelings. It was after all, a belief that had been formed when he'd only been four years old, so he'd not only grown up with it, he'd learned to turn it to his advantage. The major contributor to the *Bubba X is an Idiot* opinion had initially been based on his bulky build. From birth, Bubba had been more like a brick than a baby. The second thing about Infant Bubba was that he never cried.

Whoever heard of a baby that didn't cry?

Well, best guess would be any infant inside a houseful of people who were always taking care of the baby but neglecting to pass this information to the next person to come along and pull the baby up and out of his cot. Which meant that on some days Baby Bubba could enjoy being fed five or six times in one day. This would also explain why the baby had so quickly bloated up to the size of a toad-frog. The second simpleton identifier was that at almost five years old, and long since beyond the proper age for toilet training, Bubba continued wearing thick diapers while waddling after his mother. But the real fly in the sweet potato pie was that he had sucked his thumb into his late teenaged years.

Ergo, Bubba X—Miss Mabel's tenth child and a late life baby—was judged an idiot.

Again, none of the accrued facts were actually Bubba's fault. Being the tenth child in an overcrowded house meant that his mother's *mothering* could only be, at best, described as skewed. What with nine other children suffering pre-teen or full blown teen trials and pitfalls, and a husband who just one day up and decided that he had a bad back and consequently couldn't work any longer, Mabel was forced to take up the wage earning slack. This meant too, that like it or not, she had to depend on her bone-idle husband and drama prone children to care for the baby.

By the time Bubba X was walking, and before Miss Mabel was somewhat happily widowed, she was working primarily in the cotton fields. During those days, what money she earned was simply handed over to Jedidiah (the slacker husband) who, bad back or no, still very easily raised his hand to take her money or use his fist if she dared to argue about giving it up. With the demise of Jedidiah, one by one her other children began to leave home—as well as the meager prospects of Henrytown. Still working the cotton, Bubba was left to toddle behind Mabel as she worked along the cotton rows. She had to completely concentrate on picking the cotton. If she didn't, she risked the danger of the rough and knife-sharp bolls. When working the long hours in the fields, it was quite candidly more convenient to keep Bubba in diapers: Which she doubled up to such a degree that Bubba looked like a fat barefoot, blue rubber butt bumble bee. The thumb sucking was merely the by-product of a lively mind trapped in a humiliating and mind-numbingly boring existence. But . . . all of these conditions, when cobbled together, effectively lay the foundations of the ongoing belief that Miss Mabel's last baby was backward.

In early childhood his nimble mind had already reached the conclusion that playing stupid worked to his advantage. At home his mother couldn't bring herself to trust him with the hard chores for fear he might injure himself. At school he was never called to the blackboard to work out the math problems, something he quite easily did inside his mind while he sat at his *special desk* in the back corner of the classroom where he spent the hours happily sucking his thumb. Meanwhile, he watched as the "bright" kids were treated to the taunts and jeers of other classmates while, fruitlessly toiling away at the blackboard problem. Bubba's peers hated school, but he thoroughly enjoyed every minute of it, quietly absorbing each and every lesson, most especially history. Bubba loved history.

The school system continually passed him on to the next grade level because he was never any trouble in class and the bigger he grew the better he proved to be at sports. In fact, he excelled in the La Salle Parish passion—baseball. Bubba was the best home-base catcher anyone had ever known. For some curious reason, he could signal to the pitcher the perfect pitch and, for someone his size, he could catch a foul ball faster than a rabbit could run. Of course, each and every time he successfully tagged out the batter, the viewing fans were treated to the sight of Bubba wiping dirt from his "sucky thumb" against his pant leg and then sticking said thumb straight into his mouth, but . . . never mind.

As a fully grown man, being the town dullard meant that while he waited his turn at the feed and grain store counter, he was treated to the confidential conversations of the town gossips. Seems there were quite a few of the young ladies in town who were setting their caps for the brand-new preacher. The half dozen men loitering in the feed and grain were quietly laying bets on which of the hopefuls would eventually succeed. How odd that at no time was Cousin Libby's name even mentioned. Knowing Henrytown as well as he did, Bubba was certain that there was even more speculation on this very same subject going on over in the barber shop. And from the merest of glances he'd given to the beauty parlor, it was hard to miss the sight of the little shop being way more crowded than usual. By his own mother's telephone activity, he knew that the Crow's Nest was habitually tying up the town's lines with chatter about the Pretty Preacher Boy from Atlanta. And "*Oooooh, didn' the Preacher talk so goooood?*"

Before Bubba had set off on his walk to the feed and grain, he'd heard his mother adding fuel to the fires by informing the Crow's Nest that Libby was ". . . secretary'in for the preacher." And because Libby was blood kin, Mabel had been very quick to add, "Course me an' Bubba's gonna be there the whole time Libby's working." (With this last comment, both the Preacher and Libby's sterling reputations were duly saved. *Good job, Mama.*)

Once again at the parsonage, and presently walking hunched-style under the house as he sorted out the maze of existing piping, Bubba mulled the dangerous waters that the new preacher was unknowingly swimming. He was still mulling as he then applied himself to the task of grafting in the proper piping to accommodate a hot and cold water supply into the newfangled washing machine. Yet, what was actually on his mind was his prevailing concern about Mr. Ralph Winters. That mean old booger controlled the town and the church's Board of Deacons. From what Bubba had gleaned, he knew that Mr. Ralph would see to it that the new preacher wouldn't be around long to enjoy his brand-new washing machine. But truth be told, Bubba was far more worried for Yancy—whom he called, Uncle Yank.

Bubba loved Yancy Flowers as only a young man starved to death for a father's approval could love another man. Then too, Uncle Yank was the only person in town that Bubba felt badly about fooling with his dumb-as-mud, act. Protective of Uncle Yank's honest reputation, Bubba was bound to make certain that he did the best job that the preacher could ever expect. Even if the job at hand proved to be a fruitless endeavor, what with the preacher being on the verge of being extended an invitation to leave town an' all. Which would be a pure shame. But couldn't nobody stop Mr. Winters once he'd made up his mind about a thing.

Bubba had personally witnessed the bad things that always seemed to follow the folks who locked horns with Ralph Winters. Uncle Yank had locked horns with him over that fencing trick, which was nothing but out and out land theft, and then they'd gotten into a big whoo-ha over something at the mill. Whatever that something was, it must have been a pure doozy because that scallywag Mr. Ralph fired Uncle Yank right there on the spot. As if all of that hadn't been bad enough, Mr. Ralph had then gone and taken away Uncle Yank's high standing in the church. For the life of him, Bubba could not see how any of this low-down, dirty-dog behavior could be passed off as Christian. But Mr. Ralph-Head-Deacon-And-Mill-Owner-Winters was one mighty erratic sort of fella. Nothing he had ever seemed like it was ever enough, but what little another fella had was just suddenly the very exact thing that Mr. Ralph was convinced he'd always been needin'.

Kinda crazy really.

In these last few days with the new preacher an' all, Uncle Yank seemed like he'd gone an' put his troubles with Mr. Ralph Winters right out of his mind. Uncle Yank was even smiling and laughing again. Those good spirits told Bubba that his Uncle Yank purely thought the world and all of Pastor Aaron. So, if Mr. Ralph Winters was determined to take the preacher away from Uncle Yank as well, Bubba knew his Uncle Yank wouldn't be hardly able to stand it.

That worried Bubba. It worried him a lot.

He was finishing up the drain line when the department store's delivery van rumbled into the drive. From where he worked under the house, Bubba could see Pastor Aaron in the yard talking to the two delivery men. A few minutes later, Bubba heard all three men walking through the house. He was able to follow the sound of their footfalls until they came to stand inside the newly emptied sleeping porch. From the sound of their voices, they were standing right over Bubba's head. Earlier, he had drilled three holes in the floor, but none of the men above seemed to possess the sense to see the holes as they debated as just where they ought to set the machine. Finally, Bubba could not tolerate one minute more of all that stupid, so he stuck his index finger through the center hole as a visual aid. Well, they even failed to see his finger. That meant there was only one thing left to do.

"Pastor Aaron!" Bubba yelled. He kept his finger jutting up through the hole as footsteps neared. Then, in another of the holes, Bubba could see a portion of Aaron's face as he squinted, trying to see Bubba.

"Bubba? Did you put these holes in the floor?"

"I did."

"Why?"

"It's where the pipes run," Bubba called back. "And, it's the best place to drain out all the water that that tub's gonna hold—twice—once for the washing and once for the rinsing. Tha's just too much water to have sittin' up under the house. That water's all gotta drain out into the yard or it's gonna form a permanent pool under the house and a standin' pool will rot the floorboards."

"He could be right," one of the other men muttered.

Well of course I'm right, Bubba thought snidely. Then Bubba had another thought. "Pastor Aaron?"

"Yes Bubba X, I'm here."

"You best tell them men that they gotta tote the machine around to the back door an' then fotch it on through from the kitchen. If they bring it by the front door an' then all the way through the house, my mama's gonna be powerful mad."

"Good thinking, Bubba!"

Yeah, I know.

By seven that evening, Aaron was wearing a newly washed and ironed shirt and cotton slacks as he sat in the living room surround by the deacons and elders of the church. Eleven filled the couches and easy chairs, two sat on the piano bench, and the remainder of them had brought in chairs from the dining room. Ensconced in the best easy chair, Mr. Ralph was holding (tedious) forth and Aaron was about ready to yawn in the man's egotistical face when he felt the familiar, but relentlessly thrilling sensation stirring deep within. Then he felt himself recalling Psalms 90, verse 12.

"So teach us to number our days, that we may apply our hearts unto wisdom."

As Mr. Ralph droned on Aaron asked, in his spirit, *Father? Are you saying my time here is limited?*

The affirmation was not an answer that Aaron physically heard, it was so far and away more profound. It was a communication that rose up from the deepest part of him and then fired throughout the whole of his body. Aaron could count on one hand the times he'd experienced this type of impression; the last time had been when he'd been praying for guidance about the little church in a place called Henrytown.

And was that God speaking, a scoffer might ask?

It was indeed.

Now that he knew his time in Henrytown was limited, he could no longer afford the luxury of cautiously finessing Ralph Winters. And there was no time like the present to cast off all pretense of just who was actually in charge of Henrytown Free Church.

Aaron leaned forward on the opposing easy chair and interrupted Ralph Winters. "Deacon, thank you for your input. Your list of pastoral expectations and restrictions are indeed most helpful. Now, here are the aims the Lord has for my tenure. To begin, we will start by offering Sunday school classes, on Saturday evenings and in the homes of those selected to be teachers. The home classes will continue only until the church sanctuary has been expanded and classrooms added."

Ralph Winters' eyebrows shot straight up.

Aaron wasn't finished. "Looking the building over, I believe we will be able to kick out the back wall of the sanctuary without any problems at all. Doorways on either side of the pulpit area will then lead off into a fellowship area and toward the classrooms. Directly behind the pulpit there will be a choir loft and a baptismal behind the choir."

"That's going to cost a lot of money!" Ralph bayed. "Have you forgotten that this country is in a depression and most of the mid-west farming lands are being steadily blown away by huge dust storms?"

"No," Aaron replied mildly. "I haven't forgotten anything. And neither has the Lord. This is why He has blessed us with a lumber mill owning head deacon as well as so many strong men who are at present unable to find work. By the Lord's reckoning, this is the perfect time for the church to expand."

Deacon Ralph was near to apoplectic. "I don't give away free timbers!"

"True. But you can, by way of tithe, sell your timber to your church at cost. I believe that God has brought me here and by accepting this commission I have been charged, by God, to obey and follow His plan for Henrytown Free Church. In brief, Mr. Winters, as you have so laboriously pointed out, my presence in this church is indeed on a limited basis. And until my subsequent departure, I want to impress on you, as well as everyone here, that for the next six months it is Christ—and no one else—who will be recognized as the true head of this church."

"Before we start tearin' down church walls, we gotta call for the vote," Yancy Flowers said quietly. "You know how Free Church people gotta vote on everythin'."

"Absolutely," Aaron agreed. He hurriedly wrote on a note on the legal sized notepad. "I plan to make several announcements during the Sunday service, all of which will be scheduled for the vote during the next Wednesday night's service. In lieu of our normal service, we'll simply have a prayer and business meeting."

"Sounds good to me," Yancy said. The other deacons nodded their shared consent.

The one holdout was Deacon Ralph Winters. Not only had he been rendered speechless, he looked to be turning the most amazing shade of purple—almost a true amethyst.

Ralph Winters' mind was flying as he remembered that less than a scant moment ago that it had been he (and just as nicely as he knew how) who'd been intimating that the fair haired preacher-boy oughta resign and move himself along to a bigger and more prestigious church. For his own good, he should understand, because he was too young, too good looking and too bright a boy to be content with playin' preacher in a "little ole tiny church". Ralph wasn't mistaken when he imagined that the preacher was agreeing with him but, instead of moving on, as cunningly suggested, the preacher's solution was to build himself a bigger church in Henrytown!

Not only that, but this same preacher BOY also seemed to be intimating that if anyone was going to be resigning, then that somebody oughta be Ralph Winters! Another thing that was made so abundantly clear, was that his refusal to resign as head deacon would come at his personal cost of truckloads of valuable lumber! This lad was just way too clever by half. This caused Ralph to yet again regret having been party to the sending of the letter that had prompted Aaron's call to

Henrytown. What a terrific salesman this boy would have been! And if he'd had the sense to work with Ralph, why between them, and in practically no time at all, they'd own the entire state of Louisiana.

But no! He was a preacher and in the Lord's Name, he was skinning Ralph right down to his BVD's. Now Ralph fully appreciated the pains that Fred Flowers had suffered when the boy had driven off—and at a considerable loss of profit—in Fred's nicest automobile.

Well, this newest bamboozlement would not be borne. Something had to be done. He looked around the room, hurriedly scanning for allies. Trouble was, he saw nary a one. Without a word being said, Ralph instinctively knew that he'd already been out voted; that to a man, all of his so-called brother deacons, were siding with the preacher. Yancy Flowers was even gloating!

As Ralph now saw the situation, his choices had been narrowed to two; he either submitted his resignation or he remained seated on the parsonage settee where he would be virtually agreeing to eat his profit margin right down to its mud-sucking bottom line. There was something about this young preacher that disturbed Ralph. Whatever that something was, it successfully made Ralph feel . . . small.

He hated that feeling.

Canting his head to the left, a third option began dawn, an option that made Ralph feel big again. Slowly he began to smile. "Well, here's the rub, Preacher, before any proposed building plan can be offered the congregation, I'm afraid I'm gonna be needin' an' advanced deposit and frankly, this church doesn't have that kind of money, so as I see it," he waved a dismissive hand, "this whole church expansion deal is what they call over in Baton Rouge, *moot*. Now, if you want to propose an expansion and call for a vote so's everybody can start contributing towards that goal, fine and good. But you have to understand, something like that could take as long as two or three years before the church has raised enough for just the timber deposit."

Aaron did not care for the gleam in the other man's eye. It was quite disturbing. But what he said, and with utter calm was, "How big is a big deposit?"

Mr. Ralph's smile was most unpleasant. "One hundred dollars," he drawled. "An' to secure this low-ball advance, I hate to say it, but I'll need that money tonight."

The other men gasped. Aaron didn't raise a hair.

"How much lumber does one hundred dollars buy?"

"I can answer that," Yancy said. "Once upon a time I worked as a foreman in his mill and I can testify that one hundred dollars covered the cost of framing in a house the size of plantation manor. Which means it would frame up almost triple the space the church has got right now."

Aaron quietly thought and after a brief moment he said, "Done." Then he leaned forward in his chair, elbows on thighs, hands clasped between his parted knees. "The church has agreed to pay me one hundred and twenty dollars for my six month internship. I hereby agree to hand over every dime of that to you."

"You can't do that," Yancy yelped. "How are you gonna live if you do a thing like that?" Then he glared at Ralph. "Ralph Winters, if you take everything this boy's got, then you are just too low down to draw a clean breath of air."

Ralph's response was to broadly wave his arms as if frantic to shoo away a pesky fly. "I can't be waitin' on this lad to pay me drip by drip. I said I'd need that deposit money this very night cause I got payroll to meet and bills to pay. IOU's ain't no good to me. It's either cash down now or this preacher-boy's gotta get himself a brand-new dream."

Aaron turned toward Yancy. "Brother Flowers? Would you please take everyone into the dining room for coffee and pecan pie?"

Ralph looked confused. “Does that mean me too?”

Aaron gazed mildly back at the man. “Yes, of course. Why wouldn’t it?”

Ralph, like the cheese, was standing alone in the dining room while the other men, eating their plates of pie, were in a huddle. From where he stood he could hear them tossing around fund raising ideas. Ralph glared at them as he shoveled pie into his mouth. Then the preacher walked in.

“Gentlemen,” he announced as he handed Ralph Winters five twenty-dollar bills, “we have our lumber.”

“Where in the world did you get all this here cash?” Ralph wheezed.

“My mother. She gave it to me because, well, she’s prone to worry about her son. But,” Aaron laughed, “I’m sure I needn’t remind any of you of her worrying tendencies’.”

The other men laughed as Ralph glared at the money in his hand. Suddenly, the pecan pie had lost its sweetness and there was instead a distinct taste of ash. Thirty minutes later, as the deacons filed out of the parsonage, heading off for their own homes, Ralph remained.

Standing on the hazily lit front porch and while donning his fedora, Ralph said, “Preacher. That was a bold move.” Hat firmly in place on his head, Ralph looked the much younger man dead in the eye. “But don’t you ever think you’ve got me backed into a corner.”

“Mr. Ralph,” Aaron said, exhaustion evident in his tone. “What I think is that it’s past time that you and I came to a clearer understanding of my calling. I am a preacher of the gospel of our Lord Jesus Christ. As a preacher of God’s Word, I am directly responsible to *no one* other than Him. As a member of the congregation, you are responsible for listening to God’s Word, and I can’t actually encourage this enough, for if you carry on turning from the divine Word, it is God, not I, to whom you will answer. We both know that my time here is restricted, but never credit yourself with this limitation. My time of service here has been imposed by God Himself and I serve at the pleasure of the Great God Almighty. Therefore I recommend, and quite strongly, that you spend a good deal more of your time in honest prayer before the Lord, for He will not be mocked, nor will He tolerate the abuse of His anointed."

Ralph's mouth worked, but he couldn't utter a word. He simply could not even begin to fathom this young man—this unquestionably fearless young man. He was not someone who would preach to please a congregation, nor would he genuflect to human authority. As the scales began to fall away from Ralph's eyes, he could clearly see that Pastor Aaron didn't simply preach faith, he was the embodiment of faith. There was no intimidating or dominating a man like that.

Ever.

As the moments of silence stretched and Aaron became completely certain that Ralph Winters had been so undone by the unvarnished truth he couldn't think of a response, then it was left to Aaron to think of one for him.

"Mr. Winters," Aaron said as he stuck out his hand and Deacon Winters who, still staring wide-eyed, involuntarily shook it, "I bid you good night sir. We both have quite a bit to talk about in prayer and I would suggest that we each be about this. May the Lord watch over you as you journey home."

Ralph Winters was still staring as Aaron turned on his heel and walked toward the screen door, opened it and disappeared inside the house.

Chapter Eleven

The Henrytown hotline was in fine form the following morning. By mid-day,simply everyone was talking about the doings of the deacon's meeting. Imagine! A preacher who would fork out his very own money to invest in a church he might not even be preaching in by this time next year! Nobody had ever heard of a thing like that. There were preachers throughout Louisiana who were real good at asking for other peoples' money but coughing it up their own selves put a hard strangle on their throats. The fact that this preacher-boy would be so generous and so dedicated to a church that he was, for all intents and purposes, simply visiting for a few months, put a lot of folks to thinking on how they might be able to help. For the hard truth of the matter was that the church was either going to grow or it was going to die.

Kinda funny that it had taken an outsider to notice.

Libby was also looking at Aaron in a new light as he was ever so patiently teaching her the process of outlining. He'd set her up with her very own desk (it was the long wall table that had once been on the sleeping porch). Her workspace had plenty of room for the Royal typewriter, blank paper, a bowl of paper clips and cup of sharpened pencils, and a notepad. It all looked very professional, and it was a clear indication that he'd put a lot of thought into just how to create a comfortable workspace meant just for her. Aaron's care and consideration for her needs was more heartwarming than Daddy's tales of Aaron's generosity toward the church. And now Aaron was leaning over her, his right hand flat against the desktop, his left hand braced against the backrest of her chair. He smelled good—kinda Witch Hazel-ish—and his masculine warmth was something she preferred not to dwell on.

"All right, now we have Roman numeral *I* with the subject header, ***Honoring the Lord's Day***. Now, carriage return please."

Libby pushed the carriage lever, sending the typewriter's roller to its extreme right and the machine magically advanced the sheet of paper and settled. She began tapping the space key with her fingers until the to-be-typed line was lined up directly below the finished line above it.

"Good job Lib," Aaron said without noticing the familiarity.

Libby, her eyes slightly flaring, had most certainly noticed. She bit her tongue as it tried so valiantly to correct him and, in doing so completely wreck his implied tenderness. But bitten or not, her tongue continued to squirm, causing Libby to mentally yell, *He can call me Lib or Little Orphan Annie for all I care! Don't make me bite you harder because you know I'll do it.*

Still blithely unaware that he had caused Libby such an internal battle, Aaron continued on with the secretarial lesson. "Now, this line is known as the Subtopic and a subtopic is designated by capital letters. So, begin first with a parenthesis, then the capital letter *A,*_and then an enclosing parenthesis. Then a two-space margin and then type, *Luke Chapter 9, Verse 23 & 24*. Then we insert the chosen text." Aaron read directly from his Bible as Libby's fingers kept pace on the Royal's keyboard. "And He said to them all: If any man will come after Me, let him deny himself, and take up his cross daily, and follow Me. For whosoever will save his life shall lose it: but whosoever will lose his life for My sake, the same shall save it.'"

Aaron quickly scanned her work and happily found that it was letter perfect. "Great job Lib! Now again, carriage return, new subtopic line . . ."

Libby complied with each instruction. Ordinarily Libby was a very quick study, but telling him that she understood exactly how he wanted his sermons typed out—because she had, after all, done this before, although it was evident that he'd forgotten—would have meant that he would walk away and leave her to wade through his scrawled notes all on her own. Libby simply wasn't anxious to remind him of her previous efforts, thus giving up a single moment of his closeness. But it was rudely interrupted anyway by a horn that repeatedly sounded from the front yard. And then Aaron was gone, nothing left of him but a hint of his former warmth and the faint whiff of Witch Hazel. Glumly, Libby organized Aaron's handwritten pages and began to bang the Royal's keys with gusto as on the front porch Aaron's voice called out cheerily to whomever was intruding on their morning.

Aaron remembered the face of the man in the truck as someone who had shaken his hand following the Wednesday night service. Sadly, the man hadn't offered his name. He had merely mumbled, "Enjoyed the preachin'," and then had all but jumped out of the way for the next person standing in the line. Aaron remained on the bottom porch step as the man exited the truck, stood on the ground next to the truck's cab and removed his hat, maintaining a shy natured distance.

"Mornin' Preacher."

"Good morning! And how are you this fine day?"

The man smiled, lowering his head slightly. "Oh, I'm about as fine as can be." Then, steeling himself, he raised his head and looked Aaron in the eye as he said in a rush, "My name's Clifford Boyce an' I thought maybe you could use a couple of good layin' hens. I don't have much cash money I can afford to contribute, but I got me some fine chickens and I'm more than happy to donate a pair of 'em."

Aaron knew a proud but kindly soul when he saw one, and he also recognized the courage that Mr. Clifford Boyce was displaying by offering his hens. Turning such a man away would be to belittle both his courage and his offering. Aaron quickly left the porch step, extending his hand as he made long legged strides toward the painfully shy man. "Mr.

Boyce, you are truly a Godsend! If there's one thing we've been needing, it's our very own laying hens."

Bubba X was in the kitchen garden, weeding a row of green beans when he heard Aaron calling for him. Bubba dropped the hoe and went on the run. Rounding the corner of the house he spotted Aaron looking into the back of Clifford Boyce's truck and listening to Clifford (one of the leading members of the town's down-and-out crackers) who was being uncharacteristically chatty. Aaron surely did attract some highly unusual folk and, when they were with him, they were prone to do some highly unusual things. Bubba had known Clifford Boyce all of his life and in all that time all he'd never known the man say more than, "hey." But at the moment, Clifford was talking a blue streak, and Aaron was looking as if he was hanging onto every last word.

Out of the corner of his eye Aaron spotted Bubba, and he nonchalantly waved Bubba to join them. As Bubba approached, he heard Aaron say, "Mr. Clifford? Would you mind repeating all of this to Bubba?"

Mr. Clifford immediately retreated into his customary shyness. In a softer voice he said, "Oh, I don't need to be explainin' nothin' to Bubba. He already knows everythin' about buildin' a chicken coop." The painfully shy Mr. Clifford was now feeling awkward and he turned toward his truck, as if Bubba's capable presence on the scene was the logical reason for him to leave.

"I'm sure he does," Aaron agreed and quickly adding, in order to forestall Mr. Clifford's departure, "But wouldn't it be helpful to the hens if Bubba built a coop that seemed entirely familiar to them?"

Mr. Clifford considered this and then said, "Well, now that you mention it, livin' strange just might put them off layin' for a while."

Following Aaron's ploy, Bubba put on his best dumb-as-a-stump impression and in a monotone voice asked, "What ya wantin' me to do, Mr. Clifford?"

This one question successfully opened up Mr. Clifford's chicken farming expertise flood gates. In addressing Bubba with a fatherly tone, gone was every scrap of the man's former shyness. He was still talking as he followed after Bubba to the back of the truck and then stood behind him as Bubba grappled with the crate containing two fat Rhode Island Red hens. Once Bubba had the crate out of the truck, Mr. Clifford took the lead. Aaron's last sight of the pair was of Bubba walking a pace behind as Mr. Clifford walked on in a determined fashion. It appeared that locating a prime area for the construction of a new chicken residence was vitally important to Mr. Clifford's continuing peace of mind.

Feeling satisfied with the situation, Aaron mistakenly believed that he could return to his office and to the sounds of Libby clacking away on the typewriter, but no—there were even more trucks arriving.

The stir in the yard caused a stir with the women inside the house. Mabel rushed out and came to a stop on the porch where she stood wiping her hands inside a dish towel. Libby, wearing her high waist brown trousers and pink sleeveless blouse, was only a few seconds behind her and took up a stance beside Mabel, one hand on her hip, the other against her forehead as she shielded her eyes against the blaze of the day.

"What in the world??" Libby said ever so softly.

"They's showin' their respects," Mabel replied. "Ever'body in town knows what Aaron did last night, how he put his own money into improvin' the church. Now folks are doin' what they can to show how much they appreciate him." As Mabel moved away, aiming herself for the porch steps, Libby heard her say in an uncompromising tone, "That boy ain't never goin' no other place. He's our preacher now."

Aaron's state of mind could only be described as thoroughly flummoxed. People of all sizes and ages pressed around him, their hands stretching forth with various gifts, their voices beating loudly against his eardrums. This was his second experience at being swarmed; the first being the Wednesday night service. Even so, he still had no idea how one was supposed to behave while being swarmed.

And then, to his immense relief, Libby came pushing herself into the swarm. He was even more relieved when she took charge. "Everybody," she yelled over the noise. "Everybody! Please take your gifts up to the porch. It's there that ya'll will be given some tea and where I can write down all ya'll's names and gift items so that ya'll can get a proper thank you note from the pastor and—"

"Bless God! We got us a milk goat!" Mabel's shrill voice successfully interrupted Libby's instructional flow and all heads turned in Mabel's direction. She was standing against a truck on the far side of the yard and looking into the flatbed. Hers was the enthralled expression of a child beholding a present laden Christmas tree. The owner of the truck hotfooted it over to Mabel. As he arrived, Mabel turned to the man she knew as Mr. Harold, the best goat farmer in the whole parish. "Oh, what's her name?"

"Darby."

"An' how old is she"

"Just turned two. She was bucked for the first time just this last winter. She threw two kids. She's a good girl. She gives about a gallon an' a half every day."

"How much do we milk her?"

"Six an' six."

Mabel looked blank.

"Six in the mornin', six in the evening," Mr. Harold explained. "Ya'll only feed her when she's being milked. An' I done brung a big bag of feed for her. It's in the cab so she couldn't get into it during the drive over."

Mabel, all a quiver with excitement, cooed, "Ooh, Mr. Harold, get her out so's I can pet her."

Aaron inclined his head and whispered to Libby, "How do we milk a goat?"

"I have no earthly idea," she whispered back. "Hopefully Mabel will just pet the milk out of her."

The old carriage house was designated as the temporary housing for the goat and the two hens until Bubba X could build more suitable accommodations. In the meantime, the goat and the hens seemed more than content with the carriage house, the hens taking roost on the roof of the dilapidated one-horse buggy and the goat happy with the remaining space of the earthen floor. Now it was both Mr. Harold and Mr. Clifford who were vying for Bubba's attention on just how he should build the hen coop and the goat barn. It seemed that the only thing Mr. Harold and Mr. Clifford agreed on was that neither outbuilding should be within close proximity of the other. On the porch Libby busily took notes on each and every gift as well as the names and mailing addresses of the givers. During this activity, men were surrounding Aaron and talking with passion about the new expansion plans as well as the much-needed Bible classes. Mabel had commandeered the ladies into helping serve wedges of the gifted pies and cakes along with large glasses of tea. It was while Aaron was staring lustfully at the treasured slices of cake that one of the men standing between him and a large slice of the dark chocolate cake told a joke that completely tied in with the need for church wide Bible study.

"A new pastor come into a church over in Monroe and the first thing he wanted to know was just where his congregation stood in the way of Bible knowledge, so on his first Sunday he visited the sixth grade Sunday school room. The teacher was so honored to have him in the class that she turned the proceedings over to him and he asked the class, 'Can anybody tell me who broke down the wall of Jericho?'

"Well, the whole class was silent, and then a boy in the back raised his hand an' said, 'Preacher, I get the blame for lots of stuff but I swear to ya, I didn't have nothin' to do with that wall.'"

The jokester now had Aaron's complete attention.

"Well sir," the joke teller drawled, "that teacher was very embarrassed, but she spoke right up for the boy and said, 'He's a lot of things Pastor, but he ain't a liar. If he says he didn't break that wall, then he didn't do it.'

Despite his deep desire for devil's food chocolate cake, Aaron was grinning.

"The very next day," the man continued, "the deacon committee turned up on the pastor's doorstep and the head deacon says, 'Pastor, we heard about that broke down wall, and, while we don't know who did it, we're ready to offer enough money to cover the repairs."

While all the men laughed, Mabel, by some miracle, appeared and shoved a plate containing a generous wedge of cake into Aaron's hands. It wasn't chocolate; it was angel food. Mabel had it in her mind that when in public a man of God should only be seen eating angel food and not devil's food chocolate. Aaron had told her more than once that God's direct blessing had been in the giving of Manna in the Sinai and in the unleavened bread given by Christ during the last supper; that He was not concerned about the various flavors of modern day cake.

Mabel remained unconvinced.

Aaron took a bite of the spongy angel food cake as the wag concluded drily, "First time I ever heard that joke I swore it happened at Henrytown. It's enough said that you got your work cut out for ya here, Pastor."

While Aaron was busy with the unexpected guests and their generosity, Deacon Ralph Winters, in the office of his lumber mill, was taking a wholly unexpected telephone call. The instant he heard the lady's cultured and honeysuckle sweet voice coming into his ear, Ralph's world tilted.

"A very good morning to you Mr. Winters, I do hope you are enjoying this lovely weather we're having," Miss Cornelia said.

Ralph's tongue felt four times thicker than it ought to be. "Yes ma'am Miss Cornelia, I most surely am. An' how can I be of service to you this fine day?"

"Well," she coyly drawled, "I'm afraid this is a rather awkward call because it concerns this building expansion business that I'm hearing so much about."

For some unexplained reason, Ralph's guard went up. True he'd been humiliated by the recent set of events, but there was something . . . something that he didn't like to talk about—something he never talked about—but in the last hours it was that very same something that he was finding more and more difficult to suppress. Ralph was coming to believe that he knew exactly how a fully expanded balloon felt just before it went pop. And now here was Miss Cornelia Faraday, one of the wealthiest women in the entire state, calling him on his very own private business phone line. Four days ago, he would have given anything to be told that this great lady was waiting for him on the phone line. Truth be told, when she'd moved from the Methodist church to the Free church, Ralph had moved right along behind her. For years his need for her notice and approval had bordered on the irrational. And now here she was on the phone and actually talking to him and he wasn't in the least bit as thrilled about it as he'd always imagined he would be.

WHY??

"Mr. Winters," Miss Cornelia said without any idea of the personal crisis developing on the other end of the phone line, "I was deeply distressed to learn that Pastor Aaron felt the need to pay out monies he can ill afford in order to begin an expansion project. As the town's primary businessman, Mr. Winters, I feel confident that you possess a storehouse of knowledge as to how much of an expenditure such a project would require. Therefore, I am respectfully requesting that you personally work with the pastor in order to map out the exact square footage as well as all of the other necessities such as windows and doors and that you then very quietly pass this information on to me. Would you be agreeable to this somewhat secretive arrangement Mr. Winters?"

Ralph's left hand worried his creased forehead. "May I ask the motive prompting this request?"

"You may," she returned sweetly. "But it suffices to say that mine are the deeper pockets. Therefore, the original question stands, can you Sir, be counted on to work with me behind the scenes? I know we both want what's best for the project, but without causing undue attention to ourselves. In this purpose might we be true allies?"

"Miss Cornelia, it would be my utmost pleasure to be your trusted ally."

"Excellent," she replied. "Do enjoy the remainder of your day, Mr. Winters." And then she was gone.

Ralph allowed a moment to calm himself, and then he impatiently clicked the telephone cradle's central button until the local switchboard operator's voice came to his ear. "Hey little sweetheart, ring over to the Free Church parsonage for me, will ya please?"

Libby and Mabel were seeing the last of the guests off and beginning to gather up the display of gift items. Aaron was holding onto a star quilt, greatly admiring the fine hand stitching when he heard the phone. Still holding the quilt, he entered the house, heading for the phone stand.

Mabel nudged Libby's side. "He's mighty fond of that quilt, idn't he?"

Libby simply smiled as she decided to fetch a basket to carry the canned tomatoes and preserved fruit jars. Trying to hand carry so many heavy jars might prove catastrophic. And as she set off around the porch, aiming for the outside kitchen door, Mabel stayed with her, Mabel's voice as persistent as a buzzing fly.

"He sure got off Miss Sarah Beth. Never seen that woman blush so much, an' all on account of a scrap quilt. He embarrassed the pure sand right outta her is what he did."

Moving fast Libby said over her shoulder, "He must really like homemade quilts."

Mabel turned peevish. "Well he ought not to have called her an *artist*!"

Yanking open the screen door to the kitchen, Libby snapped, "Oh for heaven's sake Mabel! He did not embarrass Miss Sarah Beth. And in his mind, anyone with the patience to hand stitch a bed quilt has to be an artist."

Entering the kitchen a step behind Libby, Mabel fired right back, "Then this whole town is full of artists cause we all hand stitch quilts."

Finding a good-sized basket under the sink's side cupboard, Libby suddenly realized the reason for Mabel's irritation. As she retrieved the basket she quipped, "Why Cousin Mabel, I do believe you're jealous."

"Am not."

"Are too."

"Libby Flowers! I am not jealous for myself, I'm—"

Aaron came into the kitchen. He was still carrying his wondrous new quilt. "You'll never guess what," he said. "Ralph Winters just called. He said he's had time to consider and he's now all for the new expansion and that we should have an immediate meeting to iron out all of the details. He feels that by Sunday next we should be ready to make a full announcement. Isn't that grand?"

Aaron was not being snide. He actually was genuinely happy. He was just so trusting, so innocent, and just so pig ignorant of the Ralph Winters the two women knew only far too well. Mabel and Libby exchanged worried glances and, before either said something they might later regret, Libby hurriedly excused herself, brushing by Aaron as she made for the kitchen's screened door. "I have to go carry in all of those canning jars."

Mabel rapidly followed suit but with the intent of taking the outside steps down to the backyard. While in her mid-gallop, she called back over her shoulder, "I gotta run out to the carriage house an' check on my darling little girl goat."

Both women having fled off in separate directions, had inadvertently given Aaron the privacy to quietly thank the Lord for whatever miracle had brought Ralph Winters—and his lumber mill—in as a fully cooperative member of the expansion planning team. He also asked for an increase of patience in his dealings with Ralph. There was something deeply imbedded beneath the older man's display of bravado that was quite distressing. Aaron could almost physically touch the man's pain. In all his young years, Aaron had never met anyone quite so—damaged.

Chapter Twelve

That evening, following a highly active day, Aaron sat at the dining room table at which was gathered the entire deacon committee. Gratefully, Ralph Winters was in full charge of the meeting, laying out a large sheet of paper with precisely ruled lines drawn on it. The other deacons were studying the drawings. Aaron said nothing. He was impressed by Ralph's effort and, by his genuine display of commitment. Equally impressive was the fact that neither Ralph nor Yancy, had used the moment to square off against one another.

Thankfully, in the middle of all the day's hub-bub, Libby had finished typing Sunday's sermon. What with all the visitors coming and going like a determined tide, Libby's attention to her typing duties had been amazingly tenacious. Following the end of the surges of different groups of guests, there had been yet one more drama to see to, the goat and its very specific needs. Bubba X and Libby kept trying to milk the goat, each failing miserably. It wasn't helpful that Miss Mabel wept quite vigorously because her "darling little girl-goat" was in such distress. When all seemed beyond hopeless, Libby remembered that Seth Lewis had once raised milk goats and she hurried out, running for the house and the telephone.

Waiting for Seth to ride to the rescue, they'd all sat at the dining room table having coffee and sampling some of the gifted baked goods. A scowling Aaron had dominated the conversation with his ceaseless griping about the state of his white shoes. He'd looked like a sulking little boy as he complained on and on about goat poop being so highly acidic. By way of demonstration, he raised each foot, pointing out each and every green splotch staining the white leather. During one of his moans about his wonderful shoes, Libby had lost her rag.

"Aaron! Will you please just hush? I know for a fact that you have five pairs of shoes; one black, two brown and two white. So what if this one pair is spotted with a little bit of green? Just think of them now as your around the house shoes."

"How do you know about my shoes?" Aaron snapped back.

"I have my spies—don't I Mabel?"

Mabel looked guilty as she nibbled at the edges of a large cookie.

Moments later, Seth and Archie breezed in and a few moments after that, they were all back in the makeshift barn, Seth instructing Bubba and Mabel on the fine art of goat milking. Not anxious to collect any more green stains on his shoes, Aaron stood well back; Libby was on his right, Archie on his left. During the milking presentation, Archie spoke to Aaron in a low, confiding tone,

"Seth's been wondering when he's gonna get baptized."

"I was wondering that myself," Aaron admitted. "The church doesn't have a baptismal and—"

"We've got the pond!" Archie and Libby yelped.

"What pond?"

Libby heaved a sigh. "The pond that's about a half mile behind the church. Everybody gets baptized in Willard's Pond."

"Ain't much of a pond now though," Archie said. "Beavers came in and now it's more like a little bitty lake, but we can still use it for baptisms and church picnics. It's a mighty good fishing hole too. The church keeps a couple of good-sized row boats tipped up on the bank so that anybody who wants to can row out and drop a fishing line."

"Really?" Aaron said, his mind harking back to a warm memory. "It sounds perfect." Then he called to the threesome surrounding the goat. Bubba was holding the goat by the neck to keep it in place, Mabel was petting it and Seth was sitting on an old wooden crate as he milked with a dexterous speed. "Seth? How would you feel about being baptized next Sunday?"

"Sounds good to me. Do I get a hallelujah picnic?"

Before Aaron had time to puzzle that through, Libby tugged on his rolled shirt sleeve. "Baptizing time is always picnic time. There's no preaching on Baptism Sunday, just baptizing and picnicking. It's an all-day event."

Amazingly, Libby's explanation tied in perfectly with the very thing Aaron had been remembering.

His mind returned to the current business meeting just as Ralph was rolling up the committee's newly approved drawing plans. Even Yancy looked pleased by Ralph's architectural eye to fine detail. All that was left for Aaron to do was offer the closing prayer, but he had an item of business of his own.

"I propose that Sunday next we schedule as a baptism and hallelujah picnic. But this coming Sunday I shall announce that the upcoming Wednesday night service will be for a vote on everything we've discussed during this evening. Therefore, prior to this Sunday's sermon, there must be a formal presentation to the congregation on the expansion plans. Our church members should have time to carefully and prayerfully consider these plans before the Wednesday night business meeting. Brother Ralph, can I depend on you to make Sunday's formal presentation to the church?"

This request rather gob-smacked Ralph. Addressing the church would mean his having to stand before the altar. Ralph had spent too many years as a liar and a scoundrel (well, he *was* a Louisiana businessman) and standing before the altar was Holy Ground. Unwittingly, Ralph remembered God's wrath in Ezekiel and Jeremiah. It didn't help the situation that the soft lighting of the overhead lighting was casting a soft glow around a face that was framed by shimmering blond hair or that a pair of ethereal cobalt blue eyes stared out from that face. It was like looking at one of God's very own avenging angels, and suddenly, that small feeling that Ralph hated closed in. Struggling to answer the waiting pastor's question, Ralph felt the twinges of something he hadn't felt in decades: Fear.

Ralph finally found his voice. "I-I would be honored . . . Pastor."

And Yancy Flowers, sensing the head deacon's moment of true humility, genuinely, albeit fleetingly, smiled at Ralph Winters.

The next morning found Aaron crawling out of bed at five a.m. Instead of doing his routine of deep knee bends and twenty pushups, he simply lay face down on the bedroom floor rug and prayed until he found the strength to stand up and begin another day. Still clad in his pajamas, he padded into the kitchen to make coffee. Standing at the stove, he continually heard a bleating sound, wondering to himself just what in thunder that sound might be. And then, as the bleating continued there came the horrific realization . . .

The goat.

Aaron turned off the burner underneath the water kettle and hurried off to dress for the occasion. As a city dweller, he did not own country clothing. However, as fate would have it, a box of cast offs had been found by Casper on the day that they had been breaking down the sleeping porch beds. The clothing in the box was old and had seen better days, but still it seemed much too useable to be left to go to mold inside the same storage barn that the beds had been destined for, so Casper had shoved the box against the wall. The necessity of the goat had miraculously brought the cast-off's box to Aaron's panic-riddled mind. He quickly went into the newly installed laundry room and began to rummage through the box of old clothing. He found a pair of denim material trousers that everyone called jeans. They were about three inches too short for his long legs, but, as Libby would say—so what. Next there were flannel shirts. All of them were ghastly. What a blessing that the goat wasn't fashion fussy. In the wad of socks, Aaron found two that actually matched. Moments later and there he stood, in high water jeans, rumpled flannel shirt, and purple socks lost inside green, polka-dotted white leather oxford shoes.

What a sight.

Retrieving the milk bucket which Mabel had so thoughtfully scrubbed following the previous evening's milking sortie, Aaron was out the kitchen's back door and headed for the carriage house. After a few inhales of piney fresh air, he was feeling confident that he could handle this milking business. Then he opened the carriage house door and switched on the single light. His first sight was a pair of devilish brown eyes with the coal-black slashes across the large irises. That was when his confidence began to dry up faster than the morning's dew on the sands of the Judean desert.

And then, Darby the Goat decided to charge.

It was all a bit of a blur after that. Aaron remembered being butted and chased and falling and then being kicked as he crawled toward the tall metal and covered can that served as the goat's food container. The hens, in a panic, were trying to stay out of the melee, but all of their terrified flapping and squawking simply added to the surreal aspects of the adventure. The instant he reached the feed can, the goat quit the attack. The hens retreated to the far side of the carriage house, staying in a tight two hens' huddle. Aaron kept a wary eye on the goat as it watched him filling the bowl. When he began moving on numb legs, the goat began to follow like a pet dog. Being careful of the bowl, Aaron made cautious progress toward the makeshift milking stand. And then

Thank You Lord!, without any prompting whatsoever, the goat walked onto the stand and positioned herself correctly on the jerry-rigged milking platform. With shaking hands, Aaron quickly slipped the noose harness over her head as the goat contented herself with the corn mash mixture. Knowing the goat would only remain compliant so long as the food portion lasted, Aaron beat his brain bloody in the effort to remember exactly how Seth had explained the milking process.

"*Don't squeeze...just lock your hand at the top of the teat an' then run your fingers gently along the teat to push the milk out.*"

That had sounded a lot easier than it actually proved to be. And because the corn was being gobbled up so quickly, the goat was becoming threatening again. Finally, through gritted teeth perseverance (never mind there was actually more milk left on the dirt floor than there was in the bucket) the goat was successfully milked.

His mired oxfords were left to stand like ugly beggars on the back porch. Aaron was again in the kitchen, walking around on purple sock feet, as he tended to the business of making coffee. The milk bucket was in the sink simply because he had no earthly idea of what else he was supposed to do with it. He was just taking his first sip of badly needed coffee when a truck horn blasted from the front of the house.

"Oh, praise God," he groaned ". . . Company." Moments later, Aaron came to sad realization that had he but waited and not gone out to the carriage house, that a veritable team of goat herdsmen would have been on hand to help him out. But, never mind.

The six men looked so identical it was nearly impossible to tell them apart. Actually, Aaron's first impression of his new home State was that precious few men in Louisiana were razor inclined. Then he came to understand that the farming men only "barbered" on Sunday mornings in order to be presentable for church. During the remainder of the week there were too many chores and field work to worry over such "dainties" as shaving. Bubba X followed this norm meaning that by Saturday, the bottom of Bubba's face looked black. The "dandified" (finely shaven) Seth and Casper were wearing their usual jeans, the legs rolled up to the ankles; white T-shirts and cowboy boots, whereas the older men favored overalls, blue work shirts and lace-up boots. Seth and Casper's smooth cheeks stood out like beacons amid all the untidy faces and then too, theirs were also the only heads to be sans grey fedoras.

Seth and Casper came along the west facing "L" side of the wrap around porch and entered the screen door that led into the kitchen while the men they followed behind continued to walk along the lawn pathway toward the carriage house. They each carried planks of lumber on their shoulders. Aaron was watching the men from the window set over the sink while Seth and Casper went directly to the free-standing china hutch. After each had grabbed a cup, they then went to the stove. Aaron was about to ask about the men carrying lumber when Casper asked a question of his own.

"Aaron? What in the world are you wearin?"

"Goat clothes," Aaron said absently. He leaned out as far as the window screen allowed, still watching the departing men. "I found them in the box in the laundry room."

"Yeah, an' you look like you fell outta that box!" Casper hooted. "If you're gonna start playing 'Farmer in the Dell,' you're gonna need a whole better dress sense."

Aaron stepped away from the sink and raising his arms to the side he said, "These suited the situation. That goat put up something of a fight."

Casper finally getting his turn at the coffee pot, laughed, "Well seein' you comin' at her in that get-up, I bet she did!" Leaning back against the stove and blowing on the coffee before taking a sip he said, "We best take you into town an get you some day-of-the-week duds. That way you can spare your good-looking clothes for church. The ladies hereabouts think you're just about the prettiest thing they've ever seen. We wouldn't want goat poo-poo spoilin' maidenly delusions, now would we?"

"Yeah," Seth agreed. "Even Libby would have second thoughts if she could see you now."

"Hey!" Casper yelled, lightly slapping Seth's arm. "You ain't supposed to be sayin' that. It's a secret."

"What's a secret?" Aaron said.

A grinning Casper pushed away from the stove. "Oh . . . just that my baby sister's kinda sweet on ya is all. But remember, you didn't hear that from either of us."

Aaron was honestly amazed. "Libby . . . Libby . . . thinks of me? Romantically?"

Casper and Seth exchanged looks. "Now this is just pure pitiful," Seth said.

"Uh-huh," Casper agreed.

And then the pair bayed laughter.

An hour later Aaron's face was shaved, his teeth scrubbed shiny and his breath sweetened by the Pepsodent Toothbrush Powder. He was wearing his normal summer attire. Seth and Casper were in the car with him as Aaron drove toward the Henrytown Dry Goods store. The other two were laughing and teasing as the car streamed along, but Aaron only half heard them. He was thinking about Libby. She was so pretty, so intelligent, so capable and . . . she liked him! There was only one thing he could do—thump up the courage to ask her out on a date. And that would take some thumping because, well, Aaron had never actually been on a *real* date. The only occasions approximating a date were those few times when, under agreements between parents he'd acted as a young lady's escort to a formal function. Hearing the call into the ministry at a young age meant that he'd never once been tempted to attend any of the high school dances. His primary interests had been studying and hanging out in his best friend's garage where they happily tore up old cars. In short, Aaron had not one clue the effect he had on people. Most especially girl people. But he'd immediately liked Libby. He'd liked her very, very much. Yet he'd simply assumed that she only thought of him as her new pastor, so he, and daily, had pushed any romantic notions into the far, far reaches of his brain. But now, after the disclosure in the kitchen, he couldn't think of anything else! Which was evident in view of the fact that he'd forgotten all about Miss Mabel and Bubba who were still waiting for a sight of the spiffy new car that hadn't come for them.

"He's over two hours late!" Mabel's voice bawled into Libby's headset.

"Well I don't know what to tell ya," Libby said into the bulky speaking horn suspended by a flat metal bar and balanced against her chest. "I've made three calls to the house and he's not picking up."

"Maybe his dead!"

Way to reach for the worst, Cousin Mabel. In an attempt to calm the older woman, Libby said, "Listen, I'm about to go off duty. I'll go straight home and get Daddy's truck and go out there and see for myself. He's probably out in the carriage house so, try not to fret yourself."

Libby was pulling the plug on Mabel when Karen, the day girl, walked into the small office. "Boy am I glad to see you!" Libby sighed.

Removing her hat, Karen looked back over her shoulder. "Rough night was it?"

"More like a stupid morning!" Libby quipped. "The pastor's gone missing and my cousin Mabel is having a hissy."

"Oh honey," Karen grinned mischievously. "He's not missing. I just now saw him through the big window over at the dry goods store. He's with your brother. Oh, an' Seth I think." Karen lightly chuckled, "Tell the truth, I can't be sure because once I got an eye full of the pastor walking around the store wearin' a pair of skintight jeans, I kinda lost my awareness of anything else!"

"What!?"

Karen removed the headset from Libby's stunned-stupid head. "Sweetheart, if I'm lyin' I'm dyin'. And it was getting a little crowded at the window, if ya get my drift." Libby stood and Karen filled the vacancy at the switchboard. "It's a pure sight the way that man can fit inside a pair of jeans." The board began to buzz and Karen forgot about Libby.

Libby scooted out of the office, and as she rounded the block's corner, she immediately spotted the throng of female spectators peering into the dry goods store window.

Libby was then just as immediately furious.

Aaron hadn't noticed the faces outside the window because he was examining himself in the full-length cheval mirror. The jeans felt a tad tight, as did the white T-shirt. But the boots were terrific! He'd always wanted a pair of cowboy boots. The feminine audience may have been lost on Aaron, but Casper and Seth were more than aware of the young women pressing themselves against the window glass. It was a comedy that was too good to be true, and yet—it was. And the two responsible for the town's newest sideshow were thoroughly enjoying themselves.

"Are you sure these jeans are the right size?" Aaron asked.

"Oh, yeah, yeah, they're perfect," Seth said.

I don't know," Casper drawled. "I think they're still a mite too baggy in the hind-end. I think he outta try a size smaller."

"Hey! You could be right!" Seth hopped down from the counter and raced off to the jeans shelf where he found a smaller size. He took them to Aaron and, firmly turning Aaron's body away from any view of the window, Seth all but pushed him into the changing closet and pulled the privacy curtain closed. Then Seth hot footed it back to the counter and hopped up beside Casper.

"I can't thank you fellows enough for this," Aaron said from behind the curtain.

Seth and Casper waved their hands against the air, as if warding off Aaron's gratitude. "Oh, don't think nothin' of it Aaron, we're just glad to help!"

A moment later when he emerged from the changing room, the girls behind the window went into a swoon. Casper and Seth tried not to buckle over as Aaron said, "Now surely this can't be right. These are so tight I can barely breathe."

Before the counter ensconced pranksters could utter a word, Libby came through the door like one of the Furies, but with one look at Aaron, she turned positively apoplectic.

"Aaron, get back inside the changing room right now!" She then rounded on the pair of instigators. "I will deal with you two later." She turned on her heel and strode toward the window, shooing away the spectator gallery who were none too pleased to be ordered off. But Libby Flowers looked mad enough to fight every last one of them, so reluctantly they began drifting away. Next, she marched herself over to the curtained off changing room.

Aaron was behind the curtains where he hadn't budged since pulling the curtains closed. He all but jumped when he heard Libby's voice coming from the other side. "Aaron Brooks! Just what do you think you're doing?!" She sounded unreasonably angry. This made Aaron angry. He stuck his head through the curtains.

"If you must know, I'm buying working clothes and boots. If I'm going to be lumbered with goats and hens and whatnot, I have to take care of them, and I can't take care of them in my best suit trousers."

"That's reasonable," she said, anger still evident.

"I'm so pleased you concur!" he fired right back.

"What isn't reasonable is your pulling on the tightest pair of jeans you could possibly find and then blaring yourself to the whole town!"

Aaron's eyes flew wide.

His surprised expression caused Libby to point to the display window as she said behind clenched teeth, "Are you going to stand there and tell me that you didn't notice that, that, horde of women watching you through the window as you shamelessly paraded around in body-hugging jeans?"

Aaron went pale. Then he looked toward the counter. Seth and Casper couldn't contain themselves any longer, they burst into gales of laughter. "Seth!" Aaron shouted. "You'd better start praying that when I baptize you, you don't accidently drown!"

The laughter spread to the store owner, his clerk, and two other male customers. Over their din Libby said, "Are you still clothed?"

"Yes."

"Good," she said, taking charge. "I'm coming in."

And she did.

From their perch on the countertop, Seth and Casper were having a wonderful time. Just when they believed the jeans buying absurdity couldn't possibly get any funnier, suddenly it did. They could see a whirl of movement behind the curtain and they most certainly heard Libby blasting at Aaron like a fishwife. The whole thing was better than a radio comedy!

Aaron stood ever so meekly as she fussed about him being a preacher and putting on a side show for all and sundry when she abruptly stopped and snapped, "Which of these felt the most comfortable."

"That first pair."

"Good. Then get out of those—things—and put this pair on. I'll go out and get a few more T-shirts because you'll be needing more than just the one. I'll meet you at the sales counter."

"I really like the boots, Lib. May I keep the boots?"

"Yes," she said while folding the rejected jeans. "By all means, keep the stupid boots."

In a much lower voice, he asked, "And would it be all right to ask you for a date?"

Libby stopped cold. Very slowly she looked up at him. At beautiful, beautiful—*him*. "W-what did you say?"

Aaron smiled as he answered, "I said that I would very much like to have a date with you please."

Casper and Seth were becoming concerned. At first everything was just as funny as all get-out, what with Libby pushing around behind the curtain like a tiny little bull and shouting her lungs loose but now—it was all very still and very quiet. At the bottom of the curtain they could still see her penny loafers, but Libby wasn't moving. Another minute passed and Libby emerged, her face kind of dreamy and she was drifting like a sleepwalker. The other store customers went quiet as all eyes were now watching Libby as she sort of drifted over to the T-shirt shelf and then kind of ran her hand along the stacks of varying sizes of woven cotton. She didn't seem to know where she was or what she was doing. Now, truly concerned, Casper and Seth slipped down from the counter.

His hands lightly grasping her shoulders Casper asked, "Baby sis? Are you all right?"

She tilted her head back and vaguely gazed up at her brother. Her voice was small as she said, "I'm goin' on a date with Aaron."

A grin spread across Casper's face. "No kiddin'? Well, then maybe he could do with a nice new shirt to go along with the new jeans."

That snapped her from the stupor. Excited now she said rapidly, “I’ll pick the shirt. Ya’ll find him a few more T-shirts.” She headed off towards the shelves of folded shirts. Then she turned and while walking backwards she said, “Oh! And one more pair of jeans. But just you make sure they’re the correct size!”

Seth raised an arm and hollered, “Don’t you worry about nothin’ baby-girl. We got this.”

Chapter Thirteen

Sunday morning the church was even more jamb-packed than the Wednesday night service. The pew which normally Miss Cornelia occupied virtually alone was also cramped. Those filling the pew on either side of her offered nervous glances and apologetic nods, but the grand lady didn't seem to be in the least perturbed by their nearness. During the praise and worship portion of the service, those within her close proximity gradually lost some of their discomfiture and as Aaron took the pulpit, any imagined offense against Miss Cornelia was forgotten.

He began with a few announcements, first thanking all of those who had seen fit to give him what he'd recently learned was known as a "Pounding," meaning that he'd been blessed with items he hadn't known he'd needed until he'd been subsequently blessed by the gifting. "And," he chuckled. "My biggest thanks go to those who turned up the very next day to help Bubba build a goat barn and hen house. Those were things I quite rapidly came to realize, most especially when being chased by the goat all around the inside of the carriage house and while the hens flew wildly, were the very things that I truly, truly needed. So, on behalf of the goat, the hens and myself, I offer our eternal thanks."

Sitting on the first row with her family, that included Seth, Libby beamed with pride as the congregation laughed and Aaron blushed crimson. While the laughter continued, Libby made a quick mental note to also write up thank you letters for the carpenters. She would add these to the stack of thank you letters that were waiting Aaron's signature and then there would be the trip to the post office. Aaron was the only person she knew during these destitute times who positively insisted on paying the expense of mailing out thank you letters. He could have just as easily asked the deacons hand them out before the services, but no—his envelopes had to be personally signed, sealed, stamped and mail carrier delivered to each recipient. The ever-practical little Libby had no idea how treasured Aaron's letters would one day be, that they would end up in frames and sitting pride of place of so many of the homes throughout LaSalle Parish. One proud recipient was known to say as he pointed to the scrawled signature, "The postman drove all the way out here just to give me this and that ain't all—the pastor himself even signed this letter to me, personal. Tha's the Preacher's own hand right there saying, 'In Christ's Service, Aaron Brooks, Pastor—Henrytown Free Church.' You know, I wouldn't take a million dollars for this here letter."

Aaron next spoke about the proposed church expansion project, which everyone already knew about, but when he called both Mr. Ralph Winters *AND* Yancy Flowers to come forward and stand together for the presentation, eyes bugged and jawlines dropped. But regardless of congregational astonishment, the duo rose from their respective places, and together they stood shoulder to shoulder in front of the altar.

Oh, it was a mind boggling, miraculous sight is what it was.

Yancy held the final drawing of the future look of Henrytown Free Church, displaying it for all to see, while an inexplicably nervous Ralph acted as spokesman. Ralph only spoke for a moment or two, explaining that the drawing would be available for viewing both after the Sunday service and then again on Wednesday night where, in lieu of normal preaching service, there would be a question and answer session followed by the congregational vote.

"In the meantime," Ralph's voice most definitely held a tremor, "we're asking all of ya'll to be in prayer for our church because as ya'll can tell, we are really beginning to need the additional floor space."

The roof and walls fairly shook with a resounding "AMEN!"

Ralph bolted for his former place while Yancy stood where he was and rolled up the drawing before sauntering back to his compact portion of the pew. He was just sitting down when Aaron offered a thank you for the hard work and dedication of the deacons. Then the pastor made the morning's final announcement. And brother, it was a pure corker; even more dumbfounding than the sight of Yancy Flowers standing beside Ralph Winters.

"I am blessed to pastor a congregation that isn't ashamed to kneel before our Lord during prayer. But to make the kneeling more comfortable, a lovely and talented lady has agreed to take charge of a ladies' group to make kneeling cushions. Miss Cornelia Faraday, would you stand please?"

Amid the united shock and awe, Miss Cornelia stood. This woman who never spoke to anyone, now turned to address the entire assembly. "It will be my pleasure to welcome all of the ladies of Henrytown into my home on Tuesday mornings for a full day of stitchery and luncheon. These Tuesday meetings will continue as long as the church has need of our talents."

A beaming Aaron then said quite loudly, "Would all ladies willing to serve in this ministry please indicate by a show of hands?"

Hesitantly, Libby's mother raised hers. This brave act emboldened the others. Within a moment, the church was filled with raised feminine hands. Unsteadily, Miss Cornelia sat down. Sympathetically, Libby thought; *first the normally bombastic Ralph Winter's voice had threatened to crack wider than the Mississippi, and now the lofty Miss Cornelia Faraday looks as if she's on the verge of weeping simply because a few dirt-poor country women have agreed to come to her house. As David once said, "Oh, how the mighty have fallen*."

If one could bring themselves to believe it, the sermon and then the altar call had been even more impressive than the opening announcements. Ten more people were subsequently added to the upcoming baptism listing. Following the unanimous approval to accept these new people as both church members and baptism candidates, Aaron said "Folks, what say next week we have ourselves a hallelujah baptism and picnic?"

The idea prompted an immediate—and loud—hallelujah. And the general opinion throughout the congregation was that the Holy Spirit was again in full charge of Henrytown Free Church. Hardscrabble Depression Era blighted or no, the people of Henrytown Free Church were sensing the immeasurable blessing of renewed hope.

To God be the glory!!

After the service, Aaron held over the baptism candidates and their families in the sanctuary. In Seth's case, "family" meant the Flowers family. Seth had come up hard in life. As the son of unrepentant drunks, he had been on his own during his teenaged years, finding work as an oil field gofer. Now, he was a full grown roustabout. The summer following their graduating from high school, Casper and Archie joined him working the "Patch" but because they were educated boys, they hadn't started out as low on the food chain as had Seth. But that hadn't made Seth resentful. It was just the opposite. He was glad to see them whenever he could, which wasn't all that often, due to the fact that Seth ran with the Patch rowdy crowd and church boys Casper and Archie, didn't.

For most of Seth's younger life, he had lived (or more correctly, hid out) in the Flowers family home, and they'd informally adopted him. It was Yancy Flowers who had managed to keep him in school until he was sixteen. That was the age when Seth took to running wild and drinking just as hard as the parents who had neglected him. Nevertheless, Yancy and Mildred continually prayed for him no matter how much trouble and strife he seemed bent on stirring up for himself. So yes, the

Flowers people were Seth's family and now they were all with him as Aaron gave the hurried instructions to all of the candidates.

"Saturday afternoon I would like all of you to come to the parsonage. During the week, make certain you jot down any questions you may have regarding the necessity of baptism. Never think your questions are foolish or embarrassing. This week should be spent in prayer and contemplation. Baptism represents the ending your former life and the rising up into a new life. It will be a serious time, and a joyous time. You will need to hold tightly to the blessing and the memory of your baptism day, because Christianity isn't a comfortable religion. It's a way of life. The true translation of *Christian* means, "Little Christ." It was a name given to the Christ followers during the first years and in the ancient town of Antioch, and it was meant as an insult. But it worked to the favor of the early believers in that it meant that those outside the faith were closely watching the way Christians treated one another; that they were not self-seeking but giving. They were not quick to anger but quick to forgive. The reasons for this is that Jesus hadn't simply taught the Law of God, He actually made the Law harder. Too many people thought—and still think—that if they are seen behaving rightly, that they're all right with God. Jesus said that's not true. He said that God knows what's going on deep within your heart. Therefore, God judges the internal.

"But here's the good news of salvation: God is patient. He's not expecting a complete and overnight change. In His mercy and grace, He's giving us the remainder of our lives to become fit for heaven, because at this moment, we're all in desperate need of the Holy Spirit's cleansing work. So, that's where studying the Bible and encouraging one another comes together. Being a Christian is the hardest and yet the most fulfilling commitment you will ever undertake. All right, now that I've thoroughly boggled your already boggled minds, does anyone have a question they'd like to ask at this particular time?"

"Yes," Mildred Flowers said. "What about the hot dishes?"

When Aaron looked entirely confounded, Yancy offered an explanation. "Pastor, you're addressing Louisiana women. They don't usually go nowhere without totin' something hot and delicious."

Aaron's mouth worked, but no sound was produced. Libby quickly spoke for him. "Mama, all you ladies can talk about that tomorrow. An' never bother askin' the pastor what he wants to eat because he can't tell ya. Eating just isn't on his list of primary concerns."

"Except for biscuits," Aaron mumbled.

Libby made a tsking sound as she rolled her eyes. At that same second, a brain cell triggered inside Aaron's skull. Dismissing the assembly of candidates and families, he said quickly to Yancy, "Mr. Flowers? May I have a private word with you please?"

Once they were alone in the church, Yancy couldn't dispel the notion that Aaron was suddenly looking as nervous as an egg-bound hen. Yancy waited while Aaron, seated next to him, made three failed attempts at what he wanted to say. On the third try, while running his hand through his hair, Aaron simply blurted, "Mr. Yancy—I'm quite smitten with your daughter. The absolute truth of it is, I was smitten the very instant I saw her. I have recently summoned the courage to ask her out on a date and now I'd like—"

"Hold it right there, Preacher," Yancy said. "If you're lookin' for my blessin' to court my girl, you got it. You're a fine young man an' I'm partial to ya. But I want to put in a quick word of warning. This is a small town and malicious gossip has a way of running twenty miles before truth ever has a chance to put its shoes on. So, here's what I'm proposing; you an' Libby can do all your datin' at my house. You can come to dinners and suppers and then the pair of you can go for walks or sit on the back-porch swing. But you don't never take her off alone in your car. There's a whole bunch of young girls—and their mamas'—who have set their caps for you an' not one of 'em would hesitate to attack a rival. Things could get real ugly real fast for my little girl. An' I can't have that. No sir. Not for you nor nobody."

"But, I don't understand. Libby drives around with Seth—"

"You ain't Seth. Don't get me wrong, I love Seth like he's my own, but he ain't the one that the girls are all dreamin' over. You are. You're the big catfish in this little bitty pond and the young ladies are settin' their hooks. If they get wind that my Libby's got the right bait, they're gonna do everythin' they can to cut her line. So, for as long as we can, we'd be wise to keep this courtin' business a secret."

"I'm not entirely comfortable with this idea, Mr. Yancy."

"Why not?"

Aaron began to stammer. "B-because it's so d-deceitful!"

Yancy sat back on the pew and let go a long soulful sigh. "Son, you're looking at this secret business in the wrong light. There's a big old long list of the kinds of secrets folks just naturally have. First are the *Light Secrets*, this is generally the stuff everybody knows already but don't talk about no more, not even over at the barber shop. Then there's *Secret-Secrets*—generally the family secrets about great-great granddaddies. Next comes *Unholy Secrets*—these are generally secrets that concern an especially noteworthy trip into Alexandria. Them's the kind a fella prays his wife won't find out about until after he's been dead for so long that she's become too feeble to bother with diggin' him up an' knockin' the pure stuffin' outta his corpse. The last on the list are the *Protective Secrets*—an' that's the kind of secret that we're talkin' about for my Libby. "

Aaron had never known such a lengthy rationalization. His stammering increased as he struggled to speak. Yancy placed a hand on his arm, effectively ending Aaron's exertion.

"Listen to me son, I know Atlanta's got a long an' bold as brass proud history, but Louisiana is a muddy little country built on big muddier secrets. It all started with Napoleon playin' it close to the chest when he offered the French territory of Louisiana for sale to the Americans. And then President Thomas Jefferson made certain the Lewis & Clark expedition was kept top secret. When all of this eventually came out, Louisiana was sold for gold an' the sons of the French nobility who'd been playin' at gentleman planters, went to bed one night as French nationals and woke up the next morning as Americans. So, ya might say that Louisiana people have an inborn talent for secret keepin'." Yancy gave Aaron's arm another pat. "And now that you've got this one little puny secret to call your very own, you can start thinkin' of yourself as one of us."

All Aaron could do was shake his head. "How long do you think I'll have to keep it?"

Sitting back in the pew and looking up toward the ceiling, Yancy pondered a moment. "Oh, I reckon we could let the cat outta the bag probably about the time you and Libby are expectin' your third or fourth child. But even then, there are no absolutes." He chuckled softly as he glanced in the direction of the markedly dazed Aaron. "It's all your fault for bein' so dern good lookin'. It's your curse an tha's a fact. But what can't be helped has to be worked around."

Aaron lowered his head. He had never had a secret before. The entire idea went fully against his nature. Besides, he wasn't completely sure he could even keep a secret. Granted he had no trouble keeping the confessional type confidences of others, but his own life had always been open and above board. And yet, Yancy Flowers was an intelligent man who knew his own people; how they thought and how they reacted. Aaron could only bow to Yancy Flowers' wisdom, however disappointing.

"Son," Yancy said. "You're lookin' a mite peckish. What say you follow us on over to my house an' have yourself some Sunday dinner followed by coffee and blackberry pie."

Aaron's face brightened. "Would it be permissible for Libby to ride with me?"

"No. She's gonna be with me an' her mama. Seth an' Casper will be ridin' with you." Aaron's expression was discouraged again. Yancy laughed as both he and Aaron stood to their feet. He slung an arm around the younger man's shoulders. "May as well get used to it son, this is your life from here on out."

In the Flower's family truck, after hearing her father's edict, Libby was pitching one of her infamous wailing fits. Oh, and it was ugly. Not even the fact that Aaron was tailgating her daddy's truck could calm her down. And in that car, Casper was in the back, but he was leaning so far forward that he might as well have been sitting in the front seat between Seth and Aaron. "I know Daddy's probably right about all this," Casper said, trying to cheer Aaron up.

"He usually is," Seth agreed. "Wonder how come we didn't think of all the ramifications?"

"Boy I swear to Pete!" Casper yelped. "Now that you've taken to learning a new word every week, you're becoming a pest about using them everywhere you can!"

"Ramifications is a good word," Seth coolly replied. "Plus, it's really fun to say."

Casper smacked the back of Seth's head. "Stay on the subject, would you just mind doin' that?"

"I was doin' exactly that when the ramifications of expressing my opinion ended with a smack upside my skull."

Casper smacked Seth again.

"I was thinking," Aaron said, ignoring them both. "If all of us went places together, then the only thing anyone would think is that the two of you were showing me the interesting sights and Libby was simply tagging along."

"That would work for about a week an' then we'd run out of interesting sights."

"And," Seth offered. "The women around here are natural born suspicious. Libby working for you one day a week an' then taggin' after us durin' all the other times would start to smell as nasty as a bayou rat."

Casper sat back and said dejectedly, "Them women in the beauty parlor would have our little Libby dyed, fired and laid to the side faster than any of' 'em could say, 'Permanent wave please!'"

"I never imagined, "Aaron said as he concentrated on following the truck, "that dating could be so complicated."

"Hey!" Casper cried. "Welcome to courting Louisiana style!"

They were all seated around the table trying to enjoy their post-meal coffee and pie, but Libby and Casper were both making this impossible. "The very least he can do," Casper was saying, "is sit at the table next to her."

Seated across the table and facing Aaron who had been placed in between Seth and Casper, Libby was quick to agree. "I fail to see the point of this Daddy. It's not like people are lurking around outside and peeping in the windows. Besides, nobody even knows he's here!"

The telephone rang. Wordlessly, Mildred left the table.

Aaron was the only person at the table who wasn't yelling as Mildred answered the phone. Less than a minute later, Mildred was standing behind her seated husband who was still being hounded half to death. Out of necessity she raised her voice against the racket. “Pastor Aaron! Your mother is being put through on our phone line. Seems you forgot to call her. Again.”

Mildred resumed her place at the table while Aaron rather meekly rose and went off to speak to his waiting mother.

His point fully made, Yancy was finally able to enjoy his pie in perfect peace.

He had wanted to be alone with her. He’d thought of all sorts of wild schemes to be alone with her, but now that they were alone—relatively—he was coming to the conclusion that sitting with her on the back porch swing while Miss Mildred made her presence known by loudly clattering about in the kitchen was actually better than being alone—alone. This way he could mask his nervousness by playing to the illusion that he was extremely worried that a member of the family could simply appear within a second’s time. So, they sat in the glider swing, hands almost (not quite) touching as Aaron gently propelled the sway of the swing. The afternoon was turning Louisiana Morbid Muggy. The porch ceiling fan was doing its best to make some movement in the heavy air but failing in the attempt. Libby didn’t notice the building heat as she thumped her brain trying to find a topic of conversation. The bitter truth was, she was beginning to wish he would leave because she had never known him to be so . . . quiet.

“So,” she said more brightly than she felt. “How’s your mama doin’?”

“Oh, she’s fine. She was just a bit anxious to hear how my sermon went.” He shook his head as if trying to clear it. “I’ve no idea how she keeps finding me.”

At last! A topic! "Switchboard girls," Libby immediately said. "We know everything."

Aaron half turned in the swing and, to her relief, he was looking more like himself, not a gentleman's clothing mannequin pretentiously posed in a glider. His genuine amazement had animated him. "But how on earth would the switchboard girl know where I was?"

"To answer that, I first have to swear you to a dark secret."

"Oh," Aaron said sarcastically. "Yet another Henrytown secret. Goody."

Libby burst into laughter and lightly touched the back of his hand. "Will you just swear please?"

"I don't know Lib. That will make two secrets in one day. However am I to keep up this frenetic pace?"

"But do you swear?"

"Yes. Fine. I so swear."

"Hope to die?"

"In this heat? When I'm expecting death at any second?"

"Well, if that's the case, then it's safe to tell ya." She leaned in closer. "We girls like listen in on conversations."

Aaron was instantly surprised. "And no one knows you're there?"

"Nope." A smug smile stretched her lips. "There's a switch on the main board that blocks noise. When we want to listen but not be heard, all we have to do is flip the switch."

"That's eavesdropping!"

"Blatantly."

"And you're not ashamed?"

"Most of the time I'm too bored to be ashamed."

Aaron backed away from her. "You're a fallen woman, Libby Flowers."

“Oh, hush. And let’s go for a walk down by the creek before we melt and leave nothing but two big old sweat puddles on the porch swing.”

Mildred watched from the kitchen window as the pair walked across the lawn heading down to the trees that lined and shaded the creek. Aaron wasn’t wearing his suit jacket and the sleeves of his shirt were rolled up to the elbows. The sight of those bright red suspenders caused Mildred to laugh and say softly, “Oh my sweet Lord!” But what deeply touched her heart was the sight of Pastor Aaron taking her daughter’s hand and helping Libby walk down the embankment.

Casper and Seth had taken off, heading out to meet up with Archie. Those three would rather fish than breathe and Casper had announced that they’d best go over to the pond before the sight of Seth being baptized scared all the fish into mortal shock. With Mildred busy in the kitchen, that only left Yancy to keep an eye on the courting pair. He was walking close to the land boundary, paying so close attention to the distant pair that he missed entirely the sight of Ralph Winters standing on his side of his infernal stanchion and four-planked fence. A stupid fence like that didn’t keep anything out, it only gobbled up land that didn’t belong to Ralph Winters to begin with.

“Hey, Yancy,” Ralph said.

Yancy turned at the waist, shocked to see Ralph so close that they were almost within handshaking distance.

Ralph went back to examining the condition of his idiot fence. “Had the preacher over to dinner I see.”

“Yeah,” Yancy grunted.

“Real gentlemanly of him to hold Libby’s hand and help her walk down the embankment to the creek.”

“He’s a considerate young man,” Yancy said, trying not to sound mistrustful.

"Funny how you an' me are takin' a walk at the same time an' along the same stretch."

"Yeah," Yancy replied. "It's a true coincidence all right."

Ralph used both hands to try to shake the top board of the fence. "How much plank board you reckon is in this fence?"

"Well, there's almost five acres of it runnin' straight an' true, so that's a real good bit."

Ralph lifted his head and looked Yancy in the eye. "By my reckoning, we've got most of a church wing right here. Don't know how we'd use the stanchions though. They been stuck in the ground so long that the bottom half's probably on its way to rot, but there's nothing wrong with these boards."

Yancy could not go beyond his innate suspicion of Ralph Winters and it was telling in his reply. "You thinking about selling off used wood to the church, Ralph?"

Ralph looked ashamed. In a low tone he replied, "No. I was just out here thinkin' how this fence has made me a pretty bad neighbor an' that maybe it's time to give all that over to the Lord."

Yancy approached the fence and both men, still maintaining a healthy space between them, leaned against it, their folded arms resting on the top plank as they looked off in separate distances, Yancy toward Ralph's pristine, park-like property, Ralph toward Yancy's large vegetable garden, animal pens and tin roofed outbuildings.

After much contemplation, Yancy finally said, "May I ask what has brought you to this conclusion?"

Ralph took a deep breath and slowly released it. "I'd really rather not go into all that right now."

Still looking out toward Ralph's property, Yancy nodded his head. "Understood," he mildly replied.

After yet another long silence, and Ralph's growing appreciation of how Yancy and Mildred had worked hard to make do with what little they had, he said, "So, you gonna help me take this fence apart or what?"

Yancy turned to face Ralph. "Well you of all people know I ain't got nothin' but time! I could take this thing down all by myself if you want me to."

"Naw," Ralph said lowly. "It's something we gotta do together because I'm sorta needin' you to come back to the mill."

Libby and Aaron took a seat in the shade of lofty pines, enjoying the coolness of the shade and the light breeze wafting from the quickly moving water of the shallow creek. Aaron was glad for the relief; Libby was worrying about chiggers and ticks crawling around inside the pine straw they were sitting on. She was wondering if she should voice this concern when Aaron began to speak.

He wasn't looking at her; he couldn't bring himself to do that, his gaze remained locked on the sunlight dappled water as it danced around and jumped over the large stones inside the creek bed. His one remaining good pair of white oxfords were solidly planted on the edge of the creek embankment and his legs were drawn near his chest, his arms resting on top of his knees. "Libby," he said in a serious tone, "I'm quite a boring person. Mine is a life that consists primarily of study and prayer. I have never courted a young lady before, so I have no idea what is considered to be the normal courting procedure."

Libby put her hand on his bare forearm. "Aaron, have you ever in your life kissed a girl?"

Aaron gasped sharply. "No!"

Libby tossed both hands dismissively. "Well Aaron Brooks, I'm just not going to sit here and believe that some girl has never tried kissing you!" Aaron's head spun on his neck as he looked at her with unnaturally wide cobalt eyes that were truly scandalized. For her part, Libby couldn't bring herself to understand why in the world the thought of a girl wanting to kiss him would so confound or scandalized his pea-sized brain. "Aaron? When you're standing in front of your mirror and shaving your face, do you ever *really* see yourself?"

"Of course, I do," he jeered. "How else would I know I've gotten all the shaving soap off?"

"Oh, good heavens," she snipped. "Lord!" She said to the heavens. "You've sent me a lunatic."

When she began to act as if she were about to stand, his hand stayed her. "Libby, this is not the time for your temper. This is the time for you to hear me out. And then if you decide you'd rather flounce off, then flounce away. But first, you listen. Agreed?"

"Fine." Libby settled while Aaron regathered his thoughts.

"Libby, I am never going to be able to offer a wife anything more than small wages, and in all probability, not even the hope of a permanent home. My father disapproves of my calling, and he has said that he will only continue to grant me an allowance for six months. After that, if I'm still unwilling to take his advice and follow his action plan for my life, then he will cut me off financially." His knees were now drawn in more tightly to his chest as he lay the side of his head against his arms. He was looking at her through eyes that were going misty as he said in such a soft voice that she had to lean in to hear. "I can't do that Lib. I have to go where the Lord calls, and cling hard to Psalm 91 verse 2." When her expression remained vacant, he obliged by quoting the verse.

"I will say of the LORD, He is my refuge and my fortress; my God, in Him will I trust."

Her voice became as soft as his. "That's the verse that brought you here, isn't it?"

His head was still resting against his arms and knees and his eyes were locked on hers as his head slowly nodded.

Well, that just tore it. Now she knew without even a trace of doubt that God had sent Aaron not only to be the pastor of Henrytown Free Church, but He'd sent him to be her husband. "Aaron!" she said crisply. "Sit up. And you ought to brace yourself because I'm about to kiss you."

He sat up smartly. "We have to be engaged before we kiss!"

"Trust me you goof, we're engaged."

Chapter Fourteen

The days of the following week flew by at breakneck speed. Libby was at the parsonage more days than not, primarily because Aaron badly needed a full-time secretary, never mind that he couldn't pay a full-time salary; secondly, because she couldn't stay away from him. When they were together, she could barely believe he would want to marry her. When they were apart, she couldn't believe it at all. Ergo, her need to be continually in his company. But then too there were the many letters that needed typing and mailing, appointments to be arranged and then the making certain that Aaron left on time in order to keep said appointments. The most time consuming of all were the "show-ups;" people who just walked into the parsonage carrying in a host of troubles with them and crying to see the pastor. Most annoying of all were the show-ups of single females who had not one living thing wrong with them except their need for Aaron's attention. The many on-the-hunt-females quickly became another crucial reason for Libby remaining on the scene.

Yet the long hours she was putting in without any hope for payment was worrying her a bit. Since her father's dismissal from the mill, she and Casper had been the only source of cash income for the family. It bothered her greatly that her parents might be expecting a bigger pay envelope than she would be handing over at the end of the week. During a lull on Thursday afternoon, she confided her worry to Aaron, only seconds later to deeply regret having done so because he instantly demanded that she speak to her father. But he'd only meant that she should confess the working for free bit. Never once had it occurred to him that she would also spill the beans about their secret engagement. Yet that's exactly what she did; and right after supper when her parents were seated in the living room listening to the Fibber McGee and Molly Show on the radio.

Mildred's motherly heart began to flutter. "Oh, my little sweetheart. How did he propose?"

Libby waved off her mother's question is if batting away an intent mosquito. "Well, to be brutally honest, he didn't. I kissed him on the mouth and then he felt all obligated to make an honest woman of me. But that's fine. I can live with myself."

Mildred put the knuckles of her fist against tightly pressed lips as she did her best to suppress laughter.

"Well, catch as catch can I always did say," her father said dryly. "But little girl, you don't have to worry about helpin' to support your mama an' me no more. I got my old job back at the mill."

"You did?" Libby squealed.

"You would have known it if you'd been around here long enough to see me going off every morning with my food bucket. Old Ralph hired me back last Sunday. Not only that, but him an' me are both workin' to take down that fence durin' the hours we ain't over at the mill."

Libby looked positively floored.

"So, you go on ahead an' kiss that young man of yours. But this next time, you kiss him a good one for me too. Any preacher who can break through to old Ralph, needs him some good kissin'."

Mildred rose from her chair and went to where her daughter stood, enfolding Libby in her arms. "My baby girl," she cooed against Libby's hair. "An engaged woman." Then she pushed Libby back, holding on to her daughter's shoulders. "Engaged to a preachin' man." Then Mildred made a disapproving tsking sound.

"What?" Libby demanded.

"Them britches," Mildred answered. "Preacher's wives do not wear britches."

"But Mama," Libby whined. "Trousers are the style these days. An' I wear dresses to church!"

"You gonna have to wear dresses all the time now because in a preacher's family, he's the only one who wears the pants. You march yourself on off to your room young madam and you don't come out exceptin' you're wearin' a dress and stockings."

"I'm gonna feel like a big old doof!" Libby cried as she slunk out of the room.

"I didn't tell ya to like it, I just told ya to do it." A minute after Libby was gone, Mildred went back to her chair and sat down.

Yancy reached across the small space dividing their separate chairs and took his wife's hand. "You don't have much longer to be tellin' her what to do ya know."

With her free hand, Mildred wiped the tear tracing her cheek. "They'll be engaged for a few months. I've still got that amount of time to be her mama. An' now I'll treasure each and every day."

On Saturday, the baptism candidates and their families gathered at the parsonage for final counseling session followed by supper. Mabel was in a flap because the ladies who had brought the requisite hot dishes hadn't seen fit to confer with her about what type of hot dish each was planning to bring. Nor would it appear that they'd done much conferring with each other. And not a single one of them had given a thought about the dessert. The upshot being there were three butter bean casseroles and one puny bowl of potato salad. Mabel was going to have to scramble if this celebration meal was going to be anything short of a culinary disaster. There was nothing for it but to sacrifice the weeks' worth of pork chops and bake up some corn bread and a batch of biscuits. There was also the chocolate cake she'd made special for the Sunday picnic. Now it seemed she'd be sacrificing the cake into the bargain. In one of her notable panics, she'd had to send Bubba off to pick blackberries for a cobbler. A plain old blackberry cobbler would now have to make do for the picnic. But the lone light in this dark storm of kitchen troubles was that Bubba would not be there to plunk himself down at the table and hog the food that was, things being what they were, barely enough to feed everyone else.

As she mixed the two different batters and kept a close eye on the frying pork chops, she turned her mind to the subject of her son. All week-long Bubba had been acting peculiar—secretive peculiar. Bubba had never been a talker, but now his long silences were just pure strange. If she didn't know better, she'd swear her son was in deep thought about something. But Bubba having a deep thought about anything wasn't even possible. Was it?

Sunday morning, the weather was truly remarkable. There wasn't a cloud in the cerulean blue sky and the humidity was bearable. It was the perfect day for a picnic. Cars and trucks bypassed the church building, making straight for the pond where families unloaded and set up saw-horse and plank board tables. Individual family blankets were spread out on the grass, and folks greeted one another in their high expectations of a truly wonderful hallelujah picnic Sunday.

Miss Cornelia arrived in her father's classic Bentley. In the open portion of the estate car, the place once the domain of the chauffeur, Miss Cornelia now sat, and driving the big car as easily as if she'd been born to it. Oh, the woman could easily afford to hire a new chauffeur; she simply didn't want one. But the true corker was that this time, there were other people in the car with her. Lofthouse people! The car was so filled with the Lofthouse family that Archie Lofthouse had to make do with sitting in the opened front with Miss Cornelia. If the sight of all that—*democracy*—didn't positively harelip Huey P. Long, then absolutely nothing ever would. But the real boggler was that after all those Lofthouses waterfalled out of the car, that they proceeded to fetch out from the car's trunk five large picnic baskets and two heavily packed and ready to go, ice cream churns. However, the most disconcerting thing was that it wasn't Miss Cornelia who called out the orders to the clan. Nope—it was *Becka Lofthouse*, doing all the tellin' everybody what to do, just like she was some kind of irritable queen bee.

Archie escaped that whole embarrassing mess just as fast as his legs could carry him. He bolted for Flowers family and straight into the company of Casper.

"What in the world is goin' on over there?" Casper asked.

Archie blew a long sigh. "It's been like this all week long. Right after last Sunday's preachin' Mama glommed onto Miss Cornelia an' now you'd swear those two have been friends their whole lives. First Mama had to help Miss Cornelia choose some likely patterns for the prayer cushions, and then she had to help fix the ladies meeting day buffet, and since then, Mama's been spending her evenings over at Miss Cornelia's helping to draw out extra pattern papers. Oh, and then there was all the fuss for this picnic day. But the worst part is that those two haven't minded using me for their slave labor."

"You didn't cook nothin' did ya?" Casper cried. "Cause if you did, point it out so's I won't accidently eat any of it."

"Heck no, I didn't cook. What they needed me for was to haul and push heavy furniture from one end of Miss Cornelia's house to the other. Then I had to clean up the back garden and set up the outside tables and chairs. Five minutes after the buffet, I had to haul all that back to the storage shed so the weather wouldn't spoil the wicker tables and chairs. And as soon as the stitchery ladies left, I had to push all the house furniture back to where it belonged and then push around the Hoover to clean up the rugs. The whole while I was doing that, Mama an' Miss

Cornelia were in the kitchen cookin' an' talkin' an' laughin' like a couple of little girls. Neither one of 'em seemed to care a single whit that they were killin' me. I swear, my whole body hurts so bad I can't wait to go off to the oil patch where them two can't get at me."

To add to Archie's pain Mildred Flowers said, "Oh Miss Cornelia's made herself a good, good friend. Ain't that the sweetest thing?" Ignoring Archie's groan, she turned to Yancy. "Isn't that just so sweet you can't hardly stand it?"

"It's so sweet my back molars are aching." Yancy replied as he turned to the two younger men. "Well, now that the mystery of Archie's unusually long absence from the Flower's supper table has finally been solved, I believe you two should go on over an' be with Seth. He could probably use the brotherly support."

They did not need to be told twice. Casper and Archie proceeded to make a dash for the clump of trees where a throng of people surrounded Aaron. He was wearing a white robe and there was no mistaking the sun-blazed blonde curly hair. They arrived at the back of the crowd just in time for the prayer.

"Father God, I ask Your blessing on this day, and on these who have come by faith into Your family. We thank you for Your grace, and Your mercy that You have bestowed on all those who love You and take pride in that Name—the Name above all other Names—Jesus. Because it is only in that Name that we humbly pray and dedicate our very lives. Amen." When Aaron raised his head and spotted Casper and Archie he cried, "Oh bless God! The boatmen have arrived!"

As the four young men walked down to the large pond, Miss Cornelia called out to them. They paused, Aaron standing in front of the other three as they all looked back at her over their shoulders. Miss Cornelia snapped the Kodak Brownie camera, quickly whirled the winding spool and, just as she was about to snap a second photo, Aaron lifted his arm and waved. Luckily, she got a perfect still shot of that as well. But, in the following week, after all of her photos had been developed, there was something about that photograph of Aaron waving that didn't simply break her heart, it shattered it. She had no idea why such a simple snapshot would evoke such raw emotion; nevertheless, Miss Cornelia hurriedly stashed the photo in a drawer in her little secretary desk where she wouldn't think of it again for a very long time. The first photo however, the one of Seth, Casper, Archie and Aaron all looking back at her and smiling, that one she framed and set out on a table in her living room where it would reside throughout the remainder of her very long life.

"Mama?" Libby said, her tone hurried. "Let's go help with the tables."

Yancy sat down on the picnic blanket watching the two women he adored carrying the weighty picnic basket between them as they hurried away, calling out greetings to the other women who were setting out food on the tables. It was a beautiful day. A blessed day. A day to treasure. Yancy was an avid follower of the daily radio broadcast of statewide news however, of late the news had been rather sketchy. This did not bode well. Any time the Long family, most especially Huey P., went quiet, something was up.

Huey P. was now a senator in Washington D.C., but the consensus of opinion was that the Kingfish still retained full control of the governor's office, and that the current governor, Governor Oscar Allen, wasn't anything more than a figurehead; merely a means for Huey to still remain governor while being in Washington D.C. Personally, Yancy didn't know whether to believe it or not. He did agree that such a thing would be a swindle—oh, it might be *legal*—but no matter how you viewed it, it sure took a hard turn to the left of ethical. But his lingering disbelief was simply due to the logic that such an arrangement would require way too many Louisiana people continually cooperating with one another. In all his life Yancy had never known four or more Louisiana politicians to continually do anything together for longer than a day—if that.

And he'd lived a while.

Over at the barber shop there were whisperings of a highly secretive club of Blue Bloods calling themselves the Square Dealers. According to barber shop lore, the list of members included doctors, lawyers, large landowners, four state congressmen, the mayor of New Orleans, and even the former governors Parker and Sanders. The Square Dealers were hotly united in the defense of two highly conservative judges who were known to rule so far on the outside of Huey's approval, that Huey had taken the bold step of publicly vowing that he'd either run them out of judicial office or he'd lay his life down trying. The Club was in full favor of the latter.

The rumors might be flowing as dark and muddy as the Mississippi but, on the latest doings of Huey P. Long, radio newswise, there was only silence. To this Yancy surmised that something was happening, and that it was something probably bad. But Yancy refused any further thoughts on the subject of what the old Kingfish may or may not be up to. This was the Lord's Day and not even the almighty Huey P. Long would be allowed to intrude on that.

"I don't know about this," Archie said.

"It's going to be fine," Aaron replied. "Just aim for the deep section, preferably in the center where we can be seen by everyone on the bank."

Like George Washington crossing the Delaware, Aaron stood in the in the center of the rowboat while Casper sat on the left, manning the left oar and Archie sat opposite manning the right oar. To make certain they rowed in concert, Casper and Archie counted out each tug of the oars. Within a few hardwon moments, they rounded the curve along the tree lined embankment, surprising the people on the shore. When Aaron decided they were perfectly positioned, Casper and Archie stopped rowing. There was still a bit of a drift to the rowboat but not enough to dissuade Aaron's intent. People began to walk toward the muddy beach area and then cluster on the less muddy areas of the shoreline.

Their new preacher was still all robed up for a baptismal service but, instead of wading out into the shallows, he was standing inside a rowboat. This was most certainly a new wrinkle on the way to baptize folks. (Had to be one of those curious Atlanta customs.) When everyone had gathered, Aaron began to speak, and even stranger than the sight of his standing in a rowboat, came the surprising fact that everyone could hear him just fine.

"I know you're all familiar with the New Testament story about Jesus getting into a boat and having His disciples push off from the shore in order to teach the multitudes of people who came to hear Him. Now as you can hear for yourselves, His distance from shore did not affect their ability to hear Him clearly. Sound actually carries better over water. So, not only are we having a hallelujah picnic, we're also having a Sea of Galilee type sermon. Matthew eight, verses twenty-three through twenty-seven tells about Jesus sleeping in a boat during a storm and over troubled waters. It's a powerful image of God's Sovereignty. When the disciples were terrified, in fear for their lives, Jesus simply stood up and said to the storm and the sea, 'Peace, be still.' It's a perfect picture of when troubles or illness have us feeling helpless, desperate, and in terrible fear, that it's all right to yell for Him, because He will hear and act His perfect will for your lives."

As Aaron was about to add more to the sermon, Casper shouted, "Is it okay to start yelling now? Cause we're sinking!"

"An' kinda fast!" Archie wailed.

Aaron looked from one to the other as they first tried to bail water with their cupped hands and then, having abandoned that, tried to row toward the shallows. Unfortunately, the boat simply caved, and all at once. Before the startled eyes of the many onlookers, down they went, Casper and Archie reemerging immediately, but without Aaron.

Libby screamed and then her brother and Archie surfaced dived in an effort to find their heavily robed pastor. Things were mighty tense on the old creek bank, but soon there came a wave of relief as three heads bobbed in the water. And all three of them were laughing. Before her mother could stop her, Libby wearing a dress, a pair of stockings and her best shoes, was splashing out into the creek and was there to help Casper and Archie with the grappling of a waterlogged robed Aaron. The next thing anybody knew, Archie and Casper were walking out of the water while Aaron walked with his arm around Libby as she helped him wade the final few steps to safety. Then Aaron was looking down at her and he was still laughing the whole while Libby busily fussed him up one side and then down the other. Arriving on the rocky shore, Aaron paused just long enough to shake like a wet dog and rain water down on an already equally soaked Libby.

The whole thing was just like watching that romantic movie that had played at the picture show theater for nearly all of the months of 1934, but no one had minded because it had starred Clark Gable and Claudette Colbert. To further this impression, one man turned to his wife and asked, "What was the name of that movie you kept draggin' me off to see just about every Saturday night last summer?"

"It Happened One Night," she answered.

"That's the one!" someone else cried.

When the pair on the beach then realized they were not exactly—*alone*—Aaron took Libby's hand and they stood together to face the spectators.

"Um, brothers and sisters," a sodden and bedraggled looking Aaron said. "It is my profound pleasure to announce that Miss Libby Flowers and I are seeing one another socially, and with the intent at some point in the near future, of announcing our formal engagement."

Booming laughter came from the men. Shrieks (no one was ever quite certain just what all of that shrieking actually implied) came from the women.

And Yancy, in his drier than sand tenor, said to Mildred, "Ya know Mama, this family never could keep a secret worth a flip."

"Oh, amen to that Daddy-Bear."

"Well," Yancy sighed. "At least it was a good whole week of tryin'."

Far behind the crowd and standing guard over the food laden tables, Bubba X beamed with pure joy. Of all the people his age, Bubba loved his cousin Libby the best, because she had always been so patient and so kind with him. And now she was about to be married to the very best of men. This news was far and away better than the sight of all those separately brought blackberry cobblers lining the desert table.

It was promptly decided, what with Aaron already wet and barely able to walk inside the soaking robe, that the baptisms should begin immediately. Seth, happy to go last, stood at the back of the line. Casper and Archie stayed with him. Seth seemed nervous which seemed a tad irrational because Seth was a strong swimmer and, Aaron was only standing in waist deep water. The little kids and young women weren't worried—all right, except for the little ten-year old girl who went into such a panic about being immersed that she'd spun like an alligator's death roll inside Aaron's arms. The situation had been a bit tricky (and all right, hysterically funny) until Aaron finally managed to dunk her. If

Aaron hadn't drown that kid, then what in the world was wrong with Seth?

As the line inched forward and Seth continued to act uneasy, Archie blatantly asked, "Seth, what in the world is wrong with you!?

"It's all this here!" Seth whispered loudly. "It all feels so . . . permanent."

"That's because it is," Casper said snidely.

"Well, now I'm worried about goin' back to the Patch, you know, as a baptized Christian."

Casper and Archie exchanged looks, then looked again to Seth. "We work the Patch," Casper said, "an' we're baptized Christians."

"Yeah," Seth grunted. "But ever'body there's used to ya'll. Ya'll went in there as Christians. Me, I went in as a heathen. I got no idea how ever'thing's gonna go once I show up carryin' a Bible."

"Yeah," Archie agreed. "You were a wild one all right. Those old boys are gonna let you have it pretty good. But ya know, Paul used to kill Christians before he was converted. It took him about eight years before the Christians would trust him, an' them other Jewish fellas he used to run with never ever did leave him alone. They were either beatin' him half to death or stoning him an' leavin' him for dead. Now you, all you ever done was shoot dice an' drink hard liquor with the patch boys. Do you really think a little bit of teasin' is gonna hurt you so awful bad that you just can't stand it?"

Seth looked ashamed and answered softly, "No." Raising his head and squaring his shoulders he said with more conviction. "No. I do not believe there's anything that they can ever say or do that's gonna change the way I believe in Jesus."

"Good answer." Casper said. "Now from here on out, it's always gonna be the three of us. The three brothers who stand up for Jesus an' for each other. Now, go on out there to Aaron. He's waitin' on ya."

Aaron's smile was radiant as Seth stepped into the water and wadded toward him. As he'd seen the others do, Seth turned so that he was standing sideways to Aaron. He felt Aaron's hand touch the center of his back, and he knew this was the cue to settle his nose between the V of the second and third finger of his right hand.

"Seth Lewis," Aaron's strong voice declared, "you have come by profession of faith to be baptized into the Body of Christ. So, by this profession, I now baptize you in the Name of the Father, the Son and of the Holy Spirit—"

Seth felt himself being rolled back and then the water washed over him. His eyes were open and through the dimming water he could see the ball of the sun directly overhead. *Wow, it sure looked round*. He'd never seen the noon day sun so clear before. And then he was being lifted, and as his face broke through the water, the sudden brightness and clarity and dazzling colors of his surroundings were astonishing.

"Arise my brother!" Aaron's voice seemed to be booming. "Into your new life in the everlasting love of God!"

In that instant, Seth understood just why Paul had endured the beatings and the stoning.

To be with God, even if only for a measly second, was worth everything.

Chapter Fifteen

It was nearing the final days of August 1935. Summer had become a season that only ever alternated between sunny and unbearably hot, to thundering rainstorms that still managed to be unbearably hot, but with the\enhanced aspect of clammy.

There is nothing as comforting as a warm bed on a cold morning; most especially when someone is loving enough to bring you a cup of coffee. Conversely, there is nothing worse than trying to sleep on a hot night when even the slightest touch of the sheets felt like a physical offense. And in the morning, hot coffee, even if lovingly brought, would be viewed as an unforgiveable insult. This was the time of year when sleeping was done mostly as a long afternoon nap that was aided by a rattling, oscillating fan running set on full speed. In the weighty brunt of summer natural born residents of Louisiana knew to wear light, loose fitting clothing and as precious little of that as modesty would allow.

Mildred Flowers had, over the passing weeks, kept her Singer sewing machine gainfully employed in the production of summer dresses for her daughter. Libby grudgingly wore them, but she hated dresses; they required thoughtful sedateness, most especially when sitting. If she felt inclined to cross her legs, there was too much to think through; legs had to be crossed a certain way; knees had to be covered at all times: It was exasperating, and the oppressive mugginess was not helping her plight. It was a lucky thing that Aaron was so dreamy, otherwise all of this effort would have seen her throwing him over. As for Aaron, he was trying his best to reinforce Mildred's dressmaking efforts by continually complimenting Libby on her new sense of style. Truth be told, he found it all just a little befuddling that Libby had no idea how utterly adorable she looked in dresses. Yet, had Libby walked in wearing a gunny sack, he would have most certainly held the same opinion. Other than the entire town existing on scant sleep (and Libby moaning her fashion dramas), things were moving along rather well in Henrytown.

Libby was working almost full-time as Aaron's secretary. Her labors were free, of course, but now that the family was no longer so dependent on the money she and Casper brought home, *free* was an acceptable wage. The money she earned as a telephone operator, along with covering the co-pay fees for her correspondence secretarial course, was only just managing to keep her mother in the extra money she was so happily paying out in the fabric section of the general store. And when her mother wasn't at the store choosing just the right fabric, she was sitting at her sewing machine whipping up yet another dress that Libby would thoroughly hate.

In a month Libby would be taking the final exam in Baton Rouge where her typing and shorthand skills would either prove the success or failure of all her time, expense and dedication. Hence Libby's need for as much dictation and typing that Aaron could throw her way. Happily, having a secretary was something he was becoming accustomed to, and so both course subjects were being steadily applied. Frankly, Aaron didn't care if Libby passed or failed the exams because he already saw her as an invaluable gift. Her having, or not having, a school certificate would make precious little difference to him. She was already managing both his life and the office with the skill of a seasoned secretary. But unknown to Aaron, she had also begun running a file of his sermons that she secretly favored.

As the weeks passed, there was nothing left of the original church except the floor, and one could easily tell the original flooring from the new lighter colored boards. The old floor now looked like a discarded rug left to lie in the center of a room. Closer to the pond was a large waterproof tent. This was where the church was holding services while the *construction* of the new church did its best not to look too much like a horrific *destruction*. The thing baffling Aaron was that the project never seemed to run out of money. Only last week the deacon committee informed him that the windows had been ordered from a specialty window manufacturing company in Baton Rouge. They'd even shown him a drawing of the windows. He was immediately taken by how the proposed windows arched so gracefully; how they would contain wonderfully multi-colored stained glass images. There were to be twelve such windows and an even larger window was to be set behind the baptistery. When Aaron looked stymied, Ralph Winters was quick to explain.

Unrolling the blueprint drawing of the new building, Ralph used the tip of a pencil to point out the details. "See here? On the backing wall, there's gonna be the three top lights, and just under the window there's gonna be three more. The lights lights will shine through an' make this baptistery window glow. An' we need it to do that because a master artist has designed the baptism of Christ. There ain't gonna be nothin' like it, not even in New Orleans."

Aaron was hesitant. "That sounds . . . expensive."

"No, it ain't," Yancy said. He shoved the order form across the pastorate dining table toward Aaron.

Aaron's thumb and index finger worried his lower lip as he carefully read each listed cost of the especially designed baptistery window.

"I don't understand this," Aaron said. "At last count the building fund account was just shy of sixteen hundred dollars. Where did we find this kind of cash for just one window?"

"We didn't find it," Yancy said. "This pre-paid form sheet came tucked inside these fancy new blue prints an' all of it just showed up at Mr. Ralph's office."

Aaron looked to Ralph, his expression amazed. "Ralph!" he cried. "You've been more than generous, but this is over and above generosity."

"Well, I would be the first to agree with ya if I'd done it, but I promise you, I surely did not. Everybody here knows just as much about the baptistery window as I do."

Aaron slapped the table-top. "Miss Cornelia!" he cried.

"That was my very first thought too," Ralph truthfully admitted. In all of his secret reporting's to Miss Cornelia on the rising costs of the expansion, she had been faithful in making up the shortfalls. But at no time had she so much as mentioned a baptistery window. Ralph cleared his throat then said, "Then I took a look at the back of the form."

Aaron hurriedly turned the paper over and read the window's intended dedication plaque: *In loving memory of Archibald Lofthouse.* Aaron's golden brows knit together. "Who is Archibald Lofthouse?"

Yancy answered the question. "Tha's Archie Lofthouse's granddaddy. He's been gone from this earth for goin' on ten years. I don't see how that family could raise this kind of cash in so short amount of time, especially not when most of their days are spent rubbing hard on a penny an' prayin' it'll turn into a dime."

"Then we're back to Miss Cornelia," Aaron said as if that settled the matter.

"Don't see how," Ralph said. "I grew up knowing that man. He was a good man, but when he died, he didn't leave nothing behind but a grieving wife, a bunch of kids an' grandkids and thirty acres of spent land. I fail to see how a dirt-poor cotton farmer could have had any connection with a lady like Miss Cornelia. At least," Ralph concluded with a toss of his hands, "any kind of connection that would have her paying out almost three thousand dollars on a window dedicated to his memory."

The late-night meeting was giving Aaron a pain between his eyes. Certain that the outcome of all their speculation would simply end in chasing this mysterious rabbit from one field to another, Aaron called for a decision on the baptistery window. As the window had already been paid for, had been crafted into the building plan, and was currently under construction, the deacon committee unanimously voted on its approval and the meeting was adjourned.

Casper, Archie and Seth had gone back to work the oil fields two days following the church picnic. Things had not gone well. The leaders of the camp instigators that were set against Seth were none other than three of the old boys who had gone to the church service with him the very night he'd run the aisle and declared Jesus to be his Lord. Seth hadn't seen them since, but back up in their old stomping grounds of the Patch—the Rodessa Field in Caddo Parish—they were waiting for him.

Their anger against Seth's life altering decision had started out with mild teasing. Over time teasing progressed into heckling. As more days passed, their unexplainable anger resulted in punches being thrown. Seth tried turning the other cheek and further enraged, they all but broke his jaw. That's when Casper and Archie jumped in and between the three brothers, they were turning just as many cheeks as those that were turning theirs.

Over the next weeks, Johnny Walker (no relation whatsoever to the famous whiskey), the general manager of the field noticed the many black eyes and facial bruises. What he began to notice more was that the injuries were not healing, if anything they seemed to be getting worse. Running a low-key investigation, he learned that when his roustabouts weren't working, they were busily trying to kill each other with their fists. In further investigation, he came to know why; the Rowdy Boys had declared open warfare on the Christian Boys, and never mind that it was three standing up to the stronger crowd of Rowdies, the Christians were actually winning. What worried Mr. Walker was the certainty that at some point a bright spark Rowdy would think to bring a knife to the fist party. The worry of that would be that he, Field Manager Mr. Johnny Walker (again, no relation to the whiskey but now wishing mighty hard that he had himself some) would be held directly responsible for the lethal outcome. And the Company would be liable! There was only one thing he could do and, making a hurried phone call, he did that one thing.

It was nearing dawn when two gang bosses entered camp house number five and woke Seth, Archie and Casper and told them to pack. Judging by the look of the place and the bruises and contusions on the newly roused three, camp house five had been the scene of yet another flurry of flying fists. What had truly impressed the bosses was that at no time had any one of the three run to the general office and filed complaints. They'd simply taken care of themselves as best as they were able and then had concentrated on doing a full day's work. These were three fine young men and a proven credit to their faith. Looking at each other, the bosses shook their heads. They were suddenly very sorry to be losing the three, but orders were orders.

Casper, Seth and Archie had been on the train almost a full hour before any one spoke. As dawn gave way to bright mid-morning, Casper was staring out the window watching North Louisiana rolling by. Seth was sitting with his head back fighting yet another bout of blood seeping from his nose. The only one not fascinated by the view or concerned about blood loss was Archie who tried to cut the prevailing silence by making conversation. "Have either one of ya'll ever been to the Sterlington Camp?"

"No," they answered curtly.

Realizing that neither of them were in the mood for banter, Archie ended the conversation with, "Sure hope it ain't as dirty as the Rodessa Camp."

Another hour later they arrived at the Sterlington depot. A big burly man approached with an impressive speed. The three stood shoulder to shoulder, quietly awaiting whatever new brand of trouble might be coming. The bigger man came to a stop before them and speaking in a voice so loud that it gave the impression that he was almost deaf, said, "Well you boys have gotta be the God-Fearers!"

"We're Christians, yes," Casper said.

"Wa-hat?"

(Oh—he was deaf)

Seth took a deep breath and shouted as loudly as his aching head and face would allow, "We're Christians!"

"Tha's what I heard about'cha," The man laughed. "An' it looks to me like ya'll have been sufferin' mightily for Christ. Well, pick up your grips an' follow me."

They complied, and then they jogged in order to keep up with the man's rapid pace. With each gargantuan stride, he talked very loudly and seemingly to the sky. "The Sterlington Camp is a great place and the town's even nicer. You boys fell mighty fortunate to get sent up here. Sterlington only has the best of the best Patch workers. The food's good an' the housing is A Number One. First stop will be the mess hall where we'll get ya'll fed, an' then ya'll can check into your cabin and get some rest. We pull eighteen hour shifts here at Sterlington an' you'll start your first shift bright an' early tomorrow."

As the three boarded the small camp bus the man said, "My name is Wilber Bouchard. I'm a Christian too. Welcome to Sterlington, brothers."

The food was amazing. They could have their eggs any way that they wanted them, and as much bacon as they could pile onto their plates. They were also given big bowls of grits, and there was toast and four kinds of jams and, of course, all of the coffee they could handle. Casper and Seth concentrated on their plates. Archie complained a lot about how his loosened teeth were making it hard for him to chew, but still—he managed. When they were taking their licked clean plates to the long kitchen counter and surrendering them to the dish washer man, Archie noticed a large platter of newly fried and powder sugar coated beignets, the Louisiana French idea of a doughnut—sans center hole—and these tasty treats were achingly within his reach. Beignets in his mama's house were strictly for Christmas mornings. Loving beignets almost as much as he loved his mama, Archie spread the cloth napkin out on top of the steel counter and as Seth and Casper politely thanked the kitchen workers for the wonderful breakfast, Archie proceeded to pilfer as many of the beignets as the napkin would hold. (And if he got fired for being a beignet thief, so be it.) But, when he chanced a look back over his shoulder, the head roustabout, Wilber Bouchard, was blowing the steam off his mug of coffee. He was seated at a small table and listening to the woes and worries of the camp cook. He sent Archie a conspiratorial wink. In that instant, Archie felt happier and more relaxed than he had been in weeks.

As the bus rolled to a stop, Casper asked, "This is for us?"

"Sure is," Wilber said. "These are good cabins, but they all look exactly alike. Your number is Twelve . . . just remember the number of Apostles an' you won't wander into the wrong one."

"These cabins have lawns!" Seth hooted.

"They surely do. An' ya'll are responsible for keepin' 'em mowed nice an' neat. The mowers an' such like are down at the supply house at the end of the block. Just make sure you turn 'em in just like you found 'em, clean and sharp." Wilber opened the bus door. "Okay boys, let's go have a look inside your new digs."

The street was paved with two separated lanes that were divided by a raised median containing neatly trimmed grass, trees, and streetlights. All of the "cabins" were fronted by paved sidewalks and there was a paved walkway leading to each screened in front porch. There were four rocker chairs on the porch as well as a lighted ceiling fan. Wilber unlocked the front door and then passed the key back to the first hand to grab it. (Archie's) They all stepped inside a nicely furnished living room.

"Rule one," Wilber said to the young men who were still in a state of shock, "there's no sitting on the furniture in grimy clothes. If you're smart, you'll shuck off your boots before you step up onto the porch because you will be held responsible for any damage done while you're living here, so consider yourselves duly warned. There's three bedrooms and a bathroom and a small kitchen. There's a camp laundry facility that's always open. You can either do your washing yourself or you can turn it over and have it done for you. There's enough camp wives who are happy to make a little extra money by workin' in the laundry." Wilber picked up the folder from the coffee table. "I know this is a lot to remember so, when you have questions, just look inside this. It's got all the camp information you need, plus information about the town of Sterlington, such as the whereabouts to the movie theater, different churches and what-not.

"There's also a camp bus schedule, so once you've learned that, you won't have no trouble getting around. The telephone is connected to the camp switchboard, and you can use it all you want to, so long as you keep in mind that all of your calls will be recorded in the billing log and your pay packet will be docked accordingly. You'll also be docked for cabin rent, but that's to cover stuff like electricity an' water, it ain't really what you would call a real rental fee. We want all our boys an' their families to be comfortable, but you gotta pay a little bit for the comfort, otherwise the company will go bust."

"Families?" Seth asked.

Wilber chuckled, the sound coming from deep inside his chest. "I guess that one does come as a revelation to ya, on account of ya'll used to livin' rough with nothin' but a crowd of hairy legged men, but yeah, we got families here. An' I hope ya'll like kids cause there's a slew of 'em on this block. The fact is, a high number of the kids in the Sterlington School are Patch kids." He handed the folder over to Casper. "Well, I'm gonna push off so you boys can get settled and get yourselves some rest. The shift bus will be here to pick up at five a.m. You just follow the other men you see walking toward the bus stop tomorrow mornin'. You got any questions before I go?"

"I got just the one," Casper said, his voice hoarse. "Have we all died an' gone to heaven?"

Wilber laughed heartily. "Not yet son. Not yet."

Chapter Sixteen

It was early Tuesday evening, the setting sun painting the sky with rich and vibrant red and gold colors. Libby was not on switchboard shift, which was a good thing, in spite of the fact that her hours off meant money out of her pay packet. Tuesdays were, as a rule, the quiet days of the week and they were simply that because so many of the town's womenfolk were holed up for the whole live-long day at Miss Cornelia's. The Tuesday sewing day had begun as a women's ministry, but now it was also a club. They even kept minutes. Libby thought this truly absurd because you were talking about a group of women that made up the infamous Crow's Nest, so they were on the telephone as a group twice a day, every day, and they saw each other every Wednesday night, for prayer service and then again every Sunday morning for worship. What kind of business could they possibly have that could ever conceivably be considered *NEW*?

Yet, their hands kept busy with stitchery meant that they didn't have as much time to swim a few laps inside the town's small-minded pool of gossip; work themselves into a flap over what they'd heard and then come rushing in to ask the pastor for spiritual guidance. So, Tuesday mornings, for both Aaron and Libby, were truly days when Aaron could pay calls on shut-ins and Libby could catch up with the piles of work held over from the previous week. The fly befouling this jar of honey was that beginning next week, Aaron would begin training the Sunday School teachers. The new schedule would begin this next Monday evening when he would be working with the teachers for the adult men and women classes. Tuesday evenings would be training the teachers of the teenage boys and girls. Wednesday night was, of course, Prayer service. Thursday evenings would be teaching the teachers of Kindergarten through sixth grade. These classes were slated to go on for the next three months. The schedule would be grueling, but Aaron had faith that at some point the church would have a Sunday School administrator able to assume this mentoring role as well as be able to field any and all problems connected to the Sunday School program.

But for now, with tummies full from the cold supper that Mabel had served (it was much too hot in August to even entertain the notion of turning on the oven) Libby, Aaron and Mabel sat on the front porch in the futile attempt to cool themselves. The rockers being used by Aaron and Libby were close together. Mabel was seated off to the side where she could easily keep a sharp maternal eye on the courting pair. Pushing the porch flooring with the tips of her toes, Mabel moved the rocker ever so slightly as she fanned herself with one of the wood handled cardboard fans that she'd shamelessly snatched from the church. Watching the pair from the corner of her eye, she couldn't help thinking that they were just too cute for words. Libby had kicked off her penny loafers and, with her legs stuck out she was treating Aaron to the sight of her wiggling toes.

"These little piggies are nice and cool—*niiice* and *cooool*—while your toes are all bound up like a Chinaman's. They're probably as sweaty as little hogs. You need to take your shoes off Aaron! It's too hot for socks and shoes."

"But you'll see my feet."

Libby turned at the waist to face him, and while dramatically elongating each word she asked, "Are they cloven?"

"No," he laughed.

"Then show me those tootsies, toots."

Aaron leaned down, slowly untying the shoelaces. "Promise you won't laugh at my long toes."

Leaning along with Aaron and watching the extended ceremony of shoe removal, Libby quipped, "I promise nothing. My concern now is for my unborn children, that they might never forgive me for falling in love with their father's face without ever once wondering what nasty secrets he had hiding inside his shoes."

"Yes, but what about me? I'm in love with a woman with stubby toes!"

"Daddy says my toes are precious little pink peas," Libby said dismissively. "Okay, now the socks." When Aaron made aggravatingly slow work of this task, Libby cried, "Good heavens! This is like watching a strip tease but without the hope of the nudity!"

Laughing helplessly, Aaron collapsed back in the rocker.

Aggravated, Libby took charge, pulling the socks from his feet. "Well, now I swear that I just give up!" she yelped. "Mabel! You've got to see this. Even his idiot feet are beautiful!"

Mabel hid her face behind the fan, her shoulders quivering with mirth. Needing relief from the pair, she managed to say, "If ya'll want to get the vanilla cream bowl outta the ice box an' then pour the cream into the churn, I believe some ice cream surely would go down a treat."

She didn't have to tell them twice. All but leaping out of their chairs, the barefooted pair chased each other for the front door. And characteristic of Libby, she was barking orders. "I'll whip the cream while you go change into your jeans. I don't care how good that washing machine is, vanilla will stain on those infernal white trousers."

The screen door banged shut, and they were gone, leaving Mabel to sit and fan herself while the sun set and peace ensued. In that peace, she thought about Bubba. He was changing. And right before her very eyes, the boy was changing. It was as if he'd found a big bottle of smart pills and had gobbled them down all at once. And now he even had his own truck and the boy was driving all over the place and acting so normal about the whole thing that a person would believe he'd been driving for years!!

***

Mabel wasn't the only one in town to be surprised by Bubba. Mr. Fred, of Fred's Friendly Autos and third cousin to Bubba X, had been set back on his heels as well. Oh, he was used to seeing Bubba turning up on the lot to buy himself an ice cold RC Cola out of the vending chest and then walk around the lot while drinking his soda pop, but Fred had always marked that down to Bubba being fascinated by the sight of the shiny trucks and cars. Kinda like the way a crow picks up discarded shiny things off the ground like shiny trash was some kind of special bird treasure. Bubba never bothered Fred and Fred never bothered Bubba. Hey! A no sale is a no sale and not worth the waste of a minute thinking about it.

Until last week.

As per usual, Bubba turned up at the lot, went straight for the soda chest situated just outside the office front door. Without raising a hair on anyone's head, most especially Fred's balding pate, Bubba put in his nickel, and after running the chosen bottle through its maze like bars and lifting the bottle to freedom, he popped the cap in the chest's built in opener and proceeded to sip his co-cola while aimlessly wandering the lot. And likely as not, making soft *brum-brum* noises, like a child playing with tiny toy cars. However, when glancing out of the office window, Fred did find it unusual that Bubba seemed so taken with the Model T that had just recently been acquired from an estate sale. Well, it wasn't really what anyone would call an *estate*, but it had been a right nice little farm.

The son of the newly deceased and his young family were moving into the farmhouse. The son already had two vehicles. What he needed more than three vehicles was the twenty-five dollars due for the death taxes. (An' wadden't that just like the government to think of taxin' a body just for dyin'?) Well, Fred just happened to have the twenty-five dollars in his pocket, so the deal was struck and he drove off in it, slowly following his mechanic who was driving one of the lot specials they'd used in order to make the trip out to the farm. Once back at the lot, the new purchase had been carefully washed up and Turtle Wax shined and there it had sat with no interest paid to it until the town's idiot-boy turned up and started puttin' his big meaty paws all over it. Which just fried Fred's bacon to a pure old crisp. Throwing his pencil down on his desk, Fred stood and hastened outside to give Bubba X a thorough talkin' to.

As it happened, Bubba was the one to start the talking. Watching Fred beating feet towards him Bubba hailed, "Hey Cousin Fred! What's the askin' price on this here truck?"

The fact that Bubba X was *talking* and not just standing there all dumb and bovine blank-eyed, put the skids on Fred. He knew, as everyone did, that Bubba and his mama were working for the preacher, but even with a job, there was no way Bubba could come up with the seventy-five dollars Fred was asking for that truck. Actually, Fred was only counting on gaining seventy. The extra five was the dickering cushion. Folks got right mad if there was no dickering. They wanted to go away happy, thinking they had gotten the best of the deal. But now here was Bubba, wasting Fred's time and paw-marking the wax shine into the bargain. His momentary surprise of Bubba's initiating a bona fide conversation vanished. Fred was becoming angry again.

"Tha's a seventy-five dollar truck Bubba X!" Fred's stocky legs picked up speed. "An' I'll thank you not to put your big ole hand prints all over it!"

"I'll give ya fifty!" Bubba yelled to his approaching cousin.

Fred put on the skids again. Sticking his balled fists against ample hips, Fred bawled, "You'll do what now?"

Bubba took a pull on the long-necked soda bottle, draining the last of the cola. Then he sucked his teeth as he looked at his thrice-removed cousin. In a milder tone Bubba said, "I'll give ya fifty an' right now, cash money."

Fred experienced the overwhelming sense of Deja Vue. In fact, he felt all sweaty with it. He would have sworn . . . *The Preacher*! The preacher must have done some kind of layin' on of hands that had not only healed Bubba's simple mind but had also imparted some of the slickerin' bits of the preacher's brain into Bubba's empty noggin. *Well, fool me once . . .*

"Now you just look here Bubba Flowers," Fred said, heavily stressing their shared surname, Fred's way of reminding Bubba that they were FAMILY. "That's a real an' honest like-new truck. Hardly got any miles on it an' it's not got one dent nor scratch to its name."

While Fred ranted, Bubba calmly pulled a wad of cash out of his overalls side pocket and silently counted it.

Fred was still belaboring the truck's fine points when the heady perfume of cash threw him off his spiel. "Bubba? Where in the world did you get all that money?"

Still slowly counting the bills Bubba mildly replied, "Saved it."

Fred nervously licked his lips, swallowed hard and then ventured, "You got seventy of them dollars?"

"Nope. Counted twice. I only got fifty-two an' the two dollars I'll be needing for gas."

The exotic aroma of virgin cash so close, and yet so far, far away from his pocket, proved to be Fred's undoing. The voice screaming in his head, *The Preacher's euchring you again*! was ignored. Fred wiped his mouth, then removed his hat and with a handkerchief, he mopped the top of his head. Resettling the hat he said, "Tell ya what Bubba, seein' as how we're close kin, I'll take the fifty an' I'll spot ya the twenty-five, cause, us bein' family an all, I know you'll be good for it."

Bubba put the fifty-two dollar bills back inside the overalls' pocket. Then he shoved his hands in both of the side pockets and treated Fred to one of his very best slack-jawed and blank-eyed expressions. "Well," Bubba said with a deliberate slowness, "this is your world Mr. Fred; I'm just tryin' to live in it. But fifty is all I'm gonna pay for a fifteen-year-old truck. As far as us bein' family, third cousins ain't exactly close kin. Fact is, if you was a woman, I could marry ya."

Euchred! *Euchred*! Fred's screaming brain echoed relentlessly as from his office window he watched Bubba driving the truck off the lot. Seeking solace, Fred picked up the telephone and told the switchboard girl that he wanted Ralph Winters' office. The process only took two minutes, yet they were important minutes that might have allowed Fred to think through his actions because of late, Ralph too had been acting mighty peculiar. Too late Fred realized that there was no hope of being consoled by his old business friend because one split second after he regaled Ralph with the news of Bubba's sudden spurt of shrewdness, Ralph burst into roaring laughter. Fred could clearly hear Ralph banging his fist against his desk with each and every guffaw. A horrified Fred thought that Ralph was sounding a whole lot like a demented hyena, and he had never heard Ralph laugh like that—not about nothing—except maybe a puppy being run over. Okay, maybe not an actual puppy, but Ralph had most assuredly been known to laugh just as hard as he knew how whenever something equally as devastating had befallen a business competitor.

The fact remained that Ralph had most certainly never laughed about the loss of profit for himself or for one of his close friends. Combined with Bubba's sudden onset of extraordinary intelligence and Ralph's highly galling laughter—were enough to convinced Fred that the Preacher was behind every slap dab of it—because this was just way too many spontaneous miracles for any rational man to rationalize away. The clincher came when a wheezing Ralph asked, "An-and did Bubba say you had to put a ten-dollar tithe in the offering plate? Ya know, the building fund can always use—"

Fred slammed the phone down on Ralph.

Two days after the purchase of his truck, Bubba appeared at the mill. He talked to Yancy for a few minutes, then Yancy sent him in to speak to Mr. Ralph. Bubba X looked nervous as Mr. Ralph leaned back in his high-backed swivel chair. Looking at Bubba with a new interest, he carefully listened to everything the former town's Idiot-Boy nervously stammered.

"I can give you a nickel for every throw away plank, Mr. Ralph. I can't give you more than that. Wish I could, but I just can't."

"Whatcha gonna do with the boards, Bubba X?"

"Well," Bubba said hesitantly. "Tha's kind of secret."

"Bubba," Mr. Ralph said gently, "I'm good with secrets. Truth is, I got a slew of 'em myself. You have my sincere promise that whatever you tell me, will stay put right here in this room."

Bubba canted his head to the left. For all of his life he had never once trusted Mr. Ralph, but now, what choice did he have? Bubba heaved a sigh. "Okay, Mr. Ralph. Here's the thing . . ."

Five minutes later, Bubba was back in the yard and carrying a handwritten note that Uncle Yank first carefully read, and then took a hard long look at Bubba. Confusion evident, Yancy said, "This here says I'm to give you whatever you want from the discard boards. That there's no charge ticket needed. How much you wantin'?"

"All of 'em."

"Well good gooble-dee-goo!" Yancy cried. "Tha's a lot of board footage. What in the world do you need all of that for?"

"Mr. Ralph said I didn't have to tell ya."

Yancy was fit to be tied. Bubba had always been special to him, but now Bubba was keeping secrets and Yancy was feeling the wasp sting of rejection. "Well, have it your way then. If Mr. Ralph says you can have 'em, then you take 'em. But he didn't say nothing about anybody helpin' ya with the loadin', so you're on your own Bubba-Boy."

"Tha's fine. I don't wanna be puttin' nobody out. Just point me in the direction of the boards an' I'll do it all myself."

For the next three days Bubba's coming and going from the mill became a regular sight. No one helped him, no one asked him any questions. And from his upstairs office, Mr. Ralph watched from the window and chuckled.

Miss Mabel wasn't the only one curious as to what Bubba was up to. That very afternoon Aaron had spotted Bubba's truck heading along the track that led into the deep woods of the parsonage property. Aaron had never been back there simply because he was afraid of the woods. There were things in there—living things that had teeth and claws, or worse, fangs—therefore, he didn't feel compelled to investigate Bubba's activities. Aaron had merely contented himself with remaining curious. He and Libby were resettled on the porch, sitting on the floorboards and taking turns at the ice cream crank, and Mable was safely out of earshot, busy with cleaning up the mess they had made in her kitchen. Simply a means of making evening conversation, he now brought up the subject.

"Bubba is of late doing something I find a bit odd," he said.

Libby made a light disdaining sound. "Yeah? Well you an everybody else in town. All anybody can talk about is how he just woke up one morning being kinda smart."

The ice cream mixture inside the ice packed metal canister was getting thicker, making the canister's built-in paddles harder to turn, which caused the exterior crank harder to turn. Aaron didn't possess a lot of upper body strength, so the harder the cranking, the more he sweated. "Do me a favor," he panted as he sweated even more profusely. "Throw some more salt on the ice before I completely dislocate my shoulder."

Libby lightly shook the salt scoop over the chipped ice inside the wood barrel and compacted around the central canister. She was being careful about the salt as she mused aloud, "The talk in the beauty shop is that you laid hands on Bubba and preformed a miracle."

Aaron laughed so hard that the crank slipped out of his hand, and not wanting to fool with the thing another second, he said, "I'm calling the ice cream finished."

"Oh, for heaven's sake!" Libby cried as she took up the task. "There's lots more turning room in this. That means that so far all we've got is ice cream soup. The idea is to eat it, not drink it."

Aaron watched Libby's well-formed arm turn the crank with surprising ease. He knew his masculine pride should be wounded, but it wasn't. God had sent Libby into his life to make up for his shortfalls. Aaron wasn't good at typing; Libby was. Aaron's idea of filing was to shove papers and notes around on his desk; Libby put them in created folders. Aaron wasn't good at physical activities; Libby was a tomboy. Conversely, Libby was impatient with people; Aaron had all the time anyone might need when pouring out their woes. Libby saw each new day as a personal challenge; Aaron saw it as an incredible one-time-only, gift. And it was these differences, when put together, that were the cause of

Aaron and Libby fitting together like a hand in a glove. So, instead of being defensive about his lack of gallantry, ice cream crank-wise, he watched her with genuine pride.

I'll bet she could chop wood and have a baby all at the same time. Those would be extremely handy skills should we be sent out into the mission field.

"So?" she asked, her impatient tone intruding into his thoughts. "Did you do it?"

"Did I do what?"

Libby let go of the crank and lightly clobbered Aaron's shoulder. Then speaking very slowly and using little words in the vague hope that he might actually listen to one or two of them, she said, "Did you lay hands on Bubba X?"

"Why would I do that?"

"To make him smart!" she yelled.

Aaron's hands closed on her shoulders as he leaned in so closely that their noses were almost touching. "Listen to me my little sweetheart. I am only a messenger of Christ's gospel. I am not in any shape, way, or fashion, a faith healer." Aaron let go of her and sat back on the porch flooring. "Besides, I don't believe in faith healers."

"Really? Why not?"

Crossing his arms against his chest, Aaron shook his head. "I believe absolutely in the power of prayer as well as miracles. What I don't believe in is charging money, or more politely, 'accepting donations,' from the frightened and the desperate. But that only makes me more afraid for the so-called Faith-Healers, than for those needing a cure. It's a terrible thing to fall into the hands of an angry God, and to perpetrate a carnival hoax in His Name tells me that they have utterly no idea what's awaiting them."

Libby could still feel her bones melting from the warmth of his hands. Her head was feeling a little swimmy too! She had to look away from him before she did something completely brazen, as in, throw him down on the porch floor and kiss the pure fire out of him. And she knew that she could do it too because when it came to muscle, Aaron was a bit on the stringy side. So, while looking away and at nothing in particular, she said, "Fine, you're not a faith healer. But, how do you explain Bubba?"

"Oh, quite easily actually. Bubba X is now and always has been, highly intelligent."

Her head sharply turned in his direction. "Are you crazy?" Libby screeched. "Bubba has always been the town half-wit!"

"Yes," Aaron agreed. "That was my primary impression as well. But as an outsider, and as I came to know him, I could more easily see the real Bubba whenever his mask slipped."

"Mask," Libby said dully. "Bubba has been wearing a mask?"

"Yes, and quite effectively really. I imagine it's worked to his advantage in no end of ways."

"Such as?" she demanded.

"As in always being ignored when people were expressing their honest opinions in confidence and, presumably, in private. Being able to work at what interests him and not having to work at more boring jobs just because he felt forced. Everyone's low expectations left him completely free to develop all sorts of interests. And he did. But on several occasions, he's given himself away, as in offering sound advice when sound advice was badly needed. Then there have been the times when he was sitting in the car with me and looking out the passenger window. While he was doing that, I watched his feet. Whenever my feet pressed the brake and the clutch peddles, his feet mirrored mine.

"It was always in those unguarded moments when who we really are is fully exposed. That is why I wasn't surprised that Bubba could drive. Oh, and how can we forget the installation of the washing machine? It was Bubba who worked out the plumbing calculations and he did all of those mathematical calculations in his head. There are more examples I could cite, but there's no need, it's sufficient to say that Bubba isn't stupid; that he is in fact quite intelligent. And his intelligence is because of God alone and nothing to do with me. But there is a new thing that he's been doing lately that has me most curious."

Libby was still trying to wrap her mind around this boggling revelation. In a colorless tone she asked, "Curious about . . . what?"

"I'd like to know where he's taking all that lumber he's hauling in his truck."

This comment instantly perked Libby up. Her eyes flashed with their customary light and her sagging body straightened. "Daddy said something about lumber! He said that Mr. Ralph was giving Bubba all of the mill's irregular planks. Daddy couldn't get boo out of Bubba and all Mr. Ralph would say is that he could have all the boards he wanted to haul away. That doesn't make any sense because the mill usually sells that kind of planking to folks wanting fencing board. Is it possible that Bubba's building a fence?"

"Out in the woods?" Aaron laughed. "Why would the pastorate need a fence in the woods?"

"Are you talking about the woods behind this property?"

"Yes. Bubba drives by the house three and sometimes four times a day. Going in the truck is full of boards and coming out the truck is always empty."

"And he's driving the old track?"

"Yes."

Libby became thoughtful for a few moments. Then she started working the churn's crank handle, her mind as busy as the turning canister. Finally, she gave voice to her ponderings. "Those were once old Grandpa Flowers' woods. The church property fronts it and then the creek runs right behind it. Nobody has thought about that spit of land for decades. There's only about five acres of it and most of those are boggy. As a member of the Flowers family, Bubba has as much right to that land as I do. But we've all considered those woods to be less than worthless."

"Yes," Aaron grinned, "and aren't you the very same people who thought Bubba was simple?"

Libby gasped sharply. Then she gave Aaron a squinty look of disapproval. "Well I'll tell you what we're going to do Mr. Smarty Pants. We're gonna take this churn back in to Mabel and then you and I are taking a little walk in the woods."

"But it's really, really dark now."

"Oh hush! I promise I won't let anything eat you. Now help me tote this ice cream freezer into the kitchen."

It really was quite dark. Now and then the crescent moon peeked through the Spanish moss draped trees. As they walked the hardpan track, they carried between them the elongated handle of the barn lantern. A single candle burned inside the glass walls of the black wrought iron frame. In order to break the unnerving spell of the too many noises that Aaron couldn't identify, he asked Libby the point of having a lantern that hung so closely to their shod feet. All around his head and shoulders there was nothing but suffocating darkness, whereas the flickering light near his ankles treated him to the sight of his beloved cowboy boots and Libby's penny loafers.

"Well," she replied, and much too lightly for his tastes, "when you're walking in the country, it's just as a good an idea to see what you don't want to be stepping on. Snakes are Louisiana's number one critter; gators are number two. Both love old track roads."

"Why?"

She chuckled and said, "Hardpan's just easier to slither and crawl, I guess. The idea of a long-handled lamp is, that the light will be so close to the ground that varmints can't help but see it and will crawl off and hide."

"And that works?"

"So far."

"Libby Flowers!" Aaron yelped. "You're like a roller coaster. You build up hope only to send it plummeting down again."

"That's funny," she giggled.

"There's nothing funny about what you're doing to my nervous condition—"

"Hush!" she suddenly demanded. She stopped moving and Aaron, worrying about what might be using the old road with them, stopped with her. "Do you hear that?" she asked, her voice now whispery.

Aaron was turning his head in all directions, but he saw nothing but black and he heard nothing other than his flailing heartbeat. Keeping his voice low he asked, "This something that you think you're hearing, does it sound like . . . hissing?"

"No! It's banging."

"Oh. Then that would be my heart."

"It is not your heart you big goof. I'm hearing the sound of hammering. That means we're getting close to Bubba and that he's building something."

She wrenched the lamp's handle out of Aaron's hand and scampering off to the side of the track, she set the lantern on the track's grassy verge. Coming back to him, she grabbed his hand and pulled him forward. The diminishing light of the stationary lantern helped to keep them on course. But when they rounded the gradual curve of the road, the meager light was lost, and they were immediately inside absolute blackness. Libby in the lead, continued forward, Aaron the reluctant drag-along. He was a breath away from calling a halt to the adventure when—hallelujah!—lights were shining through the outlying trees. With each step forward, it began to seem as if they were heading toward a bonfire. Or rather, several bonfires.

"He better not be slappin' up a still," Libby said, huffing out each word. "Daddy will tear his hind-end up if he is."

Bubba was not building a still.

As they came fully into the light of the large pitch torches, they saw a square structure balanced on tall bricked pilasters. The mysterious structure looked to be supporting the beginnings of a roof. Bubba was coming down the fronting steps when he saw them standing between two of the torches stuck into the newly cleared ground of what would one day be a verdant lawn and a rose garden. But at the present, the torches only highlighted newly cut tree stumps and a lot of tire ruts.

Bubba froze on the middle stair.

In a playground bullying sing-song drawl Libby called out, "Whatcha doin' Cousin *Buuub-ba*?"

Bubba, shirtless under his overalls, sat down on the upper riser and answered guiltily, "Runnin' away from home."

Chapter Seventeen

In Bubba's truck, the only one doing the talking was Libby. Seated between the two stone quiet men, she was really spraying the words around. She didn't even pause for breath when Bubba stopped the truck, and Aaron retrieved the barn lamp. Libby was still talking when he climbed back inside the cab. He could feel Bubba's pleading stare, but Aaron scrupulously avoided eye contact. In Aaron's mind, if Bubba X felt he was old enough to run away from his mama, perhaps he should begin with the lesser trial of running away from his little cousin. And if he survived that, then odds were favorable for his surviving his mother's notable histrionics.

Jesus correctly said that there were none so blind as those who refused to see. Aaron had told Libby less than two hours ago that Bubba was intelligent, this truth enhanced by seeing Bubba's capabilities for herself. Evidence aside, she was dressing him down as if he were little more than a hapless imbecile. But Aaron couldn't entirely fault Libby. A lifelong lie doesn't die in a blink. Bubba was responsible for the lie, and he was responsible for making it right.

And all by himself.

"Mother of Pearl!" Bubba finally yelled, slamming his hand against the steering wheel. "Cousin Libby would you just shut up!?"

Well, though far from diplomatic, Bubba's solution was . . . effective.

Libby looked thunderstruck. Aaron's hand quickly covered his mouth as he looked beyond the rolled down window as if he'd just spotted something in the darkness that was of keen interest. The parsonage was still a distance ahead, but as the glow of the porch lamps became more visible, Bubba stopped the truck.

"Pastor Aaron?" Bubba said, his voice an apologetic whine. "Would you mind awful bad walking from here? I'd like to speak with my cousin in private."

Aaron opened the cab door and, once outside, and while as he was closing the door, he said, "Take all the time you need, Bubba."

Aaron walked away, the twin headlights giving him an ethereal glow. The only thing recognizable about Aaron's backside was his trademark blonde hair, otherwise, with his white T-shirt, jeans and cowboy boots, he looked like any other LaSalle Parish boy taking a lonesome walk in the moonlight.

One thought triggered another, and Bubba said almost tenderly as he watched Aaron, "Hey Lib? Have you noticed how much folks in Henrytown have started to change since Aaron's come here?"

"I'm certainly noticing a whopper of a change in you!" she snapped.

"I ain't talkin' about me," he sighed. "I am what I've always been. I'm talkin' about Miss Cornelia, Mr. Ralph, Seth Lewis an' even your own daddy. It's folks like them that have changed. Me, I'm just a fraud. But watchin' other people changing for the better made me think that maybe it was time for me stop bein' a fraud."

"Well why in the world would you even want to play dumb in the first place?"

"Mama." He said with a shrug of his massive, shirtless shoulders. "She's had a hard life. I was her very last baby, so she kinda treated me like I was her little pet, and that seemed to make her happy, so I just played along. Then when I got to school age, nobody expected me to be anything besides quiet, so I did that too. An' then the older I got the more scared I got about being anything else. But since Pastor Aaron's come here, I think I come to know that me pleasing the low opinions of other people is a big insult to God. It was Him who made me a pretty smart fella, so me hidin' it was just what Aaron preached about—you remember—the sermon on how not using our talents was just like puttin' a lamp under a bushel basket, an' that if we hid who God intended us to be, we weren't helpin' nobody, especially not ourselves?"

A tear streamed Libby's face as her pride and her respect for her older cousin began to grow. To ward off the threat of her rather infamous wailing, she pressed her lips into a hard line and concentrated on really listening to Bubba; as in, hearing the very real voice of the very real man whom she was literally meeting for the very first time.

"I thought about that sermon Lib. Then I prayed on it. Then after a while it come to me that I didn't want to be Mama's pet no more, that I just couldn't go on insultin' God. That's when I decided it was time for me to be a grown-up man an' that grown up men look after themselves an' live in their own houses. So," he shrugged again. "There you go. That's the reason I'm buildin' me my very own house."

Libby tenderly placed her hand on her cousin's bare arm. "Even in the darkness I could see that it's going to be a wonderful house, Bubba."

He immediately brightened. "But, you'll still come see it in the sunshine won't ya? You promise?"

"I promise," she smiled as she hugged him.

There were about a hundred developing current events in the town and in the state that the coffeeshop lollygaggers could have chosen to discuss over their coffee, served with a smile and a generous dose of patience in the Bayou (local pronunciation, *Bye-ya*) Café. Topic number one could have been the ongoing news reports of the Dust Bowl disaster getting worse, as in the topsoil of the Midwest states was now covering the buildings and pavements of Chicago and New York City. Topic number two could also be the grim reality of the national economy close to all out collapse, and topic number three was the prevailing rumors of Senator Huey P. Long being in a death grip feud with the most prominent men in Louisiana. Then, when those topics ran dry, there was always the topic of the truly phenomenal growth of the Free Church. That new preacher was such a corker that the congregation was even bulging out of the temporary tent. But not one word of any of these principal topics were being discussed. No sir. What had the café patrons all in a flap was the truly astonishing news that Bubba X Flowers had suddenly gone from being slap stupid to slap genius.

It was this discussion that the café waitress, Myrna Dupree, found entirely interesting. Myrna was a quiet careworn woman who had only just recently turned thirty and about four years senior to the subject of the discussion. A five-year widow of a Cajun fella who'd died in his own vomit after a hard week of drinking poisoned still-whiskey, Myrna was pragmatic enough to know that her chances of finding another husband in a little backwater town ranged from slim to nonexistent. She didn't personally know Bubba, but she'd always seen him around. Bubba was always alone, walking to or from some store or another.

Just like Myrna.

Their mutual aloneness was what had drawn her eye. And then there had been that one day when she'd noticed him in front of the movie theater. He didn't see her because he was intently staring at the colorful poster advertising the new feature movie that was starring Mickey Rooney. And while studying the poster, Bubba had smiled. After that day, she began to think it was such a shame that he was simple minded because he had, in her opinion, just about the nicest smile that God had ever stamped on a man's face. True, he was on the portly side, but her late husband had had him some more than ample meat on his bones, so Bubba's weight had not been the deterrent. Nope; what had stopped Myrna from putting herself in Bubba's path was his feeble-minded nature. So, hearing that Bubba was suddenly smart enough to slicker Mr. Fred and then somehow slicker Mr. Ralph out of free lumber from the mill, from which he was said to be building a big house for himself (a thing also said to be just about to be killing Miss Mabel half to death), well, that was a bit of gossip which peeked Myrna's interest to no end.

"You know it was that there new preacher who wrought this divine miracle on Bubba X, don't-cha?" one old buzzard said to the table filled with other old buzzards.

Myrna quietly refilled the coffee cups as all buzzards agreed this to be a stone fact. As Myrna was about to leave the table, she paused just long enough to ask in her customary soft and shy way, "What time does that church meet on a Sunday?"

"What you wanna know that for girl?" Buzzard #1 asked, eyeing her up and down.

Holding the emptied pot in her hands, Myrna looked down at it as she said, "I don't know. I ain't never held much with churchin', so maybe that church ya'll are all talkin' about won't even want me."

Her humble nature struck their old hearts. Buzzard #1 was downright tender when he said, "Little girl! They'll throw their arms around your pretty neck is what they'll do. Them people love ever'body an' they'll probably love you goodest of all!"

The very next Sunday, Myrna Dupree was in the church tent and sitting on the pallets that were spread over the mown grass. Myrna did not own a vehicle, so she'd set out on foot from her little rental house that was set back on the edge of Henrytown. She was just walking by the Methodist church when a truck headed in the direction of the Free Church, and loaded to the gunnels with a crowd of people, stopped and offered her a lift. It had been a friendly squeeze in the flatbed, but everyone acted glad to have her. For the first time in too many years, Myrna didn't feel alone.

Myrna and some of her truck companions paused briefly to look at the church. The walls and roof were up, and the window frames looked as if they were just waiting for glass. "Won't be long now!" someone said. That pronouncement was rapidly followed by a chorus of "Praise God!" Then there was a stampede down the gentle incline toward the big blue tent. Myrna followed the thundering herd. Once under the tent's shading cover and being mindful of where she stepped, she sat down as close to Bubba Flowers as the crowd permitted. After the service, she was greeted with a welcoming hug from the church members and, when Bubba hugged her, their eyes locked for a second and Myrna experienced a distinct click. It was too much to hope that maybe Bubba felt it too. It was inside this moment when the preacher had spoken to the crowd:

"God wants to be involved in every aspect of our lives. There is nothing too big or too small for Him. He is a God who can create the highest mountains and the deepest oceans and then create the smallest and most delicate flowers. So, we can trust Him absolutely with all of our cares and all of our deepest hopes and dreams."

That preacher did not look like a liar, so Myrna took a chance. Sunday evening, Myrna had a long talk with God. She poured it all out, her loneliness, her feelings of inadequacy, her heartbreaks and her many disappointments. She laid it all at His feet, and then she sobbed for how long she just didn't know. It was only when she crawled into bed that she remembered that she'd wanted to talk to Him about Bubba. But by then she was so emotionally drained that she simply put out the light and fell asleep.

The very next morning—Monday—Bubba was driving through Henrytown. He was an hour too early to meet with Mister Wayne who had agreed to talk to him about the sheets of roofing tin that Bubba needed for his house. And since he was way too early for the meeting, Bubba just up and decided to stop in at the café for a cup of coffee and maybe a bacon biscuit.

Myrna's face lit up like a marquee when she spotted Bubba walking into the café. He took a seat on one of the counter stools. She was dutifully writing up his order when he said, "Didn't I see you at service yesterday?"

"Yes, you did," she replied. And after that—oh my—they had just the nicest conversation.

Monday turned to Tuesday, and on Tuesday morning Aaron was driving from the grocery store, the car loaded with Mabel's listed items. As he passed by Miss Cornelia's, he happened to see the lady herself standing on her front porch greeting the Tuesday Morning Stitchery ladies. They all spotted Aaron as well and they playfully waved for him to stop and join them.

Trapped.

But if he didn't stop in for a cup of coffee with the "girls," he knew he'd never hear the end of it. With a wearied sigh, he parked in front of Miss Cornelia's house, and to their near giddy cries of welcome, he walked the pavement dividing the neatly trimmed lawn.

Miss Cornelia was nothing if not efficient. Within minutes she had every lady set up with individual small tables containing all of the stitchery accoutrements as well as delicate china cups filled with coffee and petit fours plates containing tasty nibbles. When all ladies were well into their stitching and nibbling, Aaron broached a subject that he'd long wanted to discuss with her.

Keeping his voice low he said, "Miss Cornelia? What exactly can you tell me about the baptistery window?"

Without revealing so much as a flicker of emotion she replied in that smoothly sophisticated way of hers, “Pastor? I’m so honored that you would stop by to see my roses. They truly have bloomed gloriously this year.” And with that, she led him through the French windows and into the garden that was fragrant with the perfume of roses.

They walked the gravel path between the rose beds, bees busily working the perfect blooms. Miss Cornelia’s chin was lifted skyward as she avoided looking directly at Aaron. While they walked in silence, he studied her remarkable profile. Even in advancing age, the woman was stunning. In her youth she must have been amazing. Perhaps Ralph and Yancy were right all along; a poor dirt farmer and a beautiful heiress could have had no connection whatsoever. He was on the verge of apologizing for having taken up her time when her voice, as faint as the hum of the bees, met his ear.

“My parents raised me to be frightfully aware of our class, and as a member yourself, you surely know that we never divulge nor explain.”

“What I’m hearing inside all of this,” he said with a chuckle, “is that you have no intention of ever telling me anything you might happen to know regarding the baptistery window.”

“Your hearing, young sir, is indeed finely tuned.”

She stopped and directed his attention toward a particularly stunning rose bush, the blooms huge and bright with a unique blend of vibrant orange and ruby red. “I bred that rose. I have a potting house at the end of this pathway. I spent many years grafting various types until I had just the color mix that I wanted. So far, it’s the only rose bush of its type in existence. It has to mature a bit more before I can trust it enough to cultivate additional cuttings.”

“Have you named your rose?”

“Yes,” she said as she turned them back in the direction of the house. “I’ve decided to call it, *Unrequited.*” Then with a bright smile she said, “Rather suits the color, wouldn’t you agree?”

And the distinctive red and orange tones vaguely reminded him of something familiar, what, he couldn’t put a name to. Still, the name she’d chosen for her rose did indeed seem rather perfect. On reaching the house, Aaron paused on the slate-stone veranda. Bringing her hand close to his face he bowed at the waist. As his lips timidly brushed the back of her hand he murmured, “Good day to you my lovely lady.”

“And to you Pastor.”

He watched as she turned away and passed through the French windows. He clearly understood that a woman of character would never confide her precious memories, for the very reason that once confided, the memories would no longer be exclusively hers.

***

He had been six years her senior when she first saw him walking in the very garden that she had just walked with Pastor Aaron. Archibald Lofthouse had been a grown man of twenty-two and she, newly turned sixteen. It had been her Coming Out season and the entire household was in a frenzy with the preparations for her formal presentation into Louisiana Society. The season, and her presentation, both culminating with the Debutantes’ Ball in New Orleans. But oh, the maddening dreariness of the preparation. Two seamstresses were constantly accosting her with new patterns, new materials and endless fittings. Added to the misery was Mother’s ceaseless twittering around like an agitated sparrow. The cool spring morning was ruined for her with the boredom of the final fitting of the debutante’s traditional white evening dress. The bedroom’s French windows that allowed access to the balcony stood open and she could clearly hear father in the garden below. He was being extremely loud, shouting about the blasted flagstones and the blasted moles having made them all out of kilter. Father could be quite comical when he was upset. He never meant to be, he simply was. While the seamstresses worked in tandem at pinning her up like a doll, and she on a stool with her raised arms stuck straight out to the sides, she chanced a peak through the bedroom windows.

She easily saw her father striding through the garden, still thundering on about the blasted flagstones and the blasted moles, "double damn and blast their sightless eyes!" During his amusing outburst, he was being obediently followed by an older man. The older man, in turn, was being followed by a younger man who, even from a distance, caused the oddest reaction in Cornelia.

He had the most extraordinary hair. In the sunlight it shone with such an intense red and gold that she really couldn't force her eyes away. He must have felt himself being spied on because he looked up and caught her staring down at him. Cornelia's heart skipped, then slammed against her tightly corseted ribcage. He was shatteringly handsome. There was also, as Father would have said, a bit of the "Olde Puck" about him. Meaning that Father would view him as a born mischief maker. In order to maintain the stare between them, he began walking backwards as he continued following the other men. Then he smiled, and oh my heavens, his smile was glorious. The next thing she knew, he was throwing his arms wide as if daring her to make a leap for it; and that if she did, he would readily catch her. That her expression turned to alarm struck him as incredibly funny. Bent on scandalizing her further, he then began to urge her on with quick, short waves of his hands. She tossed her head, indicating she would do no such thing. Lifting her chin also treated him to the sight of her splendid profile. He should have been immediately smitten by the sight of her best feature, and yes, immediately become her senseless devotee. (Well, since she'd turned thirteen, there were so many young swains who were.) However, instead of pledging her his heart, wealth, liver, kidneys and spleen, he merely tossed his hands in surrender and left her to enjoy her day of captivity. And then she lost sight of him as he disappeared among the long shadows of the house.

"Who is that red haired young man with my father?" Cornelia asked softly.

The head seamstress, busy with the hem alterations and with straight pins clasped between her teeth said matter-of-factly, "Only redheaded young man I know of Miss, is Archie Lofthouse. Bit of a hellion that boy. But he's a good worker, so's there's that. Young Archie will see your father's fair done by. Turn please Miss. We need to be measurin' the front of you now."

Cornelia stood in that dress for another hour. When she was about to swoon, the two seamstresses opened the windows even wider so that she would have more cooling air while they finished the last of the pinning. It was then that she could hear his vibrant young voice drifting up towards her, and simply hearing him laugh and tease the older man he'd been following along the grounds, was enough to keep her contently quiet during the final process of playing the dress shop mannequin.

Two months. That was all the time she'd had to get to know Archie Lofthouse. At the end of those months, his work in the garden was finished and she, only a day away from being spirited off to New Orleans. But those two months had been more than enough time for the pair to fall completely and desperately in love. Their mutual misfortune was having been born into an era when the classes were forbidden to mix.

In New Orleans, Cornelia made her stunning debut and was earnestly sought after by many young men of distinguished families. But only the man she wanted was working on a sharecrop farm, and he was about to be matched with the neighbor's daughter.

He and Miss Cornelia would never see each other again. But he kept a small lock of her hair in his pocket watch just as she kept a lock of his bright red hair hidden away inside her cameo broach. When decades later he fell gravely ill, his one deathbed request was that he be buried with his watch. Cornelia had no way of knowing his final request, but nevertheless, she had likewise listed in her will that she was to be buried in her favorite blue dress and with the cameo she had so faithfully worn every day of her life.

Now, mercifully, there was another Archie in her life. If he had been her very own grandson, she couldn't have adored him more. And there would be nothing less than the very best for her Young Archie. And to that end, she said a silent prayer as she took up her pen and wrote a letter to her second cousin in Baton Rouge.

Chapter Eighteen

Emma Templeton was a lively, bright and attractive, ultra-glamorous modern girl. She'd newly turned eighteen-years-old and she was driving her mother—literally, and—in a white roadster—to tears. Gracia Templeton, second cousin to Miss Cornelia Faraday and fifteen years Miss Cornelia's junior, wasn't one for histrionics. Instead, she was a martyr to migraines. The day after Emma graduated high school she'd been given by her father, Preston Templeton, the gift of the white roadster. Subsequently, Gracia hadn't known a migraine free day. Adding to the agony was Emma's announcement that she had no immediate college ambitions. Nor did she seem prone toward any other ambitions. All she did was attend parties and roar around in that stupid car. Amid all of this headache riddled pandemonium came the unexpected letter from her elderly maiden-lady cousin.

The letter didn't surprise her. Cousin Cornelia was known for keeping a sharp eye on her relatives. Well, other than standing on the outside and observing the more interesting lives of kith and kin, what other activity did the old dear have? Therefore, Cornelia's unexpected letters habitually cropped up throughout the family. Gracia dismissively assumed that receiving such a letter meant that this had simply been her turn. And yet, the invitation for Emma to visit in order "to properly celebrate her recent graduation," as Cousin Cornelia had put it, did hold the heady pong of respite. The invitation was intended for a two week visit but, Cousin Cornelia also intimated that Emma would be more than welcome to stay longer. Henrytown, she'd added, was simply so charming and the young people so very wholesome and cordial that, "I can well imagine your Emma falling in love with this small section of Louisiana."

Gracia could well imagine Emma rattling around inside that big old house and putting up with the frail attentions of an old lady only just long enough to La-De-Dah it over the less cultured bayou rubes. After successfully making others feel less about themselves, if not forcibly run out of town on a rail, she'd come roaring happily home. Emma might possibly survive Henrytown, (and visa-versa) the maximum of two days. But at this point, two days of peace seemed like bliss, so without further ado, she hurriedly penned the acceptance note and had the maid rushing out to the post office.

She had been braced for a fight at the dinner table when she broke the news of Emma's pending departure from hearth and home. Both daughter Emma and husband Preston had listened to her small speech quite attentively. And when she finished, Preston was opening his mouth to protest the absence of their only—and thoroughly precocious—daughter, when said precocious daughter cut him off.

"That sounds a perfect hoot! I'd love to spend some time with the old darling. She's utterly fascinating, don't you agree?"

Preston tried, "I-I don't know if I'd bandy the term *fascinating*—"

"Oh, come on Pops! The most beautiful woman this state has ever known locking herself away for yonks and yonks, only to reemerge in her retiring years. It makes me wonder if during all of those lost years she'd been playing the Lady Chatterley tableau."

Gracia began to strangle. And on mashed potatoes of all things.

"Think about it Mommy," Emma continued ruthlessly while her mother choked and fought for her life by gulping down the entire glass of water. "All this time that the family's been pitying poor ole Cornelia, she's been happily dallying with the gardener. He must have gone toes up in the flower patch or something, which just might be the cause of her reemergence."

"My impudent child," Preston said firmly. "You watch far too many tasteless films. This is not a film. Your great-Cousin Cornelia is a well-respected lady who has never once put a foot wrong in proper society. She has been gracious in issuing a lovely invitation and you will not sully that invitation with unseemly pretenses."

"Daddy, you've just made the whole thing seem boring," Emma pouted. "And now I don't want to go at all."

"You leave at the end of the week," Gracia managed to say. "I've already sent the acceptance letter. And do sit up straight in your chair. When you hunch you look like a blond gargoyle."

Aaron came rushing into the office, already late for his next appointment, which was a homebound and bedside situation, therefore he had to retrieve his Bible. Libby knew better than to get in his way when he was in a mad dash, so she remained at her little desk and simply spoke over the noise of his crashing about in his desk that he never once allowed her to touch or organize. Consequently his desk-top was a rat's nest. Hence, the crashing around.

"Two items of interest," she yelled. "First, Casper, Archie and Seth are on their way home for their three week furlough. Second, a package came by special delivery. The postage mark says it's from Atlanta."

Aaron whirled around. He looked excited. "Where is it?"

Pointing with the eraser end of her pencil she answered, "It's there somewhere. I placed it where you would see it. I wasn't to know that you would charge in here and start tossing everything. It's a very small package, so you better keep hunting. Pretend it's an Easter egg."

Aaron was busily rifling the desk-top when he said tersely, "It's not an Easter egg. It's your blasted engagement ring."

"What?" she squawked, propelling herself out of the chair. An instant later she was by his side and madly hunting right along with him. "Why didn't you tell me you were getting me a ring?"

"I wanted it to be a pleasant surprise."

"Well surprise!" she jeered. "Now it's lost somewhere in this mess. Why will you never allow me to spring clean your desk?"

"A man has to have something that's all his own. My desk is my something."

"Not when there's a ring in it for me it isn't!"

"I've found it!" he cried, holding the package in his hand. "Oh look, and there's my Bible. Whatever is it doing shoved all the way into the back corner?"

Libby snatched the package out of his hand. "I don't care. I want to see my ring."

Aaron forcibly took the package away from her. "Libby Flowers, this is something that must be done properly."

He had to fend her off as she cried, "Properly, shmroperly. Gimme, gimme, gimme!"

Aaron could be aggravatingly stern when he wanted to be. "No, we're doing this properly or not at all. Kindly take a seat please." And to prove he wouldn't be bullied, he didn't make a move to open the package until she complied. During the scant amount of time required to carefully remove the packaging, he told her a story.

"I telephoned my parents almost two weeks ago and informed them of our engagement plans. Mother wept, Father blustered, blah, blah, blah. Other than that, the upshot was Mother agreeing to send along Grandmother's ring. Hers was a ring that has been in the family since before poor Old Mad George lost England the Colonies of America. It arrived in Georgia on the ship from London and worn, on the hand of the then newest Brooks bride. It has been passed down in our line of the

Brooks family ever since. My mother wore the ring until her fingers became a bit arthritic. Or so she said. Quite honestly, her fingers have always looked perfectly fine to me. At any rate, she put it away until such time it was to be passed along to my bride."

The package wrapping was discarded and lying on the bare wood of the office floor. In the center of Aaron's palm sat a small silver box encrusted with tiny amethyst gems. Tears were blinding Libby's eyes as Aaron went down on one knee and extended the valuable little box. "Miss Libby Flowers, would you be ever so kind enough to grant me the singular honor, as well as the greatest joy, of consenting to become my wife?"

Libby couldn't contain herself. She bolted out of the chair and into his arms, hugging him for all she was worth as she sobbed quite loudly against his neck.

"This is a yes, is it?" He felt her nodding furiously as she continued her highly vocal weeping. "Really darling, I'm absolutely awestruck by your enthusiasm, but wouldn't you like to see the pretty ring?" Libby's answer was one of her dreadful, middle ear piercing, bawls. Aaron's cheeks puffed as he blew a long stream of air from his mouth. "Well, perhaps in a moment then." He wrapped both arms around her and held onto her as they stood on their knees in, what turned out to be, a very lengthy embrace.

In the early morning of Tuesday, August 15, 1935 the boys—Seth, Casper and Archie—happily climbed onto the train. They were headed off for home and, for three whole weeks. The new camp was ideal and the townsfolk of Sterlington more than amiable, but they were Henrytown born and bred and they couldn't wait to get there. After what seemed like an endless journey, but only actually involved three hours—scheduled stops on the line and the detraining and cargo loading times included—the train finally pulled into the sparse Henrytown depot, and they quickly thundered to exit the train as if in a run for their lives. Standing on the platform, Yancy did what he always did when he saw the boys come off the train. He gave thanks to the Lord that the boys were all home again safe and sound. The second thing was to break out in hard laughter because no one could fall out of a train car quite like those three. If those boys were the Keystone Cops, the sight of their stampeding method of detraining couldn't have been funnier.

It was mighty cramped in the truck cab, but four happy men gladly squeezed in together. "Whadda ya boys want to do?" Yancy asked. "It's only about ten thirty, plenty of time for a little sightseeing before dinner-time if ya'll would like to give that a whirl."

Archie, pushed up hard against the passenger door, spoke for the group. "Mr. Yancy? What kind of sights can we see that we haven't already seen over a go-zillion times?"

Yancy craned around to face Archie as he chuckled. "There's one fair old doozy of a sight. It's the new church building. Wanna give it a gander?"

"I'm game," Seth said.

"Well yes, Daddy," Casper said. "You're only gonna take us over there whether we want to go or not."

"Tha's a fact," Yancy replied. "Seth? Move your knee a bit son. I'm fixin' to slam the gears into third."

"Oh, sweet Lord!" Casper wailed. "Everybody hang on. Daddy's gonna blast us up to thirty miles per. I pray I don't pee myself in the excitement."

"Amen to that," Yancy laughed.

Yancy looked as if he couldn't be prouder of anything in his life while the other three stood and gawked, all three of them speechless.

The church grounds were in a high gear of activity, and everywhere there was the strident noises of sawing and hammering. All of it punctuated by the voices of the nearly fifty men who were applying themselves to the business of heavy construction. The walls were up, and the fronting porch looked wider than most houses. Six four-by- fours acted as temporary columns for the porch roof that was, like the main roof, still in skeletal form. The windows were framed in, but as yet there wasn't any glass. Also missing were the front entrance doors. The thing seemed to just split off from itself in four different directions in the back area, while the front, the main sanctuary, had been completely swallowed up by the new construction.

Seth asked the question that he and the other two were all thinking. "What in the world is Aaron building? A Redneck cathedral?"

"I told ya it was a doozy," Yancy crowed. "But to be truthful, the whole thing has kinda snowballed on the boy. He just wanted plain and simple. It's everybody else tha's been fancying it up. We even got them whaddayacall colored glass windows coming in. An anonymous contributor went an' paid to have them special made."

"Well who did a thing like that?" Archie cried.

Yancy shook his head. "Son, the word *anonymous* means, don't nobody know. What we do know is that the window for the baptistery has been dedicated to the memory of your granddaddy."

"You have got to be kiddin' me," Archie said in disbelief.

"Well, I ain't. Mr. Ralph showed us deacons the paid in full bill. An' on it was the dedication to the memory of Archibald Lofthouse."

"My old grandpaw?" Archie said in a stupefied tenor.

"Tha's the only Archibald Lofthouse we know of. That is, except for you. An' you ain't a memory. You're still alive an' a big old pain in everybody's backside, so whoever our anonymous is, he ain't meanin' you." Yancy shoved his hands deep into pockets as he took a long and loving look at the distant building. “Gotta be someone from the olden times,” he mused aloud. “Tha’s all any of us can figure. Someone Old Archie must have done a big favor for, like saved his life or some such. It would be just like Old Archie never to brag about doin’ something like that. So, unless Mr. Anonymous steps forward an’ offers up a stirring testimony, I guess we’ll never know the truth of it.”

“Does my family know about this?”

“Yeah, an’ they’re in just as much of a quandary as the rest of us.”

“I-I just don’t know what to say to all of this,” Archie stammered.

“Well,” Yancy shrugged. “Those are the very best times to say nothing at all.”

The four remained silent for about five minutes and then Seth asked, “How’s Aaron?”

Yancy chuckled in his chest. “Oh, he’s a whirlwind that boy. Libby’s working for him full time now and even she can’t hardly keep up with him. But the deacon committee’s got a surprise for both of them. We’ve just unanimously voted him in as our permanent pastor.”

“That’s great!” the three said in unison.

“Well, we kinda had to. If we hadn’t, every man-jack in this town would have strung us up. Folks around here purely love Pastor Aaron.” Yancy turned at the waist, a smile twitching his lips, his eyes squinting slightly. “An’ speakin of surprises, I gotcha some even bigger news about Bubba X . . .”

It was close to five p.m. when Aaron drove the road to home. It had been a very busy day. There had been the homebound visits, and then the drive to Myrtle Hedge’s Regent Hospital to visit with three different church members who were either extremely ill or locked in the drama of bringing a baby into the world. However, the expectant father had been harder to counsel than all of the sick people cobbled together. At the end of it, Aaron came out of the father's waiting room reeking of cigar and cigarette smoke, as well as feeling desperately ill from smoke inhalation. He'd then stopped off at the Methodist church where Rev. Waite had kindly helped him wash the taste of tobacco out of his mouth by readily supplying him with glass after glass of iced tea. The outcome of their meeting was that both churches would hold weekly suppers to feed those in need, a good balanced meal. Sad truth be told, the weekly church supper would most probably be the only balanced meal many of the families would enjoy from one week to the next.

The two pastors even decided to name the weekly event, Stone Soup Supper; after the old fable about a wandering trickster who came into a medieval peasant village with nothing more in his pocket than a supposedly magical stone that he claimed would transform plain boiling water into a vat of delicious soup. All the villagers had to do was provide the boiling pot and water and, if they felt inclined, a spare onion, a potato and perhaps a scrap of bacon; whatever they might have to contribute. And then, thanks entirely to the stone, everyone would eat like a king.

And that's what the weekly meals would be all about, everyone offering something to feed an entire community of souls having to endure endless meals of little more than cornbread and clabber—a thickened and partially soured milk concoction. Aaron was offered some of the stuff by those families who wanted to provide him something during his visit, but they'd had nothing else. It was disgusting but nourishing, and he was always careful never to take very much of it for fear the many children would be left to go to bed hungry.

He was close to home when he decided to pull in for a quick look at today's progress on the church. He'd all but just stepped out of his parked car and was crossing the work-zone yard when he heard familiar voices. Looking up he saw three shirtless men waving to him from the roof. And with a happy cry, he started running as Seth, Archie and Casper began making their way down the tall ladder.

It was indeed a very happy reunion. Aaron had missed them all so terribly. They were his brothers more than his friends. As the four locked arms in a group hug, Aaron never wanted to let any of them go. This emotional sensation offered a small inkling of how Jesus must have felt about His beloved disciples. The realization that He would too soon be leaving them all behind must have been crushing. But oh, that heavenly reunion, how glorious! Aaron broke the group hug and began hugging each one individually.

Her house was filled with ladies again. Of late, it seemed as if it was always filled with women. With the church expansion, the need for cushions had expanded right along with the architecture. The ladies were in a flurry to have as many cushions completed as possible before the first service in the new sanctuary, which was why they were still in her house even though their husbands were home and wondering about their suppers. In the heat of the day, the stitchery sessions were either in the back garden or on the spacious front porch. Such a front porch session was still in progress when a white convertible roadster came roaring up the street and swerved dangerously into Miss Cornelia's drive. Just before it crashed on through the detached garage at the end of the drive, the sports car came to an abrupt stop. Then the driver, a very blond young woman wearing a sleeveless white blouse and baggy navy-blue linen trousers, stood up in the fancy top-down convertible and yelled up to the porch lined with seated—and as frozen as ice statues—women.

"Hey ya'll! Is my Aunt Cornelia home?"

They all slowly nodded.

In a snippy manner she said, "Would one of ya'll *mind* telling her that her darling niece has arrived?"

The lady closest to the front door shot out of her chair and bolted.

Auntie Cornelia was astonishing. In real life she had to be at least going on one hundred, but she looked no older than Darling Mommy. And, she had more energy to boot. Within minutes she had those ladies working, carrying in Emma's cases, setting her up in the freshly aired guest room located in the formerly closed off north wing of the house. The ladies, over time, had made it their secretive business to examine every corner of the house, but even then, they hadn't dared to try the door at the end of the second floor. But today that door stood open, and today they were treated to the sight of yet another hallway that accommodated three more doors and all of them open. Inside one door there was a room that had the look of an old nursery, complete with a small school area. The next rooms were freshly aired bedrooms containing hearths and spacious sitting areas. Other than the nursery, Emma was given a choice as to which bedroom she favored.

"The light mauve," she said ever so grandly. And then with a quicksilvered shedding of said grandeur, she raced into the room and immediately fell backwards onto the bed. She was being partially enfolded by the down filled comforter as she issued a cry of, "Wheee! This will do me!" Far from being offended, Miss Cornelia merely smiled. "Auntie, this must have been your bedroom once. It looks like you, you know? But as a young debutante."

"You are very correct. This was indeed my girlhood room. And now it's yours."

Emma pulled herself up just enough to balance herself on her elbows. "Really? As in for only two measly weeks or as in forever and ever?"

Cornelia turned away, directing the ladies as to where the suitcases should be placed as she said quite casually, "The latter I should think, sweetheart." Auntie Cornelia then shooed the other ladies out. "Come down whenever you're ready, dear."

"What?" Emma cried. "You mean there's no time schedule? No four o'clock tea, aperitifs at seven, dinner at eight?"

As she was closing the door Cornelia laughed, "I'm a tad too fractured to hold to the customary house schedule. I do hope this doesn't prove to be too heathenish a lifestyle for you."

Emma plopped herself back down on the bed. "That's a joke, right?"

Cornelia's twinkling laughter could still be heard from behind the fully closed door.

Becka Lofthouse was tidying up the living room when Cornelia came down the stairs and entered the room. There were still a few women washing up and drying dishes in the kitchen, but for the most part, the ladies were outside and walking for home. Setting the cushions to rights on the settee, Becka glanced up, saw Cornelia, and shook her head. "You're gonna have your hands full with that one," Becka grimly predicted. "A little corker that girl."

"Isn't she just," Cornelia beamed.

Becka wasn't finished complaining about Emma's rash intrusion. "Why you would invite that girl to come for a visit when you've got more to do than you can manage? Now that is a flat mystery to me is what it is."

"I've brought her here for Archie."

Becka, still bent over while arranging the settee pillows, instantly stood upright, her eyes wide. Open mouthed, she stared at the face of the high-born lady who had only just recently become the dearest, truest friend she'd ever known. Becka's mouth began work, but it took a moment for the sound to flow. "M-My Archie? My oil patch workin' son, Archie? An' a rich man's girl?"

"They're a perfect match, wouldn't you say?"

Well, now Becka just absolutely had to sit down. And she did. Ever self-conscious of her rawboned hands, she entwined her fingers together and tried to hide her hands against the fabric of her dress. Cornelia joined her on the settee and lightly patted those work-worn hands.

"Becka, I will not allow you to worry about her parents. You are my good friend and Archie is like a grandson to me. I think the world of that boy. In my opinion he deserves the best, and while at the moment you might think my niece is a handful, I'm asking you to trust me when I say that the best thing for Archie is right this minute upstairs and wallowing around on the bed comforter." Becka's eyes were still the size of dinner plates as Cornelia sat closer and said conspiratorially, "All we have to do is shove them together and let nature take its course."

"Oh Cornelia," Becka moaned. "I don't think—"

"Then don't. Leave that to me."

Still looking positively terrified, Becka's voice quivered as she asked, "What are you gonna do?"

"Well, the first thing on the agenda is trading in the Bentley."

"I don't understand."

"You don't have to. Just send Archie over tomorrow morning. Tell him I need him to drive the Bentley over to Fred's."

"An tha's all I tell him?"

"Yes."

Chapter Nineteen

Archie was still asleep in the narrow bed of his private bedroom, a lean-to addition that had been added on to the house during his teenage years. Archie was the eldest of the five children that Becka and Frank Lofthouse had brought into this world, and of the five, Archie was the only redhead—like the grandfather he'd been named for. His one brother and three sisters teased him about his hair, and in the Lofthouse home he was called Carrot more often than Archie. But being the eldest had its perks, one of which was his own room, even if it was just something Daddy had slapped up against the back outer wall. The little addition had everything he needed, nails along the wall to hang his clothing, a dry sink and a chiffonier complete with a mirror. On top of the chiffonier were his shaving brush, soap mug and razor and an old framed childhood photograph of himself with Seth, Casper and a scowling little Libby.

Photographs of himself were a rare thing in Archie's life, and this one had been taken when Mr. Yancy had driven them over to see the visiting carnival in Myrtle Hedge. The three boys, bare foot and dressed in nothing more than loose overalls, looked as if none of them had had a bath in weeks. But that had more to do with their crawling under canvas walls to see the carney shows for free. One of the shows was a woman dancing in front of a bunch of men when she wasn't wearing anything but a bunch of scarves. Archie was looking a trifle dazed in the photograph because he'd just seen a strange woman's bare belly. Libby was looking all mad because she wasn't allowed to try most of the rides because the carnival men kept saying the rides were way too scary for a little biddy girl. Again, these were traveling strangers. None of them had known Libby Flowers at all.

The one thing his room didn't have was an alarm clock. When he was home from the patch, the last thing Archie wanted to hear was a blasted clock. This also meant that he intended to sleep for as long as he wanted to. And because it had been a very hot night with not a single breeze wafting through the room's only window, he'd gone to sleep in the nude. Consequently, when Becka opened the door to her son's room, his bare buttocks stared her straight in the face. She walked over to the bed where he lay sprawled out and face down and retrieved the discarded top sheet, draping it over him as she thought sourly, *Oh you're right Cornelia. This here boy of mine is every rich young girl's hope an' fancy*. Rather loudly she said, "Archie! Wake up!"

Less than thirty minutes later, Archie was riding shotgun in the truck with his dad, Frank Lofthouse. His instructions had been to drop Archie off at Miss Cornelia's before going off to his temporary job at Mr. Ralph's mill. The hope was that Frank would become hired on full time, but times were bad and Mr. Ralph was forced to hire men on a week to week basis, this way as many that needed work might have some, even if it meant the work only amounted to a few weeks at a stretch. But no one held that against Mr. Ralph, least ways, not since the Lord had finally gotten hold of him. Since that miracle, Mr. Ralph had been doing what he could for as many as he could and for that the people of Henrytown purely blessed him. The shame was that this could not be said for his wife, Miss Alma. But then, she'd always been something of a hard nut.

Archie hadn't had time for breakfast because his mother had been in a tizzy to see him washed and shaved and dressed in his best clothes. So, while she ironed his summertime Sunday pants and shirt, he'd had to sit out on the back porch steps polishing his shoes. Now his stomach was growling as Daddy went on and on about how he was sure looking forward to his dinnertime bacon sandwich but most especially to the apple. Apples were the rarest of treats, and Frank Lofthouse only had one because Archie had been taking an apple each night for his suppers up in Sterlington. He had wanted to share something of the rich fare he was being given and apples traveled well. They had to, seeing as how they had come into Louisiana from the State of Washington via the trains. Packing six of those apples in his carryall, those apples were on the move yet again, having seen far more of the United States than Archie ever would. So now, at seven in the morning, his stomach was rolling with hunger as his father droned on about the apple in his dinner bucket. It was a good thing they arrived at Miss Cornelia's when they did because Archie was about a second away from wrestling his father for that apple.

Miss Cornelia opened the front door before Archie had time to ring the pull bell. "I hope you're hungry," she said. "I'm making French toast. You like that, don't you?"

"I wouldn't know ma'am. I don't rightly know what that is."

She opened the door, waving him inside. "Well, wipe your feet and come in and you'll find out. My," she sighed as he entered. "Don't you look nice this morning?"

She was wearing her almost fully grey hair in the usual carefully pinned chignon. She was also wearing her favorite blue day dress with empire waist and long billowy sleeves. The dress collar and bodice were white lace and the cameo broach that she wore with everything was centered in the front of the collar. It was a very old-timey dress, the hem brushing the tops of her sensible lace up shoes. She kept rattling on about how nice he looked and how the errand she needed him to do would not be spoiling his clothes as she led him into the kitchen and then had him sit down at the table of the kitchen's sunny snug.

She was still talking as she went to the opposite end of the kitchen and worked at the stove placing thick slices of bacon into the frying pan.

Archie was no longer listening. He loved the kitchen snug best of anything else that the grand house had to offer. It was enclosed by big bay windows, each window raised high to bring in the cool and rose fragrant air from the garden. The table was round and horseshoed by a pale lavender colored and padded leathered bench with a large matching back rest. This was a table where a man could sit enjoying either the early morning or the late evening cup of coffee. And all the while he would be either hearing the songs of the early birds or the evening crickets while God's peace rolled over him. Archie was busy promising himself that one day he'd have a house with a table just like this when Miss Cornelia walked over to the back stairs that connected the kitchen to the upper floors. She yelled up those stairs, "Sweetie! Get dressed and come down for breakfast!"

Archie jumped slightly in the padded bench when he heard a heavy thump, and practically right over his head, and then the sounds of racing footfalls, followed by the slamming of a door. What in the world did Miss Cornelia have up there, he wondered. Some kind of heavy-footed monkey?

"Archie!" Miss Cornelia chirped. "Drink your orange juice. I squeezed it fresh myself." Now that the bacon was frying, she was standing at the counter, slicing thick portions of bread and then dipping the slices into a wide bowl and then bringing the slice back up again with an eggy looking mess that was clinging and dripping from it. He had no idea what she was planning to do with any of that. She said it was French, and he guessed that meant the original French settlers from France, not the late coming Cajuns from Canada. Archie didn't know if he wanted to eat something so foreign but, his mother had given him instructions that whatever he was offered, he was to be grateful and act as if he enjoyed it. So, Archie steeled himself for the worst as he sipped the small glass of freshly squeezed orange juice, very grateful that he was at least thoroughly enjoying the juice.

A young woman came down the kitchen stairs and into the kitchen. She was barefoot but wearing flowing navy-blue slacks and a pinkish hued cap sleeved blouse. She had bobbed curly blond hair, very large blue eyes with artificially darkened lashes, thin eyebrows that looked like crescent moons drawn onto her forehead and extremely bright red lipstick. Archie's first impression was that she needed to flounce right back on up those stairs and scrub her face. Barring that, he was more than willing to hold her down and scrub it for her.

"Sweetie" didn't seem to be all that smitten by the sight of him either. She stopped mid stride and gave him the once over, and the curl of her too bright upper lip exposed her immediate disdain for the young man wearing modest clothing and his red hair unnaturally slicked down by his insistent mother. Walking over to the counter and wrapping an arm around Miss Cornelia's shoulders, she said in a voice that made him feel as if she'd just inspected a bug with a magnifying glass, "Who is he?"

"He," Miss Cornelia stressed as she kept on dunking bread into the wide bowl, "has a name. It's Archie. He's the son of my dear friend Becka and he's come to do me a great favor. And I'll thank you to behave."

"Oh, Auntie," the girl sighed dramatically. "Behaving is just so tres boring."

"Yes, Sweetie I'm sure it is, but you'll just have to bare up. Now go sit down at the table. Breakfast is almost ready."

She slid into the opposing side of the snug's bench with all the enthusiasm of a wet rag doll. "I'm Emma," she said, her tone equaling her body language. "I'm from Baton Rouge."

"Good for you," Archie replied in matching attitude. "I betcha miss it." And then he looked away as if captivated by something that was just outside the window.

Emma had never been shot down by a male before. The experience was unfamiliar as well as rather unpleasant. She picked up her glass of juice and quietly sipped at it while she pretended that she too was watching that same something just beyond the window screening.

The egg toast was better than anything Archie had been expecting. There was real powdered sugar on it, and after Miss Cornelia invited him to help himself to the maple syrup pitcher, the whole stack of fried egg bread toast was really good. She also served him six whole pieces of bacon and refilled his juice glass. If he had liked her niece, he would have worried that he was making a pig of himself. But he didn't like her, so he could care less what she thought. He thoroughly enjoyed the meal while listening to Miss Cornelia talking about cars.

"I just can't manage the Bentley anymore and I don't want to hire a driver. What I want is a modern and easy to handle car that I can drive all by myself." She took a quick drink of coffee. "I called Fred Flowers, and he assured me that he has three brand new cars on his showroom floor, and he's willing to consider taking the Bentley in on a trade basis. But I don't trust that man, Archie. I want you to stand up to him for what's fair."

Archie chuckled. "Maybe you ought to call Aaron or Bubba. They seem to know just how to handle Mr. Fred."

"And don't think I didn't consider it," Cornelia laughed. "But the man is wily. If he saw either one of those two coming in with the Bentley, his defense walls would go straight up. No, for this business, I have to send in someone he'd never suspect."

"You not gonna come with me?"

"I am not. Haggling over automobiles is man's work. I have all the necessary papers you will need in an envelope. For the rest of the business, I'm trusting you to be my agent." She turned to her sullen niece. "Sweetie, I'd like you to go along with Archie. As a woman, you'll better understand your frail old auntie's needs far better than a couple of men." Neither Emma nor Archie knew what to say to this request, so both remained silent. But inwardly both were groaning.

Emma went upstairs to her room to fetch her shoes when she heard Cornelia and Archie in the garden below. They were walking toward the garage where the Bentley was housed.

"I only get to have her for a couple of weeks," Cornelia was saying. "And I so want her to have a good time."

Archie replied, "I bet Casper and Seth wouldn't mind showin' her a good time. They're a good couple of fellas, an' you could trust either one of 'em with her."

"Are you saying you don't like her?"

"Miss Cornelia, I was trying my best not to say it, but since you asked me flat out, then flat out I gotta say, no ma'am, I don't like her."

"Why ever not?"

"Well, she wears too much lipstick. A big red mouth makes her look ridiculous. The worse thing is all that lipstick smears all over stuff like it did her juice glass and coffee cup. An' then her eyebrows look like something a clown would paint on himself if he was wantin' to look surprised. If there's anything pretty about her, I just can't see it. If I was to pick a girl, I'd pick somebody like Libby. But not Libby because she's like one of my sisters. But I am looking for a girl who's real close to being Libby but without being Libby. Miss Cornelia? Am I making any sense?"

Cornelia placed her arm inside Archie's, and she bumped the side of her head against his shoulder. "You're making perfect sense. If Emma's not your type, then she's not your type." She stopped their walk. "But would you mind doing me one more favor?"

"Anything for you Miss."

"Thank you. Please allow Emma to assist in the car business. After that's accomplished, you'll be free of her."

Emma couldn't decide which was worse, being so hurt that she wanted to cry or being so mad she wanted to flatten that hick for even thinking that he was too good for *her*! So, she stormed off to the *en suite* bathroom to splash water on her face. Her mistake was looking into the mirror of the medicine cabinet. And suddenly, the makeup style that was ever so chic in Baton Rouge and New Orleans, now seemed . . . "Oh sweet heavens!" she wailed. "My eyebrows do belong on a startled clown!"

She picked up the bar of beauty cleanse and energetically applied the rich suds to her face. Next, she simply used the eyebrow comb to smooth her rumpled brows. That done, she bent over at the waist and briskly brushed out her hair. Standing to face the mirror again, she used her fingers to rumple her permed curls into a semblance of order. Lastly, she remembered the soft coral lipstick her mother relentlessly begged she wear. Retrieving it from her cosmetics bag, she applied it to her lips and then blotted to make absolutely certain that it would not smear. She ran for her shoes and shoulder bag then sped down the grand staircase like a tornado.

She was standing in the drive as Archie carefully backed the Bentley out of the garage. Emma waved merrily to Cornelia, and then she promptly climbed into the back of the car, leaving Archie to sit alone in the chauffer's area. Archie's irritated response to this intended snub was to slam shut the sliding window that separated the driver from the passenger's compartment. Fred's was only about five minutes away, but it proved to be a very long and uncomfortable five minutes.

Fred couldn't believe his eyes when the Bentley came rolling onto the lot. Sure, Miss Cornelia had telephoned saying that she was seriously thinking about trading in the fine old car, but thinking and doing were two entirely different things. But obviously she'd thought, and now she was doing. Fred called Ralph to share the news of his good fortune. On the collector's market, the Bentley, old or not, was worth twice over any one of the three new cars parked in his showroom.

"I know an old boy in the Garden District who'll pay thousands in cash money for that car," Fred gushed into Ralph's ear. "As soon as the trade is made, I'm callin' him!" Fred took the receiver away from his ear and left it on the desk as he stood to his feet and watched out of the office window. From the receiver, he could hear Ralph's voice buzzing like a hornet, but as the receiver bell was lying on the desktop, Fred couldn't make out what Ralph was going on about. And too, he really didn't care what Ralph was saying anyway. When the car doors opened, Fred picked up the receiver bell and the candlestick telephone and yelled down the line, "They're getting outta the car! Gotta go!"

Ralph was so mad he was about to spit. He knew Fred Flowers well enough to know that the man was more shyster than Christian. And Miss Cornelia, that refined and gentle lady of the old, lost South, was just too trusting is what she was. A modernday cracker-barrel rouge like Fred Flowers would gobble her down like penny candy, and smile the whole while he was chewing her bones. Well, not while Ralph Winters had a single breath left in his body he wouldn't! Grabbing his key chain, Ralph stormed out of his office.

Fred didn't know what to make of the sophisticated young woman calling herself Miss Cornelia's niece when he knew perfectly well that Miss Cornelia hadn't any siblings. But Archie Lofthouse was standing right there beside her and he didn't raise so much as a slickened-down hair the whole while she was saying it. So, obviously there was a close blood connection somewhere; even if that connection wasn't as readily apparent as both young people supposed. And again, Fred didn't actually care anyway.

Leaving two topnotch mechanics to go over the Bentley with kid-glove care, he ushered the young people into the showroom. As he led Archie in the direction of the new car that was the exact Tudor model currently owned by Aaron, the girl fled off towards the sporty Ford convertible Model B Woodie. The fly hoods were up and locked open in order to show off the V8 engine. It was painted Mohave Sand with Old Barn gray rag top and matching rubber on the running boards. The wood paneled sides were blond oak. It had red rims and white side wall tires. It was the very last word in estate touring cars. Not for one second did Fred believe Miss Cornelia would ever be caught dead in it. Which was why he was temporarily flummoxed by the young lady yelling across the floor, "I want a test drive in this one."

Fred looked questioningly to Archie. Archie merely shrugged. "Uh," said Fred. "I'll fetch the key."

The girl—Emma—snatched the key off Fred and ensconced herself behind the wheel. Archie rode shotgun and Fred sat in the back as Emma carefully steered the new car through the double bay doors as a workman pushed them open. And once the car was clear, Fred was knocked back in his seat when she floored the accelerator, and the car shot out of the lot like a rocket. Archie was laughing like he was having a high old time while Emma sped along the curvy back roads like a professional racer.

"It has more pep than my poor bucket," she yelled to Archie. "Listen to that engine hum. It's like a silken symphony. What say we let her run to the limit?"

"Fine by me," Archie answered.

Fred, who had clawed his way forward and managing to poke his head between the two young people, tried to sound reasonable. "Now Miss, you got her up to near fifty. Tha's already a mighty high speed on this little road."

"Nonsense!" Emma replied. "That numbering thing-a-mie says it'll do seventy. Let's see if it really means it." Without waiting for an answer, Emma put her foot down, and once again, Fred found himself being thrown backwards. This was quickly followed by his being tossed from side to side as the car careened around corners, dodged one tractor and then overtook a hay truck. The pair up front were downright giddy, but in the back a terrified Fred was trying to stay upright. It was by God's mercy that at a four-way intersection the car to come to an abrupt halt. But not so merciful in that the sudden stop had also flung Fred to the floor.

"Hey, great brakes," Emma declared. This stop involved waiting for a very early 1920's Model T to quiver and sputter its right-of-way-self through the intersection. Archie and Emma used the opportunity to turn at the waist and look back to Fred who was, at that moment, crawling his way back into the seat. In perfect unison the two young people hollered, "We'll take it!"

Ralph Winters leaned against the side of his car watching with interest as the two mechanics went over the Bentley. One man was inside the hood, and the other man was, flat on his back on a wide and wheeled board. Moments later, said man came rolling out from underneath. He stood up and picked up the rolling board, pausing long enough to confer with the mechanic at the hood. The confab concluded, and still carrying the board, he walked off and disappeared into the bowels of the darkened and noisy automotive works garage. Using a rag, the man still at the car first wiped his hands, then he wiped the car, erasing all traces of his handprints. He was lowering the hood when Ralph left his car and approached the Bentley.

"Pretty old car," Ralph said casually.

"Wouldn't guess it," Chet Evans said. He was a man Ralph knew purely on a nodding acquaintance, but he knew him to be a singularly honest type of fella. Chet put his hands on his overall wearing hips as he looked at the car with an expression of unreserved admiration. "We just went over every inch of it and there ain't one sign of age to be found. In fact, it's gotta be the cleanest car either one of us has ever even seen, an' that includes the ones standing right now on the showroom floor."

"So, you wouldn't hesitate to buy it would ya?"

Chet emitted a soft laugh. "If it was anybody but Mr. Fred sellin' it, I'd buy it in a heartbeat." Then, fearing he'd said too much and to the wrong person, Chet excused himself and hastily walked away, disappearing inside the garage. However, as it happened, he'd made that comment to the very best person.

Ralph took a step back and examined the luxury British car. "Well Alma," he said aloud to a wife who was not there. "You always did lust after a ride in this here car. What say you just own it outright and ride in it any old time you want to?"

The Woodie entered the lot at breakneck speed and screeched to a stop. It was a flashy car and thoroughly suited the two young people popping out of it. The girl impressed Ralph immediately. He did not miss the close resemblance to Miss Cornelia. Ralph still carried boyhood memories of a young Miss Cornelia. And, Archie Lofthouse standing next to her triggered another hazy memory. It was something from long ago, when he'd been just the little boy who had been hired to pull weeds from Mr. Faraday's flowerbeds. And he could dimly remember seeing something way back then. But what? Ralph canted his head to the left as he watched the pair, vainly trying to call up the wispy fragment. His effort was thwarted by the sight of Fred wobbling his way toward him.

"Stupid girl," Fred growled. "She almost killed me!"

"You hush about that girl." Ralph snarled. "You are *not* her equal." Fred was instantly cowed. And while Fred was fleetingly intimidated, Ralph added, "I'm tradin' my car for the Bentley. It's a fair deal Fred. My car's practically new, as you well know because you're the one who sold it to me, and the Bentley's better days are long gone. Still, Alma will like it, so here's my key," he said handing it over. "I've already got the Bentley's key so there's no need to trouble yourself. Anything owing for the new car's taxes and such are on me an' Miss Cornelia is not to be charged a single dime. And now that we got all that settled, introduce me to the fine young lady."

Cornelia instantly fell in love with the new car. She ran back inside the house and changed out of her day dress and into a blouse and skirt. Then she, Archie and Emma set out in the new car, Emma in the middle of the front seat and Archie by the passenger door and both busy instructing Auntie C in the driving of a modern automobile. They ended up at the parsonage where Cornelia gaily honked the horn, bringing the house occupants out onto the front porch. When Libby spotted Cornelia in the driver's seat, she raced down the steps, Aaron two steps behind her. Mabel didn't budge. She stood in the shade of the covered porch glowering at the new spectacle Miss Cornelia was making of herself.

For as long as she could remember, Mabel had held nothing but admiration for Miss Cornelia Faraday, but now she couldn't abide the woman. Not since she'd heard Miss Cornelia expressing her own admiration for Bubba's house building skills and that she could hardly wait to see his house when it was completed. The topper had been her solid approval of that trollop from the café that Bubba was so busy courting. In Miss Cornelia's own words to the ladies noted for hanging on Miss Cornelia's every word, "Myrna is a kind hardworking young woman and Bubba is fortunate to keep her company." Every bit of this had cut Mabel straight to the core, so now, as far as she was concerned, Miss Cornelia could just go hang. To prove it, while the preacher and Libby danced to Miss Cornelia's current tune, Mabel sat down in a rocker and pouted. But, of course, she listened to every single word that was being said out there in the yard.

Pastor Aaron and Archie Lofthouse were busy doing what men did, inspecting the new car. Meanwhile, the three women formed a separate cluster, Miss Cornelia and her niece oohing and aahing over Libby's engagement ring, a dark sapphire surrounded by diamonds. Then before Mabel knew it, all five were heading for the porch, the three women in the lead, the two men still talking together as they followed the women. Miss Cornelia stepped on to the porch first and grandly announced, "Mabel, we've come to give you a hand with making the sandwiches for the church workmen."

In the kitchen Libby taught Emma how to peel hardboiled eggs while Cornelia whipped up her special mayonnaise, and Mabel carefully sliced the cooled loaves of bread. Then the two men walked in and Emma almost swallowed her tongue. Out in the yard she had, of course, noticed Aaron, but he'd been nattily dressed and being from the state's capitol, Emma was quite used to seeing throngs of well-dressed handsome young men. But now Aaron was turned out in jeans, T-shirt and scuffed boots and the sight took her breath away. Her mouth was still hanging open as he walked by, heading straight for Libby. He gave a quick kiss to the top of Libby's nose before informing her that he was going to "give the fellows a hand at the church."

Libby visibly cringed, but Aaron failed to notice.

"First,' Aaron continued, "I'm taking Archie home to change, and when we get to the church we'll tell the other fellows to expect the sandwiches in . . ." he looked to Miss Cornelia, not Mabel, who quickly supplied the answer that the food would be delivered in two hours.

Mabel began to untie her apron. "I'll just go run down the track an tell Bubba—"

"No," Cornelia cut in. "The girls and I will be bringing the food. There's no need to take Bubba away from his house building."

A seething Mabel retied her apron as the two men left the kitchen. The other women ignored her fit of pique as they talked among themselves, Libby going on and on about Emma's slacks and how much she missed wearing trousers.

"You're not comfortable in dresses?" Cornelia asked.

"No ma'am. Especially on hot days like today. But Mama says I've gotta wear them."

"Your mama's right," Mabel said snidely. "A preacher's wife can't be lookin' like no common *cafe* hussy."

As Cornelia took the bowl of mayonnaise to the refrigerator to cool, she said offhandedly, "I've always held the opinion that a lady sets the standard by her manner and not so much for what she wears. If I were young, I'd be wearing trousers myself."

"You're not all that old, Auntie C.," Emma laughed.

Cornelia closed the door of the refrigerator and said, "You know, I don't feel old. But I am feeling the heat in this long skirt." She turned to face the younger women. "Girls? What say we make a quick trip to Myrtle Hedge? I suddenly have the urge to go shopping."

In the ladies clothing section of the Myrtle Hedge department store, the salesgirls were in a dither. First of all because Miss Cornelia Faraday was in their department, and secondly, she said that the two young women with her could have the run of the place; that all of their purchases would be on her account. Two seconds later, the girls were hitting the racks like intent locusts. Miss Cornelia went off in a separate direction toward the more sedate section and with a saleswoman who knew a fine lady's requirements. It wasn't long before the girls were racing off to the changing room, their arms loaded with a veritable haul. From the stash of outfits they planned to buy, they selected new trousers and blouses that they decided would be fun to wear right out of the store.

"Do these look too tight across my backside?" Libby worried.

"No. You have a perky caboose. You should show it off."

"Well, if Aaron hasn't managed to kill himself by falling off a ladder, he might not like me in this."

"I don't care if he is a preacher, the man's not dead. He's going to love you in those pants. What kind of diet do you have?"

Libby turned away from the full-length mirror. "I don't know what you mean. What's a *die-it*?"

"Oh, for pete's sake," Emma scoffed. "A diet is when you guard against calories like a millionaire miser guarding against spending a few pennies."

Libby was still confused. "So worrying about calories, is kinda the same as worrying about . . . polio?"

Emma clapped her hands over her mouth and laughed into her palms. "Libby! Stop it. You'll make me pee!" Quicksilvered Emma moaned as her attention switched to her feet. "Oh no. I love these trousers, but my shoes aren't right."

"Yes, well," Libby sighed. "Mine have seen better days and that's the awful truth."

Emma brightened. "Not to worry, I've got this." She flung open the dressing room door and said to the waiting saleslady, "A pair of white patent pumps please, size six and," she looked back to Libby who was nodding fiercely, "correction—two pairs in size six. And T-strap pumps if you have them."

"Yes miss, we have them!" and off the salesgirl flew for the shoe section.

When Emma and Libby emerged in their new and matching outfits, none of the saleswomen dared to call attention to the fact that they looked like feminine versions of sailors, the sort featured in a tap-dancing chorus line. Both were wearing dark blue pants with white sleeveless blouses that had the signature sailor look of back shoulder flap. In the front, their blouses were complete with a jaunty dark blue scarf tied in a knot at the décolletage. Neither cared that they were twins—or a tap-dancing team—because Emma dearly loved the new clothes and Libby was so happy to be back in trousers and wearing brand new shoes that she was on the threshold of tears. Then too, she wasn't worried about her mother kicking up rough because the new clothes were gifts from Miss Cornelia. How could Mama possibly refuse Miss Cornelia?

Libby's life was suddenly so very good—trouser-wise.

They were escorted to the more mature section of the ladies clothing department and the girls, heavy shopping bags surrounding their legs, sat in wing backed chairs as they waited for Miss Cornelia to emerge from the store's most secluded dressing room. They were running out of things that those of brief acquaintance might find of interest, when Emma looked at her wristwatch.

"If we're going to get back in time to deliver those sandwiches, we'd better get a wiggle on."

Libby stood and walked toward the dressing room, then she paused and looked back to Emma. "Do you suppose she's all right?"

"What?" Emma smiled. "Are you worried that the sight of seeing herself in the mirror wearing trousers has done the old dear in?" Emma rose from her chair. "Trust me, Auntie is made of sterner stuff."

And they would have knocked on the door if it hadn't opened. Suddenly, Miss Cornelia and the saleslady were walking out of the changing room and seeing the startled girls, she stopped, the saleslady stopping behind her. Libby and Emma instinctively clasped each other's hands to ward off falling down in astonishment. The sight of a trouser attired Miss Cornelia was proving to be somewhat staggering. The trousers were flowing cotton but with the look of raw linen. The blouse was a pale grey silk with a large opened collar. Her trademark cameo had been looped through with a wide dark grey ribbon and then tied like a choker around her neck. On her feet were modern black patent ankle strap pumps. Her hair was. of course, still immaculately coiffed in her signature chignon. She had always been a stately woman and, even while wearing her loose fitting dresses, there remained a subtle hint of a slender and well-formed figure. But now her figure looked . . . well, it didn't look like it belong to someone a hundred years old!

"Your mouths are open and you're both stone silent. Am I to make of this that you find me too absurd for words?"

"No," Emma breathed. "Auntie, you're amazing!"

"Why can't we be blood related?" Libby squeaked

To the chuckling saleswoman Cornelia said, "I believe that's meant to imply that I'll do." Then to the still staring younger women she said,

"Come my beauties. I'm suddenly finding myself quite eager to thoroughly horrify the whole of Henrytown."

Chapter Twenty

At the parsonage, Cornelia remained with the car, and putting the top down exactly as Emma had instructed. She'd also left the engine idling, indicating their need for haste. Then too, Cornelia was feeling a mounting distaste for Mabel. The girls went in, grabbed the packed sandwiches, the metal coolers containing tea, the basket containing drinking jars, and then they were dashing out of the house. Mabel was barely on the porch as the three in the convertible roared off. From her vantage point, the only thing Mabel noticed was that Miss Cornelia had treated herself to a nice new blouse, never suspecting even for an instant that that blouse might be tucked inside the waist band of a pair of trousers. So, for the present at least, Miss Cornelia's reputation, remained unscathed.

At the church, Cornelia feared for her car's tires, what with the menace of nails all over the building site, so she steered toward the outer edges, thus avoiding any possibility of a puncture. She parked close to trees, keeping the new car inside the tree line's protective shading. But they were still too far away for the workmen to have spotted them, so the girls stood outside the car, waving their arms over their heads as Cornelia blasted the car horn. That was all the signaling the men needed to come sliding down ladders and heading in the direction of the car. Aaron was the only man still wearing a T-shirt, the rest were bare chested. Having only ever seen masculine bare chests in swimming costumes, and city men at that, the sight of these barechested men caused young Emma's eyes to stand out on their stalks.

Staring at Casper, who was leading the charge for food, Emma asked, "What is wrong with his arms? Why do they look so . . . bulged?"

Libby pealed laughter. "Those bulges are muscles. Don't men in Baton Rouge have muscles?"

"Let me assure you," Emma laughed. "If the young men in Baton Rouge had bulging muscles like that, I'd still be in Baton Rouge."

It was all happily chaotic as the men were served sandwiches and tea, however, Miss Cornelia didn't care for the way Seth and Casper were competing for Emma's attention. Above the din of so many voices, Cornelia managed to shout, "Where's Archie?"

Casper turned his face away from Emma just long enough to say, "He's still on the roof. He'll be down directly."

Archie was doing what the men had secretly labeled, *Aaron Cleanup.* The preacher was so happy to be part of the roofing process that none of them had the heart to take the hammer away from him. It had been left to Archie to surreptitiously follow behind him, prying out the hopelessly bent and tangled nails, and then hammer in the replacements. So, while Aaron stood there happily boasting to Libby about how hard he had been working, and even showing off the blisters that were coming into bud on his palms, Archie was working even harder to make sure that Aaron's section of the roof wouldn't come down during a thunderstorm. After mending the very last nail, Archie began to descend the ladder and pray mightily that at least one sandwich had been saved for him.

Emma was laughing because Casper and Seth were proving to be such a pair of cut-ups. But when she spotted the bare-chested Archie walking toward her, laughter stuck in her throat like a swallowed fish-bone. His red hair was wet from sweat and glistening in the sun like a dazzling ruby. His arms—and chest—were all . . . bulgy with those muscle thing-a-mies, but the biggest stunner was that his skin was golden. She'd known a few redheaded boys, but they were pasty and freckled, and they were terrified of the sun turning their milky flesh as crimson as a boiled lobster. Suddenly, Emma was feeling a bit flushed. Her gaze fixed on the approaching Archie, she no longer heard a word

Seth or Casper said. However, she did feel Auntie C., bump her arm and reluctantly, she turned her stupefied attention in Cornelia's direction.

"I saved Archie these two sandwiches, and here's a jar of iced tea. Would you make certain he gets these please?" Emma grabbed the sandwiches and the Ball canning jar of tea and sprinted off to meet Archie. Cornelia averted everyone's attention away from the pair by saying in a loud voice, "Alright, ya'll have been kind enough not to mention my being in trousers, but Pastor, since you are unable to lie under any circumstances, I would like to ask your completely honest opinion of this particular sight that's been set before your eyes."

"Miss Cornelia," he said with a broad smile, "you are magnificent."

Archie was glad to see Emma hurrying toward him and not just because she was bringing a jar of tea and wax paper wrapped sandwiches. For some reason she looked way better than he remembered. The pair met yards away from the others. Archie started with the tea, almost draining the jar while Emma looked up at him, watching his neck muscles work as he swallowed, inhaling the pleasant cinnamon-ish sweaty odor of him. Added to all of this the fact that his bare V shaped torso ended inside the loose waistband of faded blue jeans and then those long legs ended with frayed cuffs from which protruded worn and dusty cowboy boots. Emma felt on the very edge of a collapse. There was no doubt in her tightly permed little noggin that she was not in the presence of just another flirtatious, arrogant boy but was instead standing before a self-confident and fully grown man.

"You look different," she heard him say.

"Oh!" she blurted. Still discomfited, she said quickly, "Auntie C took us shopping. This is one of my new outfits. Do you like it?"

"Yeah," he drawled between drinks from the jar. "It's real pretty, but that ain't what I meant." He looked her over again. Then it came to him and he blurted, "Hey! You're not wearing lipstick!"

Emma's hand flew to her mouth. Turning away she said, "Oh gosh! I'll go put some on!"

Before she could escape, he grabbed her arm. "No, you don't! I hate that stuff. Believe me, you're a lot prettier without it." When she settled and looked down at her feet, suddenly all nervous and—shy—he broke the awkward silence by asking, "Are those sandwiches for me?"

The next two weeks flew by in a blur. Henrytown Free Church somehow survived the sensation of Miss Cornelia continually wearing trousers and roaring around town in her wood paneled sports car. Much to the delight of Miss Cornelia and Archie's mother Miss Becka, Archie and Emma had been keeping steady company. Casper, never able to fully make up his mind, was sparking three different girls. In the meanwhile a young lady from Olla, named Verda-Louise, came to Henrytown to visit her cousin, but it was Seth she primarily visited. Bubba and his sweet friend Myrna had become a solid couple and as such were inducted into the group. As there weren't many places for young couples to go, and what with money being a high discouragement for venturing too far, the couples ended up spending the majority of their evenings at Miss Cornelia's, where there was an abundance of food, soda pops and iced tea, gramophone records, radio programs, and long private walks in the moonlit gardens. For four young couples falling in love, Miss Cornelia's house was a positive haven. And once they got wind of it, and dearly wishing to escape Mabel's incessant mourning the loss of her *baby* to "that trollop from the café," Aaron and Libby too ran for sanctuary at Miss Cornelia's. Consequently, the four couples became five, and the big house was filled with the voices of young people, music and laughter. Miss Cornelia and Becka Lofthouse were the official chaperones, (never mind that they were holed up in the kitchen and working on their stitchery), and the racket the young couples made was, for Cornelia, as sweet a sound as the finest hymn.

The morning of September third was Archie's final full day at home in Henrytown. By the next afternoon he would be on the train and returning to the oil patch. When Emma didn't come down for breakfast, Cornelia climbed the back stairs and found her still in bed and lying face down and weeping into a pillow. Cornelia rushed to her, making all the sounds a mother makes when trying to soothe a hurting child. But instead of being soothed, Emma sobbed more wretchedly as she flung herself fiercely into her auntie's arms. It was only when she'd gained a modicum of control that Emma tearfully spoke.

"Oh Auntie! I'm so miserable!"

"Yes darling, I know. Archie's leaving but—"

"That's not it," Emma snapped as she sat up smartly, flinging tears from her face. "He won't be gone that long, and we've promised to telephone and write. What's making me miserable is that Mommy and Daddy called yesterday to inform me that they have enrolled me in an all girl's school in New Orleans. It's all to do with my debut, and Mommy's demanding I come home straight away. She sounded positively elated about shipping me off. I don't want any of that Auntie! I don't want to be stuck off inside a girl's school preparing myself to be presented like some prized heifer on the marital auction block. The whole thing is barbaric! Besides, I already know that I want to marry Archie! And that he wants to marry me too."

Cornelia felt herself thrown into a time-warp. She knew precisely how Emma felt. But there was still a question and softly, Cornelia asked it. "Just how do you know Archie wants to marry you?"

"Because, you darling goose, he proposed! And I have the cigar band to prove it." Emma held up her left hand with fingers splayed, and there on the third finger, was the paper band that read, *White Owl Cigar*. "Of course, I daren't wear it while washing my hands or it will end up circling down the drain, but I love it regardless; and I absolutely do not want to go home. In fact, I never, ever want to leave Henrytown." Emma was on the verge of a new sob-fest.

"Then you won't leave," Cornelia said firmly.

That one small sentence had the effect of a slap. "What? You mean I can stay here? With you? But Mommy will never allow it!"

"She won't have much of a choice if you are married." Emma went bug-eyed. "What? You mean . . . today?"

"Yes, my darling. I mean today." Patting Emma's hand, Cornelia smiled confidently. "Wash your face and please do something with your hair. I have a few telephone calls to make."

After fanning the face of her thoroughly dumbfounded son, Becka was on the run for Cornelia's. She was met on the walkway by Mildred Flowers and Libby. All three spoke hurriedly and crisply as they jogged toward the mansion's porch.

"Daddy dropped us off," Libby explained. "Aaron and Casper are out running a thousand errands. Aaron is so excited. This is his first marriage ceremony. He's so nervous, you'd think it was our wedding!"

"Why is this happening so fast?" Mildred asked.

Becka quickly answered, "Because if they're not married today, Emma's parents will make sure they never get married. Miss Cornelia is determined they don't have that choice. A judge she knows has even rushed through the license!"

"She's such a romantic!" Libby sighed.

Behind them a horn sounded, and they stopped short of the porch steps. Out of the parked truck popped Seth and Verda-Louise, a girl nearing twenty with very blonde and crinkled waved hair whose pleasant heart-shaped face was set in a perpetual smile. Verda was from a strict orthodox family, and though she envied the slacks favored by the other girls of the group—and even matronly Miss Cornelia—Verda hadn't yet stumped up the courage to wear anything other than dresses. She was simply not the type of girl that anyone would have imagined Wild-Boy Seth ever being sweet on. But, judging by the way he held onto Verda's hand, he most certainly was.

"This is so exciting!" Verda squealed. Managing to break free of Seth she raced up the walkway ahead of him. "It's such a perfect day for a wedding."

Seth arrived a pace behind her and placing his hands on Verda's small shoulders he said, "Just what do ya'll need me for?"

"You're to go to my house and sit on Archie," Becka said. "When I left him, he looked like he was havin' a spell. But I know that boy. He'll snap out of it an' when he does, he's gonna come runnin' over here an' then he'll climb the trellis if he has to, just to get in to talk to Emma."

"Why?" Both Libby and Verda asked.

Mildred shook her head and turned away. Of course she knew why, but how was she to explain it to these utterly clueless young people? But Becka, brave soul that she was, simply spoke the truth of the situation.

"Because my son's a poor boy. But he's also honorable an' he's gonna want to give her every chance to change her mind about marryin' beneath her station."

Libby faltered as she said softly and thoughtfully, "That's just so—so—"

"Stupid," Seth quickly cut in. "Emma ain't never gonna do better than Archie." Then he tapped the highly worried Libby on the shoulder, and she lifted her eyes to meet his. "An' Aaron ain't never gonna do better than you, little missy-bug, so you can stop frettin' yourself about that one too."

"So, you'll go stay with him?" Becka asked.

"I'm goin' right now. What time am I supposed to have him here?"

"Miss Cornelia said five sharp."

"He'll be here," Seth promised.

"Well of course I want to marry her!" Archie cried as he stuffed clothes into his carryall.

"Then why are you packin' like you're about to scurry outta here an' run for the first train outta town?"

Archie stopped stuffing the bag and slumped down on the bed, the old springs sharply complaining under his weight. "Look," he said dejectedly. "This is just one of those things I didn't think all the way through. I love her with all my heart, an' I guess I just got carried away with the emotion or something, plus it was fun, you know, givin' her that cigar band an' everything. But the truth is, I don't want to trap her with somebody like me an' then for us to spend the rest of our lives with her hatin' me while she's standin' at the sink scrubbin' clothes on a washboard an' worryin' about feedin' a bunch of kids." He looked forlornly at Seth, "An' that's all the life I can offer her. An' that just ain't enough for a girl as fine as Emma."

"Yeah," Seth agreed. "That does sound pretty miserable all right. An' my first impression of these miseries is, that I'm not hearin' one word about what God might be thinkin' about any of it." Archie gasped and Seth continued. "Arch my man, do you really think God went to all the trouble of bringin' that girl into your life just to make you unhappy? I gotta say no. If you'll just trust Him to succeed more than you're trustin' yourself to fail, then I predict you'll be a lot happier kind of fella. Now there's a pretty girl who is getting herself all primped up to be your blushin' bride and a house full of people working like bees to make you a special wedding. An' ever bit of this is because they all love you. But," he raised his hands in the air in exasperation and then let them fall with a slap to his thighs, "if all you want is to run off like some kind of demented squirrel, then I ain't gonna stop ya. I will feel sorry for you for the rest of your whole sorry life, but I won't stop ya."

Archie looked at the canvas carryall and then he looked back to Seth. With a heaving sigh he said, "What time am I supposed to be at Miss Cornelia's?"

"Five."

"An' just where am I supposed to be takin' my wife after the weddin'?"

Seth laughed as he rubbed Archie's slumped shoulders. "What say we let the Lord surprise ya?"

"Oh yeah," Archie jeered. "Like the big surprise I'm havin' right now just ain't enough."

"Well, He is a pretty big God ya know. Big surprises are kinda His specialty."

Aaron felt panicky. Libby, as Maid of Honor, was upstairs with the bride, so Aaron was left alone to buck himself up when what he knew he needed most was a good healthy dose of her sarcasm. It was quite mindboggling really, how Libby's barbed tongue never failed to put things into perspective. As the house began to fill with wedding guests, Aaron ran off to hide in the library where he could read over his notes. This would be the first wedding he conducted. Added to that, it was the wedding of one of his dearest brothers. He was terrified he'd make a mess of it. Miss Cornelia and her all-volunteer company of wedding planners had put forth a remarkable amount of effort into this wedding, somehow even managing to make a three-tiered cake as well as decorate the garden like an al fresco chapel. Folding chairs had been set out in rows, standing baskets were filled with freshly cut flowers and, from somewhere they'd even found a small raised platform for Aaron to stand on while wearing the same robe he'd once almost drowned himself in. Safely hidden in the library, Aaron could hear the voices of people in all parts of the house, but only one was able to rouse him; that of Casper's when he opened the door poked his head in,

"Groom's here!"

"How is he?"

"He ain't lookin' anywhere near as panicky as you, but then again, he don't look like he has a whole lot of blood flowin' up into his face neither."

"Bring him in here. In fact, I'd like all four of us in here."

"You got it." The door closed; Casper was gone. A moment later, Casper, Archie and Seth trooped in. As reported, Archie was indeed looking exceptionally white, the ashen effect thoroughly quashing his normally healthy-looking tan.

"Fellows," Aaron said. "I believe we badly need to pray."

Fifteen minutes had gone by. Miss Cornelia and Becka Lofthouse had everyone seated in the garden. The gramophone was treating the small assembly of guests to a recording of the Viennese Orchestra playing a selection by Bach. All that was missing were the wedding's most essential persons. The bride and her maids were waiting and looking impatient while Miss Cornelia went on the hunt for the groom, the groomsmen and the pastor. She found all of the latter in the library, standing on their knees with their arms around their shoulders as they prayed. As they hadn't heard the door opening, she closed it slightly with the intention of knowing only when she might intrude without interrupting. Aaron's prayer ended and then she heard Archie's voice

"Father-God, I'm so nervous I can't stand myself. Emma's such a fine girl an' I love her so much. I want to marry her so bad I can taste it. But I'm scared of the life I might be forcing her to live. I don't have money or education. I don't have a house or even a good car. Heck, I don't even have money in the bank. Which ain't such bad thing what with all the bank robbin' goin' on these days. But still, what can I offer a girl like Emma? All I got is my love for her and my faith in You. Please Lord, help me make that enough. It's in Jesus' Name that I pray."

Cornelia extracted the hanky from the sleeve of her summer silk frock, wiped her eyes and squared her shoulders before softly knocking on the door. She came into the room as the four young men stood to their feet. "Gentlemen, I believe it's a perfectly marvelous day for a wedding."

Aaron's nervousness evaporated as from his small dais he watched Libby walking down the garden aisle wearing a white floppy straw hat that was festooned with flowers around the headband. She was wearing her best Sunday dress, a pale gauzy lavender, and her new white shoes. It was too easy to imagine her as his bride coming to meet him at the altar. But today, she was the maid of honor, not his bride. The real bride, her arm entwined with Casper's, was behind Libby and walking toward a waiting Archie. Emma's dress was white swathed with a myriad of tiny blue butterflies patterned into the fabric. Her hat was almost identical to the hat worn by Libby. He wondered briefly where they had gotten them in such a short amount of time. But knowing Miss Cornelia's eye for detail, he was certain she'd either had them stashed in her attic or she'd simply pulled them out of thin air. Neither option would have troubled her in the slightest. But Emma's bouquet, almost three times the size of

Libby's, looked responsible for denuding Miss Cornelia's prized rose bush, the one she'd named, Unrequited. How very odd that those rose blooms exactly matched Archie's red hair!

As the bride and groom stood before him, Aaron forsook his high flown "The Importance of Marriage," notes and simply went to the heart of the occasion. Nor did he address the assembly. When he spoke, his words were strictly for the couple standing before him with their nervous and hopeful, young faces.

"I am here as God's representative, reenacting a sacrament He introduced in the Garden in the ages past when he brought a man, Adam—and a woman—Eve, together and blessed them with the giving of one to the other. Marriage is a holy sacrament and a lifelong commitment, but what it is without question is a joyous blessing that's been given to both man and woman directly from the hand of God the Father. So, do you Archie, joyously give your body, your love and all of your utmost care and respect to this woman standing beside you?"

"Yes, I do," Archie promised while looking deeply into Emma's tearing eyes.

"And do you, Emma joyously give yourself—"

"YES! I do. I really, really do!"

Aaron couldn't stop the chuckle as he concluded, "Well, right then. That's certainly clear. In which case I now most joyously pronounce you to be man and wife." And leaning forward toward the quivering Archie he said, "Kiss her. Kiss her now!"

A heartbeat later, Archie was lifting Emma off her feet and kissing the pure whey out of his bride. It was such a vigorous action that Emma's hat came off her head, and while the young couple was so fondly entangled, Libby made haste to retrieve the hat before it became damaged in the mash. In the middle of this maid of honor duty, Aaron bent at the waist and said only loud enough for Libby to hear, "We're next. And it's going to be soon even if that means I finish building that church all by myself."

As she stood up, her hands now loaded with both bouquets plus Emma's hat, she answered, "Fine. But please don't maul me at the altar."

"No promises," he hurriedly said.

When Archie finally set Emma back on her own two feet Aaron raised his arms and loudly said to the gathering of guests, "Ladies and gentlemen, it is my profound pleasure to present to you, Mr. and Mrs. Archibald Lofthouse."

As this had been a highly sudden soiree, there had been no time for the guests to shop for appropriate gifts, so packets of money were offered instead. Alma Winters, so undone that she and Ralph had actually been invited to attend a social function at Miss Cornelia's, had made certain that their packet contained one hundred dollars in the form of five crisp twenty dollar bills. It irked her to no end that due to the penury of the other guests, that none of the packets were opened publicly, that only the names inscribed on the packets were announced, followed by the profuse thank you's from the bride and groom. Which meant that her packet had simply been cobbled in with those only containing a dollar or two—and worse yet, that Miss Cornelia was not made aware of Alma's generosity—and to a Lofthouse of all people! Then the cake was cut, and guests were invited to enjoy the buffet while the cake was whisked off to the kitchen to be portioned out onto dessert plates.

Miss Cornelia approached Bubba as he and Myrna stood in the buffet line. "Myrna? Would you mind my stealing Bubba for just a few minutes?"

Bubba had lost such a fair amount of weight in the passing weeks that his one good suit was as loose as a goose. As a result, when he turned to look questioningly to Myrna, the suit didn't completely turn with him. Before he could speak, Myrna patted his arm. "It's all right honey. I'll fix you a plate an' find us a place to sit. I'll be just fine while I'm waitin' for ya."

Miss Cornelia walked with Bubba through the garden, beyond what had been the wedding area, and then on further and further back into her substantial property. All of this was well tended and not a weed anywhere that Bubba could see. One day he planned to have a sweeping garden with mown lawns, raised flower beds, and neatly trimmed trees with circular iron benches surrounding their bases and two water gardens—that's Miss Cornelia said they were. Which sounded way better than just, "a couple of big old ponds." At any rate, the water gardens were selectively and widely spaced into differing sections of the property and each were filled with a variety of water plants. He had no idea where she was leading him or why, but the scenery, and the ideas he was able to collect on the way were eagerly filed away inside his lively mind.

She stopped just as the flagstone path began to look so disused that it was all but hidden by verdant overgrowth. Then she raised her arm and pointed toward the shadows of large oaks. In that darkness, Bubba could make out what appeared to be an abandoned two storied house.

"That was my daddy's retreat," Miss Cornelia explained. "It's been locked up since he died. I'd like to reopen it, clean it up and modernize it. Having heard the marvelous reports of your abilities, I'd like you to take on the job. That is, of course, if you feel you have the time for such a project."

"Well," he answered speculatively. "That will be a project all right. An', it could be a pretty costly one."

"Would you not have the time to spare?"

"Oh, I'd have the time Miss Cornelia. I'm just about done with my house and outside of running errands for Mama and tendin' the goat, Aaron never has all that much for me to do, so time ain't the issue. I'm just worryin' that the house is maybe too far gone for repairin'. I'd have to come back in my work clothes and look it all over before I can say if it can be saved an' just how much it's likely to cost to save it."

"You're a fair man, Bubba Flowers."

His hands clasped behind his back, he turned slightly toward her. "Would you mind my askin' what you need that house for?"

She turned at the waist to face him, a soft smile playing her lips. "Bubba X? Can you keep a secret?"

Bubba had a great laugh and she enjoyed the sound of his laughter at the irony of her question.

"Why yes ma'am, I rightly believe I can!"

Chapter Twenty-One

Miss Cornelia and Bubba returned to the wedding reception, Miss Cornelia delighted that no one, other than Myrna, had missed them. Even from across the spacious width of the room she could clearly see that Archie was looking panicked again and, she suspected the reason. Making her way through the celebrants, she caught Archie by the elbow. Between the heat of the day and his nerves, he looked as if he were nearing the state of collapse. She pulled him off into the foyer where they could talk without having to shout over the phonograph music and socializing voices.

"Archie? Do you think you could get two or three extra days off from your job?"

"Well," he hedged. "I don't rightly know. I'd hafta speak to the roustabout foreman an—"

Taking a firmer hold of his arm she said, "The phone's in the den. Let's call him."

Wilber Bouchard sat in the Sterlington field office with the sole of one booted foot propped on the edge of the desk, the phone in one hand, the earpiece cantilevered from the lobe of his ear. He leaned back in the swivel chair, smiling and chuckling as he listened to poor little ole Archie Lofthouse sputtering on and on about the sudden change that had come on his life (bless him) and how he understood and all if Mr. Bouchard said no, but if he could see his way clear to—

Wilber spoke right up. "Son? Are you requesting some extra time for a honeymoon?"

Archie just wanted to faint dead away because truthfully, he had no idea what he was asking for. All he knew was that Miss Cornelia was forcing him to make this embarrassing phone call, and she was standing right there sharing the earpiece with him in order for her to hear both ends of the conversation. And then when all Archie could manage was more stammering, she simply took the candlestick phone and the ear bell away from him and spoke to the foreman herself.

"Mr. Bouchard? My name is Cornelia Faraday and this fine young man was just married here in my home. It was a lovely service and the buffet was particularly splendid. But I know you will agree that a wedding also needs a honeymoon."

"Ma'am, I am neither a heathen nor am I cold blooded."

"How excellent. Then how many extra days do you believe you can spare him?"

"The company will allow him three and as his boss, by way of a wedding gift, I will grant him a fourth. Will that do for ya Miss Cornelia?"

"Sir, you are a gentleman. It's been a pleasure speaking with you." She passed the phone back. As Archie stood there stammering his beet-red-faced thank you's, Cornelia left him to it because she was now on the hunt for Emma.

Twenty minutes later, a stupefied looking Archie was sitting in the passenger seat of Emma's white convertible roadster. Emma, still in her impromptu wedding dress, was behind the wheel and her suitcase was in the trunk. Archie didn't have a suitcase but standing beside the car, a laughing Casper assured him that his carryall would be waiting for him in the Sterlington cabin and besides, on a honeymoon, the groom didn't need extra clothes anyway. When Archie's poleaxed expression instantly changed to one of sheer terror, Casper realized he'd taken the honeymoon jibe a trifle too far and so Casper hurried away, joining Aaron and Seth.

It isn't known if Archie was yelling his happiness or pleading for his life as the roadster roared off. But, having turned in the sports car's seat, their last sight was Archie was of him hanging out over the car's trunk while curbside guests threw handfuls of rice at a set of black skid marks Emma had left on the pavement. All the women commenced to weep while the men snickered. Standing separately from the others, Archie's remaining cohorts had their own judgments.

"Well now there we have it," Casper cried, his right hand thrown wide as he indicated the speedily diminishing car. "Proof positive that our Archie was a virgin on his wedding night. I have never in my life seen him so scared."

"Think he was trying to jump outta the car?" Seth asked.

"Probably," Casper answered. "But when Emma put her foot down on the gas, the boy was trapped."

Seth, Aaron and Casper sounded like an exceptionally soft voiced Greek chorus as they stared off at the now empty street, "Bless his little heart."

After a delightful luncheon with Becka Lofthouse on the following day, Cornelia and Becka took their coffee into the den where Cornelia placed a call to Emma's parents. Becka, terrified about this call, was fidgeting in the wing back chair like a earthworm caught on a hot rock. At any rate, given the early afternoon hour—and hopefully—long after the marriage had been consummated, there would no longer be any foundation for an infuriated Preston Templeton's demand of an immediate annulment. Which of course he did. When Cornelia mildly informed him that the happy couple were at present thoroughly enjoying nuptial bliss, as was just so predictable, Preston Templeton began to rage and threaten a lawsuit. In the midst of all this bellow and bluster, Gracia Templeton could be heard wailing and moaning like one of those awful

Shakespearian ghosts. Calmly sipping coffee from her favorite Spoke china cup, Cornelia allowed the theatrics to simply play themselves out. (All of which made the call to Baton Rouge rather costly, but some sacrifices must be made.) The farce went on for such a long time that Cornelia was thinking of something else entirely when she was abruptly pulled back into the moment by Preston's insectile voice rising to a shout.

"I'm waiting Cornelia! Just what do you have to recommend this-this-person you've allowed my daughter to marry?"

"Oh," Cornelia gasped, almost dropping her favorite cup. She quickly placed it in its matching saucer. "What do I have to recommend Archie Lofthouse . . . well, he happens to be my principal heir. Is that recommendation enough for you Preston?"

Both the distant Preston and the nearby Becka almost swallowed their tongues.

"And as a matter of fact," Cornelia went on, "I'm even now having Father's old house fully restored. That house will be for me. I always did love it. Archie and Emma will be taking possession of this house. A house of this size needs a young family filling it, and the coziness of Father's former house will suit me most comfortably. I shan't have all these stairs to contend with, which will be such a blessing. I'm changing my will favoring Archie and Emma with my remaining fortune. But you and Gracia are not to fret. I will also be adding that you Preston, are to have those cane fields that you've so many times offered to buy and Gracia will have the Napoleon era French mantel clock she has so long admired. However, if you continue to contest this marriage you will leave me with no choice but to completely change my mind and—"

"Now let's not be overly hasty Cornelia," Preston blurted. "My tirade was down to the shock of a wedding that we, her doting parents, were excluded from. I'm sure that if we'd met this fellow beforehand

and were in attendance during the marriage of our only child, this entire discussion would have gone quite differently."

"Granted," Cornelia said smoothly. "But time was not an ally in this case. Archie's terribly responsible job with the oil company did not allow for all of the normal formalities. Then, there was Emma. She's such a determined child. Rather a lot like me, actually, but with much more spunk. I do adore that about her. So, with the situation being what it was, we barely had time to pick flowers and bake a cake before the wedding well-wishers were pelting rice at the tire marks the happy couple left behind on the pavement."

Becka had to slap her mouth closed with both of her hands in order to prevent herself from laughing out loud. Meanwhile, Cornelia was heaving a heavily melodramatic sigh.

"I do so wish it would have gone differently, but the children were determined not to allow another day go by without being married and as the Bible plainly states, it's better to marry than to burn, what choice did I have?"

Preston cleared his throat. "Yes, well. I'm simply not comfortable talking about my daughter . . . burning . . . but I'm afraid that I still need more time to come to grips with this news."

"Well of course you do Preston. What sort of a father would you be if you didn't? Emma will be home here in Henrytown in about five days and I'll make certain she calls you immediately. By then you and Gracia will have had time to come to terms with youthful impetuosity and perhaps even arrive at the conclusion that no matter how bizarre a situation might seem in the moment, that with time all things do indeed work out for the best."

"Cornelia?" Preston said, now sounding too much like a hurting child. "This Archie of yours . . . you believe . . . he's the best for my Emma?"

Cornelia lowered her head, willing herself not to weep. In a controlled tone she said, "Yes Preston, I believe with all my heart that Archie is the very best for Emma. And what I *know* beyond a shadow of a doubt is that she loves him so very, very much."

On Sunday, September 8th, the sudden marriage of two highly unlikely young people was no longer the primary subject at the Bayou Café or indeed, within the Preston Templeton household. The BIG news was that in Baton Rouge and squarely inside the State Capitol building and during a special session of the Louisiana legislature, Senator Huey P. Long had been shot.

It seemed that the Washington Senator had called the special session—and on a Sunday of all days—with the aim of pushing through a number of bills, one of which would have effectively cost Long's longtime opponent, Judge Benjamin Pavy, his judicial office. While a thoroughly confident U.S. Senator Long strode along a corridor of the State capitol building, Pavy's son-in-law, Dr. Carl Weiss, shot Senator Huey P. Long at close range and in the abdomen. Long's bodyguards immediately opened fire on Weiss as Huey P. managed to run for safety. Weiss died inside the capitol building while Huey was being rushed to a nearby hospital to undergo emergency surgery. However, his wound was quite extensive, the internal bleeding requiring the skills of specialist surgeons in New Orleans. They were telephoned to come immediately.

Thanks to the then Governor Huey P. Long, there was a new 80-mile concrete highway linking both cites. Unfortunately, at this time in 1935, there was also a new spillway under construction and the doctors, mindful of the barricades, turned off of Airline Highway and onto the old River Road where they became involved in a head-on accident. Meanwhile, on the same Airline Highway, the Long family ignored the barricades, Long's two teenage sons jumping out of the car and removing the same barricades the surgeons had obeyed. The Long family arrived in Baton Rouge safely. The surgeons had not.

The entire state held a collective breath as people remained seated around their radios. The suspense of this drama more spellbinding and terrifying than any horror program that a crack radio scriptwriter could ever possibly dream up. And this electrifying saga was all too real. No one dared switch off the radio or toddle off to bed expecting everything to be all right in the morning. This particular program would not be ending well. And the majority opinion was that things would most certainly not be all right in the morning if Huey P. did not miraculously pull through. This appalling fear held the Louisiana citizenry crippled with panic; for however would the Depression weary State of Louisiana possibly survive without the guiding hand of Huey P.?

On September 10th, this question had to be squarely faced by all and sundry when Huey P. Long, in his final breaths whispered, "God, don't let me die. I have so much to do."

At the Henrytown mill, a news report was blasted by microphone throughout the lumber yard. Men stopped what they were doing as they listened intently to a sobbing radio news reporter announce the demise of the Kingfish of Louisiana. The bad that Yancy Flowers had been expecting on that bright and happy day of the Galilee Sermon/Baptism/Hallelujah Picnic, had finally arrived and with a staggering force. Of all the things Yancy might have guessed would happen, Huey Long's assassination had never once entered his mind. And even more amazingly, the person who seemed to be the hardest hit by this turn of historic events, was Ralph Winters. Ralph came into the yard and told everyone to either go home or go to their church to pray for the Long family, that he was closing the mill for the remainder of the week. He also assured them that they would receive full pay during the closure. The men turned to walk away, but they didn't just drop their tools and leave them to lie in the dirt. No, they quietly and respectfully made certain that the mill was closed correctly, that everything was stored and in perfect order.

Yancy was one of the men who moved somberly while securing the facility. It struck him as odd how ordinarily a man could barely hear anything but the whine of the gigantic saws and the customary shouting voices. But now everything about the mill yard was so eerily silent that Yancy could clearly hear the birds twittering in the surrounding trees. He was thinking only of that, the sweet birdsong that he'd never before heard while in the yard when a hand clasped his shoulder and he turned his head to see Ralph. In a voice that sounded like a rasping whisper, Ralph asked Yancy to follow him up the stairs to the mill office.

After closing the door, and with tears streaming his face Ralph said, "Yancy I need you to forgive me. For years I have cheated and undercut you in every way I could. And yes, I did steal your place as head deacon. But now, I give that place back. And it may seem like I'm giving you a raise in pay, but I ain't. I'm simply giving back all the money I cheated you out of in the overtime you had comin'. But most of all, I'm needing you to pray with me. Would you do that please?"

Removing his hat and lowering his head, Yancy first silently prayed for God to forgive him his grievous sins of backbiting, and most especially his outright loathing of a fellow Brother in Christ. Then, when he raised his head, he looked Ralph directly in the eye and said, "Mr. Ralph, you don't owe me a dime. An' truth be told, you're the better head deacon. If I wadden't such a prideful sinner, I would have voted for you myself. So, I'm asking you to forgive me that, and if you will, then me an' you . . . I believe we're square, Sir."

Ralph flung tears away from his face and barked, "You're getting a raise Yancy Flowers, an' that's the end of it. You don't hafta like it, but while you work for me ya are gonna take it. Understood?"

"Yes sir, Mr. Ralph. An' now, do you want us to let's pray together?"

Clasping hands, both men went to their knees in prayer—both men now true deacons of Henrytown Free Church. And as true Christ pardoned brothers.

In the days before Huey P.'s funeral, two hundred thousand people lined up outside the Louisiana State Capitol, each and every person more than willing to stand and wait however many hours were necessary in order to have that brief moment of standing before the coffin containing their fallen hero. The day after Long's funeral on the Capitol grounds, Germany adopted and raised a new national flag. It bore a symbol that few outside of Germany understood, but in the years to come and then for generations after, it would be easily recognized as . . . the Swastika.

Preston Templeton now had more to think about than his headstrong daughter's questionable marriage. As a recognized well-connected Louisiana gentleman, Preston Templeton was doing his best to keep a low profile. The radio was bombarding the airwaves with Redneck hatred of anyone owning an impressive family pedigree or holding anything above an eighth-grade education. As there is simply no arguing with deliberately enraged people, Preston was wise to fully expect bricks to be hurled through his windows at any given second. Subsequently, he ordered the hurricane shutters to be closed and locked. At which point, the house staff decided that the kitchen—what with its thickly walled walk-in pantry and heavy door—just might be the safest place for them. Their retreat left Preston and Gracia to sit alone, in the gloom of the house, worried and afraid.

In Henrytown, Aaron and the men hauled the pews off of the trucks and into the nearly completed sanctuary. It had walls, lights, and a roof.

Its exquisite hand carved altar and Cross, choir loft and baptistery were in place. All that was missing were the windows and the feminine touches of the Ladies Decoration Committee, but Aaron decided that the congregation needed something more substantial than a tent during this time of crisis, so he called Mr. Ralph to open up his back lumber barn where the pews had been stored and Yancy called every man with a truck. Now they were doing the grunt work of hauling the pews up the front steps and into the new sanctuary. And for a man like Aaron, with just barely any noticeable upper body strength, this truly was a grueling labor of love. But the effort was not in vain, for as they began setting the pews to the left of the altar, stricken people shyly entered, some pausing to ask Aaron if it was all right to come in to pray where as some, their faces streaked with tears, were not able to speak at all and so they simply moved past him and made their way to the first available pew and sat down. From that point on, Aaron was relieved of the heavy labor for he was indispensable when it came to counseling those who needed it and praying with others who badly needed that.

And still more came.

Most were members of the congregation, but there were many whom Aaron had never seen before. But pews were being steadily supplied for everyone as the pew haulers were now taking the task to heart and were moving with a quiet speed. Yancy raced his truck to the parsonage, bargaining in with such force that he scared the pure wits out of Mabel who was sitting in front of the living room's standing radio and listening to the live broadcast of all the mournful happenings going on in Baton Rouge.

"Mabel!" Yancy yelped as she hurriedly dried her eyes with the skirt of her apron. "You're gonna have to make up some butter and jelly sandwiches and fill the jugs with tea. A whole bunch of folks are turnin' up at the church."

"Well how many sandwiches you reckon?"

"I don't know!" he snapped as he snatched up the telephone and clicked the receiver's arm to signal the switchboard. "A bunch is a bunch." Then into the telephone's speaker. "Hey, this here's Yancy an' I gotta find Ralph Winters kinda *rapide*." Listening to the operator tease him about using Cajun French made Yancy smile. "Yeah, I kinda do that when I'm all flustered." He listened again. "Sure, I can hold. You just find him for me—*cher*."

Mabel was dramatically bawling in the kitchen as she sliced bread. He was getting ready to yell at her again when Bubba's truck came into the yard and Libby and Myrna hopped out. The second they were clear of the truck, Bubba zoomed back out of the yard. The two young women hightailed it up the front steps and then came into the house. Libby, wearing her new favorite trousers and white sleeveless blouse, strode straight to her father.

"Daddy? Bubba X fetched me and Myrna sayin' that Aaron needs help. What on earth is goin' on?"

"Mourning people are turning up at the church is what's goin' on. We just barely got some pews inside an' there they came. I sent Mabel to the kitchen to make sandwiches. I'm trying to find Ralph because we need all the deacons to help Aaron with the grievers. You two could make yourselves useful by helpin' Mabel."

Myrna, who had sworn to Bubba that his mother would not intimidate her and that he shouldn't worry so much, felt her former courage melt, and she began to fold in on herself. Myrna's sudden onset of blatant terror aggravated Yancy to the very core. Mabel's fit throwing over her son daring to have a life of his own, was getting worse, not better. Mabel needed a good telling off is what she needed. Bubba wasn't going to do it, so . . .

Yancy still had the telephone bell to his ear, but the body of the candlestick phone was down by his waist when he bellowed, "Mabel Flowers! You get yourself in here right now!"

Mabel immediately came scooting into the dining room, but seeing Myrna, she stopped on a dime. Again, Yancy had no patience for his older cousin.

"I said to get in here!"

In full pout mode, Mabel was simply inching her way passed the dining table at precisely the same moment Ralph came on the line. "Hang on Ralph," Yancy testily said. "I got a real stupid situation goin' on here." Then to his glowering cousin, "Mabel Flowers, I ain't gonna tell you a third time!" Mabel picked up speed, and when she came in close, but not too close, she stood there looking mad enough to spit nails. "Mabel, as you know this here is Myrna. As you also well know, Bubba X loves her. What you're so mad about is that one day soon they're gonna get married. An' if you don't start to behave about it, this whole town is gonna line up just to turn you over their knees an' I promise, I will be the first one in that long, long line. Now Myrna an' Libby are here to help ya make the sandwiches an' you're gonna be nice about it, or that spankin' line will start today. Are you hearin' me woman?"

Mabel meekly nodded and the three women promptly adjourned to the kitchen. In his ear Yancy could hear Ralph laughing and saying, "Hey Yancy? Would you mind every now an' again comin' over to my house and havin' a word with MY wife? I promise I'll pay ya overtime for it."

"Ralph, you're about to give me a big old conniption. The church is in crisis and what we need for you to do is call the other deacons an' then all of ya'll get to the church just as fast as you can."

"An' should I tell the other wives to make sandwiches?"

"That'll work. We're kinda getting us a mournful multitude over here."

Serious now, Ralph said, "The deacons—and sandwiches—it will all be there within the hour."

No one quite knows how the town of Henrytown, or La Salle Parish, or indeed the entire state, made it through the subsequent weeks. Aaron said that it was God's grace that had shielded His children from the worst of the emotional and political devastation. The congregation took his word for it because quite honestly, for so many it was as if, with the coming of the month of October, they were finally escaping a mild form of amnesia, in that no one could rightly remember where they were or what they were doing during the remaining days of September. Huey's wife Rose was appointed to fill Huey's seat in the U.S. Senate. (She would be elected for that seat—and on her own merit—in the following year, making her the second woman of the 20th Century to be elected to the U. S. Senate.)

By mid-October, the Henrytown Free Church was officially completed. Despite emotional and economic hardship, the sacrificial giving of dimes and dollars and volunteer labor had wrought a pure miracle. The church had been painted a shining white, and with its tall steeple, bright red tin roof, stained glass windows and the extra wings that went off from the sides at the back of the sanctuary, it was truthfully a sight to behold.

In those wings were Sunday school rooms and a fellowship hall that included a working kitchen. There were even two indoor bathrooms, a true luxury for those souls who had never known an indoor bathroom in their entire lives. The sanctuary had a choir section directly behind the pulpit, and behind them was the baptistery with that amazing stained-glass window that was just above the heads of the standing choir members. Because of the lights on the backside of the baptistery, the image of Christ coming up out of the water during His own baptism in the Jordan River, shone down on the baptismal candidates as they stood inside the baptism fount with Aaron. That window, a gift from some unknown contributor, was so big and so costly that the glass artists themselves had traveled with it to Henrytown, and the four of them had bunked in at the parsonage during all of the ten days it had taken to install it properly. Those four men had been very proud of their work and they had unobtrusively etched their names into the glass at the bottom left, where their names would always remain but would need to be intentionally sought out in order to be read.

Mr. Wayne, the longtime cantor of Henrytown Free, was made the official choir director. He was a humble man before the Lord, and during the remaining years of his life he directed the choir. As the voices sang he looked up not at the choir, but at that window above them, and he blessed God for that gifted sight as well as the privilege of his faith.

Chapter Twenty-Two

It was scheduled to be a pre-Thanksgiving wedding, and the entire town was in a flap, most especially Mildred Flowers, mother of the bride, Miss Libby Flowers. Aaron's mother had arrived by train from Atlanta, so Aaron was more involved with being with her, ergo, he was of no help whatsoever. No one knew why his father hadn't made the trip and the excuse of his being unable to get away from buisness certainly seemed odd. Aaron's mother, a highly dignified lady, with such a quiet air about her, was not the sort of person anyone dared to grill. However, the ladies of the town did try to grill Miss Cornelia because they rightly believed that, if anyone could offer an explanation, it would be her. And, of course, that was true, but she neatly skirted the issue because the truth would not have gone down well. Just as it hadn't when Preston and Gracia Templeton arrived in Henrytown and finally met the young man who was the husband of their daughter Emma.

"A cracker!?!" Preston raged.

Mercifully Bubba X had restored Father's old house in a blindingly short amount of time. There were still things that needed doing of course, but in the main it was clean, water-tight, cozy and bright. Best of all, in the moment of Preston's unseemly tirade, it was completely private.

It was November and quite a chilly day. They sat in chairs before the generous fireplace, the fire snapping at the logs with the same energy that Preston's angry glare snapped at Cornelia. "Yes," she said, "I do grant that Archie has one or two rough areas—"

"One or two?" Preston scoffed. "He's nothing more than a back-woods clod! Can he even read?"

Cornelia waved a hand, “Oh of course he reads. I think. But never mind any of that Preston. Have you truly seen how much those two love each other? Have you opened your eyes to how happy Emma is?”

“Well of course she’s happy Cornelia. She’s sitting up there in your house like she’s the new queen of this town, and she has her red headed ape dancing her attendance. What eighteen-year-old girl wouldn’t be happy?” Preston turned in his chair so that he could face Cornelia fully. Either she had no idea what the upper classes of Baton Rouge and New Orleans had had to endure in the last weeks, or she simply didn’t care. However, Preston allowed her a third option.

“Cornelia, you have lost your mind. But the worst part of it is that your insanity has infected my child’s life. For that I will never forgive you. Now Gracia and I will front out the next two days of this very unfortunate visit, never mind that Gracia is terrified to be in the same room as her son-in-law, and she verges on hysteria in the company of his lamentable family, but I will only—politely—address you while in the company of others. When we are alone, and after I am returned to Baton Rouge, I will have nothing more to say to you. But I do promise I shall make certain that all the doors of polite society are slammed shut in your face.”

He leaned in closer, spittle foaming in the corners of his mouth as his mounting hatred of her, like rabies, began to consume his heart and mind. “You and I both know that you do not have nearly enough money to open those doors again. If the Rockefeller’s many millions won’t budge them, then with your meager few, you don’t have so much as a single solitary prayer. You are ruined Cornelia. And let these following words be my final words to you,” he rose from the chair and with his straight back turned to her, said, “I no longer want, nor will I under any conditions accept those cane fields of yours. As far as I’m concerned, they can go to rot just as I so earnestly pray you will as well.”

As Preston Templeton slammed his way out of her snug home, Cornelia rested her wearied forehead against the palm of her hand. The centuries old class divide that Huey P. Long had so distastefully dragged out into the open, making it a political issue, had—with his death—become an all-out war. This war was now spilling out over the borders of Louisiana and rampaging its way throughout all of the Southern states. There was absolutely nothing wrong with the marriage of Archie and Emma, that is, with the exception that at the close of 1935, it was being publicly viewed as the worst form of class betrayal—and by both classes. During the days when Cornelia had dared to love the first Archie Lofthouse, it had been he who had adamantly refused to cross that line.

"I can't do this to ya girl," he said, his breath softly caressing the curls of her hair. "I just love ya too much. You gotta live in your world an' I gotta live in mine. It's just the way of things Cornelia." His arms fell away from her and he was walking away, becoming a shadowy figure in the moonlight of the garden. This scene had occurred so many long years ago and right outside this very house. She had wanted to call after him, but coward that she was, her throat was frozen, not a single sound could she utter. He was lost to her, the pain of that, overpowering. Without her Archie, her young life had effectively come to an end.

And now, because they were in love with people socially unsuitable, Emma Templeton-Lofthouse and Pastor Aaron Brooks, were themselves casualties of a class division that should have been left to die in the same way it had always lived—in tightlipped seclusion. But in the political world, nothing was private. The Kingfish had continually waved the flag of class division like a soiled rag. And that, as far as Cornelia was concerned, no matter what else others might gleefully accuse, was that man's one true crime.

Preston would of course make good on his promise of publicly ruining her, of that she had not one shred of doubt. Preston Templeton was a southern gentleman and a gentleman always kept his promises. Yet the trouble with his plan for launching his grand expose against her was that she no longer gave a flying fig what anyone in the upper class society said, did, or thought. So, did Cornelia understand why Aaron's father wouldn't spare the time or expend the effort to attend his only son's wedding? Oh yes, she understood only too well. Which was why she was fully prepared to do whatever was necessary to make the wedding of Aaron and Libby truly spectacular. She would also stand by that noble lady, who was his mother, throughout her courageous effort to support her son during the most significant moment of his young life. That kind of courage was rare. Cornelia knew that during her moment of testing that she had most assuredly had not had it.

But she did now.

There were so many things about this place her son called home that had, on first sight, truly baffled Emilia Brooks. For one, why were there so many run-down shacks everywhere? And dogs. Dear Lord, every yard belonging to every shack was virtually teeming with long-eared, and pronounced rib-cage scrawny dogs. And right behind the loathsome dogs stood long-faced, raw-bone thin, vacant expressioned, and bedraggled children.

Then there was the town. With just one prolonged blink, like a cheap magician's trick, it disappeared. Yet prior to the blink, there hadn't been all that much to recommend its continuing existence anyway. But to hear Aaron talk about it, as they drove the main thoroughfare, one could not help but have the distinct impression that for him this little nondescript town was akin to his finding the lost Garden of Eden.

"And Mother? Wait until you see the church. Except for the stained glassed windows, we built it all by ourselves!"

"Oh my," she said as she fanned herself with a lavender scented hankie. "That does sound most enterprising."

And she really had held only good thoughts regarding the self-help church building endeavor: Until they arrived.

Aaron's church was very white, very large and very . . . disjointed. Firstly, because it was built so high above the ground and resting on a series of bricked pillars. Secondly, because there were separate buildings coming off from the sides, of the main worship area which, if viewed from the air, would have made the entire structure resemble a topless cross.

"I designed it myself!" Aaron exclaimed, his face beaming with happiness.

"Did you dear?" She fanned her hankie a bit more vigorously. "How very . . . adventurous . . . of you. Well done my darling boy."

"Would you like to see the inside?" he asked while reaching to turn the key and kill the car engine.

She placed a hand on his arm and said, "Perhaps after I've had a chance to wash my face and recover from the train trip."

"Oh yes, of course. I'm sorry Mother. I'm afraid I've been here for such a long time that I've completely forgotten about the ghastly amount of travel involved. And anyway, Libby's at the parsonage and she's dying to finally meet my family."

Having already seen the shacks and dogs and those many poor little children, Emilia was now expecting the worst when meeting Libby. In fact, during the brief drive to the parsonage, her busy little mind was already dreaming up the profuse apologies she would offer Albert during the first moment she had to telephone him. All of the apologies would begin, "You were absolutely right dear. I shall never doubt or question any of your opinions ever again. I do so beg your forgiveness for having disobeyed your decision that we not attend this wedding, for like you, I cannot approve of our son marrying one of these . . . people."

And then, as Aaron drove the car into the yard fronting the time-worn house with its big covered front porch, she saw the loveliest girl standing on the edge of the porch. She was a very healthy looking, pretty and happily smiling young woman dressed in grey slacks and a pink blouse. Judging from the way she sprinted down all of those porch steps, she was also highly athletic.

"Darling?" Emilia asked hopefully. "Is that . . . Libby?"

Stopping the car, Aaron turned to his mother, giving her one of his most beautiful smiles. "Yes. Isn't she marvelous?" he said. "Would you believe I fell for her the very first moment I saw her?"

Emilia placed her hand on her son's arm and lay the side of her head against his shoulder. "Yes, my sweet love. I can quite easily believe you did."

Well now, Albert would certainly not be getting Emilia's sniveling apology as coming up fast toward the passenger's side of the car was the very daughter Emilia had prayed for so many years God would send her.

"Hello Mother Brooks!" Libby called through the opened window.

"And hello to you!" Emilia laughed. Turning hastily to Aaron she said, "Darling boy, please open this infernal door so your mother can hug her lovely daughter."

"Never wait for him!" Libby laughed. "He's pokey." With that Libby opened the passenger door and climbed into the front seat, all but flinging herself into Emilia's opened arms. "Welcome home Mother!"

Emilia Brooks had never overtly defied her husband before. When the wedding invitation had arrived, her husband, Albert looked as if he was in the throes of a stroke.

"Oh, but we must attend our only son's wedding!" Emilia cried as Albert tore the invitation into shreds right before her horrified eyes.

"We certainly must not," he countered as he continued to shred. "This is utter folderol. Aaron's devotion to going *native*, means that he's simply become smitten by this little bayou beauty. He will not marry her. He wouldn't dare."

"But," Emilia mewled. "Grandmother's ring—"

"Stop it Emilia," Albert snapped, tossing the ruined invitation like confetti. "I know my son. He'll have that off her hand the very instant she skins a coon and the ring is subsequently coated in gore. I tell you this wedding business is simply preposterous. The very idea of traveling to that horrible state is nothing but a complete waste of time and money and we will not do it."

She had not argued further. There was no point; Albert was always right, always knew what was best, and that was the unquestionable end of it. However, what she did instead was pilfer money from his wallet, pack two bags and then wait for him to leave for the university the following morning. Twenty minutes later she was in a cab and headed off to the train station. Despite how calm she might appear on the outside, inside she was a trembling mess, imagining all sorts of scenarios that might play themselves out within Albert's fury. He could demand a divorce. *No, he'd never do that. The scandal of it would drive him mad.* He could confine her to a section of the house where they would never have to see or speak to each other for a long period of suitable punishment. *Yes, that's what he would do. It's clean, thrifty and secretive, in that he'd only be bothered by her company whenever forced to trot her out as a hostess*. Feeling ever so much better about her blatant rebellion, Emilia bought her ticket, sent a telegram to Aaron with the details of her arrival and then boarded the train for Louisiana. Not once in any of her very vivid imaginings, as she settled in her compartment for the long trip across states, had it occurred to her that she would never actually see her husband Albert again.

Aaron decided it would be best if he placed the call to Atlanta. He suspected his mother was a runaway; that she had defied Father; and in so doing meant that she was not in Henrytown by his grace and favor. It was never any good confronting her with the truth. As was her wont, she would deny it and then offer tissue thin excuses. But this did not mean that she wasn't terrified. Mother was only ever brave up to a point and for her, direct confrontation had always been yards, possibly even miles, beyond that point.

As it worked out, there was none of the studied hostility that Aaron had been expecting. Primarily because all conversation was being so effectively blocked by the housekeeper Mrs. Avery.

"I should like to speak to my father please, Mrs. Avery."

"I'm afraid Dr. Brooks is unwell," she said brusquely.

"Indeed. Will you please inform Dr. Brooks that Madam has arrived safely?"

"I shall do, yes."

"Thank you Mrs. Avery. And please convey to my father my very good wishes for a prompt recovery and that I shall be praying for him."

"As you like, Pastor Brooks." Mrs. Avery hung up.

Sitting on the settee with her soon to be mother-in-law, and watching Aaron hanging up the phone, a chill raced through Libby. That had been the most formal and loveless one-sided conversation she'd ever heard. How in the world did such a cold fish manage to raise a son like Aaron? But the warm soft hand nestled within her own, answered the question. The father had had precious little to do with any of it. It had been the mother who had raised the fine and caring man that she, Libby Flowers, was about to marry.

Yet as a thoroughly trained supporter of her husband, Emilia Brooks did not miss a beat. "Is your father still unwell dear?"

Aaron knew how to play the game, but now instead of the pretenses hurting him, he merely found it all so sadly amusing. Lowering his head, he chuckled lightly. "Yes Mother. Father remains quite unwell."

"Such a shame," Emilia tsked. "It's his allergies you know."

Preston and Gracia Templeton left the next afternoon, leaving the very misguided impression with the Lofthouse family that they were in full support of their daughter's marriage, and their acceptance of Archie as their son-in-law. As none of these innocents needed to know the ugly truth, Miss Cornelia did not share it. What she did instead was hold her head high as she and the entire Lofthouse family stood on the lawn of what was now the home of Archie and Emma as the Templeton's were being waved farewell. That done and dusted, Cornelia walked back to her modest home, redressed herself in the slacks she had come to adore and then proceed to the garage where she climbed into her spiffy sporting car and drove for the parsonage. Twenty minutes later, she was standing in the parsonage living room and introducing herself to Emilia Brooks.

Here was yet another boggling conundrum for Emilia to cope with. This stately woman was quite obviously a woman of breeding, but highborn women of a certain age did not drive themselves about in flashy automobiles and they most certainly did not wear trousers. At least, not in Atlanta they didn't. Louisiana was such a foreign country Emilia had no idea how she was expected to endure all of its suspect peculiarities. But at least here was a woman of her own age with whom she could communicate. That Miss Mabel person's dialect was beyond understanding, and it strained Emilia's nerves whenever she tried. This morning Aaron had been called away and Libby was expected to be out all day attending to bridal details, so this had left her alone with Mabel. In other words, Emilia had endured a nerve rattling morning that first began with a breakfast of the strangest looking toast and accompanied by grits and greasy bacon. Then the coffee was so thick and so strong she couldn't guess if she was expected to drink it or eat it with a fork. While Emilia struggled with the breakfast, the Mabel person had gone out to see to the chickens and the goat. Emilia had no idea what any of that meant, but she was grateful for Mabel's prolonged absence.

Noting Miss Emilia's glazed over expression caused Cornelia to smile. "You're having quite a time of it, aren't you?"

"Oh dear," Emilia breathed as she placed both hands against her cheeks. "It's that obvious?"

"Only to one who knows the signs," Cornelia returned. Cornelia patted Emilia's cold hand. "Wait right here. And try not to be alarmed. I'm about to yell."

Cornelia went to the screened door and stepped out onto the dining room section of the wrap-around porch. Forewarned or not, Emilia did jump when she heard Miss Cornelia yelling. "Mabel! I'm taking Miss Emilia for a drive. Make certain Pastor Aaron knows his mother is with me."

Cornelia came back, walking quite rapidly. "Grab your handbag and quickly follow me."

"Why quickly?"

"We have to outrun Mabel."

Emilia was quite taken by Cornelia's confident air. That and the fact the Cornelia was the only woman of her acquaintance who actually knew how to drive a car. It was just all so modern and . . . independent. Yet Emilia did feel one or two qualms when Cornelia drove, not in the direction of the dreadful little town, but down a hardpan track leading off into the dense woods.

"I have to have a quick word with my contractor," Cornelia said as she concentrated on staying in the middle of the track, thus avoiding tree branch scrapes to her car. "He's Mabel's son. He's a remarkably capable and thoroughly likeable young man. Your son certainly thinks the world of him. Everyone knows him as Bubba X, and before Aaron's arrival, the entire town steadfastly believed Bubba to be little more than an idiot."

"And my Aaron helped him overcome this?"

"He did indeed."

"By the power of prayer?"

"Yes, that and the fact that as a newcomer, Aaron was able to see through Bubba's lifelong disguise."

Emilia gasped sharply. "Why on earth would anyone disguise himself as an idiot?"

"It made his mother happy."

Emilia gasped again and Cornelia, glancing quickly, gave her a smile. "Your son has been a God sent blessing for all of us. It's for that reason that everyone you will soon meet will immediately love you; myself included."

The house in the woods was big. As was the young man who owned it. When they'd rounded the corner, they saw him on a tractor. Cornelia parked behind a truck and then got out, waving both arms over her head to attract the man's attention. Emilia clumsily fumbled with the car door handle, needing several tries before meeting with success. It seemed such a trivial thing, opening one's own car door, but for a pampered city woman, opening a car door all on one's own was something of an accomplishment. Feeling a bit proud of herself, Emilia came to stand alongside Cornelia as the young man clad only in overalls and boots climbed down from the tractor and walked toward them. He looked like a half-naked bear and the very sight of him made Emilia afraid. She took solace in Cornelia's assurance that he was friendly, and, one sincerely hoped, more intelligent than he appeared. Emilia relaxed completely when following the introductions, the man known simply as Bubba X, smiled. He had an amazing smile, and his dark eyes sparkled with a truly affectionate kindness.

"Bubba?" Cornelia said as she surveyed the acre of ground he had been plowing. "Is all this going to be your yard?"

"Yes ma'am!" he exclaimed. And then, waving a massive arm, he began explaining his vision for the large yard fronting his newly built house. His plans did sound extraordinary, and he was so detailed that it was easy to imagine the grassy areas, the shade trees and the many kinds of flowering beds.

"Are you going to try for a rose garden?" Cornelia asked. "Because if you are, I have some cuttings I'd love to donate. And what about a magnolia? What's a yard without a magnolia tree?"

"Well, now you're sounding like Myrna," Bubba groaned.

"Bubba X?" Cornelia asked smartly. "Do you want a long and happy marriage?"

Bubba blushed scarlet. "Yes'um. I purely do."

"Then you're going to need that magnolia tree." Cornelia turned and walked back to her car where she retrieved her handbag from the backseat. She came back, counting cash as she walked. Then she handed the cash to Bubba. "Here's the hundred I owe you and there's an extra hundred in advance for the work that still needs doing on my cottage."

"That roof ain't leaking on ya is it?"

"No. You did a fine job. I've been cozy and dry."

Bubba was looking at the money in his hand, his lips twisted to the side. “I still don’t understand why you’d want to live in that little house.”

“Bubba X, now you’re sounding like your mother.”

Well, that just got off with him so badly that Bubba looked like he wished the earth would open up and swallow him whole. “Oh Miss Cornelia,” he whined as he turned his embarrassed face away. “I am so sorry. Your business is your business an’ none of mine.”

She placed a motherly hand on his thick arm. “It’s all right, Bubba. Some things just need extra time to outgrow. But, as you’ve come so far, I trust God to take you even farther.” When he could lift his eyes to meet hers, she smiled and asked, “Now, do you want those rose bush cuttings?”

His smile was bright enough to light up the entire parish. “Ever’one you can spare me, yes ma’am I surely do.”

“And the magnolia?”

“Yes’um. And the magnolia.”

Cornelia made many logical observations in her life and one of the primary logics was that services rendered to people of lesser means were considered to be luxuries. For the well-heeled, the well-offs, the moneyed, the frightfully rich—services were seen as entitlements. Aaron had been cut from that bolt of cloth and when he arrived, his pedigree—and his helplessness—blatantly apparent. But he laughed at the jokes made about him, he gladly turned his entitled hands to any task anyone might trust him with, and never once did he turn up his nose to the offerings of his improvised parish. To one and all, no matter their condition or circumstance, he was kind and loving. Emilia Brooks had raised a spectacular son, and when the time came, she’d turned him over to the Lord. And now, here she sat, in the car with Cornelia Faraday, quietly, bravely and admittedly, a trifle desperately, doing her very best to come to terms with this strange Spanish moss draped world in which her son so happily lived. And Cornelia admired Emilia Brooks all the way to her bones. In just one afternoon, Cornelia had come to realize that beneath all of that flutter and finery, that deep within Miss Emilia Brooks there beat a true and loving heart. However, once Emilia let it slip that she was sleeping in Aaron's bed while he made do on the settee, Cornelia turned the car and headed back for her house.

"What a lovely home!" Emilia said as the car pulled into the drive of the imposing house.

"Isn't it just," Cornelia answered, pulling up the parking brake. "But don't fall in love with it, Emilia. I've given it to the children in the hope that they will fill it up with even smaller children. I have become the in-residence dowager, and, as such, I have been relegated to the garden cottage."

Emilia—bless her golden little soul—oohed and aahed over the garden cottage, saying how much it reminded her of the English countryside. Cornelia canted her head to the right as she studied the cottage. "You're right Emilia. What it needs is a thatched roof. But how Bubba X will work that into the roof-line of the screened-in back porch I've no idea." Emilia burst into giggles and then into hearty laughter as Cornelia's outrageous version of an English accent asked, "Will you take tea m'lady?"

A relaxed Emilia played along. "Yes, thank you Jeeves."

"Cup or canning jar, Madam?"

"Canning jar I should think. But do use the Spode jars."

***

Aaron was astonished as he followed his mother around the bedroom while she repacked her luggage cases and while Miss Cornelia sat waiting for her in the living room and talking with Libby.

"Mother," Aaron stammered. "You don't have to leave. This is a comfortable house and I'm quite content on the couch."

Emilia turned from her packing and placed a hand on her son's chest. "My darling boy, I'm not content for you. And I really do not like the feeling that I'm in the way. I get quite enough of that in Atlanta, thank you very much." She returned to her packing. "I've grown quite fond of Cornelia and she has extra bedrooms in her lovely cottage. I was thrilled to be offered accommodation. I've accepted and now I'm afraid that's simply the end of it m'dear."

"You sound just like Father," Aaron said in a little boy, ill-humored tone.

"Do I dear?" she chirped as she snapped shut the cases. "Gracious! Imagine that."

"Well, when will I see you again Mother?"

She wrapped an arm around his waist and placed her head against his chest. "I'm afraid that it shan't be tomorrow darling. Cornelia and I are motoring off to see some pottery works. She tells me that Louisiana pottery is becoming quite nouveau among the New York people. But it would do, seeing as how Yankees are nouveau-riche themselves. But then darling, and this is truly the exciting part, we'll be having luncheon in something called a Creole-French café. Doesn't that positively scream the word, precious?"

"But Mother, all of that is in an entirely different parish!"

"Yes darling. Your mother is becoming quite madcap! But never mind. You're a grown boy now. I have every confidence you'll survive the shock." She tiptoed and kissed the side of his moping face. "Now darling, promise you'll behave while I'm away and I'll see you in service on Sunday morning. Oh, and I love you very much." She snatched her hat from off the bed as Aaron took hold of the handles of the suitcases. As she put on her gloves and led the way through the parsonage, she said merrily, "I'm very much looking forward to hearing your sermon darling. But I do hope it's not all about Job. I'm afraid I've never actually had that much patience for the man."

Chapter Twenty-Three

Emilia loved the bedroom in Cornelia's cottage, and heeding her hostess's advice, she was careful not to overdress for Sunday service. She wore a modest grey sheath, sensible lace up staked heel shoes, and a gray suede hat with a deep crown, rolled at the side brim but with a jaunty feather on the opposing side. And of course, she never went to church without wearing her white gloves. Grabbing her Bible and her handbag, she hurried to meet Cornelia who was already and waiting for her in the car. When she opened the car door—and all on her own—she and Cornelia burst into giggles. As the car backed out of the drive, Emilia brazened to say, "You know Cornelia, I was wondering where you acquired those very comfortable looking trousers you tend to favor during the weekdays."

"Wonder no more," Cornelia gaily replied as she expertly shifted the car's gears. "Tomorrow we shop!"

Emilia despaired that she would never remember the many names of those she was being introduced to, but the three quite vigorous young men who announced themselves as the Preacher's Boys,—Archie, Casper and Seth—these were names she would never forget. Cornelia took the arm of Archie, and Emilia took the offered arms of Casper and Seth and quite grandly the ladies were escorted down the center aisle and then seated on the first pew to the left. Libby, already seated there, readily welcomed each beloved woman with a hug. From where Emilia sat, she had a clear view of her son as he beamed his love for all three women. The church was truly rustically beautiful on the inside and the voices of the choir, enchanting, but it was Aaron's sermon that both captivated and thrilled his proud mother to her core.

"If you will all turn to Colossians chapter three, we will begin to understand the point Paul is making when he is teaching the church of Colossi the true meaning of Sanctification . . ."

Emilia every now and again had to pinch herself in order to believe that this was real, that the devout man of God delivering the sermon was indeed her son. He was so handsome, so sure and his voice floated like the finest silk over the attentive congregation. Libby was sitting with her back ramrod straight, chin lifted, eyes fixed on Aaron as her left hand rested in her lap and on top of her right; the engagement ring on prominent display. This was truly where Emilia's son belonged, and this young lady was the woman he was meant to belong to. Finally, Emilia was certain that God knew what He was doing when he sent Aaron to Henrytown, Louisiana. In that moment, she also knew that she was free of ever having to worry about her son again. And instead of feeling distressed, she felt—well frankly—liberated.

Emilia tuned back in time to hear Aaron saying, ". . . by fully acknowledging the very real fact that everything outside of Christ is chaos, let us begin each new day with a renewal in Christ, clothing ourselves in mercy, kindness, humility, gentleness and patience. Let us all recognize that each new day is a holy of obligation to be lived entirely to the glory of God the Father."

After the service, when Emilia had the opportunity to tearfully hug her son, Aaron chuckled against her ear, "It wasn't about Job, was it Mummy!"

"No, my darling son. It wasn't. It most assuredly wasn't."

Three days later, flyers appeared in the stores and shops and lumber mill of Henrytown.

The wedding of Pastor Aaron Brooks and Miss Libby Flowers has been postponed until further notice due to an unexpected death in Pastor Brooks' family.

Aaron, Libby, Emilia and Cornelia boarded the train for Atlanta. Aaron and Emilia were somnambulistic, Libby and Cornelia having to guide them through all the iffy movements of climbing onto the train, sitting down and, whenever necessary, eating food in the dining car. The only things they were capable of doing on their own was holding one another's hands and quietly blaming themselves for Albert Brooks' sudden heart attack. It was complete nonsense of course, but grief just naturally drifts toward the nonsensical. At long last, the train arrived in Atlanta, and on the day just prior to the funeral.

Libby had never seen a city as large as Atlanta. Both the cities of New Orleans and Baton Rouge would have easily fit into just one section of Atlanta. Her first reaction to Aaron's family home was one of pure panic. Two seconds over the threshold, three people were clinging desperately to Cornelia, Aaron, Emilia, and Libby.

Aaron's boyhood home was large and bright and airy—and old. Pre-Civil War old, having survived Sherman, Carpetbaggers, Reformation and all the wars and woes that followed these primary disasters. It had always been the home of the eldest son of the Brooks Family. Now it was to be Aaron's. Trouble was, neither Aaron—nor Libby—wanted it. Aaron also knew that on her own, his mother would never be able to cope with the old manse. After the highly attended and stiffly formal funeral of Dr. Albert Brooks, a reception followed at the Brooks home. Libby only had the one black dress, but mercifully it suited all of the somber occasions. Emilia seemed to be rallying but Cornelia remained close by her side.

Libby was largely ignored by members of the family. Long-time friends, taking this familial cue, ignored her as well. The girl seemed nice enough, and she was certainly attractive, but prior to his death, Dr. Brooks had pronounced Aaron's rumored attraction to the backwoods Louisiana belle to be merely a youthful dalliance, and that, no matter what Emilia might believe of the situation, any subsequent marriage was completely off the table. Even in death, the Brooks family and friends went right on believing Albert, and so, Libby was dutifully avoided.

Which left her standing alone in front of a fireplace that was large enough to roast an entire ox. Wearing her little black dress, black stockings and black patent shoes, she looked elegant, however, she felt more like the ghost attending its own wake. In the meantime, Aaron was holed up in the library with the family's attorney and three of his male cousins. He emerged briefly, had a quiet word with both his mother and Miss Cornelia, and then quickly led them both to the library. With their exit, Libby gave up trying to be social. She left the reception and climbed the stairs to her room, not missing for a second the pleased expression held by the housekeeper, Mrs. Avery.

An hour later, Aaron softly knocked on her door. The instant she opened it he kissed her hard on the mouth. Then as he held her in his arms he said, "I'm so sorry sweetheart. I know you've been treated abysmally."

"I hate it here, Aaron!" she sobbed.

"I know, I know. But the good news is, you and I are leaving tonight. We're going home."

"But what about the house? Didn't you just inherit this humble pile?"

Aaron laughed as he set her down on her feet, and oh, it felt so good to laugh. "Yes, my darling, I did indeed inherit this somewhat imposing pile and I owned it just long enough to sell it off to my cousin Nathaniel.

Therefore, it remains the Brooks Family seat, but I'm no longer the one required to do the sitting."

"But what about Mother Brooks? Where is she supposed to go?"

"Wherever she wants. Other than the twenty thousand dollars I've claimed as commission for brokering the sale, she's an independently wealthy woman. She's free to go wherever, and do whatever she pleases. Amazingly, what she pleases is to take up painting, and where she pleases to go is Miss Cornelia's cottage."

"You're joking!"

"Not a bit. Call me conceited, but I also believe that she enjoyed my preaching so much that she also wants to join the Henrytown Free Church. At any rate, she and Miss Cornelia will be packing her up and then following us in about a week."

"Does your mother even know how to paint pictures?"

"My darling, I have no idea. Quite candidly, the woman has begun to baffle me."

Libby threw herself into Aaron's arms. "Oh! I don't care if she can or can't. I'm just too happy that we'll all be together." Aaron was thoroughly enjoying the hug until Libby began squirming. "Hang on a minute," she said, pulling away from him. "Did I hear you correctly? Did you just tell me that you have twenty thousand dollars?"

"No, my little love, I said we—***we***—have twenty thousand dollars."

Libby drew a sharp breath. "Aaron! We're rich!"

"Well not quite, but certainly we have enough that it would be wise to follow the dictates of the wealthy."

Libby rolled her eyes. "Aaron Brooks, would you please stop speaking Atlanta and start speaking Louisiana?"

"Oh. Right. What I meant was, people with money never talk about it." When her face began to purple with the threat of an impending explosion of temper, he quickly said, "Libby—we never talk money with other people. And besides, Miss Cornelia has agreed to open accounts in her bank in Baton Rouge for both Mother and for us. Therefore, for as far as anyone is to know, Mother is just a nice little widow lady and you and I are still as poor as a pair of church mice."

"But what if somebody asks about the house?"

"We tell the truth. The house and its contents became the immediate property of my eldest first cousin, Nathaniel Roberts-Brooks Esquire. And that's all we say Libby. I firmly believe that the Lord is preparing us for something and that we are to consider this new money as part of that preparation. Agreed?"

"Agreed," she said as she hugged him again.

"There's just one other thing, sweetheart. Will you please marry me?"

"Aaron! We're already engaged!"

"Yes, but what I meant was—now. Will you please, please, marry me now as in tonight?"

He didn't need to ask her a third time.

It was a very private wedding, attended by Emilia Brooks, Cornelia Faraday, and the newest owner of the house, Nathaniel Brooks, who stood as best man. Ironically, the wedding took place right before the very fireplace where only hours before Libby had felt so lost and alone. Judge Delbert Matheson, as an honored guest, had with one well-placed telephone call cleared all of the pesky legal details that might have taken days to manage. Pastor Buchanan, who had officiated Dr. Albert Brooks' burial, happily officiated the nuptials. Now that she was a widow, Emilia slipped the wedding ring off of her finger and gave it to Aaron who placed it on Libby's. He kissed the ring on his bride's hand and then he kissed his bride. It truly was a lovely wedding, even if the whole thing was done and dusted within a matter of minutes. Which meant of course that the pair would not need to be chaperoned for the long trip back to Louisiana.

In the very moments the cab was whisking the newlyweds off to the train depot, Miss Cornelia was telephoning the Western Delivery Telegraph Office because—well, sometimes the contents of a telegram were just more carefully thought through than any news broken by way of a telephone call. There were a lot of people in Henrytown, principally the bride's parents, who were going to feel cheated by this quick marriage. Cornelia had already trod that road: she wasn't all too eager for a second go. Therefore, she measured each telegraphed word most carefully.

Am obliged to remain in Atlanta. Stop. Due to fears of any hint of indiscretion, Aaron and Libby chose to marry. Stop. Pastor and Mrs. Brooks will arrive Henrytown late tomorrow afternoon. Stop. They beg your understanding. Stop. Signed; Miss Cornelia Faraday.

Standing in the center of the living room with his son by his side, Yancy read the telegram out loud to Mildred and Casper. Yancy and Casper grinned, then laughed as they shook hands. Mildred, who had been working on the hem of Libby's wedding dress and having it spread out all over her lap, collapsed back against the couch and dissolved into tears.

"Mama!" Yancy barked. "This ain't no time to boo-hoo. Those children did the right thing. A preacher an' his fiancé can't be riding a sleeper train without a chaperone. Such a thing would have too many people snickering about our daughter walking down the aisle in that white dress you're getting so upset about."

"Well I just don't understand how Cornelia couldn't be on the train with them!" Mildred bawled.

Yancy went to his wife and retrieved the silk dress before Mildred's tears ruined the fabric. Lovingly, he began to fold it neatly. When she began to protest, he said, "Hush woman. I'm savin' this for the granddaughter we're gonna have one day."

Without another word, Mildred got up, went to the bedroom and came back with the packing box and protective tissue papers. Together Yancy and Mildred wrapped and boxed the dress. "I'll store it in the cedar chest," she sniffled. "I may not be around to see my granddaughter marry, but I'll be with her all the same."

"Yes, you will, Mama. Yes, you will." When the box was closed and sealed with a blue ribbon, Yancy said, "I think you need to start workin' the phone now sweetheart. This town's got a train to meet tomorrow." Hearing Casper going for the front door he yelled, "Where are you off to this time of night?"

"I'm gonna find Seth an' then head over to Archie's. We got some plans of our own to be makin' ya know."

As the train began its slowing for the Henrytown platform style depot, Libby, who had been a mountain of courage throughout the ordeal of the funeral, wake and hurried wedding, was now a bundle of nerves and holed up in the tiny sleeper compartment's bathroom. Aaron was fully clothed and stretched out across the bed and on his stomach staring somewhat misty eyed out of the compartment's little window. His first day of marital bliss had begun with him getting dressed, leaving Libby asleep and heading off for the dining car where he had a breakfast tray prepared. Then he'd carefully carried the tray back to the compartment. Luncheon had been a repetition of breakfast, but with the exception of carrying back the tray with dirtied dishes. The porters tried very hard not to smile as he handed the tray over. Neither did they ask if Madame would be coming to the dining car. The couple were honeymooners, and other than some sandwiches, there was nothing outside of their sleeper compartment that they needed nor wanted. It was now three in the afternoon and, as the reality of facing her hurt and angry parents drew closer by the minute, Libby was beside herself.

Aaron had no idea how to comfort her because, quite frankly, he was just too happy about being married. As he was now only preoccupied with the same glee that Adam must have known when God had married him to Eve, Aaron could not remember a word of the lectures on grief and fears counseling that he'd attended during seminary. Therefore, Libby was left to struggle through her fearful emotions all on her own—and in the little bathroom because she knew that if she had to look at Aaron's euphoric face for one more second, she was going to clobber him. She was blowing her nose into a wad of toilet paper when she heard him calling out over the noise of the train.

"Sweetheart! I don't think anyone is especially angry with us!"

Libby opened the bathroom door just enough to look out. Aaron, still belly down across the bed, quickly waved for her to join him. "You've got to see this Lib!!"

The compartment was so small that with three quick steps and then an inelegant belly-flop, she was on the bed beside him, their faces framed inside the little window as they looked out at the crowded platform. Simply everyone was there, the men holding up large pasteboard and hand painted signs on long handles while the women alternately wept into and then waved their hankies. The signs read:

Welcome Pastor & Mrs. Brooks.

Oh you kids!

Welcome home!

Happy Daze Ahead!

The largest sign had three handles and each handle was held by Casper, Seth and Archie. In excessively large painted lettering the sign read: *Did you sleep all right Aaron*?

Reading their sign, a horrified Libby shrieked, "I hate my brother!"

A laughing Aaron said, "Lib, you don't know the sign was Casper's idea."

"Yes I do! He's the only one in that trio of goons who actually knows that "all right" is two words not one. I keep telling you he's a horrible brother, you just continually refuse to believe me."

Aaron raked the corner of his mouth with his teeth. "Well sweetheart, we've been spotted." Libby looked closer and saw Mabel busily pointing to the pair of faces in the window. As soon as others saw what she was seeing, they waved directly toward the compartment window.

As Aaron and Libby waved back, Aaron said, "Put on your shoes and hat my darling wife. We officially belong to the masses now."

There remains to date and secured to the west wall of the Henrytown Free Church Fellowship Hall, marking its first ever function, that reads: *In the celebration of the marriage of Pastor Aaron and Mrs. Libby (Nee Flowers) Brooks—1935.*

In the next months, life moved at a quick-silvered pace. Miss Cornelia and Aaron's mother, Miss Emilia, returned to Henrytown to find Archie and Emma living in the back cottage. "That house is just too big for us!" they declared. "So, we switched. Ya'll don't mind, do you?"

As it happened, the house trade worked out to be a blessing. Emma felt more comfortable managing a smaller house when Archie was home but when he went back at the patch, she brought her nightie, bathrobe, slippers and toothbrush and slept in her former bedroom. She called it "camping with the girls." Over the passing of weeks, both Cornelia and

Emilia became involved with various church committees and having a larger space in which to gather the committee ladies proved highly advantageous. Then too, Emilia was finally allotted the time as well as the space she'd always wanted in order to take on oil painting. Painting was an art form she'd always enjoyed. Unfortunately it was also one that Albert had declared to be a waste of her time. Not that she lacked talent, she most assuredly had that. No, his objection was that her hands were mired by paints and that no matter how well she bathed she continually reeked of turpentine. As a dutiful wife, her function was to attend to his son as well as her required hostess duties. If she then had any free time, he strongly recommended she take up crewel stitchery.

But, she was a widow now and as such, Cornelia not only encouraged her to emerge from her stifling cocoon, she'd also helped Emilia clean out the attic. Then they hired Bubba to install skylight windows in that section of the roof. Then Cornelia drove Emilia to the artist supply store in Alexandria where the two of them bought brushes, canvases and paints—and an entire gallon of turpentine.

But the big shock to Aaron's senses was that his mother, Miss Emilia Brooks, was not just wearing trousers. Nope, her favorite clothing was now overalls worn over a feminine short sleeved blouse. The legs of the overalls were rolled up to the ankles and her feet were shod in odd looking little canvas slip on shoes. Whenever he wanted to see his mother, he typically found her either working on a painting up in the attic studio, or she was out in the back garden digging in the earth. She had even joined a type of ladies club whose sole purpose was to trade cuttings and tulip blubs. As his mother, she was also deeply concerned about the ragged and half-starved children of the area, and by pressing Cornelia and Becka into service, the three had taken over the Stone Soup Suppers, relieving Aaron and Reverend Waite of the Methodist church of this shared responsibility.

On the heels of all this, Emilia had felt the call to donate twelve treadle sewing machines to the Henrytown Free Church and before Aaron or the deacons knew it, twelve sewing machines were lining the walls of the fellowship hall. It was on these machines that the ladies of both churches sewed clothing of all sizes for both boys and girls. The suppers soon not only provided weekly meals, they had become the means of distributing new clothing for the needy local children.

Mabel had been worrying that now Aaron was a married man, his wife Libby would take over the house, which meant Mabel would again join the national ranks of the Depression's unemployed. However, Aaron was now busier than ever and Libby, as his full time secretary (she never did get her official certificate), had all she could do to keep him on schedule while she managed the brand new church office. One of Libby's most infuriating duties pertained to an especially horrible kind of paper that had a top sheet and a stencil sheet. The two pages came connected together and a box of these papers were so costly that typing errors were not encouraged. After carefully peeling the (hopefully error free) typed top page from the stencil sheet, she then had to fit the stencil onto the barrel of the brand-new mimeograph machine. Then the barrel was filled with foul smelling blue ink and she turned the handle on the barrel while the ink inside squeezed into the stencil and the machine spat out as many copied pages of the typed original as was needed. It was on this contraption—that gave Libby no end of fits—that the first church bulletins and orders of service were printed and given out to the congregation. Thursdays had become Libby's dreaded Mimeograph Days and every Thursday evening she came home swearing blind that had she known that that blasted machine was to be the third party in her marriage she would have more carefully thought through Aaron's marriage proposal.

In the light of all this high activity and Thursday drama, Mabel's role as cook/housekeeper was more vital than ever. And now that the church office had been relocated to the church itself, Mabel was finally allowed to clean the parsonage study. The bookcases and the roll top desk had been hauled over to the new office, and the horde of money that Aaron had kept locked up inside the roll top desk had been safely deposited in the bank in Baton Rouge along with the rest of the monies he'd inherited. In total, the account registered to Pastor and Mrs. Brooks was twenty-five thousand, nine hundred dollars. But, it might just as well have been twenty cents for all they cared because, as far as they were concerned, every single dollar of it was the Lord's Money.

In December a joyous Christmas came and on New Year's Eve, a hectic 1935 went. No one knew what 1936 would bring, or why the radio news was so captivated with the foreign names, Adolf Hitler and Benito Mussolini, when everyone knew perfectly well that the important news was that the late Huey P. Long's "Share Our Wealth" programs were rapidly dwindling. Then came the news that the very men who had promised Huey so faithfully that they'd carry on his programs were now being exposed for corruption. The only light left to flicker on the statewide horizon was the rumor that Judge Richard Leche was about to run for governor, and that Huey's brother, Earl K. Long, was going to run as Leche's Lieutenant Governor. To firm up the rumors both men were almost nightly on the radio promising how they would revive Huey's work of helping the poor; that what the state needed were more roads, bigger bridges, more hospitals and schools. All of that sounded quite fine and promising, but the upshot was, at present the only people actually helping the poor of Henrytown were its Christians: The men were volunteering their work anywhere they were needed, while the women served the Stone Soup suppers and were keeping the church sewing machines humming. The politicians talked, the Christians quietly worked and, as a witness to all of it, Aaron continually fell to his knees and thanked God for the privilege of being a member of the Christian Family.

The first wedding in the expanded Henrytown Free Church was the marriage of Bubba and Myrna, on February twenty-third, 1936. Bubba, having lost eighty pounds and wearing a new dark blue suit, white shirt, brand new lace up shoes and with his hair all trimmed and slicked down, made a surprisingly handsome groom. Most of the unmarried young women in the packed-out church were both greatly surprised and then greatly upset that they had let him go to a foreigner from Evangeline Parish. Because when all was said and done, never mind that she'd lived and worked in La Salle Parish for years and years, Myrna would always be that "*Coonie*" *from Evangeline.* And as by way of proving this sore point, everyone in the church was for the groom, whereas there was just one little seventeen-year-old blonde girl with huge green eyes who had come by train to stand as family for the bride. Her name was Merci Edmond and she was the niece of Myrna's first husband. No one understood what kind of mother would name her daughter "thank you," but Cajuns were a peculiar folk. There was just no guessing their reasons for doing anything.

A week before the wedding, Merci had carefully packed her best two dresses for the trip into the faraway country of La Salle Parish, but even in Henrytown, her bayou best wasn't quite good enough. Still, she wore what she had with as much dignity as her tiny body owned. When she was introduced to Miss Cornelia and Miss Emilia both of the venerable matrons instantly loved the somewhat grubby, yet quietly regal, Merci. So, of course, they took her over. It's what they did. Any time those two found a muddy jewel, they just felt compelled to scoop it up and polish it to a high sparkle. On the day of the wedding, their polishing efforts were readily apparent, for now Merci was dressed in a brand new pink dress with matching hat, white shoes and white gloves, and her golden blonde hair had been neatly bobbed. Merci did indeed sparkle like a diamond and the combination of her inherent gracious manner and splendid appearance was so becoming that as she stood as a bridesmaid next to Myrna, she rather unfortunately made the blushing bride seem rather washed out and plain.

And one of the ushers, Casper Flowers, could not keep his eyes off of her.

Free Church people did not drink wine. Merci could not understand a wedding reception that did not involve wine. But Myrna, whom she loved like a mother, seemed so very happy. Merci sipped the too sweet punch and forced a smile, determined that she would not display any disapproval of this very strange way of celebrating a new marriage. But the question remained, if this uncomfortable gathering was how they celebrated a wedding, whatever did these people do when a child was safely born—throw ashes on their heads and wail?

"Hello," a male voice said close to her ear.

She had to turn her head in order to see beyond the side rim of the bell style hat. A very nice looking young man smiled at her.

"My name's Casper."

"I am so pleased for you," she answered with a sweet smile.

"*Caspar*—that is a very strong name."

"An' I like the way you Frenchy it up," he chuckled.

"My name is Frenchy too," she laughed. "It is Merci. Because my mother thanked the Holy Mother that I did not die the way the midwife said I would."

"Why would the woman say a thing like that?"

Merci waved a dismissive gloved hand. “I don’t know. I was only born so I didn’t yet understand French.”

Casper exploded into laughter the precise moment that Archie and Emma were walking by. Archie stopped, forcing Emma to stop right along with him. “Whatcha doin’ Cas?”

“Oh, I’m just sittin’ here fallin’ in love,” he grinned.

“Well,” Archie drawled as he began to hurry his nosy wife along. “Ya picked a fine day for it.”

As Archie was forcibly dragging Emma off, she was whispering like a hissing snake, “What is Casper doing? Didn’t he bring another girl to this wedding?”

“Yeah.”

“Well, what in the world does he think he’s going to do with two completely different girls at the very same social?”

“I have no idea. But at the first sign of ugly, we’re outta here.”

Chapter Twenty-Four

Casper Flowers was too much of a southern gallant to simply dump his date and run off with another girl—no matter how badly he might want to. But he did keep a close eye on Merci all through the remainder of the reception. And then he saw her leaving with Miss Cornelia and Miss Emilia. Which made sense seeing as how Bubba and Myrna would be honeymooning in their house and a virginal teenaged girl under the same roof would put something of a damper on their wedded bliss. But not knowing how long Merci would be remaining in town was quite frankly killing Casper. His great fear that she might be boarding the train as early as tomorrow morning had him sweating like a mule in the noon day sun.

Within minutes of Merci's departure, he took the arm of his date and they lingered just long enough to wish the newly married couple well, and then he all but frog marched that poor girl to his truck and sped her home. Once she was safely deposited on her father's doorstep, he was back in the truck and blasting his way to Miss Cornelia's where, after his arrival, he all but beat the door down.

A robed Miss Cornelia answered, and seeing Casper she folded her arms across her chest and treated him to a withering look. When Casper opened his mouth, she promptly raised a silencing hand. "I do understand why you're here, Casper Flowers. And I cannot say that I'm in favor of your presence. You are a renowned chaser and I'll not have you chasing the innocent presently residing in my house as a guest."

"But you don't understand—"

"Yes, I do, young man. You're seeing Merci as a delightful challenge because she's different from the girls around here, and you've become bored with what's familiar. But I would advise you, and most sternly, to stay with what you know. Merci was raised in a convent. She does not know the ways of young adventurous men. And remembering the number of young girls you brought under my roof, you are truly adventurous. Now, while I truly do appreciate that you would respect her physical innocence, it's her emotional innocence you would make a ruin." He opened his mouth again, and again she beat him to the punch. "Don't even try to say different, Casper Flowers. This town is positively besieged by the number of hearts you've broken. Hers will not be added to this deplorably lengthy list. She will soon be going home to her own people and to her own future, and I'm making it my business to see to it that she goes home without the encumbering shackles of a painful memory. You have no earthly idea the crippling effect that has on a young woman. If you did, you wouldn't be so quick to chase. Now you just take yourself on home, my young sir and do not even try darkening my door again before Merci is safely gone." To put paid to her pronouncement, Miss Cornelia slammed the door in Casper's bloodless face.

He was just driving, not knowing or caring where he was or where he might be going. His mind was busy on other things because frankly, his confrontation with Miss Cornelia was the first time he had ever been called to account for his habitual philandering. He'd really never meant any girl any harm; he'd just preferred to think of himself a roaming honeybee, and each girl a lovely flower. But according to Miss Cornelia, he was indeed responsible for a lot of harm, and a woman like her really ought to know a thing or two about life. Once upon a time she had been a young woman and what if some young buck had toyed with her emotions so badly that the pain of it had stopped her from marrying anyone else? If that was true, then it was not only horrible, it was a tragic waste!

Casper's booted feet simultaneously slammed on the break and the clutch, bringing the truck to an abrupt stop. The truck's headlamps shone out over the empty dirt road as he felt the awful twinges of a guilty conscience. What if the girl, Betty Jean, his date for the wedding, what if she was right now home and crying into her pillow because of the way he'd gotten shut of her just so he could go chasing after another and more exotic flower? Until this moment he'd never even given a single thought to how he might have publicly embarrassed her, how his literally dumping her off at her parents' door had left her to suffer small feelings about herself. All of that was not only brutish, it was pure heathen! A good Christian man didn't do things like that! Miss Cornelia was right to slam the door in his face. His face had needed a good door slamming. And little Betty Jean Armstrong badly needed an apology. Knowing where he was going now, he put the truck's gears into first and made a U-turn, driving back toward Henrytown.

The Armstrong house, a modest two-story, was completely dark. Casper didn't want to wake the entire household, so he made an educated guess as to which upper window belonged to Betty Jean's bedroom. He chucked a pebble at it. Then a second pebble. Then a third. He was getting ready to chuck a fourth when the window opened and a recognizable figure leaned out.

"Hey Jeb," Casper said in a loud whisper.

"Hey Casper," Jeb Armstrong whispered back.

"I'm lookin' for Betty Jean's window."

"Yeah. That's what I kinda figured. Wouldn't waste your time though, she purely hates your guts."

"Yeah," Casper said. "That's what I've been figuring."

"She said when you go straight to hell that she hopes old Satan himself boils you in a big old pot of putrid oil."

"That's some kinda hatin' all right."

"For all of eternity, Casper."

"Okay now that has just bumped up hatin' a few extra notches. Jeb, I really do need to apologize to her."

"Third window down. Good luck to ya Casper." Jeb went back inside his room and closed his window.

One pebble. Second pebble. Third. A split second after the fourth, the window flew up and Betty Jean was leaning out. "Casper Flowers, you swine, you stop throwin' rocks or I swear I'll come down there and turn the water hose on you."

"Wouldn't blame ya if you did. An' not just because of the rocks, but on the way I behaved tonight. You're a sweet girl Betty Jean Armstrong and I'm sorry for not appreciatin' just how lucky I was that someone like you would even agree to go out with me. So, I come over here to beg you to forgive me, an' maybe, give me another chance."

Betty Jean remained quiet. She had loved Casper Flowers since she was nine years old. Throughout the subsequent decade she had watched him date every girl in town. When he'd finally asked her out, she believed he'd been responding to the love shining out of every inch of her. Well, then he'd shown her only too clearly and too painfully that his asking her out had meant that it had just been her turn to have a whirl on the great Casper Flowers merry-go-round. She had been warned, oh, yes she had. But she hadn't listened because of all her stupid romantic hopes that true love would win the day. Well, it hadn't. He'd all but ignored her and then he'd made a public fool of her with his outright ogling of that Cajun girl. Betty Jean had never been so embarrassed, and it was even more mortifying to think that right now probably everybody in town was feeling sorry for her. But it wouldn't stop there, *oh no-no-no-no—NO*! Bright and early in the morning the Crow's Nest would be roosting on the party line and the lone topic would be, Betty Jean

Armstrong, bless her poor little old heart. And each and every spoken sentence would begin, “Well, I just feel so sorry for her . . .”

But all that sorry sure wouldn’t stop them from talking about it for days, possibly even weeks on end. She was a laughingstock and every bit of it was Casper Flowers’ fault.

“You just wait right there where you’re standin’,” she said as she slid the window closed.

He did. Like a long-legged determined sap, he stood there for hours, becoming dew soaked to the skin as he continued to convince himself that she was getting dressed, that she would appear at any moment, when the truth was, Betty Jean had gone back to bed. When the sky was turning a faint grey with the coming of daylight, Casper was about ready to give the whole thing up. That’s when Betty Jean finally came out onto the back porch.

He was sodden and exhausted but still earnestly repentant as she stood there looking at him with a disgusted expression and with her hands on her blue jean hips. As the morning light brightened, he could see her brown curly hair that was cropped just below a square jawline and the sides of it tucked behind neat little ears. What Casper liked best was that she looked so trim and fit in those jeans. She was barefoot, and from what he could tell at the distance was she also had nice little feet.

“I’ve given the whole thing a lot of thought,” she said. “And on behalf of myself and about four dozen other girls in this town, you can just go hang yourself Casper Flowers. I wouldn’t go out with you again even on a double dogged dare.”

“Hey,” Casper said calmly and as she was turning to go back inside the house. “I don’t quite remember you being so pretty. Have you always looked like you do now?”

To demonstrate her complete exasperation with him, her arms flew wide and then slapped her sides. "Well of course I have you stupid thing! I can only ever look like myself."

Casper's index finger punctuated each of his next words. "Then it's them britches. I never saw you wearing jeans before."

Seething, Betty Jean folded her arms under her breasts as one little barefoot beat an agitated tempo against the porch floor boards. Biting off each word she said, "In town I wear dresses, but I always wear jeans when I'm goin' out deer huntin' with my daddy."

"You hunt?"

"Yes, hair-brained boy, I hunt. An' good enough so that Mama always cooks venison roast for Sunday dinner."

"What do you shoot?"

"A twenty-two."

His cold hands deep inside the side pockets of his slacks and a smirky little smile playing his lips, Casper shook his head. "Can't shoot a good deer with no stupid twenty-two."

"You can if you neck shoot it!" she shouted. "A good neck shot will make a deer drop like a rock!"

That certainly wiped the smile right off of his face. "You're a good enough shot to neck shoot?"

Her tone became both smug and mocking. "Have been since I was ten."

Casper went thoughtful for a moment and then asked, "How are you at fishin'?"

"Not as good as some, but better than most," she replied.

And that did it. Casper started walking for the porch.

"What do you think you're doin'?" she squawked.

"I'm comin' in for coffee an' a long talk with your daddy is what I'm doin'."

Betty Jean hurried to the steps to try to block him. Casper's response was to lift her off her feet and sling her through his left arm like a killed fawn. Carrying Betty Jean hanging at his side like an upside U, he walked straight into the kitchen and said to her stupefied parents as they sat at their kitchen table, "Mr. an Mrs. Armstrong, I'm formally requesting ya'll's permission to court your daughter."

"Don't give it to him Daddy!" Betty Jean yelled down to Casper's boots.

Ignoring his daughter, Mr. Armstrong asked, "Casper Flowers, why are you lookin' all wet?"

"I'm wet because your daughter had me standin' outside all night long when all in the world I was tryin' to do was apologize to her. And now here she is trying to deny me a cup of coffee so's I can warm up."

Mr. Armstrong turned in his chair and looked back to his son who was leaning against the kitchen's door frame and smiling wider than the Cheshire Cat. "Jeb, go fetch Casper some dry clothes." As Jeb disappeared, Mr. Armstrong turned back to Casper. "Might wanna set Betty Jean down. She's lookin' like she's about ready to start buckin' on ya." As Casper complied, Mr. Armstrong said to his nearly traumatized wife, "Mama, stir yourself an' pour this man some coffee."

Two days later, Merci boarded the train for home and, the Cajun boy who was growing desperate to see her again. Casper would never forget Merci. He would never regret having flirted with her or that his efforts in playful pursuit had ended with Miss Cornelia giving him a hard talking to. It was because of all of this that he'd finally opened his eyes and discovered what had always been standing right in front of him. Casper was not on the depot platform as Merci left La Salle Parish. He was sitting in a deer stand beside the girl he knew for certain that God intended him to marry: Betty Jean Armstrong.

***

In 1935, Adolf Hitler had thoroughly violated the Treaty of Versailles. The Luftwaffe had been reformed and Germany had rearmed herself and enacted the order of conscription into the Wehrmacht.

Jews had begun to leave the country just as too many were simply disappearing in the night, their homes and businesses seized by the State. Any Christian, be they high ranking members of the clergy or simple laity, heard speaking against Hitler, were also steadily vanishing. By the beginning months of 1936, the Intelligentia were now finding themselves under serious scrutiny. Hitler's hatred of this superior class had its effect on ordinary German citizens. Books, most especially non-German books, were filled with dangerous ideas, and the people who read them were unfit for respectable German society. Panicked that they might be accused of this offense, people began to purge their households of any and all disapproved of reading materials. In droves they turned these items over to the proper authorities for disposal. In other words, to be burned.

Yet none of this was making the national news programs, and especially not the Louisiana State news. National news was all agog that the former playboy Prince of Wales and now, the newly crowned king of England, was being rumored to be playing it fast and loose with a married American woman. (And a Royal scandal involving a handsome bachelor king always trumps any doings of some ugly little spud of a German fella.) On the local front, Judge Richard Leche and Earl. K. Long were becoming a shoo-in for Governor and Lt. Governor. On April 21st, 1936 when the Election Day was playing itself out, Libby wasn't in line at the polling station. She was in the Myrtle Hedge Medical Clinic where she was weeping and carrying on in a pure old conniption fit because the girl was convinced she had cancer of the female parts. Inside all of her caterwauling was the plea, "Please let me be the one to tell Aaron! He's not as strong as I am!!"

(*Oh, sweet merciful heaven*!)

As it turned out, Libby didn't have a hideous tumor. Nope, what she had was a baby.

Another interesting aside was that Aaron, without ever realizing it, had started a new style in men's casual attire. He hadn't meant to, it was just the outcome after the crates, containing of the last of his possessions in his former home, arrived from Atlanta. The 1930's was the decade of a craze called Hollywood Pants. High pleated waistline, wide legs and soft cotton material. Young men and women throughout the United States, lived in them. But due to the tropical heat of Louisiana, Aaron decided that washing and ironing shirts all the time was just too bothersome. So, he began wearing simple crew neck department store white T-shirts under his newly recovered, cotton navy-blue blazer. As if this wasn't eye-popping enough, he shed the Oxfords for the navy-blue slip-on canvas boat shoes that he'd picked up while once spending a week in Marble Head, Massachusetts, in the family home of his seminarian friend.

Everyone in Marble Head sailed. And the canvas boat shoes were called after the small factory exclusively supplying the yachting crowd. His friend had just called them, Sperry's. Aaron bought a pair, along with several pairs of the obligatory lightweight "Crew" socks, to wear around Marble Head, and then, he'd merely kept all of it as souvenirs. Finding the Sperry's and the socks in one of the shipped crates, and recognizing these items as a Godsend, he began wearing them all over Louisiana. Most especially during the week he was in the even muggier climate of New Orleans and attending a pastor's conference. The younger pastors all wanted to know what those shoes were and where he'd bought them. He happily answered, and a fashion craze of white t-shirt, blue blazer, and slip on Sperry's duly erupted throughout the southern portion of the eastern coast.

But aside from Aaron's new clothing style, the news that he and Libby were expecting a baby was the very news the town needed to lift it from a melancholy that was so insidious that no one could even stand the thought of listening to the radio anymore. Europe, Japan and Italy seemed to be having a shared kind of crazy and the new governor of Louisiana was only offering the weary people lofty future plans and then awkward excuses when those plans either failed miserably or were simply shelved. It was just flat out embarrassing every time the man opened his mouth. What Louisiana people had to do was "stay the course" and not grumble too much because he was confident he'd soon figure something out. And as one wag was heard to say, "Governor Leche don't just favor leading from behind the lines, he's the kinda fella who's still lookin' at a map trying to find the whole dern battlefield."

Emilia Brooks was so happy about becoming a grandmother that she was beside herself. Cornelia recalled the stitchery group, but now instead of needlepoint, the ladies were given soft pastel colored balls of fine yarn, pattern books and knitting needles. Meeting again in the large living room, the ladies were soon cranking out so many delicate layettes that these too became clothing offerings at the Stone Soup suppers. Meanwhile, Emilia (who abhorred stitchery of any kind) put her painting skills to work. But now, instead of canvas, she was coming daily to the pastorate repainting the room that had been used as a linen storeroom, reclaiming the room as a nursery. As Aaron pitched in, thus saving his mother from climbing ladders, Emilia studied his profile. Each night in her attic studio she made numerous charcoal sketches. Once the nursery walls were dry and glowing a happy sunshine yellow, and the ordered baby furniture was on its way from the best nursery store in Atlanta, Emilia set to work on the portrait of her son. Three months later, the finished oil painting was quietly passed on to the head deacon, Mr. Ralph, who saw to it that the canvas was properly framed. On Aaron's birthday, May 23rd, 1936, the portrait was unveiled in the fellowship hall. It is still considered to be the finest example of her work, among the many highly sought after works that Emilia Brooks would be known for.

On May 23rd, 2000, the portrait, after being appraised for slightly more than two million dollars, was ceremoniously given over to the Chancellery office of the sprawling La Salle Parish Bible College and Seminary.

By mid-August of 1936, the African-American, Jesse Owens, thoroughly trounced Hitler's Aryan Supermen at the Summer Games in Berlin by breaking or equaling nine Olympic records; breaking or equaling three World Records and winning a total of four Gold Medals.

On the home front, Seth married his longtime girlfriend from Olla, Miss Verda-Louise and Casper married little Miss (neck-shot a six point buck and purely dropped that sucker) Betty Jean Armstrong. To save money, it was a double wedding. The Sterlington camp was building more cabins, so Seth and Casper applied and each received a brand new one. Promptly following the duel wedding ceremony, brides and grooms were on the train to honeymoon in Sterlington. They would not be seen in Henrytown again until late October.

At first, Archie wasn't clear on just where this left him—camp room wise—because Emma was now in the early stage of pregnancy and suffering from extreme morning sickness. He was terrified of risking her health in the petroleum tainted air of Sterlington. To his relief, with his agreement to share the old cabin with three other camp bachelors, Emma would remain in their cozy home in Henrytown, and under the trusting eye of Miss Cornelia. What he was finding hard to live with was Emma's fixation for soda crackers and chocolate squares mashed flat between the two crackers. It spooked him half out of his mind when he accidently found her hiding in a closet with her mouth stuffed while she protectively clutched a box of crackers and a bar of Hershey's chocolate. At the parsonage, Aaron's gag reflexes were also being given a vigorous workout because Libby's pregnancy tastes were running rather violently toward the combination of watermelons and raw hot dogs. When the two expectant father's compared notes, they could only agree that their wives' cravings had somehow transformed them into ravenous beasts in a snarling feeding frenzy.

It was truly an unspeakable sight.

Archie eagerly climbed on the train and escaped to Sterlington.

Aaron remained trapped like a gagging rat.

At ten p. m. on Friday, October 9th, Libby pushed Aaron's shoulder as he lay on his side, his back to her. "Aaron? Wake up. Something's happening."

Aaron's eyes popped open, but it was just as dark in the room as it had been behind his lids. Hearing nothing more, he closed his eyes again.

"Aaron!"

He bolted up in bed. "What? What's wrong?" He pulled the small chain on the banker's style lamp secured to the white enameled wrought iron headboard. Libby looked pale and sweaty, and she'd kicked all of the covering away from her bloated body. She was so heavily pregnant that the only way she could sleep to any degree of comfort was on her right side and with several pillows tucked up around her, and with one positioned between her knees. This arrangement also meant that she took up nearly all of the bed. Throughout this last stage of pregnancy, Aaron had felt he was sleeping uphill while clinging tenaciously to the edge of the mattress. But he didn't grumble because he knew she would hit him if he did.

"Should I boil water?"

"NO! You should call the doctor and tell him it's started. Then you should call my mamma." When he just stared at her, she yelled, "Now, Aaron!"

Wearing only his BVD's, he raced down the hallway and into the living room. The buzzing signal roused the catnapping switchboard operator. When she recognized the line and plugged into it, she didn't give Aaron a chance to say not even one word.

"Libby's havin' her baby isn't she?! Don't you worry Pastor Aaron, I've got the call list. You just go stay with Libby and I'll do the rest." She pulled the plug on Aaron. On his end, shrugged his shoulders and dutifully hung up.

Then he decided he'd better get dressed. In the bedroom every question he put to Libby was either answered with a snarl or a long drawn out moan.

This was going to be a muddle-some night.

Dressed in thick socks, jeans and flannel shirt, he decided he should eat something in order to keep his strength up. Oh, and make coffee. Yancy would be driving Mother Mildred, and Yancy would want some coffee. In the kitchen, Aaron first readied the drip coffee pot and then put the water kettle on the stove to boil. This action should have brought back fond memories, but it didn't. He was hungry. He was standing at the new refrigerator, a wedding gift from the entire congregation. Bubba X had installed it and had been purely tickled to death to relieve Aaron of the old electric ice box. Aaron stood for a long time studying the contents of the appliance's shelves; something he could do now that he had a modern refrigerator with a built-in light. There was still some roast from last Sunday's lunch. He wondered if meat that old was dangerous.

"Hey honey?" he yelled over his shoulder. "Do you think that the leftover roast is still all right enough for me to have in a sandwich?" She answered, but her hollering was reminiscent of someone in dire need of an exorcist. Then too, what was said inside the hollering truly doesn't bear repeating.

Aaron was in the living room staring out the screened door and eating his iffy roast beef sandwich when a succession of lights flashed and bobbed outside in the blackness of night. Aaron opened the screened door as first Dr. Willington, a doctor only a few years older than Aaron but already a seasoned veteran in the birthing business, rushed straight on by him. The doctor was followed rapidly by Mother Mildred, who also ran on by him as if he didn't exist. Then came Miss Cornelia—ditto. Rapidly following Miss Cornelia was his very own mother who wounded Aaron to the quick when she charged on by as well. Last but not least, there was Yancy; whom, as it turned out, was the one and only person to recognize that the coming baby's father was actually in present.

"You got any more of them sandwiches?"

"Yes. But I can't guarantee the meat. It's from Sunday's dinner."

"Does it taste kinda sour an' maybe a litte gamey?"

"No."

"Then it's all right. Is that fresh coffee I'm smellin'?"

"Just made it."

"Good thinkin'. Things like birth take a while."

On the morning of October 11th, 1936, Joshua Edward Brooks, all eight pounds and seven ounces of him, came screaming into the world.

Just as Libby was falling into an exhausted sleep, she mumbled that she'd just had a dream that she been trying to push out a pumpkin while Aaron kept asking her to take a bite of a roast beef sandwich and give her opinion on it. Standing by the bed as Libby drifted off, Aaron looked at his baby son who was swaddled and serene in his arms. Joshua's round, and a tad bit reddish, face and with his closed and squinty eyes, was indeed remarkably pumpkin-esque.

December 22nd, Emma Lofthouse gave birth to a baby girl. She came with glowing red hair—just like Archie's. They named her Katie. Three months after this birth, Betty Jean found out that she was pregnant. Casper took another long look at Aaron's uncharacteristically untidy and frazzled looking appearance, as well as Archie's. This baby business seemed more and more like a real demanding kinda job. He had been teasing both men unmercifully about it all, but now the tide was turning, and knowing what was coming; the morning sickness, the lunatic food cravings, the waddling wife who cried over the least little thing, only to be followed by an infant with a pair of lungs the size of Texas, Casper became thoroughly horrified by the rip-tide rolling his way.

Although, not nearly as terrified as his sister Libby, and when she was terrified, she was hissy-fit prone. Thankfully, the clinic in Myrtle Hedge was learning to cope.

"I cannot be pregnant!" she wailed to the extremely patient Doctor Willington. "I was told that as long as I'm nursing the baby, I couldn't get pregnant."

"Did I tell you that Libby?" he asked in his mild, longsuffering manner.

"No," she snapped. "My mamma told me."

"And she received her MD from . . .?"

"I cannot be pregnant!" Libby persisted. "I am still having to wear maternity clothes because my real clothes are too tight."

"Your real clothes are still too tight because you're coming up on being three months pregnant."

Red in the face and huffing like a steam engine she vowed, "I'm going to kill Aaron."

A month later, Vera-Louise found out she was pregnant, and with twins, leaving Seth with such a pleased expression that he looked like a perpetually grinning monkey. As more and more couples were steadily being given the pregnancy diagnosis, the ever-expanding Free Church became jokingly known as First Passionate Church.

Bubba X had become a fully licensed contractor and, because of the quality of his work and his attention to detail, he was in high demand throughout La Salle Parish. The first client for the Flower's Construction Company's team of five, was the Henrytown Free Church. Already the newly built church was needing expansion in the nursery room in order to separate the toddler's area from the infant's nursery. The parsonage also needed expanding, a new hallway and bedrooms were being planned to jut out from the former study, leaving it as a walkthrough access to the new bedrooms as well as a playroom.

The crepe myrtle and bottle brush bushes would have to come up in order to make room for the extension. Bubba told Aaron that he'd lessen his construction fees in trade for the bushes. Aaron redirected Bubba to the head deacon. The bushes were church property, as was the parsonage. Bubba obediently went to Mr. Ralph, who was by now so impressed with Bubba, that he struck a deal of his own. The upshot being, not only would Bubba get the bushes but, he would also get a considerable lumber discount if he agreed to only buy from Mr. Ralph's lumber yard.

The deal was made, hands were shaken. Mr. Ralph was more than pleased to be adding the up and coming Flower's Construction to his client base.

He and Bubba had both come up against Miss Mabel's hard brand of mothering.

In Bubba's case, she was still fighting tooth and fang to keep her last baby boy in diapers for the rest of his life. In Mr. Ralph's however, he was having to put up with the constant lash of her acerbic tongue. In any case, Mr. Ralph was learning the new grace of patience and despite his mother, Bubba was steadily growing into a fine young man and husband. A husband who was even now hurrying home to tell his wife Myrna that she was going to be adding some stately old flowering bushes to her increasingly pleasant front yard.

Thinking about that young man, Mr. Ralph turned his thoughts in the direction of why both he and Bubba had waited so long to truly value their own worth. Only a year ago Bubba had measured his worth by his ability to outsmart everybody with his dumb act, whereas Ralph had measured his worth by how much money he had inside his wallet. Today, Bubba was happy just being Bubba the pretty smart fella and Mr. Ralph was happier not caring a whit about how much money he had on him.

Mr. Ralph sat at his desk and quietly talking this puzzlement over with the Lord when the answer came. And it came with the memory of a golden-haired young preacher giving a sermon on the true freedom of simply letting go of self-love and embracing the one and only true love—God. Now that had been a sermon that had truly knocked Ralph back in the pew. Then Aaron had gone on to say that the word *I*, is actually more God's name than it is a personal pronoun. He had them all turn in their Bibles to Exodus twenty and read with him the Seventh Commandment.

“Thou shalt not take the Name of the Lord thou God in vain.”

Then he had them whip over into Exodus 3:14.

“And God said unto Moses, I AM THAT I AM.”

Next it is written, ‘Thus shalt thou say unto the children of Israel, I AM hath sent me unto you.’

“Then in the Gospel of John, chapter 18, Jesus says of Himself, ‘I AM’. Therefore, whenever we are about to use those two all familiar words, we must first ask ourselves if our egos are supplanting Almighty God. And this is a vital question because the awesome God of eternity detests idolatry, and in bolstering our own egos we are indeed engaging in the soul crippling practice of self-worship.”

Well, Ralph had a week long think about it and finally came to the humiliating conclusion that, in brief, whenever he began a statement with, “I this,” or “I that,” that he’d done so because he’s felt like a teeny-tiny man desperately needing an ocean of attention and admiration. But, when he started being more careful with that word, the less noise he had to make. And the less noise he made the more people actually listened whenever he spoke. The whole thing hadn’t been easy, of course. The first two weeks he’d had to guard his tongue closer than a miser guards a quarter. But each day proved that it was worth the effort because he was increasingly feeling the prison door of pride swinging more widely open, thus setting the real Ralph Winters free.

1940 was quite a year. In June, Paris had fallen to the German army and President Franklin D. Roosevelt signed the Naval Expansion Act in order to increase the capacity of the U.S. Navy. The young men of Louisiana, desperate for work, were joining the Navy in droves because heck, being born and raised in a state that was mostly below sea level anyway, Louisiana boys were naturals for the Navy. Worrying about the

Army's peacetime thin ranks, in September the U.S. Congress approved the conscription draft, requiring all men from between the ages of eighteen through thirty-five to register for the Draft. All of the young men in Henrytown complied. Including Aaron. On November 5th, Franklin D. Roosevelt won his third presidential election. There was not one word via the newspapers, the radio or the movie theater's *Movie-Tone News Reels* of a place named Auschwitz.

By Christmas of 1940, Aaron and Libby had four children of stair-step ages. All boys: Joshua 4 years old, Caleb almost 3 years old, Jeremiah 18 months and Micah 1 month old. As Papaw Yancy was heard to say, "Every time Libby comes up pregnant the deacons' haf'ta vote to give Aaron another pay raise. But of late we have started to get a mite suspicious."

The whole town might be joking about their pastor's flourishing birthrate, but the remainder of the world was going nuts and faster than a squirrel could scamper. On the Louisiana level of nuts, not long after his landslide election as governor, Judge Leche became heavily involved in what continues to be known as the *Louisiana Scandals.* Indulging himself in the purchase of a yacht, a country estate and a private hunting preserve, Leche had been ridiculously easy to catch at taking hefty federal backhanders. Half of the regulars at the Bayou Café believed that Leche should be immediately sent to prison for Graft. The other half believed he should be hung for the crime of Stupid, because it wasn't as if Leche could easily hide his opulent lifestyle. And, most certainly not behind the cloak of an old moneyed family. Everybody and their dog knew the man's family was only just barely middle class! And as governor he was only earning around seven thousand a year! How in the world did he even begin to believe that no one would notice that he had being living like an emperor on a picayune budget?

But the true corker came when it was learned that the LSU president, Dr. James Monroe Smith had quite busily gambled away the school's money. It took great restraint on the part of the faculty, staff and student body not to unleash the university's mascot—a real live Tiger—on the embezzler. Dr. Smith and Governor Leche were forced to resign their offices. Lt. Governor Earl Long, never implicated in any wrongdoing, was now serving as Governor. It was still early days to form an opinion about Earl, and as he was Huey P. Long's brother, and therefore inherently politically canny, the new governor knew that he was being continually watched by a highly distrustful citizenry.

Disgraced Former Governor Leche was duly sentenced to ten years in a federal prison. He was also immediately disbarred. Watching all the whoo-ha of his predecessor, the Governor Long was even more determined not to put a political foot wrong. Yet as it happened, his caution and almost excessive guardedness were exactly the attributes the inundated state had been badly needing in its new governor.

What all the regulars at the Bayou Café adamantly agreed on was that it was a good thing old Gumpy (Mr. Edward) had died like he did not long after Huey P's assassination. Because if he'd been alive for all the nonsense that came after—well, it would have just flat killed him.

Chapter Twenty-Five

In late October 1941, Libby felt supremely happy as she walked out of the church nursery. Two of her babies were napping while Caleb was pouring over his ABC's with Mrs. Everett. As she walked along the hallway toward the office, she knew she was facing yet another battle with the infernal mimeograph machine, but even that failed to dampen her spirits. Josh was in the local school's kindergarten and even though there had been one or two incidents involving his headstrong nature (where he'd gotten that, Libby couldn't fathom) he was enjoying kindergarten. Caleb was as jealous as he could be about this and was perpetually crying that he wanted to "go a-schoooo!" as the bit too proud of himself Josh climbed into the car to be driven off by Daddy. All four of her children were growing and thriving and—after years of looking like a bloated toad, she was finally getting her figure back.

Thank you, Jesus!

Libby was also wearing her beloved trousers. The struggle to get back to the size of the slacks had been monumental. Trying to remove baby weight was worse than trying to scrape off pine tar from the bottom of one's shoes, for no matter how much effort was used, there was always that little dab extra that resolutely clung on. The last five pounds had been Libby's, little dab extra. It didn't sound like much, but as far as the side zipper of her trousers was concerned, five was as good as fifty. But this morning, hallelujah! The zipper went up without any sweat beads forming on her brow and no skin had been pealed from her knuckles by zipper's metal teeth. So, she was feeling pretty fine about herself and life in general.

Until she picked up the newly delivered mail and saw an envelope from the War Department in Washington D.C. The official governmental envelope required no stamp. The American government didn't need postage stamps. An official looking round black seal where the postage stamp was normally placed was all the missive needed to be sent with all due haste. The envelope was addressed to Pastor Aaron Brooks and beside his name and church office address, there was a bold red inked imprint reading "Highly Confidential." This would mean that as his secretary—or even as his wife—she was not allowed to open the envelope. But she could stare at it as it lay in her hand and while she wondered why the bright sunny day, and a day when she was finally wearing her most favorite pair of slacks, had so suddenly lost all of its joy.

Aaron came into the office late. After dropping Josh off at school and picking up Miss Mabel, there had been household errands to run. Mabel had a list. The woman *always* had a list. Taking care of a busy household was serious business for Mabel and, when the pantry was low or she was out of Bon-Ami scrubbing powder, then conditions were critical to her continued existence. What with all the driving and waiting for Mabel, Aaron mightily wished he'd asked Libby to drop Josh off at school. But, coward that he was, he knew the reason behind his insistence on driving Josh to school and then picking up Mabel. They were a two car family now—thanks to Mr. Fred guardedly selling them the cheapest—as well as most reliable—runabout on his lot. Libby could have easily taken on the school run chore, but that would have left Aaron with the feeding, cleaning and then dressing of the three younger boys. He had no idea where Libby hid her extra arms, but he was certain his wife was part octopus. How else could she manage two lively little boys and one screaming infant all at the same time? His wife never failed to amaze him, especially when he felt he had all he could do to just to get Josh into the car on time!

Josh was a highly organized little chap. He knew exactly what needed to be packed inside his school satchel and he knew the correct order of placement. First came the Adventures of Dick and Jane Reader, then the Dick and Jane Work Book, followed by the Big Chief writing tablet, the four carefully sharpened pencils, and the one pink eraser, and lastly the ultra-box of crayons that Nana (Emilia) had given him. It was ultra because it had every crayon the Crayola Company produced and had its own built in sharpener. But the real bonus was that it had *both* the metallic silver and gold crayons. A child's coloring box didn't get more ultra than that. However, Josh's box was missing the *real gold* crayon. He had happily handed it over to a little girl named Suzie after she had consented to be his girlfriend. And not for just one measly recess, but for the entire school year. (Apparently Josh also knew how to drive a hard bargain.)

Libby was still holding onto the envelope and fretting over it when Aaron finally walked in. He was about to kiss her cheek when she pucker-blocked him with the envelope. Then she helped him remove his suit jacket as he studied the envelope with a questioning expression. This told her that he was just as mystified as she. And there she was, holding his suit coat and waiting for him to open the Washington D.C. envelope when he turned on his heel and walked into his office—and closed the door! Sometimes his exceedingly ethical behavior irritated her all the way down to her last corpuscle. How would Washington D.C. know if he shared the letter with his very own wife? Libby pressed her ear against the door on the oft chance that he might be reading out loud. (He wasn't.)

October 19th, 1941

Dear Pastor Brooks,

My name is Captain Andrew Marshal. I'm not the best recruiting officer so, I shall simply tell you the truth; that I am aware that you, as a fully ordained minister, have duly registered for any future draft. The purpose of my writing is to ask you to prayerfully consider joining the Army Chaplain Corps prior to any circumstance which might subsequently prompt a formal call up. The Corps is strictly voluntary and at present rather desperate for fit young men of God to join this special unit. There are no promises of entrance rank higher than that of 2nd Lieutenant, nor is there any guarantee of future safety. But soon, thousands upon thousands of young men will be needing Prayer Warriors dressed in the same uniform and on the same battle line to bolster their courage. It is on their behalf that I am reaching out to other young men of God.

This letter is to remain completely confidential. At present you are not even allowed to discuss it with your wife. What is encouraged my brother, is going to the Lord. Take as much time as you need and then please write to the address on the letter head and to my personal attention. Your decision will be considered final and no questions will be asked should your response be negative. We all serve Him when, where and how, He chooses.

Oh, I forgot to mention that there will be a form of boot camp. But to be fair, I did warn you I wasn't perhaps the best choice for Corps recruiting.

In Christ's Service,

Andrew Marshal

Cpt. Andrew Marshal—Asst. to Chief of Chaplains—U.S. Army Chaplain's Corps

Aaron did pray, he began immediately after reading the letter, but he didn't have to pray for very long, he already understood that he was meant to go; that he had always been meant to go. From the first he had known that his time in Louisiana was meant to be brief. He'd thought in marrying Libby, that wherever God might send him that they would go together. Now he understood the arrogance of presupposing his love and desire for her was in partnership with God's plan. Yet what God had meant was that where Aaron was meant to go, a wife and children could not follow.

He lay his head against the crook of his arm and wept against the top of his desk. Now he shared his small part in the suffering of Gethsemane. Yet, however small that portion might be of the bitter agonies suffered by Christ, the thought of leaving Libby, his little boys, was truly horrible. So horrible that it crushed his heart. But if war was—as the letter intimated—on the imminent horizon, then thousands upon thousands of husbands and fathers would be leaving their families. They too would know this horrific pain. And they would be needing Prayer Warriors marching with them.

Aaron now knew beyond any hope of doubt that he could not refuse their need.

It had taken over an hour to regain his composure, write, in his own hand, a confirming acceptance letter and then address the envelope. When he came out of his office, he saw Libby and Miss Massey, the head of the children's Sunday School department, on their knees as they examined the contents of an opened box, oohing and aahing over its contents. Looking up at him, Libby who, on the arrival of the box, had stopped thinking about the mysterious letter from Washington, and was again all smiles.

"Aaron! You really must see what the church board sent. We have study quarterlies, posters, coloring pages, Bible verse flash cards and teacher study plans! Isn't that exciting?"

Aaron went to his wife and drew her to her feet. He then bent her backward in his arms as he planted a passionate kiss on her lips. Both the dipped back Libby and the still kneeling Mrs. Massy, were stunned bugeyed.

"I have some errands to run sweetheart," he said casually as he righted her. Removing his suit coat and hat from the coat rack, he said breezily, "I won't be coming back into the office, and before you ask, yes, I will remember to pick up Josh."

Watching him walk out, and with that extraordinary kiss still burning her lips, Libby had no idea what she was supposed to say to Miss. Massey. So, she opted for redirecting the other woman's attention back to the box.

Aaron did not mail the letter from the small post office in Henrytown. There was more than likely speculation enough concerning the received confidential letter. Their handling a return letter would simply add more fuel to this speculation. Libby was his primary concern and she had to be protected from wild rumor for as long as possible. After posting the response in the Myrtle Hedge post office, he drove straight for the one person he felt he could trust. Amazingly, this was the same person he'd had problems trusting throughout nearly all of their initial acquaintance. But God had worked a change in this man and Aaron could feel God's guiding hand leading him in this direction.

Ralph looked up as his secretary opened the door to his office and poked her head inside. "Mr. Ralph? Pastor Aaron would like to see you if you have a minute."

Ralph placed the newly signed contracts between his mill and the State of Louisiana, into a folder. "Sure Ethel, I got a few minutes. Show the pastor in."

When Aaron walked in and took a chair, the first thing Ralph thought was, *the boy looks pure peaked*. Five minutes later, Ralph was looking a bit peaky himself. Then he grabbed the desk's second telephone, the phone designated strictly for in-house calling. "Hey Ethel, would you do me a quick favor an' call down to the yard and ask Yancy Flowers to get himself up to my office just as fast as he knows how to run, please? Thank you." Mr. Ralph hung up and turned back to Aaron.

Aaron was visibly alarmed. "Mr. Ralph, this wasn't meant to be shared. I'm not even supposed to be talking with you!"

"I understand you Pastor, but what you've got to understand is that this concerns not just the church but Yancy's daughter and his grand-children. I can't cut him out of this discussion. But I can promise you, as two of your deacons, that not one word of what's said will ever leave this room. You can trust Yancy an' me to be your Aaron and Hur an' hold up your arms just like they once did for Moses. An' son? From the sound of things, you're gonna be needin' us to do just that."

Once Yancy was filled in, and given a few minutes to process Aaron's bombshell, there was a lot that the three men needed to discuss.

Yancy's tone was belligerent. "That parsonage is church property, but them boys were born in it! Once a new pastor gets sent in, where are Libby and the boys supposed to go? Did ya even think about that, Aaron?"

"Yes, I did." Aaron said softly. "I'm fully prepared to pay the church for the house, the property and all the furnishings. I don't want Libby or the boys to be uprooted."

"I agree," Ralph said. "The church has plenty of usable land to build a new parsonage. Besides, we're still gonna need Libby to be our church secretary. Therefore, she needs to stay right where she is. If this country does go to war, we're gonna need to provide as much stability as we can for all the families who are all gonna be left behind. An' we first begin with our pastor's family."

"So, how much we money talkin' for Aaron buying the house?" Yancy asked.

Ralph did some quick calculations. "The furniture's old, the land is half boggy an' the only real value is the addition of the new bedrooms. All told, we're lookin' at a bottom line of replacement value of five hundred dollars." He turned in his swivel chair to face Aaron. "Son? Can you manage that amount?"

Aaron was so grateful he wanted to weep. Instead, he managed a thickly voiced, "Yes sir, I believe I can."

From there the continuing discussions surrounded finding Aaron's possible replacement. Finding another young preacher would be a waste of time, because if America did go to war, that young man would be called up too. They were going to have to find someone old, possibly retired. As this topic required more time than the subject of the parsonage, Mr. Ralph's secretary was asked to pick up Josh from school and then keep the little fella amused for as long as necessary.

Miss Ethel had been delighted. After running the errand, she fed Joshua the cookies she'd baked the night before and, was munching one herself as she listened to him read from his Adventures of Dick and Jane reader. He was a precious little boy, the pure spit of his daddy. Miss Ethel loved him, and she hated it when the private meeting finally ended, and she had to give him back to his father. But the private church business seemed to be settled as all three men shook hands, followed by manly type hugs.

Mr. Ralph said something that sounded like, "Now what we got to do is wait and pray." A remark that had Yancy Flowers looking as if he were on the verge of weeping. Miss Ethel didn't question any of this, not even in her own private thoughts. She had been Mr. Ralph's secretary for fifteen years. She was no longer the type of woman who questioned anything involving Mr. Ralph.

***

In the passing weeks, the prayers were intense and fervent. However, the waiting period was not that long. Following a joyous Thanksgiving and the beginnings of the busy Christmas Season, all hell on earth broke loose on December 7th.

On December 8th, America declared war on Japan. On the 9th and just days before the Draft Registration List was formally being used, Aaron received a telegram. On signing for the telegram, he was no longer the Henrytown Free Church's Pastor Aaron Brooks. He was now 2nd Lt., Aaron Brooks, U.S. Army Chaplin Corps and he was to report immediately to Ft. Sill Oklahoma.

Five minutes after the news, and after Aaron left for their bedroom to pack, Libby fainted. She knew the reason. After having worked so hard to slim down, she was again pregnant. She had not told Aaron, and now she had no idea how she would tell him. Thankfully, he hadn't even been there to witness the little spell. It had been Miss Mabel who had picked Libby up from the living room floor and, as Libby came groggily back to herself, she meaningfully warned, "You will not say one word. Do you understand me Cousin Mabel?"

Mabel vigorously nodded.

There was as much hoop-la seeing Aaron off at the depot as there had been when waving in the newlyweds. The older women cried, the men were stoic, and Libby not knowing what she was supposed to say to this man whom she loved only frantically. Finally she managed, "I promise I'll try very hard to save myself for you."

As he climbed the train's metal steps, Aaron was laughing. But as he leaned out of the compartment window, he shouted down to her, "I have loved you Libby Brooks from the first day you taught me how to make coffee! You do remember that day?"

Somehow, without screaming out the grief she was feeling, Libby managed a smile and a brisk nod. But as the train traveled further away, and Aaron was no longer hanging out of the window, her hands covered her mouth and she sank to her knees. Weeping uncontrollably, her mother-in-law Emilia Brooks, Miss Cornelia, Miss Becka Lofthouse and her own mother Mildred Flowers, were all on their knees as well, as they encircled her and enfolded her in their arms.

More telegrams were arriving to be signed for. And because the telegrams required a signature, the telegraph office had to telephone prior to delivery. This meant the draftee knew beforehand that the notice from the Army was coming, thus giving him just enough time to hike it out over to Myrtle Hedge to the recruitment offices of the all-volunteer Navy and Marine Corps. These two branches of the military, eager to help the Army draft dodgers, post-dated—by twenty-four hours—the signup papers with the addendum that the recruit acknowledged the owing of an extra day for *discharge purposes*. The Army screamed foul, but—as it was only the crybaby Army kicking up rough over the secretive practice—the Navy and the Marine Corps didn't care.

Bubba X was among those who ran before the telegram was delivered in the hopes that he would be accepted into the Marine Corps, but as soon as the Marine recruiting officer heard that Bubba's occupation was building contractor, he marched him next door to the Navy. Seemed the Navy was on the sharp look out for men just like Bubba for a special unit called the Seabees. The Seabees built the important things that the Marines would later need. Bubba X was treated like a highly valuable inductee and this made Bubba feel extra proud as he was being sworn in. He ran home and told Myrna the news and informed her that she was now head of operations for the Bubba Flowers Construction Company. She was already keeping the books and she had proven she could handle the work scheduling, so all he was really leaving her was the responsibility of bossing of the work crew. Bubba knew that his wife, in her waitressing days, had had to handle two temperamental fry cooks who had a wide range of knives at their disposal. That had been way tougher than her managing a few guys armed only with saws and hammers. Myrna could take over the company without even raising a sweat and they both knew it.

When Bubba left on the train for the distant and exotic sounding San Diego, California, only Myrna and Mabel were there to see him go. And as the train pulled away, Myrna turned to her sullen mother-in-law and said, "If you are ever publicly rude to me again, I will wear your mean old guts as garters. And it will go twice as hard for you if I ever find out you've written *MY Husband* any worrisome letters. The only thing you and I will ever write to him is good news. Bad news we will keep between just us. Is this clear to you Mother Mable?"

Yet again Mabel, who was growing progressively wary of the steely spines that were rampantly developing throughout the growing population of War Wives, knew better than to argue.

When Casper, Seth and Archie received their telegrams, they hurriedly signed for them because Aaron was already in the Army and they knew that without them to look out for him, Aaron would get himself killed long before he ever faced an actual battlefield. Kissing their wives and children good-bye—and to the ragged music of the platform band that Henrytown had managed to cobble together for the increasing purpose of seeing off its brave young men—the three Preacher's Boys all but jumped on the train. As the train headed off for Oklahoma, the three prayed with every turn of the giant steel wheels that they would not be finding Aaron already dead.

Actually, it was so far so good for Aaron. The Chaplin's School was a jeep drive away from the regular training post. His very first day in the camp Aaron had made a new best friend. His new friend was almost as physically helpless as he, but Aaron was much taller than the Chaplin Candidate known as Fr. John Mahoney, a Catholic priest of the Redemptorist Order, and of late of Dallas, Texas. He was also a typical Irish jokester who was astonishingly wiry and could easily wriggle through things like combat type fencing. When Aaron and Father John worked together as a team on the obstacle course, they approached—almost capable. The friendlier the two became, the more Aaron called Father John—RC—as in Roman Catholic. It wasn't long before Father John just naturally answered to it and so the nickname stuck.

All of the Christian men in the Chaplain Corps wore crosses on both lapels of their uniforms and one cross centered on the front of their combat helmets. The company had but one Orthodox Rabbi among them. His name was Morrie Wasserman. He was painfully shy but, with encouragement, he soon opened up to the friendliness of the others. The members of the company found Morrie's lapel emblems vastly interesting as they were small metal replicas of the Torah. And there was no mistaking his helmet in a rush because Morrie's was centered with the Star of David. On the right shoulders of their jackets, Aaron and RC bore the round blue and gold badge of a white dove with an olive leaf in its beak hovering over an opened Bible. Morrie's badge was white and blue and with the Star. One night at the chowhall, RC commented that if the three of them were cast adrift in a lifeboat, they'd be the perfect punch line of his favorite joke. He then told the joke. Neither Aaron nor Morrie got it, but it made RC laugh so hard that he slapped the tabletop, so they obligingly smiled.

In the next two weeks they learned how to survive climbing ropes and heave themselves over very high walls, and then how to crawl on their backs while their noses were barely touched by the low hanging barbed wire. Learning to march long distances in cadence was almost a type of holiday. There was also class work involving how they were allowed to teach to troops of mixed faiths, counsel terrified and troubled soldiers, how to comfort troops in hospitals and most importantly, how to administer crucial first aid on the battle field in order to maintain life while waiting for a trained team of medics to come on the scene.

By week three they learned how to drive Jeeps, AKA *Peeps and/or Leaping Elizabeth's*, through hilly and muddy fields and change flat tires in down pouring rain. They also learned what essentials were needed in their field cases. In Aaron's case was packed with one altar cross and one hundred pocket sized New Testaments. RC's case was heavier with folded vestments, altar cross, and candles and sealed boxes of communion wafers. Then there was Morrie's case, prayer shawl, a combat-green Yarmelke, a small Torah and Shabbat candles. After a few days of schlepping those cases through the same obstacle course they'd only barely managed to survive when unencumbered, Morrie and RC were tempted to become Protestants.

Aaron was straddling the top of the wall and was there to help pull RC the rest of the way. Once RC was safely on the wall with him, both men sat there laughing.

On the ground the Drill Sargent yelled, "If you two don't wanna get picked off by a Nazi sniper, I would strongly suggest you scramble down from there!"

With that, Aaron lifted his arms and shouted back, “People of France! Ignore the tanks and the guns! We’re men of God and we come in peace!”

RC was now laughing so hard that he almost fell off the wall.

The widely accepted version of military Chaplains was that they did not carry guns. The truth is, they were destined to be on the battlefield and in the trenches right alongside combat soldiers. As chaplains were wearing the very same uniform as the soldiers, they were considered, by the enemy, a viable target. Therefore, chaplains were obliged to defend themselves whenever necessary so as not be an extra burden to the men they had been called to serve. This meant that in week four, the chaplains were marched over to the rifle range.

Seth, Casper and Archie were excellent marksmen. They were so good in fact that they were now being trained as a three-man squad on heavy machine guns. But as soon as the company sergeant got word that the chaplains were going to be given rifle instruction, to the sergeant’s chagrin, his three best men immediately volunteered for the target pit duty. The chaplains most probably hadn’t fired so much as a popgun in their lives, and Sergeant Wil Owens wasn’t at all happy that his three Hot Shots might end up as target fodder. But, his Hot Shots had seemed oddly excited while they were volunteering.

“Preachers with guns,” Pvt. Seth Lewis was heard to laugh. “Sarge, ya just can’t let us miss the sight of that!”

“Just promise me,” the none-too-pleased Sergeant Owens said, “that you boys will keep low. And by that I mean belly down in the pit low. Only lift your heads to check the target after I blow the cease fire whistle.”

Peeking over the dirt rim of the trench, they spotted Aaron marching along in combat fatigues, boots and helmet and looking oddly natty. And the way he marched was kinda hysterical. He looked more like he was just strolling along and enjoying the sunshine. "I can't believe it," Seth said. "Aaron might march stupid, but he sure makes those boots and fatigues look good."

The Boys promptly agreed that Libby would fall over in a swoon if she could see her fearsome warrior husband. Following this brief brush of exhilaration, pit duty devolved into boring. First the chaplains sat down on the grass to hear a lengthy lecture. After that a gun rack was rolled out and, as their distant sergeant picked up an M-1 Garand and held it up high over his head, the Boys began to Improvise on the lecture they weren't, from opposite end of the range, able to actually hear.

"Gentlemen, this is a gun," Archie said for the distant Sergeant Owens.

"The skinny end ain't the part you put against your shoulder," Seth added.

"An' whatever you do," Casper said. "Don't turn to ask a question while you still have a loaded rifle in your hands!"

The six others in the trench laughed. After another few minutes, the men of the Chaplain Corps filed past the gun rack and each chaplain took one. That was when Casper hurriedly said to the other men, "You see that tall blond guy? He's mine!"

Trying to follow Aaron was like trying to follow a bouncing ball. As the other chaplains settled down on the ground and onto their stomachs behind the sandbag rifle barrel props, Aaron was still walking around as if he just couldn't seem to make up his rabbit mind as which sandbag he might prefer. This left Casper to run back and forth in the pit until finally Sgt. Owens bellowed, "Lay down Lieutenant! Sir!" Aaron obediently complied, while Casper again quickly changed places with yet another target spotter.

The best thing that can be said about Aaron's rifle-manship was that he hadn't managed as yet to blow his own head off. When Sgt. Owens blew the whistle to indicate cease fire, Casper pulled the mounted target down. To his chagrin, there wasn't so much as a powder burn on it. This could only mean that Aaron had been firing so high that flying birds had been in mortal peril.

"Well this is just embarrassing!" Casper cried. "I mean Sweet Lord have mercy, this guy's my own brother-in-law!" Thinking quickly, he yelled, "Any of ya'll gotta a pencil on ya?" One man did. Casper took it and used it to stab the target, just an inch off center. (Couldn't make this look too good) Then he used the pulley to send the target back up, which he followed rapidly with the target marker to indicate the hit. Sgt. Owens was not only surprised he was genuinely pleased. This first group of chaplains were given five more practice shots and each time Casper had had to employ the pencil against Aaron's still fresh as a daisy target. How Aaron was managing to miss a five-foot by five-foot target was truly flabbergasting. But yet, thanks entirely to a stubby Eberhard/Farber Number Two pencil, Aaron was one of the ten chaplains out of the entire company of thirty, to qualify as a marksman.

That night in the barracks, Aaron wrote to Libby on what was being called V-Mail, stationary that was a small single sheet of paper that when folded and the glues on the side edges dampened became a sealed self-containing envelope complete with a prepaid stamp.

Darling, you won't believe this, but you're married to a crack shot. It was tough work and I had to fully focus, but I managed an impressive score. Long story short, your husband is a qualified rifleman. Next week we're to have a go with handguns on the pistol range. I pray I do nearly as well. Kiss the boys for me and thank you for your prayers and letters. One is my comfort, the other my joy, and to such an extent that I make something of a fool of myself during mail call. My friend RC, a Catholic priest from Dallas, says I act as rude as a heathen. But he's a celibate so he can't understand how my wanting to be with you can make me a bit crazy. And now I'm running out of writing room. Will write again tomorrow. I miss you terribly and I love you desperately, Aaron

On the same day Libby also received a V-Mail letter from her brother.

Hey baby-girl. We finally saw Aaron today. He looks so good in a uniform you would drool. Which is kinda sickening knowing how much you drool already and also explains all those baby boys. We didn't get to talk to him because he's an officer and the 3 of us are only, G.I.'s, but it was good to see him looking so healthy. But I need you to do me a favor baby-sister, I want you to pray that all four of us end up in the same company. Don't ask why, just do it. Pray. Kinda love you some, Casper

Chapter Twenty-Six

Bubba's wife Myrna was proving to be a right pain in Mr. Ralph's backside. In negotiating the contract to build a new two-bedroom parsonage, she not only wanted to maintain the formerly agreed to discounts on all lumber, but now she was arguing for additional discounts on tools, nails, plumbing supplies and cement mixes.

"I'm working with a skeleton crew," she said, speaking more plainly than anyone would have credited the former timid cafe waitress. "Fewer able-bodied men means overtime, and the deacon committee has recently decided only to give onetime payments and with no expense overruns. So, as head deacon and primary materials contractor, I put it to you that my husband's company has other higher paying jobs that need doing as soon as possible. That leaves me with the task of seeing to it that the crews work quickly and quickly means overtime. Now, the way I've figured our operating costs, things could be counterbalanced by extended discounts on all materials, not just timber. So, you and I need to come to an agreement—and in writing—because it's got to be one way or the other Mr. Ralph. Either you extend additional discounts, or you agree to our being paid for all necessary overtime. Otherwise, I'm afraid I'm going to have to pull Flower's Construction off this job and sign a contract with the Urania Mill. I hate all this ugliness Mr. Ralph, but I cannot not allow the deacon committee to drive my husband's company into bankruptcy while he's off getting ready to fight for our country. No sir. I cannot not do that."

This is going to be a long war, Ralph thought grimly. But then, the church coffers did have Aaron's five hundred dollars that Aaron had paid in full for the ownership of the old parsonage. Ralph had quietly earmarked those monies for a bell for the church steeple. But, as a young seminarian, from the same seminary that had produced Aaron, was due to arrive from Atlanta in three weeks, the completion date for the new parsonage could not be set back. This young unmarried man had been refused for military service because of his "special requirements." The letter had not specified just what those requirements were, but if they were enough to keep him out of the Army, then they had to be quite special indeed. In any case, the interim pastor would need a place to live, so there was nothing for it but to agree to Myrna Flowers' bludgeoning terms.

As Ralph handwrote the codicil for the existing contract, he said, "Bubba's doin' okay is he, Myrna?"

"He's just fine. He says he's getting a brand-new education on building things the Navy way."

"You tell him he's missed, ya hear? An' that I'll be prayin' for him each an' every day."

"Yes sir, Mr. Ralph. I surely will tell him."

Mr. Ralph, as were most of the older men in Henrytown, was struggling to adjust to the fact that as able-bodied men under thirty-five were being steadily called up, women were beginning to fill their vacated jobs. By the time the new parsonage was completed, it had been built mostly by women working for the Flowers' Construction Company. Myrna was the over-boss and her first female hires were two wives of plumbers whose military allotment checks were not stretching nearly far enough. In these first months of the war, Myrna was the only construction boss willing to give these hard-pressed women a try. As a result, the grateful women completely plumbed that house in half the time of an all-male plumbing crew. But then the women had children at home to care for, so, as plumbers, they weren't inclined to dawdle.

A crew of women now working for the water well drilling company were responsible for the water that subsequently flowed through all of that well-soldered piping. Myrna then took on three women carpenters. The next hires were two women who proved that they could mix and pour cement almost as easily as they mixed and poured cake batter into pans. These women also had friends who were the wives of brick layers who had spent most of their married lives watching their husbands' brick up pillars for house foundations. Then two women painters finished off the effort by painting the new parsonage inside and out. There were only the three men, ranging in ages between fifty and sixty, who still remained on the Flowers' payroll. These men acted as crew bosses and it seemed to tickle them all to pieces that the women roofing crew could walk roofing beams as easily as high wire artists. By the time the new parsonage was finished, these men reported to Myrna that the women crews were proving to be highly capable and reliable workers. That report proved beyond all of Myrna's worrisome doubts that the Flowers' Construction Company could not simply survive, but that it might very well thrive. And thus emboldened, Myrna began to submit bids on all types of construction jobs.

As America geared up—and essentially overnight—to go to war, women were farming, flying the airmail, were on horseback and managing ranches, and in cities large and small, they were swelling the floors of factories. Older women were also needed in various occupations, Miss Emilia, Miss Cornelia and Miss Becka for instance, were running a day nursery out of Miss Cornelia's sprawling home to help the young mothers who were being called out of their homes.

In Emma Lofthouse's case, she was promoted as the new Chief of Clerks in the Myrtle Hedge Courthouse. And, according to both Archie and her proud-as-punch daddy, Mr. Preston (as Archie was only ever allowed to address his father-in-law), except for having to do the actual judging of case trials, Emma was in charge of that "whole shebang."

This massive migration into the workforce made daycare for under school aged children vital to the War Effort. Miss Cornelia's elegant front yard was transformed into a playground with three swing sets and two playhouses and a large tree house for the little boys, albeit as a safety concern, the tree house was on ground level and simply encircled the base of the old sycamore. It was left to the little boys to pretend that they were way up high. The swings, playhouse and treehouse had all been built with motherly love and attention to detail and completely at cost by the female crews of Flowers' Construction.

The three ladies of Miss Cornelia's Day Care also hired on a full staff of women to cook meals, help bathe and feed and supervise the toddlers while the three older ladies contented themselves with rocking babies to sleep in the rockers that lined the front porch. For all of this service, the working mothers were charged a dime a day per child. For those mothers to whom a few dimes a day was tantamount to a fortune, well—sufficient to say that no child was ever known to be turned away from Miss Cornelia's.

The Henrytown church board had been extremely upfront that the position being offered was only until their rightful pastor came marching home from the war. But Pastor Carl Hicks felt both blessed and terrified when accepting the position: not because of the responsibility, but because he had obstacles to overcome when it came to dealing with people.

A victim of polio, Carl had come to treasure Colossians 1:29: "*Whereunto I also labour, striving according to His working, which worketh in me mightily.*"

It had taken him a long time to understand that in this simple verse, Paul was confessing his own physical weakness, that he too had had to struggle as he learned to depend solely on Christ's mighty power to meet his many physical challenges. Both of Pastor Carl's legs were bound in heavy braces and, during the last decade, his legs had atrophied and had shrunken to such a degree that even when he was fully clothed his legs looked like a pair of dried sticks. The hardest burden came when the doctors told him that any lingering hope of manhood was also as dead as his legs. For these reasons, most of his young adult life had been spent as an outsider, social rejection his stale bread of life. He'd entered the seminary after graduating college with a Bachelor's in theology. Seminary had been a necessary educational continuance on the road to his earning a Ph.D. Without any confidence he would find love or a family, he envisioned his life as a solitary scholar. But then came the war and newly ordained pastors who did not qualify for military service were needed to fill the churches that standing pastors of right age and physically acceptability, were leaving behind. Suddenly, Carl Hicks found that even cripples were considered allowable pastors. Or presumably, the church in Henrytown had decided that one crippled pastor might be allowable. But Pastor Carl Hicks was not one to cling to something as vaporous as optimism.

Aaron was home from boot camp, as were Casper, Seth and Archie. They were indeed in the same company and after a brief leave, the four would be traveling to New York where they would wait to board a ship for England. But that was two weeks away and so they too were standing on the Henrytown train depot platform—and in their uniforms—amid the full turn out of deacons and as many church members as could be rallied. Aaron looked tall and confident in his uniform; he was a Captain now. Because he was in public, he tried not to appear at all scrambled by the fact that Libby was pregnant again (even though not one word of it had been mentioned in her letters). Nevertheless, he was still in a state of shock from finding his wife, who repeatedly assured him that she was just only over four months, wearing maternity clothes. He'd had to bite his tongue not to scold her about being pregnant at such an inconvenient time, mostly because scolding Libby about anything never really worked out all that well. Most especially when she was pregnant; times when she would oppose his most logical observations with language that can only be described as being, particularly harsh. Holding his nearing one-year-old son Micah, his older sons, Joshua, Caleb, and Jeremiah, were clinging furiously to his trouser legs as if terrified he would disappear off to somewhere on the train again.

The welcoming throng held a collective breath as the arriving train rattled to a full stop and passengers began to detrain. However, none of the few likely looking men stepping off the train did anything more than nod toward the delegation and make their way off the platform. When all hope was fading that the new pastor was on the train, one of the poorest wretches anyone had ever seen, appeared on the train's gateway; two porters were helping the man wearing leg braces over emaciated and stunted legs. Once safely on the platform, this man was literally dragging himself along by way of two steel canes. It was a gut-wrenching sight. Soft-hearted women turned their faces. The deacons stared in horror, unable to look away.

Aaron (with baby Micah) walked toward the detraining man. "Excuse me, I'm Pastor Aaron Brooks. Would you happen to be Pastor Carl Hicks?"

Carl raised his head, and to the left, as he relied on the grips of the hand crutches, and the toes of his shoes to act as balancing mediums to ensure that his vertical position was maintained. Learning to do this had earned him a well-developed upper body strength. He tried to fight back the tears welling in his dark eyes as he gazed up beyond the brim of his hat and at a man who was the very personification of the term, Greek god. If this was the pastor he'd been sent to replace, Carl felt his chances for any type of acceptance dwindling faster than snowflakes falling on a late spring morning. He was about to apologize for his crippled condition and then hurriedly offer to wait for the next train back to Atlanta, when this most splendid man said an even more splendid thing.

"I'm really hoping you are Pastor Hicks because you're very badly needed. Please don't let this crowd of welcomers make you anxious. We're just a highly enthusiastic bunch. Actually, we're all rather loveable once you get to know us."

The furlough was much too brief. In the two weeks that it had taken to see Pastor Carl settled and a willing housekeeper found for the new parsonage, Aaron, Casper, Seth and Archie were again on the platform with family and friends. This time there was also the Victory Band, consisting of two older men playing trumpets, one high school girl playing a clarinet while the pair of cymbals were all too liberally being employed by an overeager teenaged boy who was presumably the clarinet player's boyfriend. At any rate, Pastor Aaron and the Preacher's Boys were getting a true Henrytown send off. Before kissing Libby for one last time, Aaron raced to where Pastor Carl was determinedly holding himself up on his braces by grit and the steel reinforced cane-like crutches.

"Carl," he said hurriedly. "I know you to be an extraordinary Bible scholar, and I want to assure you that from what I've heard from you in the pulpit, you're also a fine preacher. But you'll be an even better preacher if you let go of the textbooks and hold more tightly to God's Word. Just feed your flock the pure Word and trust God to do the rest. He won't let you fail. I promise, He won't. That's not His style. And my

Libby is someone you can rely on to handle the office and keep your scheduling straight. For everything else, you have Brothers Yancy Flowers and Ralph Winters. They are truly dedicated men of God. Do not be afraid to rely on them."

Choking back tears, Carl said, "I shall earnestly pray for you each and every day."

"Thank you. I'm actually quite excellent with a rifle, but I can't manage to hit anything with this side arm the Army's given me. Please don't tell Libby. She suffers the delusion that I'm a wonderful soldier."

Officers were not encouraged to fraternize with regular G.I.'s, but Chaplains were meant to fraternize with all ranks, so Aaron shamelessly took advantage of this privilege and fraternized like crazy with Seth, Casper and Archie. Left to cool their heels for weeks on end in New York City, the four saw the sights that involved climbing all the way up the Statue of Liberty, catching an Off-Off-Broadway play (which was terrible) and finally lining up to ride various guided tour buses. The Four found it all quite fascinating, but none of them could fathom why anyone would actually want to live in a city so large and so . . . active. They sent lots of post cards home with scenic views of New York City and Libby's V-Mail notes were a daily occurrence during Aaron's stay in New York.

My darling husband, thanks entirely to you I look and feel like I'm about to explode and yes, I am only five months! The doctor thinks I'm carrying a litter. Other than that, things are going well. Pastor Carl's pride has eased enough to accept the wheelchair the Clinic offered. His sermons are getting better and people are coming in for counseling. If anyone understands heartbreak and hardship, it's Pastor Carl. You would be proud of the way he's growing in the Lord. Speaking of growing, all of the boys are climbing out of their clothes and shoes. Your mother and mine are doing what they can to keep them properly clothed, but it's almost hopeless. I believe Mabel is feeding them too much goat milk and that's the cause of their bones doubling overnight! Caleb loves school and now Jeremy is screaming to go. Our babies are becoming little men. I want to shove them in the freezer bin with the ice trays to keep them small. But they would fight being squeezed together, so I thank you for Baby Micah—who isn't walking, but running. And I thank you too for this one that's coming. But think pink, Aaron. I'm fed up with rambunctious boys. This family needs a little girl playing dolls and tea parties. Not that I did any of that but, we can dream. I love you so very much—Your swollen wife, Libby

Four weeks later Aaron, Seth, Casper and Archie were on a ship, in a convoy of ships that were crowded with solders headed for Portsmouth, England. Crossing the Atlantic was rough, with waves higher than the ship's deck railings. Then too there was the very real danger of Nazi submarines prowling the ocean's depths, hunting for targets for their silent running torpedoes. Seamen were routinely positioned all around the decks where they kept vigil and watched through binoculars for any tell-tale trails left by the torpedoes' wakes. If spotted, the only hope the ship had was to try to move out of the way. It wasn't much of a hope, but it was precious. War was suddenly all too real, and Aaron had all he could do to counsel frightened and worried men, while RC—the only Catholic priest on the ship—heard confessions chiefly on a non-stop basis. Not only was war very real, but *Eternity Itself* yawned and with that prevailing reality, there wasn't an atheist or an agnostic to be found anywhere on board. The one question that was asked again and again of the two ship's chaplains wasn't, "Why should I believe in God?" but rather, "How can God love someone like me?" And when this question was routinely followed by, "But Sir! You don't know what all I've done!" Aaron felt blessed that he wasn't in RC's cassock and forced to listen to each and every sordid detail. As a simple pastor, Aaron could cut to the chase.

"I don't need to know your past sins. God already knows all of them, and it is He who has provided the answer, the way of forgiveness and salvation. God sent us all the Perfect Lamb to take away our sins; to exchange our mortal wretchedness for eternal beauty. What you must do is repent—turn away from a terrible past—confess that your sins were not someone else's fault but that they were your own failings. You have to accept that responsibility, you have to own it, because it's only when you acknowledge the fact that your sins were entirely your own fault, in what you did and in what you failed to do, that you can then give it all over to Him and then trust Him to cast all of it as far as the East is from the West; that all of them will be buried forever under the Slain Lamb's cleansing blood so that the valuable young man God always meant you to be can then receive a brand new life in the light of His all-consuming love."

"But I'm so scared."

"Good. So am I. But fear in the face of death is healthy because what our fear means is that we're sane enough to realize that we are not equipped to live—or die—in this insane world without Him. Yet whether we die in this war or survive into old age is not the true issue because all of us are eternal souls temporarily encased in corporal bodies. For everyone born into this world the one true destiny is eternity and our freedom of choice is where we choose to live in that eternity."

"But what about the guys who don't believe there's a God?"

Aaron faintly smiled as he shook his head. And then his cobalt blue eyes locked with the soldier's. "Well frankly, I weep for them because denying the existence of God is right up there with a maniac putting on a blindfold and denying the existence of the sun. The sun will continue to rise in the morning whether anyone chooses to believe in it or not. Just as God will always be God and completely independent of anyone's belief or disbelief. And now son, are you ready to pray?"

"Yes sir. I am."

August 12, 1942

Darling Swollen, as your date begins to approach, my prayers for you are constant. I don't care what that baby is as long as it is healthy and you have an easy time of it. We're only a few days from land and hopefully I'll have a rest. The Lord's work onboard has been around the clock. So many fine young men have given themselves to the Lord and baptisms have been about 1,000 per cent. The captain arranged for a tub of water to be kept on the upper deck. There's not room enough for me, so I kneel on the outside while the young man's upper body fills the tub and his legs dangle over the tub's rim. It's a funny, but effective arrangement. I've recently heard the disappointing news that upon reaching land that I will be sent to London while our Three will continue on to another post. I will miss them. They are my brothers & my tangible contact with home and you. I love you Libby Brooks. I love you inexpressibly. P.S., if the baby is a boy, how about Matthew? I use his gospel more often than not because Matthew is so plain-spoken. Which I think is a wonderful trait in a son. Should it happen that you are indeed carrying a litter, you'll have to name the others on your own. As long as there's a Matthew in the bunch, I'm fine.

On August of 1942, the Marines had landed on Guadalcanal in the South Pacific. The U.S. Navy had begun a three-day battle to retain this first major American gain of World War II. The naval losses were heavy but after the three-day battle, the Navy had retained its control of the Solomon Islands. Bubba X wasn't one to write much, but Myrna treasured every scrawling letter. She received a letter three months after the battle for Guadalcanal.

Hey Honeybun, the Navy dropped me an the other Bees off on a place in the ocean I cant tell you about. We got to build a bunch of stuff that I cant tell you about neither. What I can say is that this whole island is just one big old dern mess. You tell that Ernie for me that I said you are the boss an if he got something else to say, he can just hike his butt out to where I am an say it right to my face. If he dont want to do that then he should just shut up. I love you Myrna. Dont you take no guff now.

Aaron would have never guessed that he had such a cast iron stomach but working as one of the many chaplains in the hospitals in and around London, he'd seen enough suffering and horrors to effectively lead-line even the most sensitive of stomachs. The *MovieTone Newsreels*, it would appear, had candy coated much of the disasters that had been faced by the British people. Yet there was something noble and thoroughly heroic about the way those who were still able, got themselves dressed up each and every morning and then walked to work as if their lives were normal. It was particularly impressive in that most of the walking was done through the mountains of debris that had once been flourishing neighborhoods. Taking note of this impressive strength of character made Aaron doubly proud of the seemingly casual conversation he'd had with one of the British doctors at Guy's Hospital.

"Your surname, Brooks, is, of course, entirely English. You might have been born a Yank, but the surname, combined with your rather striking Saxon characteristics, mark you as one of us." The doctor checked his clipboard. "You'll be on Ward 3 this morning." He looked up at Aaron, a mist clouding the doctor's sky-blue eyes. The mist cleared and any further hint of exhaustion—or sentimentality—was again non-existent. "It's the gangrenous ward I'm afraid. Means everyone in there is about to snuff it. Oh, and the stench is rather awful as well. Other than that, I bid you God's speed and a hearty welcome home. What's left of home, that is to say."

The hardest battle Aaron faced was when the patients of Ward 3 took the sight of his American uniform as a sign that the war was almost over, that their lives and their country would again soon be as "Right as rain." But for this group of people, who were over fifty-five and with wounds so grievous that they had been deemed too unfit to be given the medicines that the country simply didn't have enough of, Ward 3 was where people were sent to die in as much comfort as could be afforded.

But there was a sixty-something man that Aaron took to almost immediately. Like Saint Matthew, he was very direct. When spotting Aaron, he didn't bother sending up his thanks to heaven. No, Mr. Frank Partridge, a double amputee beneath the knees and with severe gangrene, was much too Eastender "Cockney" for any "sob-sister waffle." The first words he had for Aaron were, "Well, I must say you Yanks certainly took your time. I'd still have my chippie if your lot had pulled your thumb out sooner. But no, you couldn't be bothered, so there was I, mindin' my own mushy peas and queues, when BANG! My whole shop went. I wouldn't have minded about the shop so much, but I'd just paid dear for a new chip pan. Or nearly new, said the nearly reliable Wide-Boy I bought it off. But apart from the dandy chip fryer, I find I do miss my legs."

Neither Frank Partridge nor Aaron were at Guy's for longer than four weeks. Yet each and every day of those weeks, Frank was something of a delight, never mind that the disease was becoming more rampant and so malodors that even the seasoned nurses were having a hard time not retching. On that final day, Frank's ragged last words were, "Here, you bein' a preachin' man, what you need to do my son is take yourself on over to Spurgeon's gaff. And while you're there, tell Old Charlie's ghost that Frank Partridge sends his regards."

To honor the brave old man, Aaron found the historic church that had been founded by the legendary Charles Spurgeon. Being allowed to come inside and pray for Frank and the tens of thousands like him was, for Aaron, his most profound honor.

His next high honor was to find himself standing with the select few of the Chaplains Corps on the morning that Winston Churchill formally extended the United Kingdom's greetings to the delegation of American Allies. While he was shaking the Prime Minster of England's hand, a letter from Libby was casually being tossed onto his barracks cot.

Greetings new father. You are now the proud parent of a human watermelon, weighing at birth, almost ten pounds. It's male, healthy AND with all ten fingers and toes. His name is Matthew Aaron Brooks. I read a book in Carl's library that states the new medical theory that the sex of a child is entirely dependent on the father. So, you did this, Aaron. YOU! Our newest child is another boy. I HOPE YOU'RE HAPPY! And yes, I'm shouting. But I have to shout because Matthew screams when he's hungry and he's always hungry. But I still love you anyway.

In the frosty months of 1943, Aaron was sent to rejoin his former company that was stationed off in the Devonshire countryside. It was a wonderful reunion with Casper, Seth and Archie. The three looked fitter, more muscled, and they walked with something of a swagger. They had spent the passing months training for all sorts of things. They had jumped out of airplanes, learned how to drive tanks, they had improved their gunmanship on a truly impressive array of armory, and they had learned how to live in the field eating nothing but C-Rations. Now, they were waiting for the newly formed 4th Armored Division to arrive in England. The Boys didn't know if they wanted to be with a tank division. None of them liked riding inside tanks as much as they enjoyed being given rides on top of the tanks. Seth didn't care much for the infantry either, because he hated having to walk for miles while carrying machine guns and weighty straps of ammo "belts". But all three agreed that field maneuvers were all right when they could ride "topside" on a tank and then hop off whenever the situation called for them to choose a likely cover and set up their machine guns. It all sounded wonderfully brave and Aaron was impressed to say the least. Then he told them about Baby Matthew and the three of them were more impressed by the fact that Aaron had fathered a ten-pound baby.

"Well, actually, Libby was quite clear that I had very little to do with his being something of a whopper. But—if medical theory is of any worth, I am entirely responsible for his being born male."

"Hey!" Casper laughed. "That means that you're now the whole reason for five brand new men bein' brought into this world. Good job Aaron!"

Aaron shook his head. "This is not exactly your sister's attitude, but I thank you all the same."

Christmas of 1943 was going to be a little on the lean side. Everything was being rationed, except for red beans and rice. Of those two items, there was more than plenty. And something was going wrong with Mabel's taste buds. As a cook, the woman had always loved her salt, but now she was so liberal with it that half of the meals she produced were inedible. Before she poisoned off Aaron's entire family, effectively taking away the lion's share of her grandchildren, Mildred

Flowers took over her daughter's kitchen, leaving a glowering Mabel with the housecleaning chores.

Matthew was sitting up in his playpen and Mildred was stirring the bean pot when the glowering Mabel trudged into the kitchen. Standing at the sink and washing the morning's dishes Mabel tiresomely said, "That smells like boiling paste. Smells to me like what them beans needs is some scoops of salt an' a few more splashes of Tabasco." And with that, Mildred's patience with her cousin hit a wall.

"Mabel!" Mildred snapped. "Little boys have to eat this, and they can't take all that salt and Tabasco you keep pourin' into their food. Libby has repeatedly told you, and just as nicely as the girl knows how, that too much salt and red pepper is hurting their stomachs."

"Libby don't know what she's talkin' about," Mabel grumbled as she rinsed a plate. "Never did know. She just likes to go around actin' like she's so smart that she even staggers her ownself with all her smartness. But that's just Libby bein' too dern uppity for her own good is what I say."

Mildred had never wanted to slap the pure fire out of anyone before, but Mabel was pushing mighty hard for a good slapping. Mildred was turning away from the stove to warn Mabel of the impending consequences if she didn't mind herself, when in that moment, Mabel began to crumble and then, right before Mildred's widening eyes, Mabel fell flat down on the floor. Mildred rushed to her to find Mabel's breathing labored and the pulse beat in her wrist feeling weak and thready. Mildred ran for the telephone in the living room. While on the phone with the switchboard girl, she heard a terrible clatter in the kitchen. The clatter was followed by Mabel's piercing shriek and then a stream of obscenities involving Myrna. Then, mercifully, for both Mildred and the young telephone operator who had also heard the uncharitable comments, Mabel went quiet. After only a few seconds, Mildred set down the phone and hurried back to the kitchen. The flames of the stove's jet-ring were still burning but the pot that had been sitting over the jet was on the other side of the room and lying tipped over onto its side. Half cooked kidney beans, onions and chopped celery covered the walls as well as most of the kitchen floor. There would be no scolding Mabel for her violent temper tantrum.

Mabel was dead.

Chapter Twenty-Seven

Mabel Flowers' was the first funeral for Pastor Carl, and he was so nervous he could barely breathe. And then unbidden, the memory of a conversation with Aaron came to mind.

"Our work is the Lord's. All of it. I take great comfort—and joy—in the knowledge that there is never any part of His work that's about me. As pastors, we are never meant to take His place, we're simply asked to stand in His space." Aaron began to laugh his special brand of laughter as he concluded, "But He asks this of all of His followers, so we can't even feel superior in that!"

Carl, seated in his very comfortable wheelchair, looked at the steel canes standing in the corner of his bedroom. Using those canes would help him feel something close to being a man again, and they would again fill him with the false impression of independence. But then again, his struggling for physical things that would never again be his, would take the attention away from the newly deceased and refocus the congregation's attention on him. Pettiness—an appalling characteristic of Pride—is a hard thing to accept about one's self. Yet acceptance, followed quickly by surrendering it to God, is also cathartic. And cleansed of his ridiculous pride was precisely how Carl felt as he turned the wheelchair and left the crutches to stand forsaken in the corner.

In the final hours of 1943, Mabel Flowers was laid to rest. Strangely, her funeral was well attended, and the wheelchair bound preacher had done a lovely job of the services. But at the graveside service, things got a little tricky for him until Yancy and Mr. Ralph came to his aid, solemnly walking on either side of his chair and guiding him along through the grassy graveyard. Myrna Flowers, who had seemed especially distraught during the church services, was calmness itself as the casket was lowered into the grave. No one suspected that this composed demeanor was due to the little chat that Mildred Flowers had shared with her during the walk from the church to the burial plot.

"I want you to stop feeling guilty about Mabel's passin'. Other than divorcing Bubba X and leavin' town forever, there was not one thing you could have done to please that woman. An' the older she got the more venomous she was. An' it wasn't just directed at you. Libby was getting her fair share of abuse, an' if my Libby couldn't do nothing with her, you didn't stand a prayer. But now she's with the LORD. He'll straighten her out, an' I say bless Him. So, you just hold your head high Myrna Flowers. You are the best thing to ever happen to Bubba and the whole family knows it. Now that Mabel's not around to kick up one of her horrible fusses, I also expect to start seein' you more regular at Sunday dinner."

No one knew who in the Army was calling the shots, but somebody was sure as heck responsible for moving men from one division to another and then back again like some kind of drunk playing a fast game of checkers. Actually, the man responsible was General Dwight David Eisenhower who was holed up in a manor house on George Road in the London suburb of Kingston, where he lived and worked, twenty hours, each and every day and completely teetotal. There was a method in his seeming madness when he again transferred Seth, Casper and Archie in mid-January to the newly arrived and recently formed 4th Armored Division. The 4th needed seasoned men in its ranks and the recently promoted Sergeants Flowers, Lewis and Lofthouse, fit General Eisenhower's profile. And as oddly requested, he also approved the transfer into the 4th one Captain Brooks of the Chaplain's Corps. On February 23rd, 1943, the Four reported to their new division located in the wilds of

Wiltshire, where it was really, really cold and terribly, terribly frosty. As in always seeing one's own breath and never being able to actually feel one's own feet, frosty. For the four Deep South boys, living rough in the bitter cold was Hell in all of its infamous glory. But to make everything worse, the 4th had been born in New York State and was comprised primarily of Yankees, who had just been sent overseas after being trained in the baking heat of Texas. The men of the 4th couldn't understand a word the three new transferees said, and Casper, Seth and Archie couldn't understand a word coming out of their mouths either. And just when everyone thought nothing could become even more horrible, word came that the 3rd and the 4th's commanding general was none other than, Lt. General George S. Patton. Good old Blood and Guts himself.

"Oh, this can't be good," Casper said.

And it wasn't. The next six months the men of the 4th lived out the bitter winter on the Salisbury and Avebury plains while they were being polished to a gleaming shine as a united and effective combat unit. Aaron's one bright spot was that he had his very own "Peep" with Chaplain and two crosses enclosing it, painted in white just below the glass windscreen. He also had an assistant, a young man from Boston named Liam, a Black-Irisher (meaning he had jet black hair and startlingly blue eyes) who had been born and raised a Catholic but considered himself a non-denominational. As such, Liam had no problem whatsoever in being assigned to act as a driver for a Protestant field chaplain. But he did have a few qualms about the fact that no matter how much he practiced, Captain Aaron still couldn't even manage to shoot his own foot with his pistol. Not that Captain Aaron tried to shoot his own foot. Yet there had been two highly impressive near-misses of his left pinky toe: which rapidly became legendary within the ranks of the *Flying* 4th—a name given to the unit when their speed and maneuverability began to set the standard for other tank divisions.

While Casper, Seth, Archie and Aaron were freezing their "Uh-huhs" off in England, Bubba, in the relentlessly hot and humid South Pacific, was sweating off the last of his former weight. Thanks to the continuous sauna-like conditions and the long hours of physical labor, he was now down to muscle, bone and gristle. And he was on yet another island the Marines had turned into a dern mess, when the mail finally caught up with him. He read Myrna's first, and in it he learned of his mother's death. Myrna was full of apologies about not having been a better daughter-in-law. He next read the unexpected letter from his cousin Mildred. As was her wont, Cousin Mildred quickly came straight to the point of things.

Bubba X, I know Myrna has written to you about your mama and being Myrna she's probably tried to take the blame for all that went wrong between them. Don't you dare believe a word of it, do you hear me Bubba X? Your mama had a very sharp tongue in her head and she was not at all kind to Myrna. In fact, Myrna doesn't know this, so don't you dare tell her, but Mabel Flowers' dying breath was spent cussing Myrna. It breaks my heart to tell you that but it's the truth and I was right there so I know. You have a good wife in Myrna and she's as smart as a whip and she's running that company of yours so good you'd be nothing but proud. So when you write her you tell her how much you love her and how proud you are of her, do you hear me young man? Because if you don't do that then when you come home I will give you a whipping. Take care of yourself. We all love you and we miss you. Cousin Mildred.

Bubba sat back on his bunk and had himself a long think. Being a highly intelligent man, he knew that the worst thing Southern mothers stood guilty of was in teaching their daughters that men didn't favor smart women. But that was only true of dumb men. Myrna's first husband had been as dumb as mud, which is why he used to beat her anytime her natural intelligence accidently slipped out. Conversely, Bubba loved it whenever Myrna proved she could outthink him. Which, as it happened, was most of the time. Yet what that proved was that he could completely trust her. Bubba picked up the box of Navy issued stationary and he painstakingly wrote Myrna the best letter of his life, putting all of the love and tenderness he possessed into each and every word. When she finally received it, Myrna treasured Bubba's letter so much that she framed it. Then she hung the frame right beside the framed letter of welcome that she'd received from Aaron soon after she'd joined the Henrytown Free Church Family. For the first time in far too many years, Myrna Flowers felt truly loved and accepted; enough that she started turning up at Cousin Mildred's after church (with obligatory casserole) for the very crowded Flowers family Sunday dinners, because well—she was a Flowers.

June 5th, 1944

Libby enjoyed the bright sunshine of the early morning as she held on to Baby Matthew and sat on the front porch steps watching her four sons playing in the front yard. In the distance she could hear bobwhites calling out to one another, as in one of the high pines songbirds endlessly trilled their differing styles of melodies. It was one of those mornings that Aaron loved so deeply. It still amazed her in the way that he was able to find such an intense joy in the ordinary. He wasn't simply the type to stop and smell the roses, Aaron would stop to deeply inhale and marvel that each rose petal was in its carefully assigned place and all of it so delicate, so elegant, and so remarkably colorful. He saw things no one else bothered to see, and he found beauty in the oddest places. Case in point—Libby herself.

Aaron was forever telling her—and everyone else—that she was the most beautiful woman he'd ever seen. Yet her mirror, and those who clearly saw her, had differing opinions. A born realist, Libby knew that at best she was a snub nosed maturing tomboy who, if her mother was any example to go by, would not age all that well. Why a man like Aaron had even looked at her twice was just one of those divine mysteries that escaped her. Instead she'd allowed his delusion to flourish as she glommed onto him like a determined crawdad. But she did love him with every fiber of her being and from that love had come five healthy and incredibly beautiful sons.

The downside of this all-consuming love was that even on a perfect early summer morning her missing him was a physical torment. She didn't realize she was crying until she felt Matthew's chubby index finger poking at the tears sliding down her face. Funnily enough, his infant curiosity helped bring her back from the teetering edge of all out grief. And just in time for in that moment, Daddy's truck pulled into the yard and the older boys were running toward it calling for their Grammy. Libby stood, hoisted Matthew on her hip and then hastily wiped her cheeks clean with the back of her hand. Her mother was here to take on the house and the boys while Libby hurried over to the church where she was needed as Pastor Carl's full-time secretary/assistant.

Life without Aaron, whether she liked it or not, had to be lived for yet one more day.

Libby had only been in the office for about five minutes when the telephone rang. Taking a deep breath to steel herself for the day's business, she answered only to hear that it was a long-distance call from Shreveport, and never mind the expense, the caller seemed determined to take her time getting to the point of the call.

"Ma'am, my name is Amanda Harris and my husband, Sargent Darren Harris, attended your husband's Christmas service on the training fields in England. He said it was quite a sight, hundreds of G.I.'s sitting on tops of tanks and jeeps that were surrounding your husband who was standing all alone in the mud. But he said he never heard a sermon like it and that all the guys were real quiet so's nobody would miss a word. After the service, my husband asked the chaplain's aide for a copy of that sermon. The aide said there weren't any copies, so he just handed Darren the whole thing on account of how he swore your husband always knew his sermons by heart anyhow. Then he sent the sermon home to me and told me that I should telephone you to let you know that your husband is doing well and that all the men love him."

Libby's throat was so tight she could barely breathe. Gathering herself she said hoarsely, "Mrs. Harris? Would you mind very much sending me a copy of that sermon? I only ask because I have spent years compiling his sermons and I would like to add that one to the file."

"Ma'am, if you wouldn't mind, I'll just bring it to you. I would dearly love to hug the neck of the wife of the man who brought my husband to Christ. I'll take the morning train and see you around noon tomorrow. Is that all right?"

"Yes Ananda, it's very all right. I'll be there at the station to meet you."

D-Day was to have been on June 5th but due to foul weather, the Supreme Commander of the Allied Expeditionary Forces, General Dwight D. Eisenhower, put the largest amphibious invasion ever recorded in world history on hold as he hoped for better weather. When that hope was dashed, it was well after midnight on the 6th when General Eisenhower gave the final go-ahead. Oddly enough, it was thanks almost entirely to the inclement weather that the Nazis were caught off guard. When at 6:30 a,m. the fog began to lift off the Normandy coast, one

German soldier was recorded as saying, "How can there be so many ships in the entire world?"

He was right to say it because the Channel was crowded with ships, 5,000 to be precise. And then came the air support, the sky burdened to the point of being completely blackened by the hundreds of fighters that were proceeding the supply, and paratrooper laden airplanes. The fifty-mile coastline had been divided into five sectors: Utah, Omaha, Gold, Juno and Sword. As the hundreds upon hundreds of troop transport vessels took to the water and headed for the German entrenched beaches, Aaron went to his knees. He did not feel the cold salty spray against his face or the knobbed steel deck biting into his flesh and bone. He only felt grief for those who were about to be lost from this life as he wept and prayed God's mercy on the souls of so many fine young men. Casper, Seth and Archie were not on the first ships that crossed the English Channel. Aaron was on board one of the ships simply because he had been needed as a chaplain. Beyond that, he would have to wait for his assigned company, the 4th Division. But the distant sights he saw from the ship's forward deck ripped through his soul.

Noon on June 6th 1944 in Louisiana meant 6 p.m. in Normandy. Not one of the three young women on the depot platform; Betty Jean—Casper's wife; Verda Louise—Seth's wife; or Libby, had heard a word about D-Day. But for the detraining young woman from Shreveport, who tried her best to look like Betty Grable, and very nearly succeeded until she smiled and revealed teeth that could have done with childhood braces, D-Day meant that her husband's lifeless body was lying on that distant beach and being lapped by the channel's briny waves. It was eventually dragged off by living soldiers whose job it now was to clear the beach in order for the landing transport vessels to bring in the tanks, trucks and jeeps that the landing forces badly needed.

Other than that, it was a bright sunny day and the four young Army Wives were excited to meet one another.

Libby was at the wheel, Amanda sitting up front with her as the car drove the main street of Henrytown. In the back, Betty Jean and Verda Louise were heard to simultaneously gasp and then Betty Jean say, "White Gold!"

"What?" Libby snapped.

"Slow down and look left!" Verda Louise ordered.

Libby applied the brakes as all four looked left and saw a little barefoot girl on the sidewalk crying for all she was worth as she stood looking down at a spilled bag of sugar, an entire month's ration.

"Oh, that child is gonna get a big whippin' from her mama," Betty Jean said.

"Not while I have a breath," Libby answered. Hurriedly parking the car, all four women bailed out, Libby rushing to comfort the sobbing little girl while the others got down on their knees and carefully scooped up the sugar and with their cupped hands shoveled it into the sugar tote bag.

"It's dirty!" Amanda exclaimed.

"Then we'll take it to my house," Libby yelled. "If my mama has the patience to sift tiny little beetles out of flour, she'll know how to clean up this baby girl's sugar." Then to the child, "You hush-up crying sweetheart. Everything's gonna be all right."

"No it ain't!" the child wailed. "I'm gonna get beat!"

It was about this time that Myrna was driving one of the lumber trucks through town. Seeing the commotion on the sidewalk, she slowed and parked next to Libby's car. Libby was on her knees holding onto the arms of a distraught little girl while three other women were one their knees sweeping the sidewalk with their hands.

"What in the world?" Myrna said loudly as she approached the odd group. "Are ya'll havin' a prayer meetin' right here on the sidewalk?"

Looking back over her shoulder Libby said to Myrna, "Hey girl. You know everybody in this parish, do you know this child?"

Myrna was dressed in old jeans, boots and one of Bubba's shirts. Her hair was tied up inside a faded red bandana. (Nobody ever claimed construction was glamorous.) Without missing a beat, Myrna lifted the little girl and the encircling women stood to their feet. Holding the sobbing child close Myrna said sadly, "Yeah, I know her." Then Myrna looked off as she rocked the child and said, "She's one of the Lofthouse people. From the side of the family that the other Lofthouse people don't like to talk about. She's called Sissy. Her mama and daddy are dead. One night they got into a domestic altercation that didn't end peacefully. Especially as one had a pistol and the other one had a shotgun. Now she's livin' with her uncle Charlie."

"Oh, my sweet Jesus!" the other women chorused. With the exception of the newest arrival to the group (Amanda Harris)—everyone had heard Archie speak more than once about Charlie Lofthouse. And the things that he'd said, things which were only barely acceptable in mixed company, had just flat scalded their ears off. To think that a man like that was now the custodian of a helpless little girl was not to be borne. In other words, when the child had said she was going to get a beating, she wasn't being melodramatic.

"We cannot take her back there," Libby said.

"We ain't," Myrna said firmly. "I've always wanted a child. The Lord has provided."

"W-What do we do about the sugar?" Amanda worried.

With the child calming down a fraction, Myrna momentarily shifted her interest to the newcomer. "Who are you?"

Flustered to be the object of this strangely dressed woman's attention, Amanda stammered, "I'm—I'm just a visitor from Shreveport."

"Uh-huh. An' besides going to Betty Grable movies, what do you do for yourself over there in Shreveport?"

Libby pressed her lips together to fight back the pressing urge to laugh. Myrna was no longer shy, and she certainly wasn't anything close to reticent. Ever so gradually, she had morphed into Bubba X. But without his finer sense of charm. Which was practically none.

Her face flaming red with embarrassment, Amanda continued to stammer. "I live with my parents and I write letters to my husband who's in the army."

"Well then," Myrna said dryly. "You'll be better off stayin' in the car and holdin' onto Sissy while the rest of us corner ourselves a child beating rat."

"What do we do about the sugar?" Verda Louise asked, repeating Amanda's question. Then adding, "I vote we look around for some rocks to give the tote bag some good throwing heft?"

Myrna bayed laughter. "Now I understand why Seth loves you!"

Amanda was just as pleased as she could be to stay low inside the car. The little girl Sissy was so terrified that she was scrunched up in the foot-well and concentrating all of her six-year-old self on the stranger lady's peep-toed high heeled shoes. It fascinated Sissy the way the lady's polished toenails were all scrunched together, like they were trying to tunnel out of the confining shoes. She also wondered, as she tried to blot out everything outside the safe confines of the car, if being all crossed over that way, hurt the toes when the lady walked around. But then her attention was yanked back into the moment at the sound of Miss Myrna's yelling.

"Charlie Lofthouse! You get your sorry butt right on out here!"

"Who's that yelling in my yard?" came the reply from inside the small house.

"Myrna Flowers."

"Well what in the world do you want?"

"I want to bring you the stupid sugar that you sent a barefoot little baby girl off to walk for four miles to fetch for ya."

Sixty-year-old Charlie Lofthouse stood five feet five and weighed about one hundred and thirty pounds and that was when wearing wringing wet overalls and a pair of swamp muddy boots. He opened the door of the one-story shotgun house and came out onto the rickety covered porch. His first sight was of Bubba X's wife standing in the forefront of three other women; women he knew to be the wives of the preacher and two of the preacher's good friends. Having a delegation of these women standing in his yard and looking so downright unfriendly, didn't bode well. With an air of defiance, he said, "What are ya'll doin with my sugar?"

"Well for me personally," Myrna answered, "I only brought it so's I can tell ya that you are a mean and horrible little man and that me an' Bubba are keepin' the child."

"Ya'll are doin what now?"

Libby quickly stepped forward. "And I'm here to tell you that Sissy is now under the complete protection of Henrytown Free Church."

Verda Louise stepped forward. "And I'm here to tell you that you will never again lay one single hand on that child."

Betty Jean stepped forward. "All I got to say to you Charlie Lofthouse, is I have a gun."

"Now ya'll just hold on a minute," Charlie cried. "I am that child's close blood kin an' ya'll comin' around here to tell me that ya'll are stealin' my little niece ain't very Christian!"

"Yes it is," Libby said. "The Lord Jesus Himself would take that baby away from the likes of you. And I promise, you will answer to every Christian man in this town if you so much as try to take Sissy out of our protective custody."

Myrna threw the linen lined burlap sugar bag at the porch. Charlie ducked back as it landed on the porch floor with something of a clatter. "There's your sugar. It picked up about a dozen or so rocks during the ride out here."

Charlie watched as the women climbed into the car and then as the car made its way down the furrowed track. He would never see his niece Sissy again, primarily because he believed every word those women had said. Then there was the prevailing fact that he really didn't care enough to ever try. Plus, he'd also heard that Casper Flower's wife, that Miss Betty Jean, was known for being a pretty good shot with a rifle. Only a crazy man would mess with a woman with a gun. His much younger idiot brother had tried having a shootout with a shotgun totin' woman. Now they were both dead. And their one child Sissy, was being taken away. With the thought of good riddance to every last one of them, Charlie picked up the sugar bag and went back inside his house.

It was breathtaking how quickly the church as a whole worked to secure the safety of little Sissy Lofthouse. Emma Lofthouse, at the courthouse, used her friendships with attorneys to draw up the guardianship papers and as soon as she told the ruling judge just who it was that had been acting as the child's caretaker, the judge couldn't sign the guardianship transfer papers quickly enough. It was Yancy and Ralph who headed up a group of men who drove out to Charlie's place to formally read the documents to him. Then a more than compliant Charlie signed his name on the line that Mr. Ralph pointed to, and the thing was done. Little six-year-old Sissy Lofthouse was now to be known—as Sissy Flowers.

The next weeks were not easy for Myrna. The thing about abused children is that when they are suddenly taken out of an abusive situation, they tend to act out all of the rage and hurt they'd formerly bottled up. Little Sissy was no exception. She had tantrums, she cried, she broke things. She even spat in Myrna's face as if daring Myrna to give her a whipping. Instead what she got was an hour of sitting in a chair facing a blank wall.

For a lively six- year-old, a whole hour of nothing was way worse than a whipping. But slowly, ever so slowly, Sissy was coming around and being helpful and friendly. It was at that point that Myrna took her over Myrtle Hedge and bought her some nice clothes and two pairs of shoes. One pair for every day, one pair for church. When Sissy was even more friendly and helpful during the following week, that next Saturday Miss Myrna took her to the beauty parlor where the beauty ladies made a special fuss over her and styled her long white-blond hair. After that, Miss Myrna took her to see the first movie picture she'd ever seen. The movie was about cowboys and horses and she got to have a bag of popped corn all for herself. The afternoon was thrilling, and Sissy was learning fast that good behavior paid big dividends, whereas tantrums meant *The Chair*.

It was nearing midnight when Myrna awoke to Sissy's screams. Bolting out of bed, she ran down the hallway to Sissy's room and switched on the lamp. Sissy, tossing and turning and so wracked by the nightmare she was trapped inside, she wasn't aware of the light. Myrna scooped the little girl into her arms and rocked her, slowly bringing Sissy out of the horrible dream.

Sissy's little tear-filled eyes rapidly blinked as she tried to focus and realize that she was safe, that the bad man wasn't hitting her anymore. And then she sobbed so mournfully, the sound of it broke Myrna's heart.

"Miss Myrna! Please don't send me away. I'll sit in the chair. I'll be a good girl!"

Myrna folded herself over Sissy and as she rocked her, and said, "Oh Lord Jesus, oh Lord Jesus, thank you for everything I ever went through. As bad as it was, it was meant to teach me how to one day help and love the child that You were going to send to me. So, I thank You and I bless You for every bit of it. With all my heart, I bless You."

It goes without saying that Sissy had never been to church. Now that Sissy was settling down, this was the first Sunday that Myrna felt that she could trust Sissy not to act out. And as it was Sissy's first church experience, she was finding the early morning procedure quite baffling. However, she did respond well as Myrna dressed her in a nice blue dress with a white pinafore. Next, she brushed out Sissy's wealth of hair and tied blue bows on each side. Sissy sat down while Miss Myrna put on her feet a pair of clean white socks with lace around the edges and then slipped on and buckled nice and snug the pair of shiny black shoes. Slightly kicking her little feet and watching as her shoes sparkled in the morning light Sissy asked, "Do I look pretty Miss Myrna?"

"Why I don't believe I've ever seen a prettier child in my whole life." Myrna said as she extended her hand. Sissy took it, hopping down off the dining room chair. "Now after church we're going over to Miss Mildred's for Sunday dinner." Halfway out the front door Myrna paused to collect her handbag and Bible. "From now on this is what we do every Sunday. First we go to church and then we go to Miss Mildred's." Myrna also picked up a large paper bag. Bending at the waist and showing Sissy the bag she explained. "These are your after-church clothes. After dinner you will need to change so that you can play with your cousins. They're boys. Boys like to get dirty."

"But what if I don't want to play with dirty old boys?"

"Then you don't have to darlin'."

"An' I can stay in my dress?"

"Yes, but I'm taking the bag just in case. Now get those little legs moving. We're gonna be late."

It was seven-year-old and second grader Caleb's turn to help out with the first grade Sunday school class. The first grade and kindergarten teachers always liked having the older children helping out with the younger students. The Teacher's Helper's program had been started by Pastor Carl. It was a program met with enthusiasm by the harried teachers even though Pastor Carl saw it as marvelous way of introducing the older children into a shepherding ministry. Caleb, one of the few older boys who took the ministry unerringly to heart, was holding his five-year-old brother Jeremiah's hand and shepherding him into the noisy classroom when Miss Myrna came walking down the hallway and leading a reluctant looking little blond girl in a blue dress. Miss Myrna stopped and made the introductions.

"Sissy," she said to the little blond girl. "These are two of your cousins, Caleb and Jeremy." Looking to Caleb she said, "This is Sissy. She's the daughter God gave to your Uncle Bubba and me. This is her very first Sunday school day. Will you watch over her for me please Caleb?"

"Yes, ma'am Aunt Myrna." With that Caleb whirled Jeremy over to his other side and extended his newly freed hand to Sissy. And to Sissy as she shyly took his hand he said, "It's all right. Just stick with me. There's nothin' to be scared of."

That night Myrna wrote Bubba and informed him of the latest happenings.

Hey Bubba mine, I'm writing to tell you that we have a little girl. Her name is Sissy and she's a special gift from God Himself. I know you will love her. She had her first day in church and you would have been so proud of the way Caleb watched over her. He's a proper little gentleman. So like his daddy! After church we went to Yancy and Mildred's. Yancy took lots of Kodak's of all of us around the table and some of just me and Sissy. They should be developed by some time next week. Sissy didn't know if she wanted to change out of her Sunday dress and play with Aaron's boys, but after Caleb asked her to go fishing, she couldn't change fast enough. They caught a whole bucket of crawdads. Yancy took Kodak's of them holding up the bucket. Libby's going to send that one to Aaron too. We're a family, my husband. I would have told you sooner that you're a daddy, but it all happened kind of sudden. I love you and I miss you—Myrna.

In the very next letter in the stack that he'd received from Myrna was a photo of Myrna and a timid, but pretty little girl. Myrna looked so proud to be holding that child's hand that it brought tears to Bubba's eyes. Then the snapshot of two children (*My Lord in heaven! Is that Caleb? He looks half grown*!), struggling to hold up a heavy bucket. Both children were a mess, but they were laughing, the girl not so timid now. Bubba wrote to Myrna without even waiting to read her other letters.

Darling wife, when you surprise a fella you sure do go all out. I told all the fellas that I'm a daddy and they didn't have cigars but they sure made free with the cigarettes. I'm so blessed to have such a wonderful family. Tell Sissy that Daddy can't wait to take her fishing. She looks like she can hold her own if she can help fill up a whole bucket. I am so proud of you Myrna Flowers I'm about to bust wide open. All I can say is I love you, I love you, I love you. Your ever loving Bubba X.

The next Saturday Myrna and Sissy accidently met up with Libby and her brood of males in Henrytown's small grocery store. The older boys were well behaved, but Baby Matthew was walking and would not be contained. Libby, who was trying to sort through her rationing book, lost her patience. "Joshua! Caleb! Chase your brother before he destroys the whole store. Jeremy, if you hope to see the new Roy Rogers movie, you will hold on to Micha and neither of you will move another muscle."

With a threat that huge looming over their heads, both younger boys were immediately frozen in place. Meanwhile the older brothers were having a bad time cornering a toddler who was becoming more and more adept at escaping. Then Caleb saw Sissy standing there holding Aunt Myrna's hand. Sissy was wearing pink overalls and a white sleeveless blouse and white sandals, and her long blond hair was pulled back into a ponytail. In his eight-year-old mind, Sissy Flowers was pure perfection on wheels, and he skidded to a stop right in front of her. In the chore of cornering a dodging Matthew, Joshua was suddenly on his own.

A very astute Myrna knew when she was the third wheel in a social mix, so she left the two children and strode off to join Libby at the counter. "They're out of everything," Libby said absently.

"I only came in for some red beans and cornmeal."

Libby snorted derisively. "Well that they've got. But if we want vegetables to mix in with the beans, then we're gonna have to show up at Miss Cornelia's like a couple of blind beggars. Thank the dear Lord for Miss Cornelia and my mother-in-law increasing their Victory garden this year." Still annoyed, Libby looked up and yelled, "Joshua Brooks! Stop playing with Matthew and just grab him for heaven's sake!"

"I'm not playing Mama! He may be fat, but he's fast!"

Libby looked at Myrna. "Would you happen to have a gun on ya? I truly feel the need to shoot myself."

Myrna was chuckling as she turned to look back at the two children who were still loitering with intent at the front of the store. It was then that she heard Caleb say, "Well just ask your mama! Tell her you'll be sitting with me an', I'll be watching out for ya."

"Okay," Sissy said. She then took off running straight for Myrna. Upon arrival, Sissy's little hands, folded prayerfully up to her chin, she looked up to Myrna. "Mama? Can I go to the movies with Caleb? Please, please, please? It's a Roy Rogers, King of all the Cowboys movie!"

Myrna couldn't breathe. Then she heard Libby whispering against her ear, "That's you girl. You're Mama. Now give your daughter a quarter before you cry like a fool right in front of her."

Chapter Twenty-Eight

In the first days of July 1944, Paris was like a carnival of celebration. Never one to miss a good party, French General Charles de Gaulle swaggered into Paris in a uniquely pristine uniform and declared with ego maniacal bluster, "France has freed herself by her own hand!"

At this same time, the real liberators of France, the Allied Forces, were either on the Normandy beaches collecting their dead and removing identity tags or they were in trucks and tanks that rolled across the Seine River Bridge. The push was on for Berlin, the still disorganized German army failing to end the unstoppable Allied advance. And there was no calming a frenzied Adolph Hitler as he continually screamed down the telephone demanding to know if his ultimate order for the retreat had been obeyed. All but frothing at the mouth, he insentiently ranted at his generals on their field radios, "Is Paris burning? Is Paris burning? I command Paris to be burning!" They were too terrified to tell him that they were no longer in Paris.

It wasn't possible for Casper, Archie and Seth to keep tabs on Aaron. As the chaplain's corps was being stretched beyond its capacity, chaplains found themselves being sent from one division to the next. As "Georgie's Boys" (the 4th) were heading off more to the south, Aaron was now with a company heading northwest. It was as the Allies rolled forward through France that "Camps" were being discovered. In total, the Nazis had seventy camps spread out from France, all through the Netherlands, Germany, and ending deep inside Poland. The first few camps discovered in France were political internment camps, yet even with these it was becoming apparent that the more inland the camps, the more varied the reasons for prisoner incarcerations and the more appalling the living conditions. Yet none of these first few camps prepared the invading Allies for the true horrors awaiting discovery in the next coming months. The sheer barbarity would forever numb minds and challenge sanity.

In retaliation to the invasion, Hitler ordered the V2 missile launch against England. For six months these warhead missiles rained down on London until the advancing Allies were finally able to capture the flying bombs' launching sites. In September of 1944, the Allies had liberated Brussels. In Holland they took the city of Antwerp, but the Germans held onto the city's port making it impossible for the Allied supply ships to unload critically needed supplies—most especially the gasoline needed by the fuel guzzling tanks. Britain's General Montgomery offered a bold idea that instead of using a vast number of troops, they would instead punch a hole in the German lines with a smaller and faster force. This force of paratroopers would go toward Arnhem in Holland and then cross the Rein, outflanking the German's Siegfried Line. With Eisenhower's approval, 30,000 airborne troops (the American Screaming Eagles and the British Brigade Airborne) filled the Dutch skies, and once on the ground, they secured the waterway bridges at Veghel, Grave, Arnhem and Nijmegen. But after four days of heavy fighting, Arnhem was proving to be a bride too far.

There isn't enough praise given to the Canadian forces, but despite the failure of the Americans and the British to take Arnhem, the Canadians battled on for three weeks clearing the Arnhem river banks of German artillery, and thus allowing the British Navy to concentrate on the massive guns entrenched on the port's strategic islands. British ships steadily bombarded the islands that commanded the river's portside entrance for almost two weeks before the Germans finally surrendered. On November 28th, 1944 Allied supply ships were at last able to make good use of this viable port, but with the heavy rains turning the battlefield into mud, the Allies were being forced to wait out the weather. The rains turned to snow and with snow there was to the bone bitter cold.

Meanwhile, Hitler had devised a daring plan of his own; a plan that was even more bold than Montgomery's had been. Germany's situation was disastrous; its forces were hugely outnumbered by the Allies and lacked supplies plus the fabled Panzer tank division was becoming dangerously low on fuel. Hitler was spinning the roulette wheel in an all or nothing wager. Against the pleading advice of his most senior officers, Hitler ordered a push through the Allied lines at Ardennes and then the advance on Antwerp. If Germany could retake the occupied port city, the Allied supplies would be cut, and his army and the Allied forces would be on equal footing. In this fraught attempt at victory, Hitler had 200,000 German soldiers, field weapons and ammunition and the last of his Tiger tanks, assembled and loaded onto flat cars. To bump up civilian morale, he had the whole thing filmed and made certain the feature starred only the healthiest and bravest looking tank commanders and infantry soldiers who were told to smile confidently as they waved for the cameras. The trains were unloaded in the dead of night a few miles from the lightly manned American lines that unknowingly but directly faced this secretive German build up.

In October Libby started a sugar drive that involved all of the ladies in the church putting back one cup of sugar each from their allotted sugar rations. By the first of November there was enough sugar, butter, oatmeal, flour, eggs and pecans to bake batch after batch of delicious cookies. All of the willing bakers turned up at Miss Cornelia's where the oven was bigger and the kitchen more accommodating for so many cooks. When finished, each of the cookie boxes were packed with freshly popped popcorn to keep the cookies reasonably fresh.

It was too late for Thanksgiving and too early for Christmas when a boxed love-offering from Henrytown Free Church eventually caught up with Aaron. And being Aaron, he freely shared the unexpected flavorful bounty. It was so early the following morning that it was still pitch dark as he put the box of remaining cookies in his jeep. He didn't wake Liam, his somewhat stalwart driver who had just recently discovered that he was a Catholic after all. Aaron's old friend and chaplain's boot camp buddy, R.C., had turned up in the main camp. His unexpected appearance was one of those few times when Aaron and R.C. could split the chaplain's services properly. But then Aaron had begun to think about those men on the front lines. Fully confident that R.C. could handle both services and that Liam would appreciate attending an authentic mass, Aaron drove alone out of the camp.

The sight of the chaplain's jeep was a welcomed delight for the men who were feeling pretty forgotten, stationed as they were on the furthest line between the Americans and the Germans. Even those G.I.'s who had never actually met Chaplain Aaron felt as if they knew him personally. He was just one of those guys you could tell anything to, knowing that it wouldn't go any farther and that he wouldn't be all judgmental. And he always had a bright and sunny smile. As one guy once said, "Chaplain Aaron wears his faith the way other guys wear their combat fatigues, all up front and no messin' around." The men had a campfire and they took turns sitting around it, trading sentry shifts, as Chaplain Aaron sipped coffee and passed around a package from home that had cookies *and* popcorn inside of it. He was also telling them all about a soldier named Joshua, and another soldier named Gideon, guys who were pretty much like them, caught up in wars that they didn't want to be caught up in.

"In all wars," Aaron said. "God uses His earthly armies to bring defeat to Satan's earthly armies. We hate war and so does He, but He also despises the evil that's threatening the good. What we must hold onto is that in Him there is no death, only the passing from this world and into His."

"But Chaplain, ain't ya just a little scared of maybe dyin'?"

Aaron bit a cookie and chuckled. "Quite honestly I'm terrified. Not of death itself, but how it will come. I hate pain, so I don't want anything ouchy. And my wife would merrily walk across the Atlantic just to tell you that I am beyond horrible whenever I'm sick, so I don't want any lingering illness that will leave her feeling only relief once I've finally expired. As selfish as it sounds, one or two of her tears cried over my coffin would be nice. So whatever the Lord has in mind, and strictly to save my wife's memory of why she ever married me you understand, I'm hoping and praying that He will bless me with something that's really, really, quick."

As if on divine cue, a barrage of rifle reports was suddenly heard. As Aaron and the others stood, grabbing up their rifles, inside the gunfire there was the increasing sounds of rolling, heavy-transport vehicles. And crashing through the dense winter forest, there came that thrumming sound peculiar only to advancing tanks.

For the first two days of the German push, General Omar Bradly, Commander of the 12th Army, refused to believe that a major German assault was underway. The attack would be known as the Battle of the Bulge, simply because the enemy push caused an unseemly bulge in the center of the Allied line. It was on the northern side of this bulge that the Germans perpetrated one of the worst battlefield atrocities of the war, shooting eighty-five captured American soldiers. Yet this mass murder of infantrymen was an indication of just how desperate the German command had become. The Americans found the eighty-five bodies when the Bulge decreased slightly in the retaking of this area. There had been no time for the Germans to conceal the misdeed, so the dead G.I.'s were simply laid out where they had fallen as the machine guns had fired. Still, it seemed that Hitler's gamble was paying off and emboldened by the meager success, he sent out the last Luftwaffe fighter planes—fighter planes that Germany was unable to replace.

As the frigid weather improved, General Patton's forces took aim at the town of Bastogne while Allied airplanes steadily bombed the German lines. By the end of February, Hitler's dodgy stratagem had failed. His forces were in mass retreat, and over 120,000 Germans had either been killed, or taken prisoner. The Tiger Tanks of the once touted Panzer Division were destroyed. In pushing back to the original line that the Germans had crossed and going beyond it, making an inverted Bulge of their own, Aaron's jeep, heavily damaged by tank artillery, was discovered. G.I. dog tags were found hanging from tree limbs like repugnant garlands. A long line of dead American soldiers were discovered almost completely buried beneath two feet of freshly fallen snow.

One of the bodies was Aaron's.

News of his death went through the 4th Division faster than a bullet. And hit hardest by this news was Seth Lewis. When it was reported that this expert sharpshooter was incapacitated by grief, R.C., the Catholic chaplain and Aaron's boot camp buddy, came on the fly. He found the young soldier lying face down in the freezing mud. The young soldier's buddies known to R.C. as Casper and Archie were holding onto him as his body convulsed with sobs. It required extreme effort, but R.C. finally managed to maneuver himself between them and take Seth into his arms. And for ten long minutes, R.C. could do little more than hold Seth and grieve right along with him.

In the mid-morning of March 2nd, 1945, Libby was in the church office carefully holding the painstakingly typed out mimeograph machine master copies for the church bulletin and monthly newsletter, all steeled and ready for yet another round of combat with that infernal machine, when Ralph Winters and her father Yancy came in, their faces tight and bloodless. With them were two members of the Chaplain's Corps. And suddenly the office was filled with what Archie Lofthouse would have described as a big old *P-A-L-L.*

Libby felt her legs giving way and her father rushed to catch her. "Please," she whimpered. "Please don't tell me he accidently shot himself. I'll never forgive him if he somehow managed to shoot himself."

Ralph Winters hastened to Yancy's aid and together they helped ease Libby into a chair and they both knelt before her. Too stunned to emit her infamous bawling, Libby simply went cold all over as Yancy took hold of his daughter's hands. Ralph lowered his head, fat tear drops falling from his eyes and dotting the office's hardwood floor. For the life of him, he could not shake the memory of a very young Aaron wearing his white shirt rolled up to the elbows, white trousers and utterly ridiculous red suspenders. His blond hair was shimmering as brightly as a halo as he held Libby's hand while they walked in the early summer sunshine, heading off toward the cooling shade of the creek that meandered along Yancy's property boundary.

Ralph knew he was miserably failing as a deacon in this highly crucial moment, but he couldn't help himself, this was all so beyond sad it was appalling. Yet it was also the moment he realized just how much he'd come to truly love Aaron Brooks, that he shamelessly wept along with Aaron's wife, for when words of comfort fail, there remains the truer comfort that is only found within the unity of grief.

April 1966

Over the decades, the world had changed so much that it hurt Libby's mind to try to keep up with it all. First was the prophetic reestablishment of Israel as a country. What a truly glorious event that had been. Next came truly awful years of ugly clothes, the McCarthy witch hunts, gritty Noir movies, Elvis Presley, and then those English boys whose songs were just stupid and their haircuts worse. But, while sitting in the comfort of her living room, quietly watching her Zenith TV, she had seen the election of a Catholic president, and then while campaigning for a second term in office, there was the shocking assassination of that president.

On a personal level, in the last twenty-odd years she had walked by more opened caskets than she cared to count; with the exception of that one all-important casket. To fulfill this need, back in 1955, she and her ailing mother-in-law Miss Emilia and the ever-resolute Miss Cornelia, had made the journey to France to visit the memorial cemetery where Aaron had been interred. His had been just one of thousands of white crosses, but his death had never actually seemed real to her until she stood at his grave and read his name on that simple cross. It was only when she came back from France that she finally read his sermon that had been hand delivered by the Betty Grable look-alike from Shreveport.

Aaron's five sons had not been short on fathers. They'd had four. Uncle Casper was the jokester who always took the boys hunting and fishing. Uncle Archie was a natural born farmer and besides growing sugar cane on the fields that Miss Cornelia had signed over to him, he raised the exotic sounding Roma tomatoes as well as twelve acres dedicated to red beans. At first no one wanted to try the tomatoes because they sounded down right "I-talian," but once the women of the Parish got a free taste, Uncle Archie couldn't grow those tomatoes fast enough. From Uncle Archie they learned to respect the land and use it with love and care. Plus he paid a good wage.

Uncle Seth was the deeply serious one. Their mother swore that when he was younger that he'd been a worse jokester than Uncle Casper, but the boys found that rather hard to believe. It was Uncle Seth who was the disciplinarian, who made certain that they stuck to their school lessons and treated schoolwork like a holy obligation. Seth was always there when it came time to inspect each and every report card. If any of the boys had known what a hellion Uncle Seth had been, or that he'd never actually finished high school, they most probably would not have sat long enough to hear any of his endless lectures on the "Duty and Benefits of Study." But they didn't know, so they endured it. Mostly because following the lecturing, Uncle Seth was always good at taking them for ice cream cones. Although, ice cream cones aside, had anyone ventured to ask just which of their uncles they most admired, to a man they would have hollered, "Uncle Bubba!"

When Uncle Bubba came home from the Pacific, a hundred and fifty pounds of his former self was missing. What stepped off the train from San Diego was steel-hard muscle. And thanks to the Seabees, Bubba knew how to build fast and tight and he could run every piece of machinery known to mankind. Then too, the little boys adored their Uncle Bubba because he was so protective. When he had charge of the boys, Uncle Bubba was like a big dark-complexioned guardian angel that nobody in their right mind would ever dare mess with. Being with him meant they could just stop being "Mama's Brave Little Men," and just be little boys who badly needed the relief from being brave and simply relax inside the safety that Uncle Bubba conveyed.

When Uncle Bubba took Sissy and Caleb to the Saturday afternoon movies, their little hands were lost inside his, as he personally escorted them up to the ticket window. Then he was with them at the confection counter. Finally he ushered them to good seats, making certain that they hadn't spilled their popcorn or Juju Beans, and THEN—with the other kids sitting in their theater seats all wide-eyed and big-eared he'd say to Sissy and Caleb, "The minute this movie is over, you two are to stand at the front glass doors. Do not come out to stand on the sidewalk. You will stay inside looking out the doors until you see my truck. Then Caleb, you will hold Sissy's hand and the pair of you will come quick. And what do I mean is quick?"

Both children answered in unison, "We will neither linger nor tarry."

"Good answer," he said. Then looking out over the entire audience of squirming children he bellowed, "None of ya'll are gonna throw things or jump around in your seats. When the lights go down and the movie begins, ya'll are all gonna be perfect ladies and gentlemen. Is that understood?"

"YES SIR MISTER BUBBA X!!" (It really needn't be said that the manager of the movie theater absolutely loved Bubba) Aaron's sons grew—but as the years passed, not one of them ever felt they had grown too big to hold Uncle Bubba's hand.

Joshua at thirty, had graduated Tulane with such high honors that the graduate board waved the necessity for a Masters and had sent Joshua straight into the Ph.D. curriculum. Three years later and within days of having earned his doctorate, he was appointed the youngest man ever to sit as Head of the Theology Department. His immediate superior was a priest who preferred that Joshua simply address him as, R.C.

Yet, after only five years and considerable weeks spent in prayer, he resigned from Tulane on the basis that he had accepted the position as

Chancellor of the LaSalle Parish Bible College and Seminary that his MOTHER of all people, had started. Years prior, when Pastor Carl had returned to his scholarly calling, the incoming pastor had preferred to build his own private house. Thus, Pastor Carl's cozy parsonage had been consigned to serve as the college's Chancellor's Residence. But that newly vacated house did not suit Joshua's wife Clarisse, a New Orleans socialite raised in the exclusive Garden District of New Orleans. She immediately turned up her patrician nose at the pokey little house stuck off in the back of the beyond LaSalle Parish. It required every drop of Libby's patience when dealing with Clarisse. Yet deal with her she must. Joshua and Clarisse and their two young sons were due to arrive in Henrytown in three weeks. Striving to impress the rather aloof Clarisse, Bubba and Myrna were working like slaves in order to complete the new Chancellor's Residence. And good luck to them. Bookworm Joshua might not notice any imperfections, but Clarisse could be counted on to present them with a lengthy punch list, as if Bubba and Myrna didn't already have enough on their plate.

The college was constantly expanding as students were coming in from all over the county. So many young people were seeking admittance to the Bible College that had been built in honor of the man who had passed into legend. A man they knew only by way of the ever-increasing circulation of a single book; one that had just recently been reedited to include Aaron's last documented Christmas sermon. This newest edition had been retitled, *God's Unfailing Love*.

Mr. Ralph, God keep his soul, had been responsible for Aaron's posthumous fame. In the first months after they'd received word of Aaron's death, Mr. Ralph had gone through Libby's files and using money from his own pocket, he had seen to it that Aaron's sermons were published as a daily devotional study. He hadn't needed to pay for the second or third printings because the returning veterans, who had briefly known Aaron or had simply heard him speak, had made the little book a runaway best seller. They also wrote hundreds upon hundreds of letters. Aside from the endless job of being a mother and working as the primary church secretary, Libby spent her evenings answering each and every letter.

Little wonder then that she had entirely forgotten about the Baton Rouge bank account and the money that had come to them following Miss Emilia selling the Atlanta house. She finally remembered only after her mother-in-law's funeral and the subsequent gathering at Miss Cornelia's for the reading of the will. In her mother-in-law's will Libby was given guardianship over every last dime of Miss Emilia's monetary assets; the money was to be used to ease any and all of Libby's financial needs as well as to further the educations of Aaron's five sons. Miss Cornelia was bequeathed Miss Emilia's remaining paintings. Everything else was to go to the needy within the community.

In anyone's view, with just the inheritance of Miss Emilia's staggering amount of assets and the money steadily coming in from the book sales, Libby Brooks was rich. Her trouble was, she needed none of it, and other than saving a generous chunk for the boys, she had no idea what she was supposed to do with it. She was still working and earning a good wage, and the house and the car were paid for. But the topper to the conundrum trebled when learning that over in the bank in Baton Rouge, with the years of compounded interest, the originally deposited twenty thousand had grown into almost fifty thousand. First of all, Miss Emilia's funds had taken care of all school fees for the boys. But there was still that bothersome pile in Baton Rouge. As Libby needed next to nothing, what to do with that plus Miss Emilia's remaining monies, as well as the steady royalty income from Aaron's book of sermons, was causing Libby some very long and fitful nights. Until one morning when she was working hard to put the whole thing out of her mind the answer simply came.

And so it was that in 1951, the construction of the first classrooms and dormitories for the Bible College began. Aaron had been right. The Lord had indeed meant that money for His work. Bubba and Myrna's construction crews did an exemplary job. The college was small, but it was well built and easily expanded upon. Bubba's keen eye for style formed all four of the buildings into a square and with an opened quad that was made up of divided lawns and four graveled pathways that would cross the grassed lawns and intersect in the shape of a cross. The lawns were then accented by myrtle trees to add color to open-aired covered breezeways that encompassed the sides of the enclosing buildings. The myrtle trees were fronted by perennial flower beds that had been planted in such a way that there would always be something blooming no matter the season. But the true beauty of the place was that when this well planned and pleasing to the eye little college opened its doors to its first year of students, the Henrytown College and Seminary (thanks to Libby raiding the bank account in Baton Rouge), began its distinguished history completely debt free.

After graduating high school, Caleb had spent the next two years working in construction for Uncle Bubba. Libby fretted that he was wasting his time, but he wasn't. Caleb was intentionally waiting for Sissy to catch up and, while he was waiting, he was gaining valuable on-the-job construction expertise. Soon after Sissy graduated high school, Caleb left construction as both he and Sissy entered the Bible College together. Caleb married Sissy Flowers the day after they both graduated. Bubba was crying as he escorted his beautiful daughter down the aisle, and she was truly lovely in the wedding dress that Mildred Flowers had once packed away for her granddaughter.

Watching as her son took his bride's hand, Libby smiled as she mentally said to her departed mother, "*Well Mama, a granddaughter-in-law will just have to do. And it is a beautiful dress. Sissy loves it.*"

Two days after the honeymoon, Caleb was ordained inside the Henrytown (Redneck Cathedral) Free Church. He'd insisted the ordination take place in the old church his father had helped to build with his very own hands. His three uncles on the Board of Deacons said nothing to correct this belief. But they did look at each other from the corners of their eyes, and Uncle Casper somehow managed not to laugh.

Not long after this, Sissy and Caleb had been sent off as missionaries to Africa where all of the building and jerry-rigging skills he'd learned from Uncle Bubba were being put to good use. Caleb and Sissy had two boys of their own plus the two baby girls that they'd adopted out of a deplorable Nairobi orphanage. Sissy had such a heart for abused and hurting children and Caleb knew the importance of children needing to feel safe. Libby was so proud of those two that she wanted to bust.

Jeremiah (who hated being called Jeremy) was in the sugar cane business with Uncle Archie. Then Jeremiah graduated from LSU with a business degree and, with that degree in his hot hand, he had stepped in to take over the business end of the sugar enterprise, leaving Uncle Archie to do what he did best, the hard physical labor of overseeing the cane fields. By 1960 they were on their way to becoming millionaires never mind that Jeremiah was all but giving away money to support missionaries; his moocher brother Caleb for a start—Caleb was always needing money for medicines or water wells. Jeremiah got so fed up with Caleb and his water wells that one Christmas (as a joke) he sent Caleb a shovel. Jeremiah stopped grinning when Caleb wrote back requesting more shovels because the men in the village were having fist fights over just the one shovel. Grinding his back teeth down to powder, absolutely certain that this latest and quite costly donation—what with the shipping expense and everything, would wreak financial havoc with the company's frail profit margin, Jeremiah sent *two* heavy crates of shovels. But instead of breaking the company, the profits of the A. Brooks Cane Company doubled.

"Ya just can't outgive God," Uncle Archie told the befuddled Jeremiah. "But dogged Jeremy if you don't sometimes try your derndest."

And while Jeremiah was literally drooling over all that black ink in the profit margin, Caleb sent another letter. This time it was all about a tractor he'd found that was in perfect working order and was currently for sale at a reasonably asked price. Actually, he'd found *two tractors*, ". . . but I don't want to be pushy. We can probably make do with just the one. Although, two would be better."

Jeremiah's wife was named Maddy, and she was the niece of Seth's wife, Verda Louise. They had one son, Ryan.

Micah was the son that concerned Libby the most. He'd broken ranks with his brothers by choosing to further his education in Aaron's former seminary. He even attended the grand old church where Aaron, as a child, had given his entire life to the Lord. It was in that church that Micah met the young lady who would later consent to be his wife. At present, Micah was now the associate pastor in a growing church in a town called Vacaville, which was way off in California. What disturbed Libby was that he was also heading up the prison ministry in what Micah called the Medical Facility. In other words, it was a prison for the most highly dangerous prisoners who, if not thoroughly legally insane, were very, very nearly. Even though Micah had grown up to be more sturdily built like his Uncle Casper, he still looked exactly like his father. He even sounded and laughed precisely like Aaron. The resemblances were so uncanny that Libby had often wondered if she'd even been in the room when Micah had been conceived. But what she did know full well was that if anything terrible ever happened to him while he was in that prison that she would throw herself into a grave and pull the dirt down on herself with her bare hands.

Micah's concert trained pianist wife whom he had met and married in Atlanta, was named Linda. Linda in Spanish meant pretty. Linda was not pretty. She was far above such cliché. It was sufficient to say that whenever Micah and Linda entered a room together jaws dropped, and breaths were caught. But when Micah preached and Linda played the church's grand piano, the Spirit of the Lord rained down. As with Aaron, people of this stripe were not destined to remain long on this earthly plane. A still heartbroken Libby knew this hard truth as a firsthand witness. Yet Micah and Linda's uniqueness was both her joy and her daily torment. As yet, the couple had no children.

Matthew—always the family clown (again another son who was far too much like Uncle Casper)—was off in Colorado in the Air Force Academy. His ambition was to attend flight school and become a jet pilot and then go on to train as an astronaut. Matt's theory was that if NASA could train a chimp to do it, then he just might stand a pretty fair chance. Uncle Casper agreed that if anyone with Flowers' blood was to go into space, then a monkey was needed to set the standard.

Uncle Seth had put the boot in by saying, "Yep. Monkey see, monkey do. But, when we've factor in Aaron's superior lack of coordination, I'm thinking we just might need to drive to Colorado and save Matthew from himself."

And speaking of Seth Lewis, when retired from the oil company, he was elected as the head deacon of the new church. The former church, the one built by so many community hands and from scrap lumber and nicknamed by her idiot brother Casper, the Redneck Cathedral, had been stripped of its extraordinary stained glass windows, altar, cross and pulpit, all of which had been reinstalled in the ever so much bigger new Church that was complete with a the towering steeple and a bell tower. Mr. Ralph had lived long enough to hear the bells somberly peel as he wept with Libby as they sat together on the first pew while her father's casket stood opened in front of the practically ancient altar that Aaron had so loved; an altar festooned with lovingly carved dogwood flowers.

The next to follow was Emilia, Aaron's mother, and then Mildred, Yancy's wife, and Libby's mother. The family pew was crowded but Mr. Ralph had been there with her. A few months after her mother's passing, the bells tolled for Mr. Ralph's funeral. Libby was yet again on the front pew. But now she was weeping for a man whom she had feared for most of her younger years. Yet, after Mr. Ralph had given up playing church and had really and truly surrendered his life to Christ, he became the man she loved quite dearly. And now she missed him even more dearly.

Amazingly, in 1960, it was Miss Cornelia who had remained as the last of the older generation to go. For a woman who regularly believed herself at death's door, had outlived everybody! And, the last time she'd put out the old familiar "I'm dying" call, she hadn't been kidding around. There would be no hopping off the settee to whip up a quick pecan pie for her expected visitors. Miss Cornelia was finished with earthly hopping.

Libby knelt by the settee as Miss Cornelia's bone thin hand clutched hers. Urgency flashed in her eyes as in a gravely and laboring for breath voice she said, "Go over to the secretary desk. Look in drawer number three on the left. There's a photograph. Get it."

Libby looked up questioningly at the attending nurse who simply nodded. Then Libby rose to obey. It was easy to find the photo, as it was the only item in the little drawer. When she looked at it, a thousand memories rushed and the shock of the rush all but knocked her off of her feet. Fighting down the emotion, Libby took the photo to Miss Cornelia.

The nurse had placed Miss Cornelia's glasses on her face in order for her to see the photo. As she gazed at it, she smiled and remembered aloud, "I was Kodakin'. The day of the picnic, the day Aaron almost drowned in the pond. It was before that when I saw those handsome young men heading toward the water when I yelled, 'Smile!' And they did. Aaron was the only one to wave. I didn't think a thing of it at the time, but when I saw this print, a powerful feelin' swept over me. Made my hair stand on end. It truly vexed me so badly that I wanted to burn this picture. But I couldn't bring myself to destroy it, so I put it away in the desk. Never did look at it again. Not until two weeks ago when Elvira here," she waved a wearied hand to indicate the nurse, "was about to bore me to tears with her tales of a famous sculptor who's her third cousin or whatnot. That's when the memory of this photo came to me that I had Elvira call up her famous cousin. He came over, agreed to accept the commission, made several sketches and he's already working." Miss Cornelia sat up just a smidgeon. "Now Libby, I have instructed Seth about all this and he holds the payment money. But I needed to tell you because I didn't want it to come at you like a nasty shock."

"Miss Cornelia," Libby said, "I have no idea what you're talking about."

"Well, what I'm trying to tell you," Miss Cornelia said, sounding more alive than she actually was, "is that there's gonna be a bronze sculpture based on this photograph, and that the college board of directors have already determined that the sculpture will be placed in the main garden in the center of the walkways. Think of it, all of those future preachers and Bible teachers will walk by the man their school is dedicated to. And yes, before you ask, the sculpture will include his three best friends who are also in the photo. The sculptor couldn't separate them in his trial sketches, but it's only right that they're all together Libby. In life those four *were* inseparable. Now I understand that Casper drives you crazy more often than not, but you're just gonna have to bite your tongue when you see him in a bigger than life bronze statue."

In spite of the tears flowing down her face, Libby barked a laugh. With the tricky moment eased, Miss Cornelia settled. In a softer voice she said, "Over these many years people have often asked my opinion as to why you've never remarried. I've always told them, 'It's because she's still married to Aaron." She tightly squeezed Libby's hand. Then she said without hesitation or the slightest questioning tenor, "I said right, didn't I."

"Yes ma'am, Miss Cornelia, you said exactly right."

"That's what I thought," Miss Cornelia said with surprising strength. She fumbled at her collar, her hands shaking slightly as she unpinned her trademark cameo broach. She looked at it as it lay in her palm. Without breaking her gaze from the expensive piece of jewelry she said softly, "I had intended to wear this to my grave. But that's wrong. Wrong because it's a symbol of enduring love. Love is not meant for a grave." With tenderness, she handed the broach to Libby. "I loved once. Just the once. I loved a man I wasn't allowed to marry. Not because he was a bad man. My parents would have overlooked the bad if he had been rich enough. But he was a poor man. A good man, but a poor man. His poverty was the unforgiveable sin. I could never bring myself to love anyone else, just as you cannot bring yourself to love anyone else. So, I want you to keep the broach. Archie and Emma are getting my fortune, but I'm giving you my real treasure. Please take good care of it."

"I promise I will," Libby said gently.

Miss Cornelia lay her head back, and as the attentive nurse removed her glasses, Miss Cornelia closed her eyes. "And now my darling girl, I want you to leave. I'm not anxious to expire in front of you because unfortunately, Elvira here has explained to me in rather vivid detail the unseemly shenanigans a corpse can get up to during the first hours of death. I should both loathe and despise it if your final memories of me were of my passing gas. The very notion gives me the trembles. I've taken the precaution of swearing Elvira to absolute secrecy, which means she's not invited to my funeral. It's nothing personal against Elvira. I'm simply well aware of how some of those women will pester her for the less than ladylike details of my expiration. I have no intention of leaving them with that joy. They didn't get it while I was alive and they're certainly not going to gain it through my death."

As Libby rose to go, Miss Cornelia handed her the old photograph. With her eyes still closed Miss Cornelia concluded their final conversation. "Please frame this. I should have never kept it locked in a drawer. I loved that young man like he was my own son. And I have missed him every day right along with you."

Now in the spring of 1966 and while sitting on the concrete bench in the college garden, Libby tilted her head back as she enjoyed the warmth of the sun on her face. She remembered Miss Cornelia's funeral as something of a benchmark in elegant taste, dignity and ultra-Southern Lady Decorum. The women of the church who had always held her in such high esteem, yet at the same time were so thoroughly resentful of her, were left to suffer in positively pea-green envy the refinement of her passing.

Miss Cornelia would have loved it.

(And no, Nurse Elvira had not been in attendance.)

Smiling at the memory, Libby reluctantly stood. She had to go over to the church office and attend to Pastor Daniel's daily roster. Then too, there was that infernal copy machine with its equally infernally frequent paper jambs. It was enough to make her wish for the long-abandoned mimeograph machine. As she turned to go, she looked back to the central area of the garden with its grand bronzed statue of four handsome young men.

Aaron's arm was lifted, his hand frozen in a wave.

Libby waved back.

THE END

Within Jesus Christ, we have God's mercy and forgiveness.
Outside of Jesus Christ, there is only chaos.

Pastor A. Brooks, 1936

Coming Soon!

Murder at Medicine Lodge

A Tay-Bodal Mystery

by

Award-Winning Author

Mardi Oakley Medawar

In 1867, the Kiowa travel to Medicine Lodge, Kansas, along with the Comanche, Arapaho, Apache, and Cheyenne to meet with representatives of the U.S. government and to sign peace treaties. But not all of the Kiowa agree that the peace treaty is a good thing, and tensions between them and the U.S. Army ("The Blue Jackets") are running high. So, when the army bugler disappears and White Bear, chief of the Rattle Band, finds his bugle out on the plains, the army command assumes that White Bear has killed the man to steal it.

For more information

visit: www.SpeakingVolumes.us

On Sale Now!

For more information
visit: www.SpeakingVolumes.us

www.ingramcontent.com/pod-product-compliance
Lightning Source LLC
LaVergne TN
LVHW050917080826
845145LV00001B/109

9781645403159